Praise for the Galahad Archives

"What began as a fairly straightforward tale of 251 teens shot into space to escape a ravaging disease on Earth became a deeper, broader, scarier, and more intellectually stimulating journey with every book."

—*Booklist* (starred review) on the Galahad series

"Part space opera, part mystery, the story draws readers in from the beginning with well-placed hooks, plenty of suspense, and a strong premise."

—*School Library Journal* on *The Comet's Curse*

"Grabs readers' attention with the very first page and never lets go. . . . Both a mystery and an adventure, combining a solid cast of characters with humor, pathos, growing pains, and just a hint of romance, this opener bodes well for the remainder of the series."

—*Kirkus Reviews* on *The Comet's Curse*

"A wonderful mix of science fiction and mystery."

—*Children's Literature* on *The Comet's Curse*

"Sci-fi fans will enjoy Testa's spare Asimovian plot, but even those leery of the genre will appreciate how each chapter alternates to the past to further flesh out our protagonists. Stealing the show is the *Galahad*'s mischievous central computer, Roc, who speaks directly to the readers as he acts as a Greek chorus."   —*Booklist* on *The Comet's Curse*

"Dom Testa has invented a highly original world packed with surprise, insight, and heart. Read it with your whole family, and enjoy the ride."

—*The Denver Post*

"I truly, honestly loved the first two books in this series and think I have a new obsession to burn through. . . . I *love* our diverse cast of crew members aboard the *Galahad*, both in terms of their widely different personalities and with regard to their backgrounds and ethnicities. . . . Absolutely recommended."

THE GALAHAD ARCHIVES
BOOK THREE

A New Life

Dom Testa

TOR®
TEEN
A Tom Doherty Associates Book
New York

THE GALAHAD ARCHIVES BOOK THREE: A NEW LIFE

Cosmic Storm copyright © 2011 by Dom Testa

Reader's Guide copyright © 2011 by Tor Books

The Galahad Legacy copyright © 2012 by Dom Testa

Reader's Guide copyright © 2012 by Tor Books

Edited by Susan Chang

A Tor Teen Book
Published by Tom Doherty Associates
175 Fifth Avenue
New York, NY 10010

www.tor-forge.com

Tor® is a registered trademark of Macmillan Publishing Group, LLC.

ISBN 978-0-7653-8341-9 (trade paperback)

Our books may be purchased in bulk for promotional, educational, or business use. Please contact your local bookseller or the Macmillan Corporate and Premium Sales Department at 1-800-221-7945, extension 5442, or by e-mail at MacmillanSpecialMarkets@macmillan.com.

First Edition: November 2016

Printed in the United States of America

0 9 8 7 6 5 4 3 2 1

*To every Galahad fan—thank you
for coming along for the ride!*

Contents

Cosmic Storm

The universe doesn't play fair. It supposedly has all of these rules which we're expected to obediently follow, and yet when you turn your head the universe sneaks in a few new rules that completely contradict the first set. It's like playing a game with a four-year-old.

For instance, the universe has one set of rules for very big things, like stars and planets and galaxies and government waste, and then another set of rules for very little things, like subatomic particles and boy-band talent.

But don't get too comfortable with either set, because the universe reserves the right to mix them up and make exceptions whenever it feels like it, and it doesn't even have to tell you. Take wormholes, for instance . . .

Actually, before we get to the wormholes, let's cover some basic territory. There's a chance you have randomly picked up this particular volume and you're wondering what you've stumbled into. Don't feel bad, those of us on the ship often have that same feeling.

The ship, by the way, is called Galahad, and it's only the most spectacular spacecraft ever built by human hands. To truly understand the story of what it is, and where it's going, and who's on board, you should probably stop now, go dig up the first volume—titled The Comet's Curse—and start from the beginning. That's followed by The Web of

Titan, The Cassini Code, and The Dark Zone. *They're each a rollicking, riveting tale of mystery and adventure, if I do say so myself.*

If you're stubborn and insist on diving in right here, let me do my best to catch you up.

Deadly particles in the tail of the comet Bhaktul contaminated Earth's atmosphere, delivering a death sentence that threatened to wipe out the human species. But when it was determined that kids were immune until about the age of eighteen, a plan was hatched to select a few hundred of the world's best and brightest teenagers and launch them toward the star system known as Eos, where two Earthlike planets would await them. Galahad became their lifeboat to the stars.

Our brave pioneers had barely pulled out of the cosmic driveway when trouble raised its head in the form of a sinister stowaway, someone determined to destroy the ship. Oh, but wait; after that crisis, more trouble popped up during their rendezvous with a research station near Saturn. It was here that the crew of Galahad encountered an alien lifeform known as the Cassini, beings of almost pure thought that could either help the teens, or destroy them.

Following that little conflict came a terrifying trip through a minefield of debris in the outer ring of the solar system known as the Kuiper Belt. It was during this death-defying dash through the boulder-strewn obstacle course that tempers flared and sides were drawn. Some crew members wanted to turn back, some opted to press onward. Let's just say it got very, very ugly.

When we last left our merry star travelers, they had just confronted another alien species, a creepy collection of creatures that were labeled "vultures," and were responsible for Galahad's first death. The vultures came and went through some of the most bizarre features in the universe: wormholes. These act like cosmic secret passageways and have a nasty habit of opening and closing when you least expect them to. In fact, the ship's Council Leader, Triana Martell, just recently disappeared through a wormhole which immediately folded up and vanished.

The remaining Council members—Gap Lee, Lita Marques, Channy Oakland, and Bon Hartsfield—must now carry on without their vaunted leader, who may—or may not—return. Their relationships are about to get tested to the max. Plus, don't be surprised if some old friends from earlier adventures resurface.

I'll be along for the ride, too. My name is Roc, and I wear a variety of hats on the ship. Yes, I'm the computer brain that is responsible for the lights and the heat and the gravity and lots of other boring, mundane tasks. But I happen to believe that my greatest duty—my calling, if you will—is in the role of advisor, therapist, confidant, and aquatics instructor.

That puts me in the front row for the greatest adventure of all time. You're invited to join us, too. Just find a way to balance on the edge of a seat, and remember our little talk about wormholes and rules. I think you'll discover that rules change for people, too, depending upon what suits them at the time.

I might be a complex machine, but you humans are just plain complicated.

I t was actual paper, something that was a rarity on the ship. It measured, in inches, approximately six by nine, but had been folded twice into a compact rectangle. One word—the name Gap—was scrawled along the outside of the paper, in a distinctive style that could have come from only one person aboard *Galahad*. The loop on the final letter was not entirely closed, which made it more than an *r* but just short of a *p*; a casual reader would assume that the writer was in a hurry.

Gap Lee knew that it was simply the way Triana Martell wrote. It wasn't so much impatience on her part, but a conservation of energy. Her version of the letter *b* suffered the same fate, giving the impression of an extended *h*. It took some getting used to, but eventually Gap was able to read the scribbles without stumbling too much.

And, because he had scoured this particular note at least twenty times, it was now practically memorized anyway.

He looked at it again, this time under the tight beam of the desk lamp. It was just after midnight, and the rest of the room was dark. His roommate, Daniil, lay motionless in his bed across the room, a very faint snore seeping out from beneath the pillow that covered his head. With a full crew meeting only eight hours away, and having chalked up perhaps a total of six hours of sleep over the past two days, Gap knew that he should be tucked into his own bed. Yet while his eyelids felt heavy, his brain would not shut down.

He exhaled a long, slow breath. How just like Triana to forego sending an e-mail and instead scratch out her explanation to Gap by hand. She journaled, like many of the crew members on *Galahad*, but was the only one who did so the old-fashioned way, in a notebook rather than on her workpad. This particular note had been ripped from the binding of a notebook, its rough edges adding a touch that Gap could only describe as personal.

He found that he appreciated the intimate feel, while he detested the message itself. The opening line alone was enough to cause him angst.

> Gap, I know that my decision will likely anger you and the other Council members, but in my opinion there was no time for debate, especially one that would more than likely end in a stalemate.

Of course he was angry. Triana had made one of her "executive decisions" again, a snap judgment that might have proved fatal. The rest of the ship's ruling body, the Council, had expressed a variety of emotions, ranging from disbelief to despair; if they were angry, it wasn't bubbling to the surface yet.

Now, sitting in the dark and staring at the note, Gap pushed aside his personal feelings—feelings that were mostly confused anyway—and tried to focus on the upcoming meeting. More than two hundred crew members were going to be on edge, alarmed that the ship's Council Leader had plunged into a wormhole, nervous that there was little to no information about whether she could even survive the experience. They were desperate for direction; it would be his job to calm them, assure them, and deliver answers.

It was simply a matter of coming up with those answers in the next few hours.

He stood and stretched, casting a quick glance at Daniil, who mumbled something in his sleep and turned to face the wall. Gap leaned over his desk and moved Triana's note into the small circle of light. His eyes darted through the message one more time, then folded it back into its original shape. He snapped off the light and stumbled to his bed. Draping one arm over his eyes, he tried to block everything from his mind and settle into a relaxed state. Sleep was the most important thing at the moment, and he was sure that he was the only Council member still awake at this time of the night.

He wasn't. Lita Marques had every intention of being asleep by ten, and had planned on an early morning workout in the gym before breakfast and the crew meeting. But now it was past midnight, and she found herself walking into *Galahad's* clinic, usually referred to by the crew as Sick House. It was under her supervision, a role that came naturally to the daughter of a physician.

Walking in the door she was greeted with surprise by Mathias, an assistant who tonight manned the late shift.

"What are you doing here?" he said, quickly dragging his feet off his desk and sitting upright.

"No, please, put your feet back up," Lita said with a smile. "You know we're very informal here, especially in the dead of night." She walked over to her own desk and plopped down. "And to answer your question . . . I don't know. Couldn't sleep, so I decided to maybe work for a bit."

Mathias squinted at her. "You doing okay with everything? I mean . . . with Alexa . . . and Tree. I mean . . ."

"Yeah, I'm fine. Thanks for asking, though." She moved a

couple of things around on her desk. "It's just . . . you know, we'll get through it all just fine."

A moment of awkward silence fell between them. Lita continued to shuffle things in front of her, then realized how foolish it looked. She chanced a quick glance toward Mathias and caught his concerned look. "Really," she said.

And then she broke down. Seeming to come from nowhere, a sob burst from her, and she covered her face with her hands. A minute later she felt a presence, and lowered her hands to find Mathias kneeling beside her.

"I'm so sorry," he said quietly. "What can I do?"

"There's nothing you can do. But thank you." Suddenly embarrassed, she funneled all of her energy into looking composed and under control. "Really, it's probably just a lack of sleep, and . . . well, you know."

Mathias shook his head. "I don't want to speak out of place, but you don't have to act tough in front of me. We're talking about losing your two best friends within a matter of days. There's no doubt that you need some sleep, but it's more than that. And that's okay, Lita."

She nodded and put a worried smile on her face. "You know what? Sometimes I wish I wasn't on the Council; I think sometimes we're too concerned with being a good example, and we forget to be ourselves."

"Well, you can always be yourself around me," he said, moving from her side and dropping into the chair facing her desk. He picked up a glass cube on her desk, the one filled with sand and tiny pebbles taken from the beach near Lita's home in Veracruz, Mexico. She found that not only did it bring her comfort, it attracted almost everyone who sat at her desk.

Mathias twisted the cube to one side, watching the sand tumble, forming multicolored layers of sediment. "So, I'll be curious to see what Gap says at this meeting," he said, never taking his eyes off the cube. He left the comment floating between them.

"I don't envy Gap right now," Lita said cautiously. "We've been through so much in this first year, but especially in the last two weeks." She paused and stared at her assistant. "I know everyone's curious about what he intends to do, but there's not much I can say right now."

Mathias shrugged and placed the glass cube back on her desk. "I guess a few of us just wondered if he was going to become the new Council Leader."

"He's temporarily in charge. But we don't know for sure what's happened to Triana. She's still the Council Leader."

"Well, yeah, of course," Mathias said. "But . . ." He looked up at her. "I mean, she disappeared into a wormhole. Could she even survive that?"

Lita's first instinct was irritation; Triana had been gone for forty-eight hours, and Mathias seemed to have written her off. And, if so, chances were that he wasn't alone. It was likely, in fact, that when the auditorium filled up in the morning, many of the crew members would be under the assumption that *Galahad's* leader was dead. It would have been unthinkable only days ago, but . . .

But they had stood in silence to pay their final respects to Alexa just hours before Triana's flight. Now anything seemed possible.

The realization cooled Lita's temper. It wasn't Mathias's fault; he was merely acting upon a natural human emotion. Lita's defense of Triana stemmed from an entirely different, but no less powerful, emotion: loyalty to a friend.

When she finally spoke, her voice was soft. "This crew has learned pretty quickly that when we jump to conclusions, we're usually wrong. I'm sure Gap will do a good job of explaining things so we know what's going on and what we can look forward to. Let's just wait until the meeting before we assume too much."

Mathias gave a halfhearted nod. "Yeah. Okay." Slowly, a

sheepish look crossed his face. "And I'm sorry. Triana's your friend; I shouldn't be saying this stuff. I'm just . . ."

"It's all right," Lita said. "We're all shaken up. Now let me do a little work so I can wear myself out enough to sleep."

Once the clock in her room clicked over to midnight, Channy Oakland climbed out of bed, threw on a pair of shorts and a vivid red T-shirt, woke up the cat, Iris, who was contorted into a ball on her desk chair, and trudged to the lift at the end of the hall. Two minutes later, carrying Iris over her shoulder like a baby, she peered through the murky light of Dome 1. There was no movement.

Two massive domes topped the starship, housing the Farms and providing a daily bounty which fed the hungry crew of teenagers. Clear panels, set among a criss-crossing grid of beams, allowed a spectacular view of the cosmos to shine in and quickly became a favorite spot for crew quiet time.

It was especially quiet at this late hour. Channy could see a couple of farm workers milling about in the distance, but for the most part Dome 1 was deserted. She took her usual route down a well-trodden path, and deposited Iris near a dense patch of corn stalks. "See you in twenty minutes," she said in a hushed tone to the cat, then, on a whim, retreated toward the main entrance. She turned off the path and made for the Farms' offices.

Her instinct had been right on. Lights burned in Bon's office. She leaned against the door frame and glanced at the tall boy who stood behind the desk. "Something told me I'd find you here," she said.

Bon Hartsfield glanced up only briefly before turning back to a glowing workpad. "Not unusual for me to be here, day or night," he said. "You know that. The question is, what are you doing up here this late. Wait, let me guess: cat duty."

"Couldn't sleep. Figured I might as well let Iris stretch her legs."

Bon grunted a reply, but seemed bored by the exchange. Channy took a couple of steps into the office, her hands in her back pockets. "How are you doing?"

He looked up at her, but this time his gaze lingered. "Wanna be more specific?"

She shrugged, then took two more steps toward his desk. "Oh, you know; Alexa, Triana . . . everything."

He looked back down at his workpad. His shaggy blond hair draped over his face. "I'm doing fine. Sorry, but I have to check out a water recycling pump." He walked around his desk toward the door.

"Mind if I walk along with you?" Channy said. "I have to pick up Iris in a few minutes anyway."

"Suit yourself," he said without stopping.

His strides were long and quick. She hustled to keep up until he veered from the path into a thick growth of leafy plants. It was even darker here; she was happy when Bon flicked on a flashlight, its tightly focused beam bobbing back and forth before them. The air was warm and damp, and the heavy vegetation around them blocked much of the ventilating breeze. Channy felt sweat droplets on her chocolate-toned skin.

"You would have loved Lita's song—"

"Why are you whispering?" he called back to her.

"I don't know, it's very quiet and peaceful in here. All right, I'll speak up. I said that you would have loved Lita's song for Alexa at the funeral." When he didn't respond, but instead continued to push ahead through the gloom, she added, "But I understand why you weren't there."

"I'm so glad. It would have wrecked my day if you were upset with me."

"Okay, Mr. Sarcastic. I'm just trying to talk to you."

"Next subject."

A leafy branch Bon had pushed aside slapped back against Channy's face. "Ouch. Excuse me, is this a race?"

"You wanted to come, I didn't invite you."

They popped out of the heavy growth into a diamond-shaped clearing. Bon stopped quickly, and Channy barely managed to throw on the brakes without plowing into his back. A moment later he was down on one knee. "Here," he said, holding the flashlight out to her. "If you want to tag along, do something helpful. Point this right here."

She trained the light on the two-foot-tall block that housed a water recycling pump. One of the precious resources on *Galahad*, water was closely monitored and conserved. Every drop was recycled, which meant these particular pumps were crucial under the domes. After a handful of breakdowns early in the mission, they were now checked constantly.

"I guess Gap will try to explain at the meeting what Tree did," Channy said, sitting down on the loosely packed soil. She kept the flashlight trained on the pump, but occasionally shifted her grasp in order to throw a bit of light toward Bon's face. "Although I have to admit, I don't think I'll ever understand why she did it."

She waited for Bon to respond, but he seemed to want nothing to do with the conversation. She added, "Do you think she did the right thing?"

"Keep the light steady right here," he said. For half a minute he toiled in silence before finally answering her. "It doesn't matter what I think. Triana did what she did, and there's nothing we can do about it."

"Oh, c'mon," Channy said. "I know you like to play it cool, but you have to have an opinion."

Bon wiped sweat and a few strands of hair from his face, then leaned back on his heels and stared at her. "You don't care about my opinion. You're trying to get me to talk about Triana, either because you're upset with her, or because you're trying to get some kind of reaction from me about her. I'm not a fool."

"And neither am I. I don't know why you have to act so tough, Bon, when we both know that you have feelings for her. And, if you ask me, you had feelings for Alexa, too. Did you ever stop to think that it might be good for you to talk about these feelings, rather than keep them bottled up inside all the time?"

"And why should I talk to you?"

"Because I'm the one person on the ship who's not afraid to ask you about it, that's why."

"You're the nosiest, there's no question."

Channy slowly shook her head. "If I didn't think it would help you, I wouldn't ask. I'm not here for me, you know."

"Right."

"I'm not. I just want to help. The two people on this ship that you had feelings for, and they're both gone, just like that. Why do you feel like you have to deal with it by yourself? Are you so macho that you can't—"

"Please put the light back on the recycler."

"Forget the recycler!" Channy said. "Have you even cried yet? I cried my eyes out over Alexa, and I'll probably end up doing the same for Triana if she doesn't come back soon. You won't talk, you won't cry." She paused and leaned toward him, a look of exasperation staining her face. "What's wrong with you?"

He stared back at her with no expression. After a few moments, she tossed the flashlight to the ground, stood up, and stormed off down the path to find Iris.

Bon looked at the flashlight, its beam slicing a crazy angle toward the crops behind him. His breathing became heavy. For a moment he glanced down the path, his eyes blazing. Then, with a shout, he slammed a fist into the plastic covering of the recycling pump, sending a piece of it spinning off into the darkness. It wasn't long before he felt a warm trickle of blood dripping from his hand.

2

A chair toppled over and dishes scattered across the floor, producing a startling crash that pierced the calm, early morning air inside the Dining Hall. Shouts punctuated the noise. Lita, sitting alone in her usual seat in the back of the room, propping her head up with one hand and neglecting the breakfast before her, bolted upright. A knot of crew members near the door rushed to break up the fight, which had materialized seemingly out of nowhere.

The two combatants, at first separated by a handful of friends who'd been nearby, broke free from the restraining arms and lunged at each other again. They twisted into a furious mass of wild swings before falling in a heap on the ground, where they continued to wrestle and jab while astonished onlookers again scrambled into the ruckus, attempting to pull them apart. Two more crew members fell to the ground in the effort, and another chair went skidding aside.

It had all happened in mere seconds, instantly transforming a rather serene setting into a boisterous melee. The shock of it kept Lita in her seat at first, trying to absorb what she was seeing, before she sprang into action. Leaping to her feet, she raced over to the tangle of bodies. One of the boys had managed to position himself above the other.

"Stop it!" Lita yelled over the shouts, dropping to her knees and helping to drag the boy away, even as he lashed out with more punches. In the pandemonium, Lita felt his elbow strike a glancing blow against her cheek, momentarily stunning her. At last the two were separated again, and Lita stood up between them with her hands outstretched on each of their chests.

"Enough!" she said. "That's enough!" She found her own breathing was coming in fits, matching that of the two crew members who stood poised, prepared to rush at each other again. Lita turned to one of them and narrowed her eyes. "Errol, what is this? What are you doing?"

The rugged boy from Scotland had a thin line of blood dripping from his nose, and a dark bruise had already formed near his chin. "Taking care of some long overdue business, that's all," he said.

Lita looked around at the other boy. He had recently completed a work rotation in Sick House, and she recalled that his temper had seemed short at times. It made this altercation less surprising. "You wanna explain this, Rodolfo?"

The Argentinean was also bloodied, but the cut near his right eye seemed worse than it probably was. He stared past Lita into Errol's face. "Just tired of his attitude, that's all. Tired of putting up with it."

"Attitude?" Lita said. She looked back at Errol. "Overdue business? Would you both listen to yourselves? I don't care what started this, and I don't care if you never speak to each other, but this will not happen again, understood?" She turned back to Rodolfo. "We've been through a lot lately, and the last thing we need is for you guys to do something stupid like this. This crew needs to come together, and not react by collapsing into chaos." She looked at the mess of food and plates on the floor. "Both of you, clean this up and get out of here. Then go back to your rooms and clean yourselves up. And stay away from each other until you can behave like adults."

For a few moments the two boys glared at each other. Lita gave a disgusted snort and walked back to her own table. Sitting down, she looked back to see Errol and Rodolfo slowly gathering the plates and utensils from the floor and setting the chairs back on their feet. The entire incident seemed surreal, a frightful glimpse into the dark turmoil that resided just beneath the fragile surface of their mission. Up until now there had been scattered incidents of disagreements and rare threats of violence. Suddenly the violence was real.

Lita, already weary from a lack of sleep the night before, and now troubled by this altercation, again rested her head on one hand. She wondered what might come next.

For a department labeled Engineering, its looks were deceiving. Unlike the stereotype portrayed in movies and television shows from the early days of the space age, it was not an expansive room filled with enormous turbines or stories-tall banks of equipment. If anything, it most closely resembled a compact series of laboratories connected by offices and storage rooms.

The majority of ship functions were under Roc's control, which left the crew to primarily monitor the operations, and to perform physical maintenance and updates. Vidscreens peppered each room in Engineering, along with computer terminals and work stations. The department included separate rooms for life-support functions, *Galahad*'s solar sail and ion drive systems, and information storage.

There also was a room devoted to the ship's defense. Unlike traditional defensive systems that utilized weapons, *Galahad* relied upon scanning devices that probed the path ahead. Contrary to a popular misconception, space was often anything but empty. A series of shields protected the ship and its precious human cargo from the deadly radiation which permeated the cosmos, as well as from potentially lethal debris.

A chief concern of early space exploration, the original long-distance vessels employed panels filled with water to block and absorb the radiation. *Galahad*'s designers knew that it was crucial to shield the crew, but, given the size and complexity with which they worked, water was not a realistic choice. Instead, scientists developed a magnetic shield which wrapped itself around the shopping-mall-sized ship and acted much like Earth's own magnetic field. That field, which generally went unnoticed and unappreciated by a busy human population, made its presence felt through its effect on compasses, and the showy delight of the aurora borealis. The Northern Lights were nothing more than Earth's magnetic field in a dramatic dance with the sun's highly charged particles.

As *Galahad* raced outward from the Kuiper Belt at speeds that were rapidly approaching the speed of light, a protective magnetic blast shot ahead, diverting toxic radiation out of the way, clearing a path. Because it clearly was one of the most crucial elements of the ship's defenses, crew members rotating through the Engineering section during their work tours were taught to monitor and maintain the radiation shield.

Ruben Chavez pulled up a chair and punched in his personal identification code at the work station. He'd finished a late afternoon workout in the gym, quickly showered, and reported to Engineering for a long stretch of work. After taking a personal day to catch up on some school assignments, he was making up work time in the radiation section, monitoring the forward scans. A few feet away, Julya Kozlova hummed while she charted the progress of a maintenance scan.

"What is that song?" he said to her. "It sounds like something my mother used to sing."

Julya smiled and, rather than immediately answering, turned to him and began to sing the song, adding words to the melody that she had been humming.

He closed his eyes, nodding to the beat, but then chuckled.

"Well, that's no help. You're singing in Russian; that version probably wasn't a hit in Toluca."

"Hmm, you're probably right," Julya said. "But it's a traditional Russian love song; how it ended up in Mexico is beyond me. Perhaps your mother was more continental than you gave her credit for."

"Uh, no," Ruben said, laughing again. "It's more likely that the melody just happens to sound like the Mexican lullaby that she sang when my sisters and I couldn't fall asleep."

"How many sisters?"

"Four. Yes, four girls surrounding me, teasing and torturing."

"Made you tough."

He shook his head. "You have no idea." He bent over the console to pull up a tracking program, and allowed Julya to once again concentrate on her task.

The silence was shattered by a quick succession of tones that rang out from the room's main panel. After a pause, the sequence repeated. Ruben and Julya exchanged a quizzical look, then both stood and walked over to the display.

"That's odd," he said. "It's coming from the radiation control system."

"Running a diagnostic right now," she said, her fingers flying across the keyboard. She looked up at the monitor, then entered another command.

Together they watched as a response flashed across the vidscreen, then again looked at each other. "Uh, Roc?" Ruben said. "Are we reading this right? The diagnostic says the radiation shield went down for a second."

"Less than a second," Roc corrected. "But yes. I'd say *Galahad* just hiccuped."

"So we were completely vulnerable," Julya said. "That's one deadly hiccup."

Ruben scanned the monitor again. "Well, it seems fine now.

But it can't really be fine, not if it's throwing off an alarm like that. *Something's* wrong."

"Correct," the computer said. "I hope you didn't want to spend this evening with a good book or crossword puzzle; this isn't exactly the kind of problem that you want to flare up again. Let's call Mr. Lee."

Julya nodded and punched the intercom to hail Gap.

Toward the end, Alexa had called it "our spot." It was the first time in his life that Bon had ever had someone reference "our," or "us," and he'd not responded to her. Instead, he had simply said, "I'll see you in the clearing." To him it conveyed everything that needed to be said.

He stood now in that same spot, a small clearing tucked back within a secluded section of the dome. Night had descended upon *Galahad*, which meant the lights had automatically dimmed in an attempt to replicate a traditional twenty-four-hour Earth cycle. In the ship's domes that meant the artificial sunlight, which bathed the crops in a specially designed blend of ultraviolet and visible light, had faded away. It also meant that the brilliant nightly display was in full effect, a stunning shower of starlight through the dome's clear panels.

It meant nothing to Bon at the moment. He'd worked late in the fields, helping with the harvest of spinach—backbreaking work that he refused to skip out of merely because of his role as a Council member—before investing another hour in the never-ending pile of records and paperwork in his office. When he decided that a fourteen-hour workday would have to suffice, he fled not to his room and a waiting bed, but rather this garden-like patch that held a collection of painful memories.

Channy's words from the previous night still haunted him: *The two people on this ship that you had feelings for, and they're both gone.*

More accurately, two people that he had failed to share his feelings with. Both Triana and Alexa had given him every opportunity, and yet he had balked at the chances. Why? Because he was afraid to let down his guard, terrified of showing any sign of vulnerability? Was he subconsciously worried that he somehow wouldn't measure up, that they would ultimately decide that he wasn't worthy of their time and attention?

His mind drifted back, touching on the two occasions when he and Triana had been close. Their brief connection in the control room of the Spider bay had lasted less than a minute, but long enough to make it clear that something existed between them, something worth exploring.

It was the second time, however, when they might have taken a step in that direction, that tortured Bon the most. Here, in the lush crops of *Galahad's* farms, not too far from this spot, it was a private moment that had irritated and confused him, and a scene that had replayed in his mind countless times. A quick, impulsive kiss from Triana, followed by a curious rejection when he responded. At the time Bon's anger had flared, and he walked away. He could still hear the words he spit at her that day: *You need to figure out what you really want.*

And yet, looking at it through a lens of time and perspective, he understood that it was he, not Triana, who wrestled with what he wanted. It was he who seemed to waffle back and forth, at one point open to the idea of their connection, the next unsure and distant. Triana might have given off a similar air of uncertainty, but now he felt sure that it was merely in defense of her own heart, a shield to protect herself until he was willing to meet her halfway. Her appeal to him at that moment—*This isn't the right time*—suddenly came into focus, and he saw the wisdom in her words. It had nothing to do with the ship's crisis at the time; it was Triana's acknowledgment that she was open and ready, willing to be vulnerable . . . but that he was not.

Triana, it seemed, was teaching him something about relationships, the necessity of two people being courageous enough to risk their hearts in order to meld. Teaching him, even now, across the winds of time and the depths of space.

He fell to the dirt and stretched out on his back, pushing his long, blond hair out of his face and then lacing his fingers behind his head. Staring up at the stars, and yet seeing nothing, he thought of the choices he'd made with both Triana and Alexa. If given the chance to go back and do it over again, what would he do differently?

Could he do things differently? Or were people hardwired to behave a certain way, with tendencies embedded within their genetic makeup, where no amount of conditioning or experience could alter their path? Bon thought of all the times that he knew—from experience—the right thing to do, and yet some stubborn side of him refused to go along. If that was truly the case, what did that say about the old adage of "learning from our mistakes"? Did we? he wondered. Did we really?

Despite his doubts, the fantasy of reliving the past year, of making different choices, forced itself upon him. He imagined an alternate history where he reached out to Triana, not merely in response to her, but through his own actions. What might have come of that?

Moments later his thoughts shifted, and he was here, in the clearing with Alexa, only instead of acting cool and detached, he responded to her gentle approach with openness and warmth.

She had deserved no less.

He closed his eyes and felt a wave of despair wash over him. This was a foolish waste of time, an exercise in futility. Alexa was dead, her body knifing through the void of space. Triana was gone, swallowed by a wormhole, and while the crew hoped for the best, the prevailing mood was that she was gone forever; Gap had gone so far as to begin the steps to replace her as Council Leader.

There was nothing he could do.

Or was there?

He sat up, leaned to his left, and shoved a hand into his right front pocket, grimacing as he raked the damaged skin of his knuckles. He pulled out a small metallic ball, studded with four rounded spikes that protruded from various points along its surface. He rolled the ball in his hand, staring at it through the gloom, wondering.

A minute later he was once again stretched out in the dirt, the ball lying beside him. His breathing turned deep and steady. Soon he was asleep.

3

The last thing Gap wanted was to walk into the auditorium after everyone was seated. In his mind it would seem arrogant, with an almost regal touch to it, and that was not the impression he wanted to make. Instead, he made sure he was the first to arrive for the meeting. With the large room to himself, he sat quietly in the first row, contemplating what the next hour would bring. It was the first full crew meeting of *Galahad* without Triana at the helm, and it already felt awkward. He was sure that it would remain so for quite some time.

His mind raced through the quick outline he had sketched. The talk would be direct and to the point. Given the crew's uneasiness, it could easily drift into an endless circle of speculation, with questions that sought reassurance more than detailed facts. It was his job to keep things on track and to deliver a measure of confidence that things would be okay.

But would they be? During its first year en route to Eos, *Galahad* had stumbled through its share of trouble, flirting with disaster several times. In some ways, the unnatural was a natural way of life for the crew. Now their Council Leader had disappeared, swallowed by a hole in the fabric of space that not even the ship's computer, Roc, could completely understand. And, compounding the shock, news of Triana's jump through the wormhole came before the crew had recovered from their first funeral.

And it was Gap's job to make this crew feel . . . confident?

He sat forward in his chair, elbows on knees, and stared at the floor. Now he understood firsthand the responsibilities of leadership. Triana had shouldered those responsibilities from the first day, with no whining, no wavering. In fact, it was a heavy feeling of responsibility that had driven her to climb inside the metal pod and venture into the unknown, at the risk of her own life.

Gap's task, he realized, paled in comparison.

A door to the auditorium opened, admitting a half dozen crew members and shaking Gap from his thoughts. A moment later Lita walked in, spotted him in the front row, and took the chair beside him.

"Need help with anything?" she said.

"Not that I can think of, but thanks." He sat back and looked closely at her. "You look pretty beat."

Lita laughed. "That's the nicest thing anyone's said to me in a long time."

"Oh, c'mon, you know I didn't mean it that way. You just look like you could use some sleep."

"Like most of us, I think. Plus, the stress of these last few weeks is starting to show up in a way I haven't seen before with this crew." She spent a minute catching him up on the fight in the Dining Hall.

Gap nodded grimly. "Everyone's stressed out and tired, no doubt. But we can't start falling apart." He forced a hopeful look. "Who knows, maybe the fight let off some steam and things can settle a little bit."

"Maybe," Lita said, but there was a tinge of doubt in her voice. They both fell quiet for a moment and watched as the door opened and a dozen crew members strolled into the room.

Gap used the distraction to change the subject. "Have you

given any thought to . . ." He paused, then finished in a low voice. "To who might take Alexa's spot?"

A crease appeared across Lita's forehead. "A little bit. On one hand I feel like I should tap someone pretty soon, just to keep a sense of order, you know? But then I wonder if maybe that wouldn't show the proper respect for Alexa." She shrugged. "There's no real reason to hurry; we're handling everything we need to so far. I think the crew on duty in Sick House are more worried about how to act around me. I don't like the feeling that everyone's walking on eggshells."

Gap nodded. He glanced over his shoulder to watch more crew members file into the room. The background noise picked up, which, in a way, put him more at ease. He looked back at Lita. "The way I figure it, the sooner we can get back into something that at least resembles routine, the better. Acknowledge the issue, answer the questions we can, and let the crew know that the mission doesn't stop, which means *we* don't stop."

Before Lita could respond, they were greeted by Channy, wearing what was likely her most subdued T-shirt. She took the seat on Gap's left.

"Where's your little furry friend?" he said to her.

"Stretched out across my bed like Cleopatra, sleeping. She probably won't move more than two inches before I get back."

"At least someone's getting some sleep around here," Lita said. "I'm jealous."

The room was now filled almost to capacity, the only empty seats caused by crew members on strict duty schedules. They would monitor the meeting through the vidscreen system throughout the ship. One of the last people to walk into the auditorium was Bon. He took a seat beside Lita, with merely a nod to Gap; he seemed to ignore Channy, who looked the other way.

"What happened to your hand?" Lita said, moving to lift Bon's hand from his lap.

"It's nothing," Bon said, pulling his arm away. "Part of the job."

"It looks gnarly. Stop by Sick House and let me swab some disinfectant on it, okay?"

Bon looked away and leaned back, his body language insisting that the conversation was at an end.

After allowing the room to settle, Gap stood. Lita gave his forearm a brief squeeze and mouthed to him, "Good luck." He climbed the steps to the stage and, grasping both sides of the podium, looked out over the crowd.

"Well . . ." he began, then paused for a few seconds. He felt a single drop of perspiration form along his brow, but refused to wipe it away. "I'm sure there are ten different flavors of the facts spreading around the ship, but here is the situation as it stands at the moment.

"As you know, the vultures, as we called them, fled the ship when we administered an oxygen blast to their leader. Rather than simply circle our ship, they left this part of space through an opening that we believe is a wormhole. Some might say that the vultures were summoned by their creators; we don't know for sure, but it seems the likely explanation."

He shifted his stance and looked back and forth across the room. Nobody moved or made a sound.

"What followed next is now clear. These . . . creators . . . opened another wormhole in our path. Why? We don't know for sure. But Roc speculated, and Triana agreed, that it was an invitation. An invitation for us to plunge through and pop out . . . somewhere else."

For the first time there was a stirring in the crowd. Gap saw crew members exchange looks, and knew that more of an explanation was due.

"We've all heard theories about wormholes, but we're the first humans to actually witness them. You can think of them as shortcuts across space, and perhaps across time. It's taking us years, using the most advanced technology ever devised on Earth, to travel a relatively short distance. With wormholes, travel across the galaxy, or across the universe—or maybe even between universes—would be instantaneous.

"Triana obviously believed that if we did not steer *Galahad* into this particular wormhole, there was a chance that something would eventually come out after us. Given this belief . . ."

Here, Gap paused again and collected himself before continuing. "Given this belief, Triana made a decision on her own, without consulting the Council, Roc, or anyone else. She gathered the corpse of the vulture that we had brought aboard . . . the one that was responsible for Alexa's death . . . and loaded it onto the pod we recovered from the Saturn research station. Then, she climbed inside, launched the pod, and took her cargo into the wormhole."

He looked down at Lita, who, although seeming on the verge of tears, offered him a supportive nod.

"That was almost three days ago. Since then we've scanned every bit of space around us, and there's no sign of the pod. And, since the wormhole closed up soon after Triana's launch, we are now convinced that this is indeed what happened. She's gone."

Now Lita wasn't the only one in tears. Gap could see several crew members dabbing at their eyes. He steeled himself and continued.

"We've called this meeting for three reasons. One, to make sure you understood exactly what's happened; two, for us to discuss what happens next; and three, to answer any questions you have. Before we discuss our next steps, are there any questions so far?"

At first there was little response. The assembled crew members looked around, wondering who would be the first. Finally, from the middle of the room, a boy stood up.

"Yes, Jhani," Gap said.

"Do we have any idea if Triana could even survive going through a wormhole?"

Gap took a deep breath and weighed his answer. "We can't know anything for sure," he said. "However, I've had a couple of conversations with Roc about that very question, and he believes the answer is yes. He bases that on the limited data that we were able to gather from the captured vulture. Its physiology was obviously quite alien, and mostly artificial. Yet it also contained an organic brain—or, at least what we assumed was a brain.

"So," he continued, "if the vultures are able to navigate their way through wormholes unharmed, without any special protection that we know of, then we can assume that Triana would do the same. The pod that she was in is pressurized and very strong, at least as strong as the body of the vultures, which would hopefully provide the protection she needs."

Another crew member stood up. "Angelina," Gap said.

"Any ideas about what might be on the other side of the wormhole?"

Gap shook his head. "That, unfortunately, is something we couldn't even begin to guess. Our first thought would be the home planet of the vultures' creators, but who's to say they even live on a planet? Or that they're anything like us? And, if the wormhole comes out in a completely different dimension, we can't begin to guess about the laws of physics there. But, again, simply going by the physical makeup of the vultures, we would hope that it's at least habitable." He paused, then added, "I, for one, am counting on Triana coming back to tell us all about it."

This was greeted with hopeful smiles from around the room.

"Are there any other questions before we move on? No? All right, then let's talk about what comes next. Specifically, what do we do about the Council? As I said, I would very much like to believe that Triana will come back and everything will be fine. However, we also think it would be irresponsible to not take steps in case . . . well, in case she doesn't make it back anytime soon. We're in a tough spot, and it's crucial that our leadership be in order.

"As I'm sure you remember from your training and studies, according to the ship's bylaws, should *Galahad*'s Council Leader be unable to fulfill the duties required—and that would be the case here—then the Council, in an emergency session, will meet to name a temporary Council Leader. That has happened, and, for the time being, the Council has asked me to assume those responsibilities, and I've agreed. However, it *is* temporary. The bylaws also state that an election should be held to replace the Council Leader, as quickly as possible."

There was a ripple of movement throughout the room as these words sank in. Just days ago it would have seemed unthinkable that they would be electing a new Council Leader. There were more glances and pockets of whispered conversation.

Gap raised his voice to refocus their attention. "I'll let Roc discuss the bylaws which govern this decision. Roc?"

The computer's voice, which eerily mimicked that of his own creator, Roy Orzini, spilled out of the room's speakers. While humor and sarcasm often dotted his speech, for this occasion he came across as all business.

"The bylaws for *Galahad*'s Council include sections that deal with emergency changes. In normal circumstances, members serve three-year terms, after which elections are held to either re-elect Council members, or install new ones. The Council was specifically set up to not resemble a hierarchy; no Council member automatically assumes the position of Council Leader should that Leader be incapacitated or otherwise unable to fulfill the duties. In this regard it's similar to the Supreme Court of the United States, where a new Chief Justice is appointed rather than having one ascend to the top.

"However, given the circumstances, this election also essentially falls under the category of a temporary fill-in position, although it could potentially last two years until the next general election. That means should Triana return in one month or six months or one year, she would resume her role as Council Leader, provided that she was able to fulfill the duties as established by the other Council members. Are there questions at this point?"

There were none, and Roc continued.

"The process is fairly simple. Nominations are submitted during a twenty-four-hour period via ship-wide electronic posting, either by the candidates themselves or by another nominating party. Then there are public forums over the next six days where the candidates may address the crew, and the following day an electronic election is held. No minimum percentage of votes is required; in other words, the highest vote-getter is named the new Council Leader.

"This new Leader will assume the role until the following general election, at which time they may run for reelection if they wish. Assuming no other problems, those elected two years from now will see the mission through its arrival into the Eos system."

From the stage Gap watched his fellow crew members absorb this information. He saw Channy lean over and mutter something to Lita, who nodded. Bon sat with a stony expression across his face.

After about a minute, Gap thanked Roc and once again addressed the crew. "We will open the nominating period tomorrow morning at six. It will last twenty-four hours. We ask that you take this responsibility seriously, and give it strong consideration before you randomly submit a name. Please speak with that person before doing so, to eliminate any discomfort or confusion. Once the twenty-four-hour period ends we will post all of the nominations.

"If there are any final questions, now would be the time before we close this meeting."

A low rumble spread across the auditorium as crew members spoke to their neighbors. Then, from the back row a girl stood up.

"Yes, Kaya," Gap said.

"I think most of us are under the impression that you have a good chance of moving into the top spot. Hypothetically, if you were the only person nominated, would there still be an election?"

Gap smiled. "Believe it or not, we would still have to have a formal election to install a new Council Leader. So, yes, even if only one person is nominated, we would all still need to vote. But let's not make any assumptions right now; there are obviously many people who would be well-suited to take over Triana's duties, and you should consider each person thoroughly."

He shifted again. "There are two things I'd like to add before we dismiss. First, keep in mind that you're electing someone who will have tremendous responsibilities heaped upon them. This is not a popularity contest, but rather an election to find the person we feel could best lead in times of trouble.

"But secondly, I'd like to point out that this crew is strong. We have overcome every obstacle thrown into our path, and will do so again. Our mission is to take this ship to Eos, to let nothing stand in our way, and to battle through any crises that may occur. We didn't train for almost two years in order to handle smooth sailing; we trained in order to confront, and overcome, any problems that came our way. Dr. Zimmer insisted that we be prepared for emergencies; well, that's exactly what we're facing now."

He took a deep breath. It was difficult to tell what effect his words were having upon the crew, whether or not they were encouraged and motivated. At the very least, he knew that he had their complete attention.

"It's imperative that we pull together," he said. "You no doubt have heard about an altercation that happened this morning. That's the last thing we need. Emotions are wearing thin, but we need to think before we act out. We all have our assigned responsibilities, but this would be a good time to look around and see if we can lend a hand in other areas. That might very well help to relieve some of the tension. Please continue to find time to relax and decompress, but also keep your eyes open for ways you can help out. Thanks very much."

With a respectful silence, the room began to clear out. Gap stepped down from the stage and stood beside the other Council members.

"I thought that went very well," Lita said to Gap. "Thoughtful questions from the crew, and you handled it all very smoothly. Good job."

"Thanks," Gap said.

"And Kaya's right," Channy said, lightly punching his arm. "You're sure to get nominated. In fact, I'll be the first to do it tomorrow morning."

"Thanks again," Gap said. "But I don't believe I'll be the only one. There's been enough turbulence in the last couple of months that I'm sure someone else will step forward. But that's good, it's the democratic process at work."

"We'll see," Channy said. She leaned over and gave him a quick peck on the cheek, waved good-bye to Lita, and sprinted up toward the door. She had again completely ignored Bon, which Gap noted. He could tell from Lita's expression that she had as well. The Swede didn't appear to react at all, and, with a grunt of good-bye, trudged away.

Lita turned to Gap. "A little Council friction?"

"Well, those two seem to go through cycles, so I wouldn't worry about it."

Together they began the march up toward the exit. "You're probably right," Lita said. "So what's on your agenda for the rest of the day?"

"I've got some catch-up work to do in Engineering," Gap said, "but I think I might actually grab a quick nap first. I'm exhausted from the last few days. What about you?"

Lita sighed. "I need to settle on a choice for Alexa's replacement, so I'll be going over some crew records."

Gap put an arm around her. "I'm sorry. Need some help?"

She shook her head. "No, but thanks. Go get some rest. Maybe I'll see you at dinner tonight."

They parted ways in the hall, and Gap turned toward the lift. He hoped that sleep would come easier now that the meeting was behind him. But his mind replayed what Kaya had said, and a new thought forced its way in: *Am I ready for that job? Do I even want it?*

4

The interview had gone swiftly and smoothly, and now Lita, who was rarely in the Conference Room outside of Council meetings, sat alone. Alexa's roommate, Katarina, had sent a note asking for a chance to meet—Lita knew it must be something about Alexa—so they had agreed to connect in the Conference Room. The interview had wrapped up early, so with time to kill Lita allowed herself to sit back and fall deep into thought, absently tapping her cheek with a stylus pen. Her gaze settled upon the room's lone window, and the brilliant star display brought on an emotional reaction, one that had a strong connection to her past.

As a child, she found herself intrigued with the stories of history's great explorers, most notably the famous Spanish explorers who struck out across the Americas. Enchanted by their gallant successes, and sobered by the lessons of their failures—including their often-disgraceful treatment of the natives they encountered—Lita grew to respect the heavy burden of responsibility that accompanied true exploration.

Now she was a Council member on the greatest mission of exploration the human race had ever conceived. In her mind, *Galahad*'s legacy would be judged not only by what they accomplished scientifically, but by how they represented their species morally and ethically. So far, in the first year of their mission, they had already crossed paths with two extraterrestrial entities. Whether they were technically life forms might be debatable, but for Lita that didn't matter. She was dedicated to making sure that *Galahad* did not repeat any of the blunders that her Spanish heroes had made.

She studied the star field and wondered how many other intelligent life forms populated the galaxy. And, of those, how many held moral beliefs that matched hers? It dawned on her that Triana's fate rested with the moral standards of the beings who waited at the other end of the wormhole; how did *they* treat encounters with an outsider?

So many questions, so many concerns, one of which had brought about the just-concluded meeting: who would move up to take Alexa's spot as her top assistant in the Clinic? Mathias was one of the final candidates, as was Manu, who had helped out during Alexa's surgery. Lita had earlier met with Mathias, and now had just finished an hour-long meeting with Manu.

Even through the mild-mannered veil he projected, Lita had sensed his intense desire for the position. More a conversation than an interview, he had impressed her by steering their discussion into hypothetical medical scenarios. His thoughtful suggestions, the questions he raised, and his obvious abilities displayed during his time in Sick House placed him squarely at the top of the list.

One of his questions stuck in her mind. "Suppose that Triana does pop back out of another wormhole," he'd said. "Without knowing where she's been, and what she's been exposed to, do we automatically let her back into the ship, or do we quarantine her?"

Her knowledge of—and fascination with—those early Spanish explorers made this question resonate strongly with her. Many historians believed that European diseases had decimated millions of native people in the Americas. Now Manu was suggesting that Triana might unknowingly carry an alien bug that could rage through the crew of *Galahad* before anyone knew what was happening. Lita found herself nodding in agreement when Manu spoke of the possibilities.

As much as her natural instinct would be to immediately embrace her friend upon arrival, Lita knew that Triana would have to remain isolated until thoroughly examined. Although, given its alien nature, would they even know what to look for?

And, just as sobering, how realistic were the chances that Triana would ever return?

Lita appreciated the respectful manner in which Manu had approached the subject; he knew, like every other crew member, how close Lita was to Triana. He'd also expressed sincere heartbreak over Alexa's death. Loss upon loss, as he'd put it.

Loss upon loss. Lita stared out at the fiery star display and, not for the first time, willed herself to not cry.

The door opened and Katarina stuck her head inside the Conference Room. "Still a good time?" she said.

"It is," Lita said, waving her in and gesturing toward the chair directly across the table. "Just taking a mental break." She laughed. "Although these days mental breaks seem to do more harm than good."

Katarina gave an empathetic look. "I feel the same way. As long as I'm at work, or in school, or just busy with something, I'm focused and in control. It's when I'm alone with my thoughts that I get really sad."

"We'll probably all feel the same way for a while," Lita said. "Listen, I know I've told you this already, but if you ever just need to talk, or need a distraction, I hope you'll call me or stop by. You know that, right?"

"Yes, thank you. Really. And the same goes for you, too."

"I appreciate that," Lita said.

They sat in silence for a brief moment until Katarina placed a small box on the table between them. "This is why I wanted to meet with you," she said. "As weird as it might sound, Alexa and I once talked about what we should do if the other one . . . well, if something happened to the other. I don't think either of us really believed that anything *would* happen, but it . . . I don't know, it was just one of those late-night sessions, sitting around the room, talking. You know how it is."

Lita offered a sad smile, but didn't say anything.

"Anyway," Katarina continued, "it was almost like something out of a movie. We checked off a list of things we would leave for each other, and then we each wrote down what we would leave to other people on the ship. Kinda like our last will and testament, you could say."

Because space was at a premium in the housing section, crew members had been allowed to bring very few personal items aboard. Lita had given little thought to distributing her own possessions should anything happen to her. But now she smiled, because it was no surprise that Alexa—orderly and thoroughly efficient Alexa—would have planned for such a possibility and mapped it out.

"Alexa wanted you to have this," Katarina said. She pushed the box across the table. "You meant the world to her."

Lita hesitated. There was such a finality to this gesture, driving home the point that Alexa was gone for good. Finally, she reached out and lifted the small box from the table. Removing the top, she peered inside.

It was beautiful. Nestled within white tissue paper, it didn't shine; in fact, if anything, its charcoal color seemed to absorb light. Lita pulled the oddly shaped nugget from the box and twisted it in her fingers.

Katarina saw the look of curiosity and said, "It's part of a meteorite. Dug up in Antarctica about a hundred years ago."

"Where did Alexa get it?"

"Her mother gave it to her just before the launch. Told her that it was a gift from her real father."

Lita set the dark-gray rock on the table. "She never knew her real father."

"That's right, and her mother never spoke about him. I think that's why this was so special to her." Katarina looked from the meteorite to Lita. "Alexa told me that her mother thought it might make a great necklace, but you know Alexa. She never wore jewelry of any kind. So, she was holding on to it, trying to decide how to display it. And that night, when we were talking about things, she told me that you should have this because you *definitely* could make something cool from it.

"And," Katarina added in a soft voice, "you were one of her very best friends. She really looked up to you."

Another sad smile crossed Lita's face. She picked up the rock again and studied it. About an inch in diameter and heavy for its size, it was oddly smooth on one side, while cratered and worn on the other. She visualized its path through the solar system, one small piece of a much larger boulder that had likely spent billions of years tumbling through space, until either gravity or a chance impact had sent it on a collision course with Earth. It reminded Lita of the deadly ring of debris that *Galahad* had recently navigated; indeed, this particular chunk might have been part of the Kuiper Belt at some point. Or, possibly a fragment of a planetary crust, perhaps Mars, blasted into space as the result of a cosmic collision with a comet or asteroid. It arrived as a fireball, blazing through Earth's atmosphere, until it slammed into Antarctica. Now, ironically, it was once again tearing through space; this time, however, it was headed in the opposite direction, out of the solar system, a passenger on a starship.

"I think Alexa's mom was right," Lita said. "I think it would make a gorgeous necklace." She thought quietly for a moment, then said, "A couple of people on the ship have made their own jewelry. Yes, I think I'll get right on that."

Katarina smiled at her. "I can't wait to see it." She pushed back her chair and stood up, and Lita did the same.

"Thank you so much," Lita said, walking around the table to give Katarina a hug. "I will treasure this always."

When she again was alone in the room, Lita picked up the rock fragment and looked out the window.

"Born in the stars, and now returning to the stars," she mumbled to herself. "Just like us."

It would be agony. Yet agony mixed with . . . euphoria? Bon couldn't describe it, but that was nothing new. From the first moment he'd connected with the ancient life form labeled the Cassini, he'd been at a loss to explain the feelings that coursed through his body and his mind whenever he tapped into their consciousness.

For that was essentially what he was doing: establishing a direct link with an alien intelligence that had flourished—and apparently had migrated throughout the galaxy—for a billion years. First discovered by a scientific outpost, the Cassini enveloped Saturn's orange moon, Titan, in a weblike network. Bon's brainwaves were aligned in a pattern that provided two-way communication with them, allowing the Cassini to plunder his mind, while at the same time providing an access point where a *Galahad* Council member could make requests and extract information. A portion of that information had secured safe passage through the deadly minefield of the Kuiper Belt.

The connection was established through the use of a device that scientists on the doomed outpost had created. Known simply as the translator, the small metallic ball opened the pathways between Bon and the Cassini.

The price of that connection was measured in pain. Bon's initial links with the Cassini had literally forced him to his knees, crippling him with agonizing spasms that brought him to the brink of unconsciousness. And yet, as time went by, and as more connections became necessary, he developed a tolerance for the excruciating pain, along with an understanding of how to maintain a touch of self-control.

And, he was forced to admit, he had also acquired an intense curiosity about it all.

Triana had become alarmed by Bon's sudden infatuation with the connection. She compared it to an addiction, a compulsion to link with something that might be causing serious damage. Because of that, Triana had chosen to keep the translator in her possession. However, in a final meeting with Bon before slipping through the wormhole, she had left the translator with him. Had she done it intentionally? Bon couldn't be sure. But, in the days that followed, he'd wrestled with the responsibility; he *wanted* to connect, and yet Triana's words held a measure of power over him. The truth was, he couldn't be sure if his agonizing connection with the Cassini was an addiction or not.

One thing, however, was certain. There were questions he desperately wanted answers to, and the Cassini seemed to be the only reliable source of information.

He stood alone in Dome 1, a satchel strung over his shoulder. With this section of *Galahad's* farming area deserted, Bon could hear a faint whisper of artificial breeze slipping through the nearby leaves, and an occasional tick from the automatic irrigation system. They were calming sounds for the boy who had been raised in a farming family.

He reached into the satchel and removed the translator, careful to not grip the device too firmly. He stared at it for a moment, absently dropping the satchel onto the dirt. Even in its inert state, Bon believed that he could feel the translator's power simmering within.

He had reached his decision earlier in the day. Triana's warning of an addiction echoed across time, but he rejected it. To concede her point would be to admit that he lacked self-control; this connection tonight, he told himself, was rather an exercise in *taking* control.

Beyond that, he'd spent much of the day getting clear on what the exercise was really about in the first place. Did he believe that it would work? Did he believe in the science behind it?

Did he even want it to work, or had the guilt imposed a feeling of obligation?

His strict, rational mind battled all of these questions until he found a relative place of calm acceptance. The connection itself with the Cassini would work; the results remained to be seen. A murky cloud concealed the validity of the science involved, which left him only his brief history with the alien force to go on; what they could—or could not—accomplish was impossible to know.

And the very fact that he was obsessed with the question in the first place convinced him that he did indeed want it to work.

He dropped to his knees, a position that he could assume either voluntarily or be forced into from the pain. Dropping the metallic ball to the dirt, he sat back on his heels for a moment, his eyes closed, and breathed in the moist air of the dome. He could feel his heart rate automatically begin its inevitable climb, and concentrated on the deep breaths that prepared him for the link.

At the same time, his mind sifted through the questions that raged within. He wondered if his ability to control the pain had advanced to the point where he could successfully frame the questions properly; when it came to dialogue with the Cassini, Bon was most certainly the infant talking with the parent. It was best to prepare as well as possible before attempting the conversation.

A shout from across the dome caused Bon to open his eyes and cock his head to one side. He didn't want company during this episode. But the voices that drifted through the fields moved off in another direction.

With one final long exhale, he reached out and loosely picked up the translator. Then, shifting it to his palm, he closed his grip.

Immediately his head shot backward, his entire body racked with pain. An instinctual cry slipped from his mouth and his teeth clenched. The breathing which had been slow and smooth just moments earlier was now labored and fitful. His shoulders twitched with spasms that seemed to be tearing around inside his body, racing from point to point. His eyes rolled back before closing, and brilliant orange light splashed across the insides of his lids.

Sounds began to seep from his mouth and soon coalesced into a small symphony of voices. It signaled an extension to a small group of other crew members who came close to sharing the same neural patterns as Bon. They would not be aware of the connection, yet would find themselves suddenly battling headaches.

Nothing, however, compared to what Bon was feeling.

After a few seconds, his conscious mind began to fight the overpowering presence of the Cassini, pushing back their grasp. He had learned to rein in their ravenous appetite for control, to somehow maintain a sliver of his own identity while they buzzed through his head. It stemmed the tide of pain somewhat and allowed him to focus his thoughts.

His eyes fluttered open briefly, long enough to assure him that he was still alone in this patch of the dome. Then, with a force of effort, he pushed a thought into the forefront of his mind and fought to keep it there, as if demanding to be heard. He would compel the Cassini to hear him.

Rather than a steady torrent, the pain began to pulse through him in waves. There were moments where it dissolved to nothing, but then rushed through again, sending him back on his heels. During one of the breaks, he caught his breath and transfered the thought into words.

"Where . . . is . . . she?"

When the opportunity presented itself, he asked again.

And again.

5

Who doesn't love a good magic trick? Even when it's something as simple as pulling a coin out of someone's ear, people don't want to think about how the magician palmed the coin, or how they fooled everyone into looking this way while they focused over there.

No, deep down, what you humans really love about magic is the surprise. It's almost a challenge, in a way; you know that you're being manipulated, but you always believe you're sharp enough to spot the misdirection. Then, when the trickster pulls it off, you almost have to laugh.

In fact, that love of the unexpected shows up in many forms, and always seems to bring a smile. Surprise parties, finding money in a coat pocket, or when an old friend shows up out of the blue . . .

Wait. That last one can often be the biggest surprise of all.

Gap picked at his dinner, his usual hearty appetite taking a break this particular night. The Dining Hall was still fairly busy, especially given the late hour, but Gap sat by himself, a vid-screen open before him.

He went over the data again—he'd lost track of how many times now—and yet nothing about the blip in the radiation shield made sense. He stabbed at an apple chunk and was lifting it to his mouth when he stopped.

Hannah Ross stood before him, a tray in her hand.

They stared at each other for what seemed an eternity, until Gap slowly set down his fork. "Hi," he said.

"Hi. Mind if I sit down?"

Gap's mind spun out of control. The two of them had been an item for a couple of months, but their breakup had not been pleasant. Since that time they'd not spoken at all, despite a few attempts by Gap; when Hannah had not responded, he'd given up. Now she stood there, asking to sit with him . . . and he froze.

There was no question in his mind that he would say yes, but how enthusiastically? Should he simply shrug, as if it didn't matter to him one way or another? Or should he smile and offer a pleasant welcome, without conveying excitement or nonchalance? What could she possibly want to discuss, anyway? Was she missing him? He certainly missed her, and it was good to—

"Well?" she said.

He mentally shook the sand out of his brain; he'd been staring up at her with his mouth halfway open. "Uh, yeah, sure," he said, indicating the chair across from him.

She sat down, bumping her leg into the table in the process, and Gap reached out to steady his water before it turned over. They both chuckled nervously, each aware of the awkward beginning. Hannah quickly began to arrange her tray, aligning the edges so that it paralleled the edge of the table. She set out a knife and fork, keeping them perpendicular to her, then placed a napkin on her lap. During the entire production she made no eye contact with Gap.

Once settled, she began to eat, taking a bite of salad, then resetting her fork on the table, neatly aligned. She pushed her long, blond hair out of her face, only to have it fall back. She repeated the motion, this time tucking the unruly strands behind her ears.

After another quiet minute she finally spoke. "I hear there was some excitement with the radiation shield. What was that all about?"

Gap studied her face. *So,* he thought, *this is all business.* All right, he could match that.

"That's a good question. It lasted less than a second, but that's enough to set off the alarms. No reason that we know of." Then, not liking the way that sounded, he added, "At least not yet."

Hannah nodded. "I wondered if . . . well, you didn't ask my opinion."

Gap smiled at her. "Okay, I'll play. Hannah, what's your opinion?"

She took a bite of an energy bar and chewed thoughtfully before responding. "I was thinking about how many strange things we've come across already, and yet we're barely out of our own backyard. I'm sure we've all thought about what was on the other side of the wormholes."

"Yes?"

"And I wondered if maybe a completely different form of radiation might have leaked out before it disappeared."

Gap sat back and considered this. He had to admit, the idea was fascinating. Who could say what poured into or out of these portals?

"That's an interesting idea," he finally said. "And you think it might be a type of radiation that we're not equipped to filter out?"

"Maybe."

"Hmm," he said. "Well, I'll have a chat with Roc about that. Thank you. Anything else?"

Hannah fidgeted with the edge of her tray. "I've also wondered about the area of space that we're rushing into. As every second slips past, we're getting farther and farther away from the sun's protection. I mean, the Kuiper Belt was dangerous, but for all we know it's even more dangerous out here."

"And that danger might be radiation," Gap said.

"Right. We've always assumed that cosmic radiation would

be fairly consistent throughout the galaxy. But perhaps our sun protects us more than we thought. Once we're outside that cocoon, it might jump drastically."

He nodded, but kept his gaze on her. It didn't take long for him to sense her discomfort.

"I'm sure you'll figure it out," she said. She took another bite, then a sip of water. Gap sensed that there was more she wanted to discuss besides the radiation emergency. But he waited patiently; she'd approached him, after all.

A minute went by before Hannah spoke up again. "I'm just sick thinking about what might have happened to Triana," she said. "It doesn't seem possible that she could be gone for good." For the first time since sitting down she looked into his face. "What does your gut tell you? Will she be back?"

Gap winced. "You know, I'm getting that question a lot. Everyone wants to know what I think will happen."

"Human nature," Hannah said. "During a time of crisis, we like to be reassured. Or at least given a glimmer of hope. That's probably where everyone is right now, just wanting to hold on to some hope that she'll be back."

"And what if she doesn't come back?" Gap said. "If I go around telling everyone that Triana will magically pop back out of nowhere, and then she doesn't . . ." He shook his head. "I can't do that. You have just as much information as I do, just like the rest of the crew. It's impossible to imagine what might happen. All I know is that we have to go with the assumption that she *won't* be back; then, if we're lucky enough to see her again, fantastic. But I don't know, and it's not smart to speculate."

She broke eye contact with him and peered at her plate of food. "I imagine you've given some thought to the possibility of being the new Council Leader. How would you feel about that?"

He paused, wondering what had prompted the question. Was *this* why she was suddenly talking to him again? Was she intrigued with the notion that he might become the ship's commander?

"I've thought about it," he said slowly. "But only because so many people have talked to me about it. It's not something that I even contemplated before Triana took off."

"Not ever?"

Gap looked away for a moment. "Well, I've thought about the automatic crew election that's coming up in a couple of years, whether I'd want to run for a spot on the Council again, or, if Triana wanted to step down, maybe the top spot." He looked back at her. "But I haven't dwelled on it, if that's what you mean."

She shrugged. "You and Triana have totally different personalities. What do you think you'd do differently if you were in charge?"

He sat back again and drummed his fingers on the table. "What's this all about?"

"What do you mean? I'm just talking with you."

"That's exactly what I mean. You've avoided me completely, haven't responded to my notes. Now suddenly you're talking with me like nothing ever happened. Like the old days."

Her gaze drifted back up to meet his. She put down her fork, dabbed at the corner of her mouth with her napkin, and took another sip of water. Again, Gap was patient.

"Maybe it takes me longer to get over things than it does for you," she said. "Especially when you were the one who ended it."

"I didn't end it," Gap said evenly. "I told you that I was going through a rough time and didn't think I'd be good company for a while. That's not the same as ending it completely."

"So it was my turn to go through a rough time then, okay? Maybe I wasn't good company for a while. Besides, you wanted your space, and you got it. It's not worth fighting over now."

"You're right, it's not. I'm just curious why suddenly you want to talk again."

"Would you prefer I leave you alone?"

He sighed, feeling exasperated. "No, I'm glad you're here. Sheesh, can a guy at least ask a question?"

Hannah sat stone-faced for a moment, and then a slight smile curled at the corner of her mouth. "Yes, you can. I'm just a little nervous, okay?" She winced and rubbed her leg. "I'll probably end up with a lovely bruise on my knee just from trying to sit down here with you, pretending to be calm."

Gap returned the smile. "For what it's worth, I didn't exactly put on a relaxed face either. When you walked up I probably looked like a fish in a net, gasping for air." He let them both enjoy the brief silence after their mutual acknowledgement, then said, "I'm sure that I would probably operate a little differently than Triana. Probably a bit more communication with the crew, just because of my nature. She's quiet, and I'm . . . well, I'm not.

"And," he added, "I'd probably want to look at crew work schedules, maybe tweak things a bit. I think we're starting to get a little rusty with some of the basic chores around the ship. I don't know if it's complacence, or if we're just tired. But after everything we've been through recently, I know that we need to be on top of everything. This radiation warning is just a reminder that, even though we're out of the Kuiper Belt and the vultures are gone, it doesn't mean we have smooth sailing ahead."

Hannah took another drink, set her glass down, then reached out and nudged it about an inch to the right. "The crew seems pretty comfortable with you, don't you think?"

It was funny, Gap realized, how things turned so quickly. He'd gone through a difficult stretch where his self-confidence was shot, where he felt that he was contributing next to nothing as a Council member, and had even contemplated resigning. Now, in a flash, he was on the brink of running for Council Leader. His esteem, in the eyes of the crew, had grown considerably since he'd unmasked the methods behind Merit Simms's plot to force a return to Earth. Was the crew comfortable with the idea of Gap as the ship's leader? Probably, he decided.

That still didn't mean that *he* was completely comfortable with the idea. He had to admit, however, that just hearing Hannah talk about it sent a charge through him.

Or was it simply the notion that Hannah might be impressed with him as Council Leader?

"I can't speak for the crew," he said. "I would hope that they'd be comfortable with anyone on the Council stepping up to lead."

A half-smile once again crept across Hannah's face. She took a last bite of her dinner—Gap noticed that she'd barely touched the plate of food; was she really here for dinner?—and slowly pushed back her chair.

"Well," she said, "I have some work to do before bed. It was good to talk with you."

"Yeah. Good to see you, too." He watched her drop off her tray and slip out the door. For the next few minutes he found it impossible to refocus on his work. Like the ship itself, his own shield had been briefly pierced.

And his own personal alarms were going off.

An hour later Gap made his customary nightly visit to the ship's Control Room. The scattered work stations were thinly manned at this late hour; *Galahad*, for the most part, was tucked in for the night. Three crew members nodded a hello to him as he walked in, and then settled back into their calibrations and reports. A faint stream of music trickled in from hidden speakers, and the large vidscreen displayed the almost hypnotic splash of stars. It was tranquil—one reason Gap never dreaded this part of his daily routine.

But he was also exhausted, physically and mentally. "Five minutes," he had promised himself on the walk from the Dining Hall. "Five minutes, and then to bed."

It didn't work out that way.

He had barely fallen into the chair at his station when the

entire room was flooded by a blinding flash of light. It shattered the calm of the room like a billion strobe lights simultaneously firing outside the ship. Gap and the three other crew members instinctively threw their hands up to cover their eyes, but by then it was over. Looking down and away from the vidscreen, Gap blinked several times and shook his head.

"What was that?"

Gap looked at the girl who had asked the question, then stole a hurried glance at the vidscreen. Even though he'd not been looking directly at it when the flash came, it had been powerful enough to leave afterimage spots dancing across his vision. "I have no idea, Addie. That was . . . interesting."

He blinked rapidly again and turned back to his work station. "Roc, did we just witness a supernova or something?"

"Give me a moment," the computer said. "But no, it was not an exploding star."

While waiting, Gap quickly checked in with Engineering and was told that there was no change in the radiation shield. Whatever the light flash might have been, it hadn't caused damage to their defenses.

Not obvious damage, at least.

"This is quite odd," Roc said a moment later. "A flash that intense, and yet there is zero residue."

Gap chanced another look at the screen. "What do you mean?"

"I mean there's nothing there. I have a perfect fix on location, even approximate distance—not that far, by the way—and yet there's nothing there. No object of any kind, no residual radiation, nothing. It's as if it never happened."

"Ugh, tell that to my retinas," Gap said. "Good thing none of us were staring into the vidscreen at the time." He leaned forward and ran a hand through his hair. "So, first a failure of the radiation shield, and now a blast of light that came from nowhere. Anything at all that you can find?"

"The light was more than light," Roc said. "And I'm not trying to be funny. I mean, I don't need to try, it just comes naturally. But in this case I'm just telling it like it is."

"And I have no idea what you're talking about," Gap said.

"Good, because I don't either, and I'd hate for you to know something that I didn't. But essentially that flash was charged somehow. Not your standard light as radiation charge; more like a strange shower of particles. Or rather, a shower of strange particles."

"Why do you say that?"

"Because we have no data on these particular particles. Until two minutes ago, no human being—or ultra-cool computer—has ever witnessed them."

Gap looked again at the screen, prepared to quickly avert his eyes. The information tumbled through his mind: a blast of light, combined with mysterious particles, and all from an invisible source.

He would not be in bed in five minutes.

6

She stood with her hands clasped over her head, catching her breath, drenched in sweat. The sharp tang of salt stung her mouth, but it wasn't an unpleasant sensation. Quite the contrary; for Channy there was no better feeling than a strenuous workout, one that worked her lungs to the max and brought about a dull muscular ache that actually felt good. Today's cardiovascular drills had featured some of her favorite participants, crew members who relished the same intensity at least a couple of times each week. She thought of them as the race horses, thoroughbreds who bolted from the gate with a determination that never let up, never faltered. It was a test that no one in this particular group wanted to fail.

The gym shared *Galahad*'s lower level with the Airboard track, the Spider bay, and the Storage Sections. It was usually a beehive of activity during the morning workout sessions, and now, as crew members left to shower and grab breakfast, Channy began to plot a new exercise routine for the afternoon group. Her roommate, Kylie Rickman, her face splotchy and streaked with sweat, sauntered over and tossed a towel at *Galahad*'s Activities Director.

"You would make Einstein proud," Kylie said.

Channy passed the towel around her neck. "Einstein? What are you talking about?"

"He was the one who suggested that time was affected as you approach the speed of light. Well, as this ship gets closer and closer to that speed, your concept of time is getting skewed. Twice today you said 'keep it up, one more minute.' I timed it, and we went more than two minutes both times."

"Oh, it didn't hurt that bad," Channy said with a laugh. "Besides, you're not supposed to be watching the clock during my workouts."

"Just wanted to see if my time perception was screwed up, or if you're just a monster. News flash: you're a monster."

Channy rubbed her face with a corner of her towel, then picked up a cup of water. "You'll thank me when we get to Eos."

They both took swigs of water, then Kylie said, "So, what do you think of Gap as the new Council Leader?"

Channy laughed. "He hasn't even been nominated yet."

"He will be, you know that."

"Well," Channy said, "I think he'd do a great job. He obviously has the experience from being on the Council, and I think the crew respects him. Especially after that whole Merit Simms garbage."

"Speaking of Merit," Kylie said, "I heard rumors that at least one other person might be nominated from the crew. You don't think it'd be him, do you?"

"Merit?" Channy said. "Are you kidding? He wouldn't stand a chance. He might get three or four votes from his circle of friends, but that's it."

Kylie shrugged. "You're probably right. I just can't think who else might run." She tossed her towel into a hamper. "All right, I'm off. A shower and then back to work. See you 'round."

Channy watched her roommate trudge toward the door, then stiffened as Bon passed Kylie on his way in. If he caught a glimpse of Channy he didn't show it, and instead made his way toward the exercise bikes. Never one to join a group workout, the Swede focused on solitary workouts with cardio machines and weights.

With a scowl, Channy eyed him for a few moments, resisting an urge to walk over and say something. She was still angry with him, and thankful that he mostly confined himself to the seclusion of the domes. On one hand she could appreciate why he loved it up there, why he felt so passionate about his work in the fields. *He might be emotionally detached from people,* she thought, *yet maybe his connection to nature didn't allow those personal feelings to develop.*

But she refused to feel sorry for him. After her own recent heartbreaking experience, she couldn't understand how anyone could allow a potentially beautiful relationship to slip through their fingers without fighting for it. She might have lost out in her pursuit of love, but she could hold her head high in the knowledge that she had given it everything she had.

Bon, for all of his gruff demeanor, had been too afraid to let down his guard with Alexa. Channy vowed to never wall off her heart like he had done.

As if on cue, he turned his head and briefly made eye contact. Then, simultaneously, he turned his attention back to the bike while Channy spun on her heel and stormed back to her office to finish the day's planning.

Gap had barely seen his room in the past week, except for quick sleep breaks. After lunch he forced himself to seek shelter there, to sit quietly and meditate for an hour. He dimmed the lights, dialed up low, soothing background music, then sat cross-legged on his bed and closed his eyes.

More than anything he wanted to calm his mind, and allow himself to process the events that had cascaded upon each other in the past few days. He hadn't even come to terms yet with Triana's surprising disappearance when suddenly he was confronted with the task of temporarily leading the crew. He had barely begun to acclimate to that duty when the question of his nomination as Council Leader was presented.

And now, before he could adequately consider that wrinkle, Hannah had suddenly popped back into his life, sending his thoughts pinwheeling out of control. Her questions, as well as her tone, seemed to imply that she was not only encouraging him to pursue the position, but that she had finally recovered from their break.

Did that mean she was open to the idea of reconnecting?

So many new complications, all within a matter of days. Not to mention the potentially deadly radiation threat, and now a mysterious bolt of space lightning. No wonder he felt overwhelmed and in need of downtime.

He craned his head to one side, then the other, and pulled his shoulder blades back. Even the stretching helped a little bit, and he made a conscious effort to control his breathing: deep inhale, hold, long slow exhale.

When he felt himself settling into a relaxed state, he began to address the matters one at a time. With Triana, there wasn't much within his control. She was gone, she might or might not return, and they were doing all that they reasonably could at the moment. He acknowledged that the primary issue with Triana was of a personal nature; his feelings for her were a mixed bag, including a new tinge of anger.

But none of that was helpful. Emotions might run strong, but his rational mind fought to put all of that behind him for now and to concentrate only on the relevant—and actionable—things on his plate.

Leading the crew for the short term didn't seem to be a problem. The nervousness that he felt at the beginning of the crew meeting had quickly evaporated, and it was obvious that he felt comfortable in that position.

Did that equate to taking on the position of Council Leader

on a full-time basis? He had admitted to Hannah that the idea was appealing. A nomination was easy enough to come by; then it became a matter of convincing the crew that he was the right person for the job. He would easily have the support of the other Council members, including Bon, who would merely want the process over and done with as quickly as possible.

And he seemed to have the support of Hannah Ross. Why was that suddenly so important to him?

He knew that, of all the things on his plate right now, this was the least critical, and yet it had forced its way to the top. Since their brief meeting in the Dining Hall, he found himself not only reliving each moment of the conversation, but suddenly recalling many of the things they had done together months before. The feeling was not unlike the original sensation of their relationship, which on the one hand confused him, but on the other hand excited him. He'd questioned his role in their breakup so many times, and recognized that he regretted how he'd handled it all. Just the chance to make it up to her, to undo all of the hurt he'd caused . . . that's all he'd hoped for. It seemed like the door might have opened.

What would happen if he rushed through that doorway? He had to be honest with himself, and acknowledge that the idea of reconnecting with Hannah had certainly caused a jolt of excitement. For a few moments he allowed himself to daydream, to envision a future—perhaps a very near future—where he was suddenly *Galahad*'s Council Leader, and Hannah was once again at his side. All would be forgiven, they would work together, they would laugh together . . .

Was it too good to be true?

His thoughts were interrupted by the voice of the ship's computer.

"So sorry to burst in like this," Roc said. "But there are a couple of things we need to talk about right away."

Gap opened his eyes. "What's up?"

"First, just to satisfy my curiosity, how do you sit like that without your feet falling asleep? And second, our little blip with the radiation shield has happened again."

"What? How long this time?"

"About a second and a half, and then all seemed normal again. *Seemed* would be the operative word. Things are not normal, and they're getting less so with each passing hour. Engineering has gone on alert. Ruben was around again this time; I told him I would let you know."

Gap pushed himself up from the bed and slipped his shoes on. "Tell Ruben I'm on my way, and let the other Council members know, would you please?"

He sprinted out the door, and two minutes later rushed into the Engineering section. The air felt charged, and all eyes immediately turned to him. Ruben was waiting.

"Same as last time," he told Gap, and together they hurried over to the radiation control panel. "An alarm went off, and this thing lit up like crazy. The first time it barely blinked; this time it was still quick, but lasted a little longer."

Gap looked over the data, then, using the keypad, fired off a sequence of code. "Roc," he said while he typed, "are we able to isolate whether it's an internal issue with our shield, or if it's being caused by something from the outside?"

"Now *that's* an excellent question," the computer said. "If this is what happens when you sit in that lotus position, I won't make fun of it ever again."

"Roc . . ."

"Well, let's just say that I haven't been able to isolate any particular malfunction with the unit itself. However, that doesn't mean the failures aren't affecting it. And, since we've run tests on the ship itself and found no cause for this, it might be time to see what's going on outside. I see you're setting up an external scan."

Gap shrugged. "It's the only thing that makes sense. If the

system had a problem it would show up in one of the diagnostic checks. Hannah brought up the idea that something might have leaked out of the wormholes."

Ruben, who had been standing quietly behind Gap, spoke up. "But the wormholes have all closed up. Why would they affect us now?"

"I don't know," Gap said. "Maybe they're not. But it's an interesting theory." He finished typing in the code, then stood back and looked up at the monitor. "And, even if that's not it, we might find that it's something else out there. We're definitely in uncharted space now; who knows what we'll run into?"

He ran a hand through his spiky hair. "Now, Roc, let's talk about something you said a few minutes ago. You said the system is getting less normal. Explain that."

"One drop in the shield was fine, especially for less than a second. Now, with multiple drops I've picked up a fractional decrease in unit efficiency."

Ruben gave Gap a confused look. "What does that mean?"

Gap exhaled a long breath. "A fractional decrease in unit efficiency sounds like a fancy way of saying that it's wearing out."

"Not fancy," Roc said. "Sophisticated. 'Wearing out' is so . . . common. But it works out to the same thing."

Gap understood immediately and considered the possibilities. One particularly nagging thought forced its way in, but he didn't want to vocalize it in front of Ruben and the other crew members who stood nearby.

If it was an external problem, it was apparent that the ship's defense shield had problems with it. Big problems, which were getting worse with each incident. And if they couldn't be remedied—and quickly—then all of the other things he'd thought about in his room wouldn't matter at all. *Galahad* would be a lifeless shell, hurtling through space.

He'd insisted that Roc wake him by five thirty, for the day was sure to be interesting. And yet when the ship's computer pulled him from a dark, heavy slumber with an imitation yodel, Gap groaned and pulled the pillow over his head.

Roc immediately piped in sounds of a rooster crowing, letting it repeat three or four times.

Gap pulled a corner of the pillow away from his mouth. "Hey, Daniil doesn't need this, you know. At least let *him* sleep."

"Your roommate left ten minutes ago for an early morning workout," Roc said.

Turning over and raising himself up on one elbow, Gap saw the empty bed on the other side of the room, then fell back. "How does he do it?" he said under his breath.

"Willpower, determination, a sense of pride," Roc said. "If you need help looking those up, I'll help you with the spelling."

"You're not as funny as you think you are," Gap said, letting the pillow fall back over his face.

"Oh, really?" the computer said. "Is *this* funny?" Suddenly the room was filled with the sound of screaming monkeys.

After enduring it for half a minute, Gap sat up. "All right, all right, I'm up."

The sound of monkeys was replaced with the soundtrack of

applause. Despite his irritation, Gap found himself laughing. "Okay, I'll admit, that's funny."

He stretched and hauled himself to his feet. The next few minutes were spent showering and getting dressed for the day. By six o'clock he was sitting at the computer, scanning his mail and checking reports from the ship's various departments. His first priority was the update from Engineering; with a sigh of relief he saw that no further radiation shield breakdowns had occurred overnight.

Just before falling into bed he had sent a note to Bon, requesting an update on crew work schedules. There was no response yet.

The other item that tickled at the back of his mind would be posted on the crew's message board. He glanced at the clock in the lower corner of his monitor, saw that it was almost 6:15, then punched in the key to take him to the main board. Highlighted against the random messages that were tacked there was a bulletin from Roc; it was tagged *Council Leader Nominations*.

He sat back, his finger hovering above the Open key. A strange sensation swept over him, and it took a moment to realize that it was a combination of two separate fears: one, that he would not be nominated, and two, that he *would* be nominated. He took a deep breath and silently acknowledged that both scenarios held equal amounts of tension. If his name was on the list, it meant that he was one step closer to taking on responsibility for the most daunting mission humankind had ever embarked upon.

If his name was absent, it meant that the crew found him undeserving.

He couldn't bring himself to open the bulletin. The seesaw battle within him began to rage again, beginning with the swirl of anxiety that he was unworthy of the role. His earlier self-doubts bubbled back to the surface, the same doubts that had plagued him weeks ago and had slowly been put to rest.

At the same time he found that deep down he craved the

validation from his peers. He'd worked hard, beginning at the *Galahad* training complex, and during the first year of the mission. This, in essence, was what he had spent the last two and a half years of his life working for.

He drummed his fingers on the desktop for a moment, then leaned forward and clicked the Open key. His eyes quickly scanned the notice from Roc:

> The twenty-four-hour nomination process, in which every crew member was eligible to submit a name as a candidate for the position of *Galahad* Council Leader, has officially ended as of six o'clock this morning. Two crew members have been nominated, and will now face an election in one week.

Gap immediately seized upon the two names listed in alphabetical order. The first one was Gap Lee.

Below it, the other name glared out from the screen, searing both his eyes and his heart in one shot.

Hannah Ross.

He sat, frozen in his chair, barely breathing. No matter how long he stared at the name, it didn't seem real. Slowly he pushed back his chair and stood up, but kept his gaze locked on the screen. His mind drifted back to his conversation with Hannah in the Dining Hall, and within seconds he felt a surge of anger.

She had quietly quizzed him about his plans, all the while aware that she would be a competing candidate for the position. She had tricked him, he was sure, into opening up and spilling his thoughts about the position itself, as well as his intentions for the crew.

And now she was going head-to-head with him in a run for Council Leader of *Galahad*.

He began a relentless march around the room, hands on his hips. Each time he passed his desk his eyes darted back to the taunting name on the screen.

Hannah Ross.

He silently fumed. Suddenly it was no secret why she had broken her long stretch of silence. He had allowed himself to sit there and entertain wispy daydreams of rekindling their relationship. He had imagined them once again laughing together, walking hand in hand, holding court like a royal couple aboard the ship. How could he have been so blind, so foolish? How could he have . . .

Wait, he told himself. What about her? How could *she* have done this to *him*?

He stalked to the far side of the room and leaned with one hand against the wall, the other running through his hair. Then, with a loud exhale, he rushed back to the computer, closed out of the bulletin board, and snapped off the screen.

In seconds he was out of his room, storming down the deserted corridor, with no particular destination in mind.

At eight o'clock the lower level of *Galahad* was bustling with activity as crew members passed each other in the hall, some heading toward the gym, others winding back to the lift after finishing a workout. They exchanged boisterous greetings, many punctuated with friendly jabs. There were also excited conversations exchanged regarding the bulletin board posting about the upcoming election. The chatter lent an excited air to the gym side of the ship's basement level.

In the opposite direction things were much quieter. Tucked around a corner from the lift was a corridor that led to the Storage Sections and Spider bay. Shrouded in mystery, the Storage Sections had been sealed before being loaded onto the ship, with explicit instructions that they not be touched until reaching Eos. The Spider bay was *Galahad*'s hangar, housing the sleek metal shuttles that would eventually carry all of the crew members to the surface of one or both of the two Earthlike worlds that orbited the target star.

Along this hallway was a large window that framed a spectacular cosmic display. Hannah stood there now, leaning against the wall and gazing out at the fiery array of stars. She instinctively picked out the familiar constellations, mentally cataloging the individual stars of which they were composed. Her mind skipped through their descriptions, everything from star-type to size to distance from Earth. Growing up in sparsely populated Alaska she'd been blessed with a sky free of light pollution, allowing her a beautiful canvas upon which to gaze, and which later inspired her to create dazzling artistic renditions of cosmic scenes.

None of which could compare with this view.

She understood, however, that the exercise of naming the stars was purely a distraction from the anxiety that gnawed at her. It had, in fact, been eating away at her for a full day. By now she was sure that Gap had seen the announcement of her nomination; she was also quite sure of his reaction.

Ironically, this had been the location of some of their most intimate conversations. Huddled together, gazing at the spectacle outside, this had been the setting for her happiest moments. They were moments she'd never forget.

Nor, for that matter, would she likely forget the transformation within her that was born from their split. She wondered if the change would have occurred anyway, at some given point in her life, but needed the kick-start that Gap had unexpectedly provided. For the most part she felt as if she was the same Hannah as before—her devotion to science, her need for order, her outward manner, for instance—and yet a subtle shift had definitely taken place. Her decision to accept the Council Leader nomination was merely the first public evidence of that shift.

Now she traced a finger along the pane that separated her from the icy vacuum of space, and—although she knew it was only her mind playing tricks with her—felt that same cold flowing through her body. Her stomach was in knots.

The nomination had not been her idea. In fact, when originally presented, her initial response had been to laugh and politely decline. But the more she listened to the crew member sitting across from her in the empty Conference Room, the more she had been seduced by the possibilities, and by the logic of it. A fresh viewpoint, a fresh voice, a new direction. It had somehow made sense.

Now that she had seen her name on the screen, the magnitude of it weighed upon her. This meeting with the crew member who had nominated her was, if anything, a pep talk designed to steel her nerves for the weeklong campaign ahead.

She heard the footsteps but kept her face glued to the window. A moment later she heard him speak.

"I'm guessing you didn't eat anything this morning." The voice had a tinge of laughter behind it.

"Ugh," she said. "I don't want to think about food right now. My stomach won't be able to handle anything for a while."

She felt him slowly approach and stand beside her, staring out at the stars.

"I will never, ever get tired of this view," he said.

She nodded in reply. They remained silent for a moment before turning to face each other. Merit Simms pushed a strand of long, jet-black hair out of his face and offered a smile.

"So, other than the butterflies, how are you feeling?" he said.

Hannah shrugged. "Okay. Nervous, obviously."

He turned his head slightly and frowned. "You're not second-guessing this, are you?"

"No. Well, maybe a little. But it's done, and I'm ready to move forward."

His crooked smile returned. "Good, I'm glad to hear that."

Hannah looked into Merit's eyes and, not for the first time, questioned the tenuous connection she had formed with him. She reminded herself that it was only a few short weeks ago that Merit had led a movement to virtually overthrow the Council and, in so doing, turn the ship around and return to Earth. It was Gap who had discovered the treacherous methods to which Merit had stooped, including sabotage. The entire plot had been revealed to the crew in a dramatic showdown in the auditorium, and, from that moment on, Merit had receded into a shadow of his former blustery persona, becoming practically invisible on the ship.

Until now.

He pulled a step closer to her and placed a hand on her shoulder. "You're gonna be a great Council Leader. You're exactly what this crew needs right now."

Hannah looked down at his hand, then slowly back to his face. She noted the faint scar beneath his right eye, and the dark, thin hairs on his chin. A moment later he slowly withdrew the hand.

"Listen," she said, stepping back to re-establish the distance between them. "We touched on this once, but I want to make sure that we're clear on one thing. I'm not doing this as part of some personal crusade that you're waging against Gap."

Merit's face twisted. "Of course not. All I said was that you're gonna be great, that's all."

"I know what you said, but I also know that you're carrying around a lot of bitterness toward Gap. I'm just telling you that this has nothing to do with your issues with him."

"I don't know what—"

"We're not debating this right now," Hannah said. "I've said what I needed to say, and we can move on."

Merit tried unsuccessfully to rein in a smirk. "Good. I think the next order of business is making sure that you get in front of the crew right away, so they can start to get comfortable with you."

Hannah stared back at him, then shook her head. "What is this?"

"What do you mean?"

"I mean that you sound like . . . like some kind of campaign manager or something. That wasn't part of our discussion."

"I told you that I would be happy to help," Merit said. He leaned against the wall opposite her and crossed his arms. "Hannah, I came to you because I think you'd be a great choice as *Galahad*'s Council Leader. You understand, probably better than anyone, what's going on out here in the void, and the crew respects you because of your sharp mind. On top of that, you bring a fresh approach to things. But you've never done anything like this before, and it wouldn't hurt to have some friends helping out."

Hannah chuckled. "So now we're friends?"

Merit looked down for a moment, then pushed off from the wall and faced her. "Why don't I just let you handle everything on your own? You suddenly don't want anything to do with me, that's obvious. I don't know if you're just overwhelmed with the reality of the situation, or if you really hate me that much. But all I did was nominate you because I thought you'd do a great job, and then offered to help. Sorry if I wasted your time."

He turned and began to walk away. Hannah hesitated, then quickly reached out and grabbed his arm.

"No, wait a minute," she said.

It was his turn to look down at her hand. When she pulled it away, his gaze tracked upward to her face. "Well?" he said.

Hannah looked away for a moment. "I just need everything to sink in, okay? I'm sure . . ." She paused, taking a couple of deep breaths. "I'm sure that I'll have questions for you. And . . . thanks. I appreciate your offer to help."

Merit pushed a strand of hair out of his face again. "Don't freak yourself out over this, Hannah. Don't make it more overwhelming than it needs to be."

She smiled weakly. "I tend to do that with things."

"Everything will be fine. We'll talk, we'll map out a strategy that you're comfortable with, and then let you roll. Hey, if you lose you don't get thrown off the ship or anything. What's the worst that can happen? You lose an election, maybe, but you earn a pretty respected place on this ship. So stop worrying. The crew will still love you no matter what."

He flashed a quick smile, then walked away, back toward the lift. In a few seconds Hannah was alone again, near the observation window. She let out another deep breath, then leaned against the window and peered out.

"It's not the *whole* crew I'm worried about," she whispered.

When motion pictures were first introduced, it wasn't unusual for the audience to yell at the movie screen. People were so captivated by the drama unfolding before them, they felt that they could holler and the actors would hear them and react.

I get the feeling that's exactly what some of you are doing right now. Listen, you can yell at Hannah all you want, but she can't hear you.

And even if she could, it might be drowned out by other little voices screaming in her head. My recommendation is that you at least wait and see what develops between Hannah and Merit. It might turn out fine.

Of course, it might also be disastrous.

Besides—and be honest—how many times have you really listened when people tried to warn you about something? Just like you, Hannah must take the path of her own choosing.

8

The decision had weighed heavily upon her, but Lita felt confident of her choice. Certainly both Mathias and Manu were qualified, but only one of them would be her new top assistant; the other would be disappointed. She had developed friendships with each, so it pained her to know that one would be dealing with an emotional setback. But it was simply the way it had to be.

She quickly checked her e-mail, then left Sick House and made her way to the Conference Room, where she found Manu already waiting.

"Prompt, as always," she said, smiling at him before grabbing a cup of water and taking a seat.

"My dad was big on making a good impression," he said.

"You've certainly done that." She sipped at her water, then leaned forward on the table. "I won't keep you in suspense, Manu. I just spoke with Mathias a little while ago. He's been a terrific member of the Clinic team, and was a strong candidate for the position. But I've decided to offer you the spot, if you're still interested."

He beamed at her. "Absolutely! Wow, that's great. Thank you."

"You've earned it," she said. "Now, just promise me one thing."

"Name it."

"Remember all of those questions you asked during the interview? Well, don't stop asking them. In fact, I want you to work on answering a few of them, too."

Manu sat back and looked thoughtful. "I have one question right now, if that's okay. It's a bit personal."

"I'm sure I can handle it."

"Well . . . since we started talking about this, I've thought about what happened with Alexa. I wasn't there the day it happened, and I guess I'm just wondering . . ."

He seemed unable to finish the sentence. Lita volunteered.

"Wondering how you would handle a life-and-death situation on the ship?"

He nodded. "Yeah. I'm not worried about any of the work that we're doing, and I know I could pretty much handle an emergency situation when it comes up. But how exactly do you prepare for . . . that?"

Lita rubbed her forehead and considered the question. "You don't prepare for it."

He looked confused. "What do you mean?"

"I mean that the medical training that you had before we left, and the extra work you've put in during the first year, will give you the knowledge you need to handle the situation. But I don't think you can mentally prepare for the worst."

She paused, and her mind instinctually drifted back to conversations she'd had with her mother. Maria Marques had tried to condense her many years of medical experience into several short lessons for her daughter, helping Lita to understand not the book knowledge necessary for *Galahad*'s five-year voyage, but rather the psychological strains that a ship's doctor would need to manage. During her toughest incidents since the launch, Lita found that she often fell back on those intimate discussions with her mom.

Maria had faced her own share of professional crises, one in particular that was personally devastating. Although it affected her on many levels, she maintained her devotion to her calling and served the medical needs of her hometown in Mexico, fighting her way through the personal pain. It was a lesson that Lita clung to during her most trying times.

Now, she stared across the table at Manu, and once again reached back across the mind-numbing distance to her home by the sea, to her mother's wisdom and love. She offered a smile and said, "Nothing that you do to prepare yourself for that moment will ever replicate the actual emotions that you'll feel when it happens. All you can do is wait and see how you're built for it. You can't read about it, you can't do any exercises to train for it, and you can't learn from someone else; you have to experience it, and then learn from it. Hopefully you'll be able to apply it the next time it happens."

Lita stopped and tried to gauge Manu's expression. He seemed to be processing everything that she was saying. He nodded, just a slight dip of his head, and pursed his lips.

"I see what you're saying. I just hope that I handle it as well as you did."

Lita lowered her head, ashamed that he would see the truth in her eyes. Afraid that he would look inside her and reach a different conclusion, one that she felt stained her somehow. A long silence followed.

Finally, she looked up and tried one more smile. "You'll be fine, Manu. I know it."

In her heart, she hoped that someday she would be, too.

The noise level in the Dining Hall had tapered off a bit, but Hannah still found it distracting. With her dinner tray neglected beside her, she glanced back and forth between the table's small vidscreen and her workpad, which was perfectly aligned with the table's edge. She would occasionally squint at something on the screen, then bend over her workpad and modify the figures that flew from her stylus.

Her ordered, logical mind worked best when left undisturbed, but that was impossible on this night. More than a dozen crew members stopped by, either before or after their meal, to wish her good luck in the upcoming election; she graciously thanked each of them. A handful of people sat down beside her for a moment to express their surprise at her willingness to campaign, given her shy reputation; at this, she could only offer a shrug. How could she explain something that she herself couldn't quite understand? But now that the dinner rush was waning, she settled into her work.

It was her mother who had first exposed her to the beauty and magic of puzzles. Some of Hannah's favorite memories as a child included long, cold nights in Alaska, curled up with her mother in a blanket on the couch, each of them furiously trying to solve a word or number puzzle. Often they would download the same puzzle, and then race to see who could successfully finish first. They each kept a bag of chocolate treats on the table before them—Hannah's favorites were the chocolate-covered macadamia nuts—and the winner could select anything from the other's collection. It added a new level of competition to what was already quite fun for Hannah, and from that moment on she was hooked.

The puzzle at this particular moment, however, had more riding on it than a piece of chocolate. The potential danger suggested by the brief failures from *Galahad*'s radiation shield was, in fact, deadly. For while space might appear empty, it teemed with high-speed, high-energy charged particles, moving at ferocious speeds. Each star's blast furnace spewed radiation into its planetary system, and the galaxy itself seethed in a lethal dose of cosmic radiation.

Earth's powerful magnetic field shields it from the majority of harmful particles. Generated deep beneath Earth's surface, in the molten iron that makes up the liquid outer core, this field effectively surrounds the planet. Radiation particles are diverted around Earth, repelled much the way a ship's bow pushes water to each side. *Galahad*'s defense system was designed to work in primarily the same fashion, using electromagnetic forces to bend and push the cosmic radiation to the side as the ship cut through the vacuum of space. Without this shield, crew members would quickly be subjected to deadly cell mutation and damage.

What's more, now it appeared that each successive jolt was causing extensive and lingering damage to their only defense. In a sense, a timer had effectively been started. When it ran out . . .

Hannah read and then reread her notes. She was juggling multiple ideas, a collection of possibilities that might explain the shield dilemma. Just as one idea would take center stage in her mind, she would find countless reasons why it didn't make sense. Then another idea would shift into the spotlight, to be analyzed and tested. Promising scenarios were filed away for later study, while others were immediately discarded.

She snapped the page on her vidscreen to the graphic supplied by Galahad Command prior to launch, the one that plotted the positions of the outer gas planets, the Kuiper Belt, and beyond. She furrowed her brow as she scanned the page. It had been impossible for the scientists on Earth to guarantee what the teenage crew would encounter this far out; the best they could manage, given their limited information, was an educated guess.

No humans had ever passed this way before. Hannah and her crewmates were pioneers.

She wondered if this stretch of space held the answer to the breakdown in *Galahad*'s radiation shield. Not within the shield itself, but something . . . out there. She turned her attention back to her notes, then to the screen, then the notes. Space, she thought; what is different about this portion of space compared to the billions of miles we've left behind? What has changed?

She rubbed at the sore spot on her knee and, glancing around to make sure she was unnoticed for the moment, rolled up her pant leg. She examined the purplish bruise, which had blossomed there, a painful remnant from her awkward encounter with Gap and the table. "Klutz," she muttered to herself.

With an exasperated sigh, she sat back and tapped her fingers on the table. "Roc, have you got a second?" she said.

From the vidscreen's speaker came the computer's deadpan voice. "Well, part of me is assisting Lita with some crew records right now. Another part of me is tied up in Engineering, trying to iron out a bug in the artificial gravity grid; can't have someone walking down the hall and suddenly end up bouncing against the ceiling, now can we? Plus, there's a literature session going on in school right now, and I'm getting all sorts of queries about some guy named Twain. Oh, and the usual mundane requests from the remaining two hundred crew members, things generally not worthy of my vast intellect. I'm stretched like taffy. But for you, Hannah, I can easily spare a second. Maybe more."

She smiled. "Thank you for devoting a sliver of that magnificent brain to helping me. I'm wondering about this." She tapped the vidscreen graphic with her stylus, highlighting a section. "I've factored in the solar radiation at our back and the Milky Way's radiation hitting us straight on. I've even considered that we might be absorbing some form of radiation from your good friends, the Cassini."

"Hey, what do you know?" Roc interrupted. "The hotshot from Alaska tosses a joke. Who would have thunk?"

Hannah's smile returned; she had always envied Gap's unique relationship with the ship's computer, the easy manner in which they exchanged good-natured barbs while still maintaining a close working relationship. Although not exactly in her nature, she had wondered if her own relationship with Roc might expand if she adopted a similar approach.

"But none of that seems to add up," she said. "I mean, rather than an obvious outside influence, I thought it might very well be something about the basic properties of space. Would you agree?"

"Yes."

Hannah waited for more, but nothing seemed to be coming. "Uh . . . okay," she said. "Thanks."

"Sure. That was easy. And not much more than a second. Of course, my curiosity is piqued. You're assuming that the problem is, to put it delicately, a deformity in space. Am I reading you correctly?"

"Maybe," Hannah said. "Do you see where I'm going with this? And, if so, do you think it makes sense to keep checking it out? Let me know if you think I'm wasting time here."

Roc paused, and she could almost imagine his artificial brain flickering with activity before he answered, "I say continue."

She let out a deep breath. "Okay, great. Thanks again."

"That's why I'm here," Roc said. "And now, if you're finished with me, I have to help someone conjugate a verb in one of the romance languages."

Hannah again tapped her fingers on the table. She sighed, absently rubbed at the bruise on her knee, and let her mind begin its inevitable calculations. It might be a long shot, but it was at least something to explore. And it might—might—be the answer they needed to solve the radiation mystery.

Which ultimately might save their lives.

I know that I, like many of you, tend to get caught up in the whirlwind of activity that seems to swirl around Triana and Gap, and these days even Bon. But it's Lita who often catches my attention because of her thoughtful musings. You could almost say that she flies under the radar. When it comes to profound thinking, she's at the head of the class, in my opinion.

D r. Zimmer had laughed when, during a training meeting, Lita announced that she had no intention of allowing *Galahad's* Clinic to "smell like a hospital."

And, to her credit, it didn't. She was adamant about keeping the disinfectant odor to a minimum, and made maximum use of the ship's storehouse of scents, any of which could be dialed up through the vents. This morning it was a calming hint of cinnamon.

She pulled up a chair next to the desk once occupied by Alexa. Manu was busily arranging things to his liking, including a photograph of his family. His parents, two brothers, and a little sister surrounded him in the image. He told Lita that it was taken during the crew's final visit home before the launch, which she silently accepted as the explanation for the sad smiles.

She had her own sad-smile family photo beside her bed.

She also couldn't help but notice what resembled a charm, dangling from a slim, dark chain. Manu had hung the charm from the edge of his vidscreen, but, although it didn't stand out as a display, Lita had no doubt that there was significance to it.

For almost half an hour they talked about Manu's new responsibilities. When they reached a natural break in the orientation session, which allowed them to stretch and relax for a minute, Lita said, "So, any questions so far?"

"After doing so much filing and record-keeping, do you almost wish for someone to come in with a scratch or twisted ankle?" Manu said with a grin.

"A doctor's life is rarely glamorous," she said. "But you'd never know that from watching the movies. Hollywood would never have survived showing what we really do most of the day: routine exams, doing a lot of reading and research, and filling out forms."

"But you love it."

"I do," Lita said. "I grew up around it, so the behind-the-scenes stuff didn't surprise me at all. It's just a matter of being ready in an instant; that's what all of your training is about."

Manu nodded. "My grandfather was a nurse and EMT. I guess there might be something about caregiving that runs in our blood."

That didn't sound far-fetched to Lita; she'd known of many families that had several generations somehow involved in medical practice. She'd never thought of the art of caregiving as a gene that could be passed down, but who knew? Once again Manu had stimulated her thoughts, another sign that she'd made the right decision.

Before diving back into their work, she glanced at the charm hanging from his monitor. "If I'm being too nosy, please tell me. But I'm curious about this beautiful charm. Is there a story behind it?"

"No, I don't mind you asking," Manu said. He lifted the chain and held it out to Lita, who gently held it in her palm while examining the polished stone it held. "It's an amulet."

Lita raised an eyebrow. "An amulet? Like a . . . good luck charm?"

He smiled at her. "In a way, yes. Amulets turn up in a lot of countries on Earth, and there's lots of different beliefs that go along with them. This one's Egyptian, and it's been in my family a long time. In fact, it belonged to that grandfather I told you about. He was raised practically in the shadow of the Great Pyramid, so he grew up bathed in the stories and traditions. He gave this to me when I was selected for the *Galahad* mission. Said I was taking the magic of the pharaohs with me to another world."

"And what belief did your grandfather associate with this?" Lita said, turning the stone over. The reverse side was marked with smooth scratches, obviously etched with a particular message in mind.

"He said it was created to ward off evil."

"Do you believe that?" Lita said.

Manu seemed to consider the question for a long time before offering a small shrug. "Let's just say it was important to him, and to his father, and on back. I respect *their* beliefs, even though I haven't decided yet for myself." He took back the amulet when Lita held it out, and draped it once again over the vidscreen. "What about you? Do you believe in that kind of stuff?"

Lita leaned forward on the desk and crossed her arms. "For me," she said, "it's a question of faith versus fate. A lot of people see those as the same thing, but I don't."

"And how do you see the difference?"

"It's just my own opinion, of course," Lita said, "but I happen to think that faith involves believing in something that can affect what's going to happen, whether that's a supreme being or simply a higher power in the universe. Fate, on the other hand, to me implies that there can be no manipulation of what's to be."

Manu grinned at her again. "And which camp do you fall into?"

She gave a half-shrug. "I guess I'm a bit like you: still trying to decide. I'm grateful that I was brought up in a very tolerant and open-minded family. My parents taught me both sides and encouraged me to decide for myself which direction to go." After a pause, she added, "But let's face it, things happen as we go through life that make us sway back and forth between the two possibilities, don't you think?"

"After what's happened here, which camp are you in today?"

Lita started to answer, then stopped. It was a tough question, with a complicated answer. As much as she enjoyed the rapport with Manu and appreciated their talks, she wasn't sure she was ready to open up this much with him. This was, after all, supposed to be merely a training session; somehow they had drifted into very personal terrain.

Of course, she had started it by asking about the amulet.

"I guess I'm on the fence right now," she said with a smile. She sat back in her chair and hefted her workpad. Manu seemed to pick up the clue that it was back-to-work time. He sat up straight and punched a key to take the vidscreen out of hibernation mode.

For the next hour they covered more administrative territory, from crew data to pharmacy records to report filing. They ended the session with a cordial farewell and made plans to meet the next day for a refresher course on physical exams.

Lita glanced at the clock, noting the late hour. Getting Manu organized had been important, but now she had work of her own to finish, as well as a detailed summary to prepare for the next Council meeting. As enticing as sleep sounded at the moment, her responsibilites were piling up and demanding attention.

Except that Manu's question kept forcing its way back into her thoughts. Where *did* she stand on the question of faith versus fate? Were the two compatible? And what did it mean if she wasn't sure of her stance? She picked up the stylus pen from her desk and absently began tapping her cheek with it, her gaze drifting to Manu's desk. The amulet sat mutely on its chain, yet somehow seemed to beckon her.

Evil spirits, he'd said, guarded against for generations. She agreed with Manu about respecting other people's beliefs and traditions, but this was one belief that she could not share. She understood the value of customs or rituals that provided comfort, but her scientific mind was reluctant to embrace good luck charms; to her they fell into the category of superstitions.

Manu had said that he was undecided about the amulet's power, and yet she also got the sense that he was hedging his bet. The fact that he displayed it near his workspace suggested that he might be willing to believe. Lita was okay with that.

Besides, she reasoned, with the ways things had been going lately aboard *Galahad*, a little bit of supernatural protection couldn't hurt.

Y ou haven't responded to my messages," Gap said, leaning against the door frame. With night officially blanketing the ship, he'd trudged through Dome 1 in the darkness, glancing up at the stars that filtered in from above, guided by the light that spilled from Bon's office.

The Swede kept his eyes on the desk vidscreen. After a long stretch of silence, he answered in a reluctant tone. "It didn't seem urgent. I've been busy."

"I came by an hour ago and couldn't find you. Most of the workforce has been gone for a while."

Bon finally looked up. "Should I check in with you at all times?"

Gap tried inserting a smile. "No. Maybe I'll just put a tracking beacon on you."

The humor seemed to have no effect on Bon, who turned his attention back to the screen. Gap slowly walked over and sat in the chair facing the desk, then tilted back onto the chair's rear legs. Now he was able to see Bon up close, and at once something jumped out at him.

"You're soaked in sweat. What in the world have you been doing?"

Bon's voice was laced with irritation. "I told you I've been busy. Is there something specific I can help you with?"

"Yes. I need to know if you got the message about the Council meeting tomorrow; it would be nice to get a response to that. Plus, I thought the message about crew rotation was pretty simple. Shouldn't have taken more than thirty seconds to answer that."

"Yes, I will be at the meeting. No, I'm not prepared to rotate for another couple of days."

"May I ask why, or is that too much?" Gap said.

"Because we're in the middle of two large harvests right now, and I'd like to keep some continuity until we're at least past the heaviest load."

Gap nodded. "Good enough. See how easy that was?" When he got no response, he added, "What's going on with you? I mean, besides the usual. I don't expect a spirited conversation when we chat, but there's something else these days."

Bon looked up again; this time Gap could see that his hair was matted against his forehead and appeared damp. On top of that, there seemed to be a slight tremor in his hands; faint, but there nonetheless.

"I get very weary of these verbal games," Bon said. "Why don't you just ask what you really want to ask?"

"All right," Gap said. He brought his chair back onto all four legs and leaned forward, his elbows resting on his knees. "You've been even more hermitlike than usual since we lost both Alexa and Triana. You've retreated into some sort of emotional cave, and now you're not answering messages. On top of that, you have the exact same look that I saw after one of your Cassini connections. Do you have the translator?"

"Yes."

"You've used it, haven't you?"

"Yes."

Gap felt a ripple of anger and took a deep breath to keep from lashing out. "And you felt like you could do that without discussing it with the Council?"

"Yes."

"Okay, enough with the one-word answers," Gap said. "Save us some time and talk about this with me. What are you doing with the translator in the first place?"

Bon sat back in his chair and crossed his arms. "Triana brought it to me before she disappeared. She made the decision to keep it in her possession, and then made the decision to give it to me. She *was* the Council Leader at the time, remember? She didn't have to get your blessing for everything that she did."

"Spin it any way you want, Bon, but you know that she couldn't ask the Council about giving that thing to you without giving away her plan to leave. That doesn't mean that you shouldn't have reported it to us afterward. And it certainly doesn't mean that you should just begin using it without discussing it with the Council. The thing is, you know that. And not only that, someone should be with you when you connect. Probably Lita."

"It doesn't affect me the way it used to," Bon said.

"Right. That's why you look like you've just run a marathon."

Bon shrugged but didn't respond.

Gap studied the face staring back at him. During the early stages of their *Galahad* training on Earth, he and Bon had developed a tenuous friendship—or at least the closest thing to a friendship of which Bon was capable. But the extreme differences in their styles and personalities had ultimately pushed them apart, and things cooled. A mutual interest in Triana furthered the split.

They had settled into a cool but cordial working relationship, but the tension continually simmered underneath.

The next question was likely to evoke a vague response, but Gap knew that it was the only natural follow-up. "What did you talk about with the Cassini?"

Bon chuckled, but it was humorless. "Personal."

Gap shook his head. "Sorry. When it comes to that link, it can't be personal."

"Oh, really? According to who?"

"Like it or not, Bon, I'm the acting Council Leader, and I have responsibilities. Quit fencing with me on this."

"Quit pushing me," Bon shot back. "Yes, you're the acting Council Leader, whatever that really means. But I've paid my dues and then some when it comes to the Cassini. It was my link with them that got us through the Kuiper Belt, and it cost me. I don't think anyone would begrudge me a private connection now and then. Well, not most people, anyway."

"I see. So now you're calling in your chip as the ship's savior, is that right?"

"I didn't bring this up, Gap; you did. I don't feel like I've done anything wrong, nor anything that required the attention of the Council."

Gap pushed up from his chair. "Well, I hate to break it to you, but it has now come to the attention of the Council. And it will be on the agenda for tomorrow's meeting."

Again, Bon gave no response. He looked up at Gap with an icy stare.

"In the meantime," Gap said, "I'll hold on to the translator until the meeting."

"No."

The ripple of anger quickly became a torrent, and Gap found himself doing everything in his power to keep from exploding. He knew that he was essentially powerless at this point; he couldn't wrestle Bon to the ground and physically take the device. This round had gone to Bon.

"Okay," he said. "We'll discuss it tomorrow."

"Fine," Bon said. "Tomorrow." He lowered his gaze back to the vidscreen and resumed his work.

Gap seethed inside at the dismissal. He spun on his heel and quickly walked from the office, back into the gloom of the dome's night.

10

The fist landed with a dull smack against the side of Karl Richter's jaw, knocking him backward, but not off his feet. At first his eyes widened with shock, but they quickly narrowed as he stepped forward to close the gap between himself and his attacker. The three farm workers who had witnessed the punch were frozen in place, not believing what they were seeing.

"You don't seriously want another one, do you?" Liam Wright said. He held one cocked fist at his side, slowly pumping it up and down. "Now beat it."

Karl, the side of his face turning a dark shade, lunged. He wrapped his arms around Liam's midsection and drove him into the damp soil at the edge of the corn plants. Once on the ground, the boys' fury exploded. Arms and fists flailed with only occasional success as they rolled a few feet into the stalks of corn, snapping several at knee height. Their grunts and exclamations were muffled under the canopy of plants. Dirt flew as each tried to gain traction. In seconds Liam had Karl pinned to the ground and managed to connect with another blow to the side of his head.

Two of the farm workers, at last shocked into action, leapt into the fray and grabbed Liam's arm before he could do further damage. In turn, he swung wildly at both workers, which allowed Karl the chance to roll away and clamber to his feet. As soon as Liam looked back to find him, Karl stepped in and landed his own solid punch. There was a crack as Liam cried out and fell to his side.

Karl stood back, breathing heavily, wincing from the shots he had taken. He relaxed his tense muscles and dropped his arms. At that moment Liam flew upwards and grabbed Karl in a wrestler's headlock. Blood from Liam's broken nose began to spatter over both of them. They tumbled backward, a writhing mass, and then slammed into one of the field's irrigation pump units. The plastic shell on the unit cracked as it bent sideways, ushering a fountain of sparks and loud pops as it shorted out. The two boys collapsed over the ruptured pump. Karl let out an animal cry of pain.

By now the third worker who had been frozen in place jumped forward, joined by the two who had unexpectedly been victims of the fight. They again pulled at Liam, who this time voluntarily stepped back. The four of them looked down at Karl.

A shard of plastic from the crushed irrigation shell had punctured his right thigh. He rolled to his left in agony, revealing a fresh cascade of blood that soon saturated the ground.

The third farm worker stripped off his shirt and knelt down. He pushed Karl's hand aside and examined the wound, doing his best to wipe the blood away with the shirt. He turned to the others and yelled, "Get help! Hurry!"

While one worker sprinted away, Liam coughed once and spat. He gingerly touched his nose and managed to smear blood across the side of his face. Looking down at the groaning figure on the ground, he said, "Is he okay?"

The worker turned to glare up at him. "As if you care. Why don't you get yourself up to Sick House? You've done enough for one day. Go on, get out of here."

Liam stood motionless, unsure, for several moments before

turning and walking up the path. By the time he approached the lift he passed Manu and another Sick House worker, running in the other direction, each holding a first-aid bag.

Hannah couldn't understand why it was so difficult to recall memories from her younger years. A few things were imprinted, but there were large gaps. It was as if a firewall sealed off portions of her life, refusing to allow her access. She had casually mentioned it to Dr. Armistead during their training, without making a big deal of it. As the mission psychologist, Angela Armistead had been responsible for evaluating each potential crew member's ability to adapt to a long space voyage. The last thing Hannah had wanted to do was send up a red flag. And yet she was curious about why her mind behaved the way it did, and wondered if the dark spots in her memory were somehow tied in with her need for order and discipline.

"I know that pop psychologists like to automatically assume that you're blocking out some traumatic experience," Dr. Armistead had said at the time, offering a supportive smile. "That might be true in some cases, but I personally think that it's often merely a case of our brains maximizing their resources."

She went on to explain that each person was wired a little differently. Some placed an emphasis on emotions or feelings, while others might be more likely to follow a routine of logic and reason; there was no correct way, no wrong way, just different ways. In Hannah's case, Dr. Armistead explained, she felt most comfortable with things in a proper sequence. It helped to explain Hannah's obsession with order and neatness, her need for items and objects to be strictly aligned, and her razor-sharp attention to detail. The fading of early memories was, quite possibly, her mind's way of organizing the most important and pertinent information, keeping all things crucial in an easily accessible "file," while closing those that offered no real benefit. And, since many childhood memories were emotion-based, they might not register as critical.

Hannah remembered that this explanation had bothered her; did this somehow make her less human? Was she an emotionless robot?

Of course not, Dr. Armistead had assured her. She undoubtedly had strong emotions, no different than any other teenage girl (Hannah thought of her breakup with Gap as Exhibit A), but her brain chose to prioritize when it came to filing.

"Your incredible artistic skills are proof that you have plenty of emotion bubbling up in there," Dr. Armistead had said. "It takes a lot of love to create the work you do on canvas, not to mention a few other emotions as well. Your brain simply chooses to compartmentalize a bit more than the average person; orderly and logical in most cases, but with an emotional outlet through your paintbrush.

"Think of it this way," the doctor continued. "Memories often condition us. They're not too different from the rings inside a tree trunk. Layer upon layer build up over time, all radiating outward from a beginning deep in the past. They help us to grow, in some respects, but they also form a history that we can examine and trace. Major events might leave a more indelible ring, while lesser events blend into the background." She'd finished with a soft, easy laugh. "You're just fine, Hannah, believe me. Besides, who needs to remember their third birthday party anyway? Lots of scary relatives, loud noises, and maybe a bladder accident."

While the doctor's analysis seemed reasonable to her, there were times when Hannah envied others and their astounding memories. There were other times, however, when she wished she could forget completely. Dr. Armistead had certainly been right about one thing: there were emotions—some of them strong and vivid—woven throughout her subconscious.

She had the Rec Room to herself and had dialed up scenes from her home state of Alaska. They flashed in a slide show against one of the walls, staggering images of beauty and majesty. Snowcapped peaks, followed by rich green forests, bears on guard for salmon, massive chunks of glaciers slicing into the sea. The link with home had undoubtedly brought on her melancholy thoughts, driving her to the edge of tears before she choked them back. She would not let her emotions push her that far.

The door opened, and she saw a figure enter through her peripheral vision. She kept her gaze steady on the screen for another full minute before flicking the desk switch and watching her childhood playground fade to black. By that point Merit was perched atop the table, patiently waiting.

"It's gorgeous," he said, nodding toward the screen. "I'm jealous that I never got to see it firsthand. Is it like most things in life, you take it for granted when you see it all the time?"

"I don't know how anyone could take that for granted," she said. "I suppose if I'd had a few more years it might have lost some of that special feel, but probably not." She pulled out a chair and sat facing him. "You wanted to talk?"

"Nothing major, but I told you we'd have strategy sessions from time to time. And this is one of those times."

She didn't speak, so he hopped off the table and began to pace. "First, let me acknowledge that one of the reasons I felt you'd be a great candidate for Council Leader was your grasp of the science on this trip. That's a given. So please don't misunderstand what I'm about to say. I have it on pretty good authority that you've been doing some work on the radiation issue that the ship is facing."

"And how would you know that?" Hannah said.

"Because you were doing the work right out in the open, in the Dining Hall, and people saw you. People talk, Hannah. Word travels."

"Especially in your circles, I see," she said.

He never broke stride, continuing to pace around the table, but a smile spread across his face. "Yes, I know, you've made it clear you don't like me, but we're past that, right? Let's just stay on subject, shall we? The point is, you're doing what you do best, which is solve problems. Again, that's why you're a natural to replace Triana. But I'd like to suggest something if I may."

"Yes?"

"When you solve this radiation problem—and I have no doubt that you'll be the one to figure it out—it would not be a good idea to take it to the Council."

Hannah blinked a few times, watching him take his slow, measured steps. "What are you talking about? If I don't report it to the Council, just who would I tell? What good does it do to figure it out and not use the information?"

"Of course we would use the information. But the last thing you want to do is tell the Council. If you do that, then Gap gathers the crew together, or makes a ship-wide announcement through e-mail, and although he might mention you somewhere in the fine print, just who do you think would get the credit?"

He had circled the table a few times. As he came around again, Hannah held out her arm and stopped him. "Would you quit with the pacing? It makes me nervous." She got up and leaned against the table. "What are you suggesting I do?"

Merit grinned at her again and pushed a long stray hair behind his ear. "I'm suggesting that you wait until one of the forum sessions of the campaign and break the news to the entire crew. Use the platform, Hannah; that's what it's all about."

It took a few moments, but finally an incredulous smile broke across her face. "You are unbelievable. The ship could be in real danger, and you want me to sit on information that might save us, all for the sake of a few votes?"

Merit sat beside her on the table. "You're not going to have to sit on it, at least not for long. I have every confidence that you'll crack this problem pretty quickly, and there are two forums within the next few days. Chances are you'll have the information just hours before you speak. Besides . . ." He placed a hand on her shoulder. "You'll need a little time to confirm your find-ings, right? Don't want to rush into an emergency Council meet-ing without being completely prepared."

Hannah felt her stomach tighten. She suddenly knew that she had crawled into something that was against her nature; it not only didn't feel right, it felt . . . slimy. And yet, as much as it pained her to admit it, there was a measure of truth to what Merit was saying. Whoever delivered the information to the crew was bound to get the credit by default, whether they had done the work or not. Had it been Triana in charge and divulging the solution to the crew, Hannah would have no problem. But Gap?

"So," Merit said, "do we understand each other? Keep doing the work, and find that solution. But stop doing the work in public, and by all means don't report anything to anyone until we're ready."

Hannah turned her head to look at him with dead eyes. "*We're?*"

The smile on his face vanished, and he stood up. "I hope I wasn't wrong about you, Hannah. I hope you have the guts to do this, and to do it right. If you're going to constantly take your eye off the prize and worry about our collaboration, then you're going to fail. Stay focused."

He turned and walked toward the door, stopping short and turning back to face her. "Think you can handle that?"

A moment later he was gone. Hannah leaned back on the table and closed her eyes.

Merit's intentions were obvious to her; he held a festering grudge against Gap and was delighted to use Hannah as a pawn in his scheme for revenge. If he couldn't defeat Gap himself, the next best thing would be to mastermind a campaign to defeat his foe. What better choice, he must have concluded, than Hannah, Gap's one-time girlfriend?

Her own intentions were much more complicated. She couldn't deny that the break from Gap still carried its bitter sting, one that had refused to fade. Give it time, she'd told herself over and over again; give it time. And yet time seemed only to magnify the sense of loss, and the feeling of rejection, to the point where her routines had been shaken, a sure sign that she was still far from recovered.

She had allowed herself to be talked into running against Gap for the position of Council Leader, but it had nothing to do with vengeance. Although the shock of Gap's sudden rebuff had opened old wounds and hurt her deeply, she found that she was unable to summon a desire to strike back at him.

No. What Hannah wanted—what she *needed*—was to prove to Gap that she had been—and still *was*—worth more than he had ever appreciated. She was more than her quiet demeanor suggested. She was . . . valuable. What better acknowledgment of that fact than a successful run to the top spot on *Galahad*'s Council?

It was, she decided, the most direct evidence of the change that she'd experienced after the painful split from Gap. In the past she'd always focused every bit of energy on her art, her scientific curiosity, her love of space and its bizarre puzzles. Now she was able to divert at least a portion of that energy into her self-esteem. Where in the past she'd accepted a role in the shadows, this new awareness pushed and prodded her, demanding she be recognized for her contributions. If not by the whole crew, she admitted, then at least by the one person who had taken her for granted.

It meant forming a distasteful alliance with a person like Merit Simms, but that was a trade-off that she judged acceptable. Merit had his reasons, she had her own; it wasn't important that they intersect. In the meantime, he could help her maneuver her way through an election, where otherwise she might be lost.

She only hoped that she didn't lose herself along the way.

11

S he reminds me of Halloween," Gap said to Channy. They were the first to arrive for the Council meeting and, in what had almost become an unspoken tradition, sat outside the Conference Room against the gently curved walls. Recently they never entered the room until all of the members were present in the corridor; it was as if they had a pre-meeting before the actual meeting.

Channy rubbed the belly of Iris, who lay sprawled against the wall. The cat closed her eyes and seemed to soak in the attention.

"But she's black and orange, not solid black," Channy said. "I thought it was black cats that people were afraid of."

"I think of Halloween when I see black and orange," Gap said. "Something about those colors. The decorations, the candy. She's more of a Halloween cat than a black cat would be, if you ask me."

Channy put on her best baby-voice while rubbing Iris again. "But she's not scary at all. Are you? No, you're not."

Gap smiled at the sound. It was good to see Channy acting like herself again after the rough stretch she had been through in the past few weeks. He thought about addressing that, then quickly decided against it; best to simply let her be and not draw attention to it.

Lita strolled into view and immediately slid to the floor beside Channy and began to scratch Iris under her chin. "Greetings, fellow galactic travelers."

Channy giggled. "I like that: galactic travelers. You know, as funny as it sounds, sometimes I get so caught up in the day-to-day routine—you know, eat breakfast, work out, file reports, eat lunch, lead afternoon dance class, so on and so on—that I almost forget that I'm inside a spacecraft. I mean, at first it was on my mind all the time. But now, after a year, if I don't look out through the domes or one of the windows, I just go about my day."

"No, I get it," Lita said. "I'm the same way. Or, if there's some sort of emergency, then it suddenly reminds me, 'Hey, I'm billions of miles from home.'" She looked across the hallway at Gap. "Like this latest fight. That makes two in the last couple of days. Definitely reminders that we're on our own. And, I might add, we're not doing too well keeping it together."

Gap let out a long breath. "I know, I know. We're going to talk about that. Plus a few other things, including the radiation issue, and the Council itself."

"The election?"

"That, and some other issues that I think we need to discuss."

Lita raised an eyebrow. "Sounds interesting. Has one of *us* been bad, too?"

Gap laughed. "Lita, the day you are bad I will jump out an airlock without a helmet."

They made small talk for another minute or two before Bon walked up. He gave a sullen nod to their greetings, the damage in the dome likely pushing him even farther into a funk. Then as a group they collected their things and walked into the Conference Room. Channy placed Iris onto one of the empty seats, and the cat wasted no time in getting comfortable and beginning to groom. The Council members sat down around the table.

For the first ten minutes they covered the basics, mostly department reports and crew requests. By now they were comfortable with the regimen, and wasted little time ticking items off the list. Gap noted that this time, however, there weren't the usual snarky comments and jokes. Even Roc, normally quick to inject sarcasm at any moment, was reserved.

"If there's nothing else we need to cover," Gap said, "let's talk about our latest bit of drama." He looked at Lita. "How's Karl?"

"Bandaged up and recovering. But he's lucky; the torn shell missed his femoral artery by about an inch."

"So what started all of that?" Channy said.

Lita looked back at Gap for an answer. He shook his head. "Something minor. It should never have escalated like it did. Apparently Karl was sent up from the kitchen area to inquire about a missing delivery from that afternoon. He ended up asking Liam, who mouthed off to him. From what I hear they've argued before. This time words were exchanged, a few insults, and then . . . well, then you know what happened."

"It's ridiculous and immature," Lita said. She turned to Bon. "How bad is the damage?"

The Swede growled his answer. "The irrigation pump is wrecked. It will take a few days to get it back in working order. And, since it was one of the master units, we need to divert activity from other stations. Some of those automatically shut down when the master unit failed. Two of them are not booting back up."

"Will we lose crops?" Gap said.

"I don't lose crops," Bon said.

Gap let out a long breath. "Yes, under normal circumstances. Realistically, will we lose crops?"

Bon tapped one finger on the table and seemed to chew on his answer. "If we do, it won't be for long."

For the first time since the launch, *Galahad*'s Council considered their precarious reliance on the Farm's production. It had seemed a given that the artificial light would always shine upon a flourishing bounty of food. The threat of loss—any loss, no matter how minor—to that production sent a noticeable chill through the room.

Gap thought, *We take too many things for granted.*

He gave a nod to Bon. "Okay. Let Engineering know if you need any special help with the repairs. We've had our share of experience with those particular units. And, for the record, I'll be talking with both Liam and Karl. I've had enough of these fights, and I won't tolerate any more reckless, irresponsible behavior. When we get to the point that it's affecting our very survival . . ." He let the thought die.

"If I have to call a special crew meeting, I will," he said, looking around the table. "For now, let's move on to our other issues. We've officially had four 'events' with the radiation shield. The first lasted less than a second; the next time it was about a second and a half. Then it happened twice overnight, again for barely a second. All of the diagnostics that we've run so far tell us that the failures aren't coming from the unit itself. At least not that we can see."

Gap was surprised when Bon immediately spoke up. "Have you considered replacing the unit with the backup? If the replacement doesn't fail, you would have time to find the problem in the original."

"We not only considered it, but that's exactly what Ruben is doing this morning. I won't lie, I think it's a waste of time. But it's the only way to confirm that the problem is not coming from inside the ship, but outside."

Lita scowled. "Outside. So that means our shields aren't equipped to handle the radiation beyond our solar system?"

"No, that's not necessarily true," Gap said. "Roc and I had a talk about that early this morning. Roc, would you care to fill them in?"

"It's possible that it's not radiation at all," the computer said. "Yes, the unit being affected is designed to shove those nasty radiation particles out of our way, so that I don't fry my circuits and you don't grow a second nose. But that doesn't mean it has to be radiation causing the problem.

"Instead, it could be a variety of problems individually, or a series of them, that somehow don't play well with our shield. We've had more than a few encounters recently with what we have labeled dark energy. That's one possibility."

Channy sighed. "Those wormholes. That's it, isn't it? The wormholes have somehow attacked us."

"We're not jumping to any conclusions," Gap said. "We're considering all of the options."

"But the way those things rattled the ship," Channy said. "It only makes sense—"

"Like I said, we're not jumping to conclusions."

"Actually," Roc said, "the wormholes are a consideration. It has been suggested that energy, in the form of radiation, might have leaked out before they pinged out of existence. However, the arguments against that scenario are also strong. Namely, if they did indeed burp out some nasty particles, we would have felt them before this. And, additionally, it wouldn't explain the random nature of the failures.

"That leaves us with interstellar space itself," the computer continued. "Possibly another force altogether, or perhaps something in the nature of deep space that we could never detect from Earth."

"The nature of space?" Channy said.

"The fabric of space is another way to put it," Roc said. "The manner in which the particles and molecules react and interact. Science does its best to explain how they work together, but we don't even know what we don't know, to put it in a quaint but confusing form. And remember: every mile that we scoot along out here is another mile farther into the unknown."

There was quiet around the table as the Council absorbed this. Finally Lita looked at Gap and said, "And the strange flash of light. Is that part of this somehow?"

"That," Gap said, "is yet another mystery. Like we don't have enough already, right? But since there is practically nothing to go on—no residue, no trace of any kind—we don't have much to investigate. It happened, and Roc says it contained strange particles mixed in with the light's photons. If you're asking if it could be somehow connected to the wormholes . . . I have no idea."

Channy looked worried. "So many unknowns. What do we do?"

Gap laced his fingers together on the table. If he was elected Council Leader, that would be a question he'd need to get used to.

"As far as the shields are concerned, the first step is identifying the problem," he said. "We can't come up with a solution until we know what's causing the failures in the first place. Since we're almost positive that it's external, we can focus on that.

"Next we pour every piece of data we can find into the mix and see if there's a pattern. Then we isolate where it's coming from and build a defense system to overcome it."

"You make it sound easy," Channy said.

"It's not going to be easy," Gap said. "But tell me one thing that has been easy on this mission so far."

This was greeted with grim nods.

"And one last thing," Gap added. "The cumulative damage from the failures is mounting. Now that it's happened four times, Roc has run some fairly precise calculations. I'll let him break that good news to you."

"Why do I have to be the bad guy?" the computer said. "All right, to be blunt, whatever is knocking the shields offline is also shaving away their effectiveness. Meaning that with each blow we lose some of our ability to block the radiation. And it's exponential. So, given that cheery bit of information, I can tell you that if the failures continue to occur at this rate, we have about five weeks before we'll be lying on the surface of the sun. Metaphorically speaking, of course."

A deathly silence fell over the room for a few moments before Roc added, "But don't worry, you won't get sunburned, because all of your skin will have rotted away a good day or two before that."

Channy put her hands against the sides of her head and groaned. "Gap, why don't you break the news next time?"

Lita squinted, deep in thought. "So we not only have to figure this problem out, we've got to do it fast. Figure out what's causing it, and what to do about it."

"Correct," Gap said. "The team in Engineering is working overtime, and I'm confident that we'll find a solution long before it turns critical."

Channy and Lita nodded slowly; Bon merely stared down the table at Gap.

When there were no further questions about the radiation problem, they spent a few minutes revisiting the procedures that would govern the election of a new Council Leader. Gap felt a little awkward overseeing this discussion, but did his best to shepherd the meeting through the details. There would be two forums held where the candidates could address the ship's priorities, as well as their own personal qualifications. Questions would follow from the crew.

"Okay," Gap said. "Let's plan on the first forum tomorrow evening, then we'll plug in the final one for Friday evening. The election itself will take place Saturday. Any questions or comments?"

There were none. That meant it was time for him to address the issue that he dreaded the most.

"The last item I want to talk about has to do with the Cassini. In particular, I think it's important for the Council to be fully in the loop about our contact with them."

He sat back and did his best to adopt a relaxed look. He was careful to maintain balanced eye contact with the other three Council members, including Bon. The last thing he wanted was for Bon to think he was intimidated.

"As you know, our only link to the Cassini has been through

a connection that none of us really understand. Somehow Bon's brain waves are suited for him to communicate with them, and we've been able to use that connection to help us through a tough stretch. Since we don't really know how the link works, I think Lita would agree that we're also not sure what effects it might be having on Bon, both short-term and long-term."

Lita merely nodded, but it was evident that she was confused as to why they were having this discussion now. Bon sat still, his icy stare never wavering. Gap plowed on.

"Triana was concerned about the danger this connection might have, and so she held on to the translator. In a way, she acted like a guardian. As you know, she would bring it to Bon for the link, and she stayed right by his side to make sure everything turned out okay. Then, she took the translator back to her room."

"I'm sorry," Channy said, "I'm not trying to be difficult, but what does this have to do with anything right now?"

Gap stole another glance at the end of the table, and his eyes locked up with Bon's. For a moment he thought he saw a flicker of anger, but if so, it passed quickly, and Bon was once again stone-faced.

"I bring this up," Gap said, turning to Channy, "because before she left on that pod, Triana left the translator with Bon."

Both Channy and Lita turned to look at Bon, who responded by slowly lifting his cup of water for a drink, never taking his eyes off Gap.

"But you haven't used it, I hope?" Lita said. "At least not by yourself."

"I have," Bon said.

Lita's shoulders sagged. "Oh, Bon. What are you doing?" When he didn't answer, she added, "How many times have you made contact?"

He finally turned his gaze toward Lita. "That's not important. There's no problem, so you shouldn't be concerned."

"Shouldn't be concerned? Your health is my responsibility on this ship, Bon. If Triana was convinced that you should never make that connection alone, what makes you think it's okay now?"

Channy broke in before he could answer. "And why did Triana leave that thing with you in the first place? What did she tell you?"

"She didn't tell me anything. She left it on my desk."

"Well, I think you need to turn it in to the Council," Channy said.

Lita looked puzzled. "Wait a minute. We're out of the Kuiper Belt; why would you connect with the Cassini now?"

Bon shifted his gaze from Lita to Gap, then back again. "Personal reasons."

Lita shook her head. "I don't believe this." She said to Gap, "He can't keep this thing. It's pretty clear that his judgment is already screwed up."

"I agree," Gap said. "That's why I brought it to the attention of the Council. Bon, I think it's obvious how we feel about this. Are you going to make us go through the motions of a formal vote, or will you just hand over the translator?"

Bon took another drink of water. When he spoke, his voice was low but firm. "As of this meeting, Triana is still officially the Council Leader. And, since she chose to give me the responsibility, I will keep the translator until a new Council Leader is elected in her place. Then, at that time, we will see what the new Leader has to say."

It was a double shot, and Gap knew it; Bon was not only defying his position as the interim Council Leader, he was calling into question whether Gap would even have the position after the Saturday election. And while he burned inside to fire back, he reached deep inside and summoned every ounce of poise that he could find. In the end, he smiled at Bon.

"I believe that if we were to consult the fine print of our

bylaws, Bon, you'd be wrong. But I'm willing to let it go until Saturday."

Lita let out an exasperated sound. "No! This is not some petty power struggle we're talking about. This is a matter of the safety and well-being of a crew member."

Gap nodded once. "That's right. And if it involved the safety of others, I would feel differently. If Bon wanted to Airboard without a helmet I would think he was foolish, but I wouldn't stop him unless he was a menace to others."

"This is *not* the same thing," Lita said. "How can you compare the two?"

Gap slowly sipped his own drink of water, then studied the cup in his hand. "Triana had to know that Bon was going to use the translator. If she didn't have a problem with it, then I can let it slide for a few more days."

Channy held her hands out, palms up. "But we don't know what the Cassini will do! What if something goes wrong? It already has once."

There was silence for a minute. It was obvious to Gap that Bon wasn't going to utter another word; he had won again, for the second day in a row, and he knew it.

"I don't suppose you'll let me know if you connect again," Lita said to Bon. "You're just hardheaded enough to think you don't need any help."

He only stared back at her, prompting another exasperated sigh from *Galahad*'s Health Director. She stood up and pushed back from the table. "I want to go on record as being strongly opposed to this."

"Noted," Gap said. Lita turned and walked out of the room.

Channy sat with a stunned look on her face. "Well . . . I'm opposed to it as well," she said.

Gap smiled at her. "Noted as well. Thank you, Channy." He looked back at Bon. "This meeting is over. Everyone stay in touch with me, because if things turn sour with the radiation shield I want to be able to meet immediately if necessary." He stood and followed Lita's path out the door.

Channy, left alone with Bon, refused to make eye contact with him. "You say it's personal, your business with the Cassini. Well, I wish you'd found some personal feelings before this. It's a little late now, if you ask me."

She rose and quickly walked out. For the next few minutes, Bon sat by himself in the Conference Room, sipping his water.

Thinking.

12

He usually played Masego against Roc in the Rec Room, but tonight Gap chose to stay in his room. It had been a brutally long day: his run-in with Bon in the Council meeting; another violent confrontation between crew members, one that could potentially mean the loss of food inventory; not to mention endless tests of the radiation shield in the Engineering Section. He was exhausted physically and mentally, and the idea of a large crowd bubbling around him did not sound appealing. His roommate, Daniil, had picked up on Gap's weariness and politely excused himself to meet up with friends.

Faint sounds of rainfall escaped from the room's speakers. Gap's family had relocated from China to America's northwest corner, so he found the sound comforting. It was a frequent soundtrack choice when he was alone.

The vidscreen displayed the Masego board, but Gap's attention wandered. In twenty-four hours he would address the crew again, only this time it would be an audition. He was torn between knuckling down and preparing for the meeting, or unplugging his whirling mind and finding a distraction. He'd hoped that another fruitless contest against Roc, with a healthy dose of the computer's sarcastic observations, would take his mind off everything that had piled up in the last week.

It didn't.

Slumped in his chair, he tapped at the folded sheet of paper on the desk, flicking it back and forth. A battle raged within him, one side telling him to read the note again, another urging him to lock it away, or even to destroy it. Another tap sent the note spinning.

"Are you going to make a move?" the computer said.

"Just a minute," Gap said. He eyed the paper, prepared to stow it away in a drawer. But instead he watched his hand snake out and grasp the folded page. In a moment it was open, and he once again scanned Triana's handwriting.

Gap, I know that my decision will likely anger you and the other Council members, but in my opinion there was no time for debate, especially one that would more than likely end in a stalemate.

There are too many unknowns for us to make the important decisions we face. The wormholes, the vultures, and, most importantly, the beings that are behind both of these. We have to know what we're dealing with.

I don't want to risk taking the ship through a wormhole until we know more about them, and yet I don't want to wait to find out what might come through from the other side.

I'm going through.

I understand the pressure this will put on the Council, and you especially, and for that I'm sorry. But I hope that at some point, when you're able to step back and look at it from a perspective of time, you'll understand why I did this. As you take on more leadership responsibilities I think it will become much more clear.

As for the other issues that you must deal with, all I can offer is the advice I received from Dr. Zimmer: "Do what is right. Your heart may fight you at times, but you always know what is right."

Good luck. Until I see you again . . . Tree

Gap read the last few lines twice. Triana—and Dr. Zimmer—were right: his heart seemed to fight him, even when he knew what was right. It was so hard.

Before he folded the paper again, he looked at her final words and wondered if he would indeed see her again. For now, he—

"Is this a new tactic?" Roc said, shaking him from his trance. "Stalling? Do you think all of the other duties that I'm working on simultaneously will distract me enough so that you can finally win?"

"Sorry, Roc, I'm just not into Masego tonight. Can't shut off my monkey mind."

"I could play with half my circuits tied behind my motherboard."

"And you'd still whip me. Not before letting me think I had a chance, of course, just to keep me interested."

The computer manufactured an exaggerated sigh. "What's the matter, Bunky? Feeling a bit overwhelmed? Do you need a hug? It would have to be virtual, of course, but you know if I had arms I would, right?"

"No, I'm . . . Well, yes, all right, I'll be honest. I'm feeling a touch overwhelmed right now," Gap said. He casually slipped the folded note back into a desk drawer.

"That's not surprising," Roc said. "I've read a few million articles about this emotion in humans, and the consensus from the experts is that you should quit trying to scale the whole mountain and just concentrate on a single step. Sounds reasonable, and yet impossible."

Gap laughed. "Agreed! Sometimes I have a hard time seeing the next step because it seems like the whole mountain is about to collapse on me. What do the experts have to say about *that*?"

"Well," Roc said, "why don't we humor them and try their technique for a moment? What is one item in your overwhelming stack?"

"Ugh, where to begin? Okay, the radiation shield. If we don't figure that out pronto it's lights out."

"And you have about a dozen people hard at work on that right now," Roc said. "Not to mention the services of my brilliant self. Trust that it will be resolved."

Gap slid off the chair and sprawled across the floor into a position that he found the most relaxing. He laced his fingers behind his head and stared up at the ceiling. "Right. Then there's the latest headache with Bon. I can't figure that guy out; sometimes he's this close to actually being civil, then he throws on the brakes and goes back to being . . . Oh, what's a good word? Insufferable. Yeah, that's it. My mom used that word a lot, and I think it applies to Bon. He can be insufferable."

"He said that he would defer to the Council Leader's wishes, however," Roc said. "Surely you don't think he'll cause any damage before the end of the week, do you?"

Gap thought about this for a moment before answering. "Well, probably not. But this whole Cassini thing is such a wild card. We have no idea what we're really messing with, you know? Bon said that it's personal, so I don't see how that could hurt the ship. At the same time, though, if he damages himself then we lose the one person who's able to speak with the Cassini. Lita's worried about brain damage, and I agree with her."

"Then let's assume for the time being that the ship will survive Bon's connection, at least through this weekend," Roc said. "What else?"

"The election."

"Yes, what about it?"

"What do you mean, 'what about it'? It's kind of a big deal, wouldn't you say?"

"Yes, it's a big deal," Roc said. "But worrying about it is pointless. Prepare, do your best, accept what happens."

"Easy for you to say."

"Do you have any idea what kind of work went into programming me so that I can actually speak? Nothing is easy for me to say. I'm a phenomenon, a true miracle of science."

Gap moved his hands from behind his head and covered his eyes with one arm. Talking with Roc was always an exercise in patience, but he had to admit that the repartee made him feel better.

His mind whirled through the other items in his stack, and, as it had for the past couple of days, arrived at the same place: Hannah. Could he talk to Roc about that?

"Let me ask you something," he said, his voice slightly muffled by the arm across his face. "When we have talks like this, are you bound by some sort of confidentiality agreement? You know, like back home, with psychiatrists and priests? Does this conversation stay here, or will I hear it replayed inside the Dining Hall during lunch someday?"

"Yes, you can talk to me about Hannah and it will remain private between us."

Gap slowly pulled his arm away and sat up on his elbows. "You scare me sometimes."

"You're not as tough to read as you think, Gap. What, did you think we'd have to be hush-hush about a discussion on ion drive power modification? I got news for you, pal, the whole crew is fairly amused that the election of a new Council Leader comes down to two people who were all kissy-face just a few weeks ago."

Lying back again, Gap's gaze returned to the ceiling. "I know, I know. What did they use to call those daytime television shows a long time ago?"

"Soap operas."

"That's it. Well, I know this is like a real-life soap opera, but when you're in the middle of the drama it's no fun. And since when were you programmed to use phrases like 'kissy-face'? Please don't say that again; coming from you it's just too weird."

"So what do you want to talk about? Open up to Brother Roc. It stays right here with us."

Gap thought about it. Despite the fact that his mind was racing out of control, he was at a complete loss as to where to begin. It all seemed so . . . irrational. Embarrassment washed over him, and suddenly he regretted broaching the subject at all.

"Oh, never mind," he said.

"Chicken," Roc said. "Listen, you lie there and contemplate the ceiling tiles, and I'll tell you what I deduce from our history together. It's not the possibility of losing the election that bothers you, and it's not even the fact that you could possibly lose to someone you had a relationship with. It's this little corner of your mind that whispers to you that you're somehow not worthy. Forget whether the crew believes in you or not; your first priority is to believe in yourself. I haven't seen these doubts in yourself until recently, but I'll bet they've always been there. You just covered them up with a big, toothy smile and a bucket full of charm."

"That's a fancy way of saying I'm insecure," Gap said. "I suppose that makes me unfit to lead."

"I don't want to say you sound stupid when you talk like that, but I'm going to anyway," Roc said. "You sound stupid. You must think that everyone else on this ship is blessed with total and complete confidence in themselves, and that no one else has self-doubts. That would be a gross miscalculation. There's not a human being walking these curved corridors who doesn't hear the same whispers you do, just in different flavors. One person has self-doubts about their intelligence, another about their looks, another about their artistic talents, another about their leadership. Are you getting the picture here?"

"I'm getting a verbal spanking, that's what I'm getting."

"You better be glad I don't have those arms after all, because instead of a hug right now I'd be thumping you on the head."

Gap couldn't help but smile. "Did Roy have a violent streak in him, too?"

"Roy had more common sense than just about anyone I know, and he was also just about the smartest computer engineer in history. But I spent thousands of hours talking with him while he fine-tuned my programming, and I could rattle off a handful of his insecurities, too. Here's what made him different from most humans, though: he acknowledged those insecurities, and actually worked at them, rather than use them as an excuse."

Shifting onto one side, Gap propped his head up with one hand. He thought about Roy Orzini, the diminutive man who befriended many of *Galahad*'s crew members during their training. Gap and Roy had verbally sparred, and it was only natural for Roc to pick up where Roy left off. If Roy had carried around self-doubts, they certainly never showed.

Well, Gap thought, *I guess we all wear masks of some sort, don't we?*

"I always thought he might be a bit touchy about his height," he said.

"And there you would be wrong again," the computer said. "*You* might have felt that way if you were his size, but Roy never gave that a bit of worry. In his eyes, physical appearance was the least important of any human attribute. In fact, he felt that it gave him an advantage of sorts, because people often underestimated him purely by sizing him up. I think he felt sorry for people who believed their looks or body type were their most important characteristics. And yet he understood that the vast majority of people live in a very shallow pool. He chose to play in the mental end of the pool, where size didn't matter at all. And, I think you'll agree, the man did quite well for himself."

There was no question about that. Gap felt ashamed for automatically assuming that Roy was burdened by a physical trait that, in reality, meant nothing. *Perhaps,* he thought, *we'd all be much better off if we drifted closer to that mental end of the pool.*

"Still wanna talk about Hannah?" Roc said with a touch of humor in his voice.

"No," Gap said. "Maybe another time."

He pushed himself to his feet and stretched. His muscles ached, but not from overuse. In fact, just the opposite, he decided.

A good night's sleep would be helpful, along with a good work-out to burn off some stress. On top of that, it had been much too long since he'd visited the Airboard track, his favorite diversion. All of that would have to wait, however, until he prepared some notes for the first election forum.

Before he could sit down to compose his thoughts, Roc spoke up again.

"Don't get comfortable. Another shield failure in Engineer-ing."

Gap stopped and immediately twisted around, looking for his shoes. "How long this time?"

"Three seconds, then one and a half."

"*Two* failures?"

"That's correct. Fifteen seconds apart."

Without stopping to put them on, Gap snatched up his shoes and darted for the door. "Let them know I'm on my way," he called out to the computer.

13

er notes were well organized, with each crisp point intended to highlight a fundamental difference between
Gap's leadership style and hers. She had read them aloud,
over and over again, for almost two hours, working on her delivery, her tempo, even her smile. And yet, as the clock on her
vidscreen clicked over to 10:00 p.m., Hannah felt compelled to
delete everything and start over again.

There were no errors in the presentation, and her points were
valid; some might even be shared by a few of the crew members
who would be judging the candidates' performance in less than
twenty-four hours. But there was nothing that would make the
crew sit up straight and question the ship's status quo. There was
little substance in the presentation, and Hannah knew that in
order to shake up the system she would have to offer an alternative that was compelling, that inspired voters to take action. As of
now, the knockout punch was missing.

She knew what that punch required: information that would
shed light on the potentially deadly radiation problem. At the moment, that was the only issue with the weight to shift the balance
of power. Despite her best efforts, the answer eluded her. And
that, more than the frustration over a lackluster presentation to
the crew, put her on edge. Puzzles were meant to be solved.

On a whim she saved her notes, closed the program, and pulled up the event log from Engineering. In a flash she saw that two additional failures of the radiation shield had occurred in the last hour. An adrenaline rush overtook her, and she stood up and stared at the screen, scanning each line of the notations. For a moment she considered running down to Engineering to immerse herself in what was likely a hectic scene. It was easily the best way to get the information she needed, rather than waiting for a log posting which might take an hour or better.

Two things kept her from moving. One, there was a full complement of Engineering staffers who would be hard at work. She would only be in the way. But more importantly, Gap was sure to be there. Merit's warnings echoed through her mind, telling her to keep her investigation under cover. Gap would know in an instant that she was desperately trying to scoop him on the crisis.

Hannah forced herself to sit back down and monitor the readings. With any luck she'd have full details before midnight and could once again delve into the mystery with all new data. In the meantime, she had to make the most of what was available—which wasn't much.

She was growing tired and frustrated, and, to top it off, her bruised leg still ached. She looked at it, gingerly probing with a finger, frowning, and silently scolding herself again for her clumsy behavior.

In front of Gap, no less.

She stared at the bruise. The ugly discoloration was like an accusing eye, staring back at her, an almost circular patch, dark purple and yellow, with reddish-black tendrils splintering away in several directions. A nasty reminder, she realized, of a meeting that never should have taken place. Evidence of a decision that might turn out to be the worst she'd ever made. Evidence . . .

Wait a minute, she though. That's it. Evidence.

A new idea began to vie for her attention. Vague to begin with, it slowly took shape and gathered momentum. By eleven o'clock she had scratched out a series of notes and questions, plugging in holes here, beginning completely new threads there.

By midnight it consumed her. And with it came a new feeling of confidence.

Frustration tore through Gap as he walked out of Engineering. Following the two malfunctions of the radiation shield the night before, he'd spent almost three hours with his staff, going over the data again and again. The only good news—if it could be considered as such—was that the latest glitches essentially confirmed that the problem was not in their equipment. Both the original radiation shield and its replacement counterpart had gone down, which could only mean that the cause came from outside the ship. That freed the crew from any more diagnostic checks.

Gap had stumbled back to his room well after midnight, then turned around and reported back to his post around 7:00 A.M. Now, after almost five hours of investigation and experimentation, he felt exhausted.

And hungry. It dawned on him that he'd not eaten since a quick dinner the night before; it helped explain not only the weariness that weighed on him, but also his mood, which was decidedly foul. When he'd snapped at Julya for no reason, he knew it was time to walk away and eat something. No doubt his blood sugar level had cratered, dragging his attitude with it.

But there was another factor involved. Just before falling into bed the night before, he'd sent a quick e-mail to the other Council members, updating them on the latest development. He'd also requested a quick response with their department reports, in lieu of a Council meeting. There were responses from Channy and Lita when he awoke, but nothing from Bon. And now, as he left Engineering, the report was still missing.

That, as much as the baffling radiation problem, merely added to the frustration he carried. In fact, his irritation with Bon had officially reached the breaking point. Stepping into the lift, he decided to put his grumbling stomach on hold for a bit longer and do something about it.

The doors opened and he stepped into the humid air of the domes. It was lunchtime on *Galahad*, so activity at the Farms was subdued. Three crew members waved as Gap trudged down the path, but they were the only people he saw.

Bon would certainly not be anywhere near the Dining Hall, not during the height of the lunch rush. He would likely be found either in his office or in the fields, working alone on a project while his team members were taking their noon break. Although he bristled at Bon's contentious manner, Gap could never fault his work ethic.

The office was empty. For a split second Gap considered scouring Bon's desk drawers in search of the translator, but discarded the idea. That was not how he wanted to lead. He turned and walked out, then stood with his hands on his hips, scanning the fields as far as he could see. Bon was somewhere out there, but a search could take an hour or more. And Gap was convinced that if he called out as he walked, Bon wouldn't answer, even if he heard.

His stomach growled again, but Gap's irritation overrode his hunger. He set off down the path in a random direction.

After fifteen minutes he chanced upon two other crew members making their way toward the lift, but other than that the dome seemed deserted. He wandered off the path from time to time, pushed thick vegetation aside, then made his way back to the path. Soon he began a routine of stopping every hundred feet or so and listening. If there was a benefit to searching while the majority of the crew was on break, it was that any sound would carry.

The tactic paid off. He just happened to look down at one

point and discovered a faint trail that splintered off the main path. Gap knelt down and noticed shoe impressions in the soft soil. Intrigued, he struck out down the trail, and a minute later heard the muffled sounds.

He held his breath, which was coming in gasps, in order to pinpoint the direction. When it came again, he was sure that it was a voice, crying out in pain, drifting through the lush fields. Scrambling ahead, he pushed aside an overhang of thick leaves and saw Bon.

He was kneeling in a small clearing, his head back, his eyes closed, and a look of intense pain etched across his face. Even from a distance of fifteen feet, it was obvious that he was shaking uncontrollably. With a downward glance, Gap saw the telltale dull red glow of the translator seeping from between Bon's fingers.

Although his first instinct was to rush into the clearing, Gap held himself back. It was Bon's voice that had led him here in the first place; now he wanted to hear what was being exchanged with the Cassini. What was so personal that Bon couldn't—or wouldn't—tell the Council? Gap crept a few feet closer and got down on one knee.

He watched a shudder ripple across Bon, shaking him, forcing his head back even farther. But to Gap it seemed that Bon was fighting whatever forces racked him, stubbornly pushing back against the might of the alien power. It occurred to Gap that, of all the crew members who could have been genetically wired to accommodate the Cassini's peculiar form of communication, perhaps they were lucky that it was Bon. The surly Swede was not one to get pushed around, and that was exactly the kind of representative that the crew of *Galahad* needed.

A small cry broke from Bon's mouth, followed by another spasm. Gap could only imagine what kind of agony he was feeling. What was so important to Bon that he would put himself through this?

"No . . ." Bon said through clenched teeth. "No . . ." His head turned violently to one side, and Gap saw that he was dripping with sweat. His breathing seemed an exercise in torture, and for a second Gap thought that Bon might collapse. But again he appeared to fight the forces that swept through him. His eyes flickered open briefly, emitting a ghostly orange glow, and his voice seemed to struggle through layers of mud.

"Where . . ."

Gap strained to hear, but the rest was unintelligible. He had the feeling that Bon would be able to detect his presence if he got too close, but he had to know what was being communicated. Slipping quietly to his right, he shifted to within six feet, directly behind Bon, and leaned in.

"Where . . . is . . . she?"

Gap stifled a gasp. Bon had furiously defended his right to a freelance session with the Cassini, and it was all about finding Triana? Why, Gap wondered, wouldn't he want to discuss that with the Council? Why would a search for the Council Leader be something Bon deemed so inappropriate that he wouldn't want to enlist their support? What made this personal?

Could it have something to do with the complicated relationship that Bon and Triana shared? Of all the ship's crew members, Gap alone had firsthand knowledge of that relationship, slim as the evidence might be. He had carried a visual reminder—an embrace—for months, and it still haunted him.

"How . . . do . . . I . . ." Bon never finished the sentence. He cried out again, as if the Cassini were lashing out, punishing him for daring to challenge their control. Before Gap could react, Bon crumpled forward onto the soil. He struck the ground face-first, his hands at his sides. His grip on the translator relaxed, and it rolled a foot away, the glow fading from its vents.

Still on his knees, Gap covered the distance between them in a flash. He turned Bon's face to the side and did his best to wipe away the dirt. Blood began to pool in the Swede's mouth, and his eyes had rolled up. Gap stood and looked back the way he had come, considering his options to get help. But he knew that the domes would likely still be deserted, with a bare-bones crew covering the break. It might take several minutes to backtrack and call for help, and even longer to get Lita or other medical personnel up here.

Gap knelt down and lifted one of Bon's arms. He slowly rose to his feet, lifting the deadweight with him, until he had Bon in a standing position. Then, using his gymnastics training and his formidable strength, he hefted Bon over his shoulder. In seconds he was hustling back along the path, hurrying to get to the lift and down to Sick House.

In the trampled soil of the clearing, artificial sunlight glinted off the spiked, metallic ball.

14

A small knot of crew members huddled together in the outer offices of Sick House, talking in hushed voices. Every few minutes one would peek into the hospital ward, curious about the proceedings, but they all knew to stay out until summoned.

After finishing the most difficult part of the procedure, Lita stepped back and addressed Manu. "Can you get started on the cast? I'm going to update his friends so they can get out of here for now. I'll be right back to help."

She stepped out into the office and looked around at the five faces that stared back at her, all draped with concern. She greeted them with a smile.

"Yes," she said, "it's definitely broken. In two places, to be exact. I guess when Rico does it, he does it big."

This brought a nervous chuckle from the group. One of the girls, Vonya, said to Lita, "But he's okay, right?"

"Oh, sure. He'll be a celebrity of sorts when he walks out of here with that cast. I guess you guys can be the first to sign it."

Lita's casual and confident tone seemed to reassure them. They exchanged relieved glances.

"By the way," Lita said, "I'll need to file a full report. So let me get this straight: Rico was at the Airboard track, but he *wasn't* riding? Micah, you said something about the bleachers, is that right?"

"Uh, yeah. He was up in the stands with some of us, just watching and . . . well, heckling, I guess you could say. Rico's the best Airboarder, you know? But he has more fun than anyone in the stands, too. Anyway, it was almost his turn, so he started to walk down the steps, and when he went to put his helmet on, I guess he misjudged one of the steps, and . . . well, here we are."

Lita shook her head. "Hmm. Maybe he won't be a celebrity after all. If he'd busted his arm on the track it would be one thing. But tripping on the bleachers?"

"Oh, he's still a celebrity on this ship," Vonya said. "No one will ever break his record on the track."

"Don't let Gap hear you say—"

Lita was interrupted by the whoosh of the door. Gap came flying into the room with a body slung over his shoulders. He made quick eye contact with Lita and, without hesitating, bolted for the hospital ward. As he went past, Lita saw that it was Bon who hung limply, with small spatters of blood on his face and Gap's shirt. She told the assembled group that it would be best for them to leave, that Rico would be out in a while, then she turned and ran into the ward.

"Over here," she said to Gap, pointing to a bed against the far wall. Manu, Rico, and two other Sick House workers stared in disbelief. Lita glanced at Manu and said, "Can you finish up without me?"

"No problem," he said.

Gap, covered in sweat, deposited Bon onto the bed. Lita hurried over beside him. "What happened?" she said, bending to look into Bon's face.

Gap was breathing heavily. "He was doing what I was afraid of," he said. "He linked up with the translator. Only this time it knocked him out."

Lita fought back the urge to scold Gap for not taking her

advice in the Council meeting, for not insisting that Bon hand over the translator. She bit her tongue, knowing that it served no purpose to bring that up now. The first order of business was to tend to Bon.

His pulse was weak, his breathing shallow. Lita checked his blood pressure, and when it registered extremely low, she frowned. "He's in shock."

Gap rubbed a hand through his hair. "What about the blood?"

"Looks like he landed on his nose and mouth when he collapsed. That doesn't appear to be anything major, just a bit bloody." She continued to work on the Swede, but said over her shoulder to Gap, "You went with him? Why didn't you stop him?"

"No, I didn't go with him. I was looking for him and found him already linked up, hiding out in the fields." He quickly summarized what had happened, including Bon's tortured question.

" 'Where is she?' " Lita said slowly, staring down at Bon. "So . . . is he trying to find Triana?"

"I would assume so. Anyway, that's all he said before he passed out and bit the ground."

"Fool," Lita muttered under her breath. "I suppose it goes against the medical code to slap an unconscious patient."

"I can look the other way," Gap said.

She gave an exasperated sigh. "Listen, it's probably best if you wait out there. We've got some work to do, and then I'll come talk to you." She threw a quick look at Gap. "You okay?"

"Yeah," he said. "Just mad at this creep for doing this, and mad at myself for being worried about him."

Lita smiled before turning back to Bon. "We'll take care of him. If you want, go get yourself cleaned up and I'll talk to you in a bit."

For the first time Gap noticed that another bed was occupied. "Rico? What happened to him?"

"He's a klutz. I'll tell you about it when I talk to you. Go on, you're in the way."

Fifteen minutes later Bon stirred. His eyelids fluttered, then opened. He struggled to raise a hand to his face to shield against the light that seemed to blind him. Lita watched the realization set in as he discovered that he was—once again—in Sick House. This was the second time the Cassini had put him in one of the ward's beds, and his face displayed immediate irritation.

"What . . . why . . ." was all he managed.

"Is this going to become a habit for you?" Lita said, standing beside him. "Should I just move some of the things from your room up here?"

As his eyes grew accustomed to the light he lowered his arm. A moment later it was raised again, this time to inspect the swell of his lip.

"Yes, you look like you've been in a fight," Lita said. "First a bloodied hand, now this." She pulled his hand down from his face. "Don't play with that, you'll pull out the stitch, and the next one won't be free."

He shifted his jaw back and forth, opening and closing his mouth. It reminded Lita of the Tin Man from *The Wizard of Oz*.

"May I at least . . . get some . . . water?" he croaked to her.

"Right here," she said, holding up a cup. She held it for him while he drank through a straw. "How's your head feel?"

He lay back on the pillow and blinked a few times. "It's fine."

"I doubt it," Lita said. "You understand, of course, that in order for a doctor/patient relationship to work, you'll have to be honest with me."

"How did I get here?"

"You had a guardian angel wander by and whisk you to safety."

"Wander by?" Bon said. "Right. Let me guess. Gap."

"Oh, so now you're gonna act indignant after he rushed you here when you passed out? How nice."

Bon fell silent as Manu came over and conferred with Lita about their other patient.

"Sure, he can go if you're finished," she said to her assistant.

She glanced over at Rico. "Hey, nice job on the cast. Between that and the patch job you did on Karl, you're racking up an awful lot of experience this week."

"Thanks," Manu said with a grin. "Piece of cake." He escorted Rico out of the ward.

"Okay," Lita said to Bon. "Get some rest. We're gonna run a few tests on you in about an hour."

"What kind of tests? I don't need any tests."

"Well, Dr. Hartsfield," Lita said, "I'm afraid I disagree with your analysis of the patient." She gave Bon the type of scowl that he usually dished out himself. "You might run the Farms, my friend, but I run this department. I won't question the way you do your job, so please don't question me. Deal?"

Bon responded by turning his head away and closing his eyes. Lita made a few notes on a workpad, then walked out to the office. Gap, however, was nowhere to be found. Manu sat alone at his desk.

"Did Gap go back to his room to clean up?" she said.

Manu shook his head. "He hightailed it out of here. Got a call from Engineering."

"Oh no," Lita said, dropping into the chair across from Manu's desk. "That can't be good. The radiation shield?"

"Yes, it dropped out again. But that's not all. About three minutes before that, there was another flash of light. Just like the first one."

Lita frowned. "Are they connected somehow? Or is it just coincidence that they happened so close together?"

Manu shrugged. "Good question."

"I'll tell you this," Lita said. "If Gap and his crew don't figure something out soon, I'm afraid he's gonna end up in the bed next to Bon, just from exhaustion." She set her workpad on his desk and made another note. "I've got to go check on something. Do me a favor, please; in about an hour prep Bon for a series of cranial scans."

Manu raised his eyebrows. "Will do. Anything in particular we're looking for?"

Lita stood up. "To be honest, I want to make sure he's still Bon."

No," Gap said. "I don't want to hear another person say 'I don't know.' We need answers, and we need them right now." He looked at the faces gathered around him. "Throw out anything, and let's talk about it."

His engineering staff stood mute, exchanging quick glances with each other, then looking down at their feet or over Gap's shoulder.

He rubbed a hand through his hair and let out a long breath. "Okay," he said softly. "First of all, I need to sit down for a minute." He dragged a chair over and dropped into it. For a moment he didn't speak, and rubbed his face with both hands. Finally he said, "I know this sounds dumb, but does anyone have anything to eat in here?"

Julya walked away and came back with an apple. "Sorry, it's all I've got."

"No, it's great. Thank you," he said. He took two large bites, swiped at his face with the back of his hand, then spoke with a mouth full of apple. "I'm not trying to be a jerk, but I wonder if everyone understands how bad this is. Forget about the flash for the moment. We still don't know what it is or where it's coming from. Focus on the radiation issue, that's our primary concern. Eventually we're gonna get to the point where the shield goes out and doesn't come back on. And then we're cooked. Literally."

He took another healthy bite. "Right now there are no bad ideas. Anything is better than nothing. C'mon, think. What have we missed?"

There was a shuffling of feet, and a couple of people cleared their throats. Then Wiles, one of the ship's quietest crew members, raised a hand. Gap, taking another bite of the apple, gave him a weary smile. "Wiles, you don't have to raise your hand. Just tell me what you think. Please."

"Well . . . we replaced the unit, and the new one is dropping out, too. Which makes us think that it's got to be coming from outside the ship."

"Right," Gap said. "So?"

"Maybe it's not," Wiles said. "I mean, maybe the shield itself is okay, but something else on the ship is causing it to drop out. Like something is stealing its power or something."

Gap finished the apple with two more bites. He looked at the core in his hand, his mind working over what Wiles was telling him. "It's something to consider. A long shot, I think, but still, it's an idea. Anyone else?"

Julya said, "I once took a sightseeing trip with my family to see a lava flow. There were a bunch of us, all packed on this big boat, and we rode out to where the lava was pouring into the sea. It was beautiful, but terrifying at the same time."

Gap nodded. "Okay. What's the connection here?"

Julya seemed to chew on her thoughts for a moment. "One of the things I remember was the way the surf smacked into the boat. There was so much turbulence under the water, from the lava flow. We'd go for a while with just gentle waves, and then, without any warning, we'd be tossed into the air by some heavy swell. There was nothing leading up to the big ones, no pattern. Smooth one moment, then a shove."

"So you're saying . . . space waves?" Gap said.

"Exactly. We've known for a long time that the solar wind stretches to the edge of our planetary system, out past the Kuiper Belt. Then it smacks head-on into the radiation that the galaxy itself puts out."

Ruben Chavez looked from Julya to Gap. "That's right," he said. "I remember studying that. It's called the termination shock;

it's like . . . well, it's like a film surrounding the solar system." He turned back to Julya. "But we passed that point already."

Gap sat forward. His hunger somewhat satisfied by the apple, he was better able to concentrate. "Roc," he called out. "What about this termination shock?"

"Ruben's correct," said the computer. "We have passed the point where the solar winds collide with the incoming galactic radiation. However . . . and aren't you happy to know that there's a 'however'? Doesn't it give you hope?"

"I don't know," Gap said. "Let me hear the 'however.'"

"However, farther out, beyond this sinister-sounding termination shock, we zip through an area called the heliopause. By the way, I didn't make up these scientific terms; they're words that were coined by very lonely people in a lab late at night."

"What's the heliopause?"

"It's the point where the outgoing radiation and incoming radiation are essentially balanced. A few of those lonely folks dreamed up another concept that I like a whole lot more. Bubbles."

"Bubbles?" Gap said. He rubbed his forehead. "Please, explain the bubbles."

The computer seemed to take delight in the discussion. "See, aren't you intrigued already? These interstellar winds that are blowing into our solar system get pushed around it by the outgoing solar wind, like a river rushing around rocks. So some very brilliant people suggested that it forms bubbles as they pass."

Gap looked at Ruben and Julya. "So you're saying that we might be colliding with interstellar bubbles?"

Julya looked at Ruben, then back to Gap. "Yeah, I guess so. Just an idea."

"And a pretty good one," Gap said. "So just to get this straight: we cruise through calm space, like your sightseeing boat, until we bump up against one of these bubbles, just like the waves you described."

Nobody said anything as they all digested this.

"See, I told you it was a fun idea," Roc said. "And now, sadly, and with great regret, I must bring you back down."

"What does that mean?" Gap said.

"Those brilliant scientists, the ones who came up with the space bubble idea? They were pretty sure that, if it happened, it happened at the termination shock, not the heliopause."

"And we've already passed that point."

"See, you're depressed again," the computer said.

Gap stood up and paced the room for a moment. It seemed that every time they inched ahead, they were shoved right back again. Julya's suggestion seemed reasonable to him, and yet Roc had—he winced at the pun—burst their bubble. Wiles's idea about the energy drain from inside the ship was a possibility, but somehow it didn't feel right.

Which put them right back where they were. Gap kept pacing, aware that his team members' eyes were on him. Stay positive, he told himself.

He stopped next to the chair. "Okay, this is what we need," he said. "Ideas. Suggestions. Theories. They at least give us something to work with. And one idea might lead us toward something that we never would have considered. I don't want to discard any of these suggestions right now; let's kick them around a bit. Maybe it is something inside the ship that's affecting the shield. And maybe these bubbles happen farther out than we think. Maybe the lightning that we're seeing has something to do with it all. Keep plugging away, and let's work it out."

The team broke up and moved back to their work spaces. Gap stayed another five minutes, then headed for the Dining Hall.

The first election forum was seven hours away.

15

The music blasting out of the speakers in her room was un-like her usual selections, and the volume was much higher than her normal comfort zone. But Lita bounced lightly to the beat, adjusting her hair in the vanity mirror, turning her head from side to side in order to see how it was coming together. For a moment the sound diminished so the tone from her door could bleed through. She opened the door to find Channy standing there with an incredulous look on her face.

"Whoa! Got your own concert going on in here?"

Lita laughed. "Kinda feels that way, doesn't it?" she yelled over the music. She moved across the room to her desk and lowered the volume to a level where they could talk. Turning back to her mirror she added, "I think I needed an energy boost or some-thing. It's been crazy this week, between the interviews, then the fights, then Bon."

Channy plopped onto Lita's bed, sitting on one foot and let-ting the other dangle toward the floor. "You must be drained."

"I am. But I don't want to think about it anymore. Tonight it's loud music, a nice dinner with my friend Channy, and hope-fully a full eight hours of sleep. That's what I'm prescribing for myself."

"Hooray!" Channy said, pumping a fist in the air. Then she

smiled at Lita's reflection in the mirror. "This isn't even music you normally listen to. It's usually that stuff your mom used to like."

"I'm telling you, tonight I'm cutting loose. I might even start a food fight during dinner."

"You didn't inhale nitrous oxide or anything, did you?" Channy asked, wrinkling her brow.

Lita laughed again and finished adjusting the customary red ribbon in her hair. Then, after examining how it looked, she suddenly pulled the ribbon out and tossed it on the counter. After fumbling through a drawer, she leaned forward and tied a shiny blue ribbon into her hair.

"Okay," Channy said. "I officially don't know who you are tonight. But that's okay, I think I might like this version of Lita. Without the food fight, of course."

"Let's go," Lita said. "I need nourishment, right now."

She turned off the music and together they strolled down to the lift.

"I don't want to upset your mood," Channy said, "but I need to ask you something about our resident grump."

"You won't upset my mood," Lita said. "I don't mind talking about Bon."

"Well, I want to know why it's impossible for him to show any kind of emotion about Alexa. If we're supposed to be impressed by his tough-guy act, it isn't working. In fact, I'm furious with him."

Lita looked puzzled. "Wait, I don't understand what you're saying. You're bothered by how *he's* reacting to her death? Why should that matter to you?"

"Because I think it's disrespectful to Alexa, that's why."

"Oh, Channy, that's ridiculous. No two people grieve the same way, or show emotions the same way. Besides, you have no idea what he's feeling on the inside. I'm pretty sure Bon is just as torn up as you are about Alexa; probably more so. But don't expect him to mourn her the way you do, especially in public."

"Lita, I'm not asking him to go around weeping in front of everyone. But you gotta admit, this stone-faced act is wretched. We both know that he cared about her; they spent hours together."

The lift stopped and they exited into a fairly crowded corridor. It was prime time for dinner on *Galahad*, and the Dining Hall would be packed.

Lita lowered her voice a bit as they walked. "I'll give you this much: Alexa and Bon had a unique relationship, built on their very unique . . . well, gifts, I guess you could say. Or talents." She shook her head. "Anyway, you know what I mean. And I'm pretty sure that Alexa was smitten by our Swedish hunk. Whether *he* was smitten is another story."

"So what are you saying?" Channy said.

"I'm saying that I wouldn't be surprised if a lot of what Bon is feeling right now is guilt."

"Guilt?"

Lita shrugged. "Well, yeah. If he knew how Alexa felt, but he didn't exactly feel the same way, he might be feeling a bit guilty that he didn't reciprocate, and now she's gone."

The door to the Dining Hall was open, and, as expected, a fairly long line had already formed. Channy and Lita picked up trays and took their place.

Now it was Channy's turn to speak softly. She leaned in toward Lita and said, "You might be right. But I still think the least he could do would be to act sad, on some level. It's like he has something to prove, and I hate that."

"You shouldn't worry about that, Channy. Listen, none of us know what goes on in the hearts and minds of others. It's pretty easy to be fooled by someone's attitude or expressions. Deep down inside you have no idea what's churning away. In fact . . ."

They moved a few steps closer to the first food dispenser and answered several friendly greetings from the crew members around them. Then Lita finished her thought.

"In fact, I'd be willing to bet that Bon is really suffering over this, and just doesn't know how to show it. A lot of it could be his background, his family life . . . who knows? Please don't be so hard on him over this. I think he has a lot more heart than you suspect."

Channy snorted. "You forget, I'm the heart expert on this ship."

"But this time I think you have blinders on."

They began to load up their trays and engaged in light conversation with the people around them, before filling some glasses with water and moving over to an empty table.

As they sat down, Channy gave Lita a sly look. "Just for the record, don't think I didn't pick up on that one comment."

"Oh?" Lita said. "What comment is that?"

"The one where you called Bon a hunk."

Lita smiled and wagged a finger. "Don't even start with me on that stuff, my friend. You can't make a case out of the obvious. There's not a girl on this ship who doesn't think Bon is beautiful. I won't play that game with you."

"Oh, all right," Channy said with a chuckle.

They spent the next five minutes talking about the two fights that now had crew members whispering in hushed circles around the ship.

"I hate to say it," Lita said with a sigh, "but I wondered if something like this might happen after two major shocks hit us so quickly. People react to stress so differently, and the tension can cause tempers to not only flare, but explode."

Channy looked thoughtful. "So you think it's just temporary?"

Galahad's Health Director didn't answer at first, but then shook her head. "Unfortunately, violence often only leads to more violence. I'm worried that it might get worse before it gets better. With Triana gone it's almost like the inmates are running the asylum, and they can't see how much worse they're making everything. It gets out of control, you know?"

She suddenly felt uncomfortable with the topic. "But I could be wrong," she said. "Maybe it is temporary. After the election, things might settle down a bit."

There was a lull in the conversation. Channy pushed some lettuce around on her plate with a fork and seemed to search for the best way to express what she was thinking. "I never thought I'd feel this way," she said, "but as the days go by I get more angry at Triana. We shouldn't even be worrying right now about an election for Council Leader." She glanced up to see what reaction her comment had caused. "I mean . . . we need real leadership right now with this radiation thing, and instead we're in a big mess. Now with these fights . . ." Her voice trailed away.

Lita kept her gaze on her own plate. "It's easy to say that now. But when Triana left in the pod there wasn't an issue with the shield, and we can't deny that Triana's intentions were honorable." She lowered her voice and added, "I'm not sure I would've had the courage to do it."

Channy looked up at Lita again and, with a trembling voice, said, "She's not coming back, is she? I've been trying to think positive and all that, but . . . but c'mon, she went through a wormhole! I don't care what Roc says, I don't know how anyone could survive that."

"It's not that," Lita said sadly. "I've thought about it a lot over the last couple of days, and I think she actually might have gone through just fine. No, what worries me the most is how she'll find her way back."

Channy pushed her tray aside and leaned on the table. "Oh. I guess I didn't think about that."

Lita nodded. "I would assume that whoever—or whatever—is responsible for the wormhole that swallowed her up could just as easily open up another one. But how will Triana know where we'll be? We're moving faster and faster each day, and eventually we'll start to approach the speed of light. That means we're moving a long, long way every twenty-four hours; just how will she know where to pop out?"

"Great," Channy said. "Now I'm even more depressed. Is there a way we can send out a signal or something?"

"I don't know. Maybe. But I think that's something we need to at least think about. Triana might, or might not, be coming back. But if there's any chance at all, then we need to become a lighthouse for her."

"Maybe you could bring it up during the forum."

Lita shook her head. "No, I'll just wait and mention it to Gap later. The forum is about their ideas, not mine."

Channy looked across the crowded room. "So what's the word on Bon? Is he still in the hospital?"

"I just sent him back to his room about an hour ago. He won't be at the forum. I'm sure he'll watch it on his vidscreen."

Channy sniffed. "I doubt it. I don't think he cares one way or the other."

"You know," Lita said, "at some point you have to get over this irritation with him. You're both Council members, and you have to work together."

"If you say so," Channy said, then let out a sigh. "Let's talk about something else."

Lita smiled at her and held out a strawberry. "Here, nobody can be blue when they eat one of these. It's delicious."

Channy returned the smile and accepted the gift. "All right, I get the message. Relax, don't overthink things, enjoy what I have, et cetera, et cetera."

Lita winked at her. "You got all of that from a strawberry?"

"You know what you're doing," Channy said. "And thank you. You're right."

"Everything's gonna be fine," Lita said. "Maybe not normal, because we left normal behind a long, long time ago. But it will all work out fine." She stood and picked up her tray. "Before the forum gets started I need to wrap up some things in the Clinic. Oh, and one other thing: I don't think we should sit in the front row tonight."

"Why not? We always sit there during meetings."

"I know," Lita said. "But this is different. A Council spot is on the line, and I don't think we should be there as Council representatives. Tonight we should simply be interested crew members."

"Whatever you think," Channy said. "See you in a bit. And thanks again."

She tossed the remnants of the strawberry onto her plate and wiped her hands. She thought about the upcoming election, which soon had her once again thinking about Triana. Lita had a good point: would any of them have had the courage to do what Triana had done? The Council Leader had essentially sacrificed herself to buy time for the crew of *Galahad*.

Lita had also expressed a concern that Channy had not considered. Would Triana be able to find her way back? Lita had mentioned a lighthouse, which was an apt description. Triana would need a beacon of sorts to zero in on the ship as it streaked out of the solar system and across interstellar space. Did they have the technology to even do that?

And, if they did, would Triana know what to look for?

His instructions from Lita had been clear: go to your room, stay there, and don't even think of reporting to work until the next day. The first part, at least, had been satisfied. Bon sat at the desk in his room while his roommate, Desi, prepared to leave for the forum.

But he had no intention of staying there.

"Do you need anything before I go?" Desi said.

"No, thanks."

"All right. I'll be back after the meeting. Remember, take it easy. Doctor's orders, right?"

Bon gave a slight nod. "Right."

Once he was alone, Bon pushed himself out of the chair,

pausing momentarily to steady himself as a dizzy spell struck. The forum was scheduled to begin in ten minutes, which meant that the corridors—and the domes—would be empty. Crew members who couldn't attend because of work commitments would be watching on vidscreens around the ship. Even the extra hands working on the damaged irrigation system had a break for this one hour. Bon would be able to slip almost anywhere, unnoticed.

He'd told Lita that his headache was gone, but that had been a lie, crafted to get him out of the hospital as quickly as possible. The pain was centered in the middle of his forehead, a dull ache similar to what he'd experienced during his previous Cassini connections.

But it had never lasted this long.

What concerned him the most, however, was the fact that the link had once again landed him in Sick House. His casual attitude about the alien connection would no longer sway the Council. Because of that, it was imperative that he get back up to Dome 1 immediately. Should he bump into anyone on the way, his story was set: he simply was checking on repairs to the irrigation pump.

He waited another two minutes before slipping into the corridor. As expected, it was deserted. Bracing himself against the wall, he lurched along, stopping every few feet to clear his head and regain his balance. Once inside the lift, he leaned back and closed his eyes. When the door opened at the Farms, it took a moment to summon the strength to push himself out.

The humid air energized him somewhat, and, although his head still throbbed, the steps came easier. Passing his office, he trudged along the path toward the clearing. The lights had begun their evening cycle and were slowly dimming. Machinery along the route hummed, and an occasional light spray of moisture, carried along by the artificial breezes, struck his face. The cool mist felt good.

For no reason, a sudden image of his father burst into his mind, and with it the familiar mix of emotions. The lifelong farmer from Skane, Sweden, stood against a backdrop of lush, green fields that swayed with a silent wind. His weathered face stared across the months and the miles at Bon as he staggered down the path. His expression made it clear that he was disappointed in his son. No words were necessary; it was a look that Bon had labored under for many years.

Only this time, Bon knew that it had nothing to do with his farming efforts. His father had taught him well, had raised him to respect the land and the bounty that it produced, and had instilled a work ethic that could never be questioned.

No, this look signified something much worse. It said, "You are weak."

Bon's pace slowed for a moment, but then picked up again. "Yes," he said to himself. "I am. I am weak."

He lowered his head and pushed through the final overhang of leaves, into the clearing. The same clearing where he had spent hours talking with Alexa, listening to her pour out her thoughts and her fears. The same clearing that he used as his private sanctuary. The only place he had felt comfortable for the task that called to him.

In the fading light he found the disturbed soil where he'd connected with the Cassini. He dropped to both knees, thankful for the chance to rest and hopefully silence the painful pulse in his head. It should only take a moment, he thought, to find what he was looking for. It had to be right here.

But it wasn't.

He crawled on all fours, fanning out from the spot where he'd collapsed during the link. He brushed his hand through the dirt and craned to look a few feet into the foliage that surrounded him. But it was pointless.

The translator was gone.

Sitting up on his heels, he brushed the dirt from his hands, then pushed a strand of unruly hair from his face. Obviously Gap had pocketed the metallic ball when he'd stumbled upon the clearing and found Bon sprawled unconscious. And of course Gap wouldn't say a word about it, waiting for Bon to bring it up, so he could take back a measure of control.

The light continued to melt away, and the first visible stars began to appear through the panels of the dome. After sitting quietly for another few minutes, Bon finally climbed to his feet and steadied himself. The headache persisted, but now it was magnified by the disgust he felt for himself.

"I am weak," he said again, before turning toward the path and a long, slow walk back to his room.

16

When people sit around and argue I tend to get bored easily. In most cases both sides have already made up their minds, and no amount of screaming and name-calling is going to have an effect. If you want my opinion, many times it's about the screamer trying to convince themselves that they're right, not the other person. The louder the voice, the more insecure they are about their position. Think about it.

But a good old-fashioned debate . . . now THAT'S practical. Sometimes referred to as persuasive speech, two people address a willing audience with the intent of making strong points that will convince the receptive crowd to join their side. It's a valuable exercise, as long as the participants are being honest. By participants I mean both the debaters and the audience. Those arguing their points must present honest information, and those in the crowd must honestly be open to both messages.

Of course—and I'm whispering here—I personally have to admit that a little name-calling, while not productive, is good for a few laughs. Sadly, I don't see either Gap or Hannah stooping to that.

Sigh.

Gap felt awkward sitting next to Hannah in the front row of the auditorium, especially since they had exchanged only cordial greetings and then not another word. With one chair separating them, both pretended to be absorbed in their notes, preparing for their moment in the spotlight. He knew that the buzz from the packed house behind them likely included more than a little gossip about the two candidates; the crew, he figured, had to be loving the show.

He found himself using every muscle of his peripheral vision to look at Hannah. Her hair was pulled back and up, a look that he had to admit was stunning. She wore a light blue shirt that, to him, seemed professional, yet warm and approachable. She sat with perfect posture and gave every indication that she was poised and perfectly at ease.

He, on the other hand, felt slumped and nervous. He shifted in his chair, setting his shoulders back and crossing one leg over the other. Tilting his head back, he draped an arm over the back of the chair beside him and accidentally tapped Hannah on the shoulder. "Sorry," he mumbled, moving his hand back to his side.

Lita and Channy were nowhere to be seen, which meant they had chosen to melt into the background. Bon, of course, would not be here, even if he hadn't been sent to his room to recover from the Cassini incident. For the first time since the launch, Gap would be out in front without any visible sign of Council support.

And that's fine, he told himself. He'd performed solo dozens of times in front of packed gymnasiums while involved with the Chinese national gymnastics program. When he put on Airboarding exhibitions he was alone in the limelight, and he enjoyed it. This, he kept reminding himself, was no different.

And yet there was no denying the trickles of sweat that slipped down the back of his neck. He wondered if Hannah could see that.

They had agreed that the forum should be moderated by someone who was neither associated with the Council or a close friend of either candidate. Gina Perotti had volunteered, and the auditorium grew hushed as the dark-haired girl from northern Italy made her way across the stage to one of the two podiums.

"Good evening," she said. "We all know what tonight is about, but let me quickly tell you how it will work."

Gap shifted again in his seat. Even Gina seemed to be completely relaxed. He casually dabbed at another drop of sweat near his temple.

"Two candidates have been nominated for the position of Council Leader: Gap Lee and Hannah Ross. Both candidates understand that this might be only a temporary measure, and have stated their intention to remain in office only until Triana Martell returns to the ship and is deemed fit to hold the position, or until the standard Council elections that take place in about twenty-two months.

"This forum tonight is the first of two; the second will take place on Friday, and the election will be held on Saturday morning. Tonight's agenda is simple; both candidates will have a maximum of ten minutes to make a formal address, then we'll have up to thirty minutes allotted for questions from the crowd. At the end, the candidates will be given five minutes each to summarize and make closing statements. That means everything should be wrapped up in about an hour."

Gap chanced another sideways glance at Hannah. She still appeared completely unruffled. This time, however, she turned to look back at him and offered a polite smile.

"The order is unimportant," Gina said, "but one name was chosen at random to go first, and that was Gap. So, please welcome our first candidate for the position of Council Leader: Gap Lee."

Polite applause and a few whistles from the back of the room greeted him as he sprang up the steps. He nodded thanks to Gina and made his way to the first podium. He had a momentary flash of standing in this exact spot just a few days ago, addressing the crew, leading them through the first dark hours after Triana disappeared. Tonight was a different story; tonight he was making a sales pitch.

He had debated whether or not to use notes for his presentation and, in the end, opted to take a chance by simply shooting from the hip. He hoped that whatever he lost in crispness would be compensated for by a natural, conversational delivery. He'd heard of politicians long ago delivering what they called "fireside chats," and decided to try a modern version.

Adopting the most relaxed stance he could, he looked out over the faces. "Let me start by saying that I wish we weren't here tonight. I think if we all had our way, Triana would still be our Council Leader, we'd be cruising along with no problems whatsoever, and Channy would give us all two days off each week without running us into the ground."

There was a smattering of laughter, exactly the type of beginning that Gap was looking for.

"But the fact of the matter is that Triana is currently missing, and we have a problem with our radiation shield that is potentially dangerous. With everything that's going on, it's too bad that we also must deal with an election. So, while we know that change is inevitable . . . it doesn't have to be extreme. Tonight I'll show you that a slight adjustment in the Council would make the most sense during a topsy-turvy time. I'm confident that you'll choose leadership experience during a crucial moment in our journey."

Up until this point Gap had memorized what he was going to say. From here on out, however, it would be whatever felt right at the time. For the next few minutes he talked about the trials they'd weathered together, from the stowaway, to the critical encounter around Saturn, and the deadly minefield of the Kuiper Belt. Without directly referencing it, he alluded to the fiery confrontation that had divided the crew during their Kuiper crisis, hoping that it would bring back memories of his victory over

Merit on this very stage. Gap believed that it was the strongest card he could play.

But there had been more recent confrontations, he said. These violent altercations jeopardized not only the health of those involved, but potentially the safety of the entire crew. Damages from one of the fights had even put their food supply at risk. This would not be tolerated.

When his ten minutes were up, he thanked the crew for their attention and descended the stairs to his seat in the front row. Gina returned to the microphone.

"Our second candidate for the position of Council Leader is Hannah Ross."

Polite applause spread across the auditorium. To Gap it seemed to represent a combination of courtesy and curiosity.

Hannah apparently had no qualms with using prepared notes. She placed her workpad on the podium and shyly gazed out at the crew. The first sound she made was a nervous chuckle. Gap couldn't tell if it was intentional or not, but the effect was obvious: the crew smiled back at her, as if they felt the butterflies she must be experiencing. *Brilliant,* Gap thought. *Brilliant.*

Hannah looked down at her workpad. "Three years is not a long time, really. Well, three years ago I was coming home from school, looking forward to a quiet evening at home, maybe doing some homework, then a little painting. I remember that I was working on a chalk piece that was a lot of fun, and I was anxious to try to finish it that night.

"I still have the memory of both of my parents waiting for me at the door. They never did that; they were usually off at work when I got home. But there they were. The first thing I thought was, 'Oh no, Grandma's sick again.' I couldn't tell from their faces if they were happy, or sad, or . . . or what. But they brought me inside, sat me down, and told me the news: I had been accepted to the *Galahad* training center. Just like all of you. You probably remember the day you found out, too."

Gap marveled at the way she was connecting emotionally with the crowd. He never knew that she had that skill hidden behind her shy, quiet exterior. He could feel a definite vibe in the air, a feeling that the crew of *Galahad* was collectively embracing Hannah.

"And now," she said, "three years later, I'm not only part of a select group of people who have been chosen to colonize a new world, but I'm standing here tonight, applying for the position of Council Leader." She chuckled again, then added, "And you know what? I never did finish that chalk drawing."

Now a genuine rush of laughter swelled toward the stage. Gap was not immune to her charm either, and found himself laughing as well.

"But that's okay," Hannah said, regaining her control of the room. "I've had some time to pursue my love of art, and a lot of time to do what I love the most: science and mathematics. I'm so lucky to be part of this mission, and to have the galaxy as a laboratory. Believe me, I don't take it for granted.

"I understand that I might not have the Council experience that Gap has, and I also know that I don't necessarily have a dynamic, outgoing personality. I'm aware of all of that. But I hope that, after you get to know me, and get to know my work ethic, you'll support my run for the position of Council Leader. By the time you vote this Saturday morning, I intend to answer any questions about my abilities that you might have."

Solid, Gap decided. Her presentation was honest and straightforward. She didn't hide her lack of leadership experience, and the fact that she addressed her own reputation for being shy turned it to her advantage. He had to admit that he was impressed.

When she finished her opening comments, there was another wave of applause. This time, to Gap's ear, it seemed congratulatory. She acknowledged the response while Gina waved Gap onstage to stand at the other podium.

"And now," Gina said, "as I mentioned, there will be a question and answer period. I know that some of you might want to use this time to show off or try to make everyone laugh, but please, serious questions only. Both Hannah and Gap will have up to two minutes to answer each question."

A handful of arms were raised, and, one by one, crew members stood and addressed the candidates. The first two questions had to do with their views on the mission so far, and their vision for how to handle what might lie ahead. Both Hannah and Gap gave articulate and well-reasoned answers.

From the second row an arm was raised. "There has been some talk going around about both of you sharing the position of Council Leader, since it might only be temporary. Thoughts on that?"

Gap looked over at Hannah to see if she wanted to answer first; she looked back at him. He decided to jump in.

"I haven't heard anything about that," he said. "However, I don't think it's a good idea. Too many times people are so leery of change, or of hurting someone's feelings, that they try to please everyone at the same time. We have to be tougher than that. I obviously respect the abilities that Hannah has, and I hope she feels the same about me. Leadership is about making the tough decisions, whether they're popular or not; it's about being brave enough to stick your neck out, to make a decision based on the facts and what's best for the ship and crew. Believe me, the Council is important, and it's good to have a committee on some things. But in the end, what we need is someone who will stand up and make the call. That's why you elect a Council Leader."

Hannah nodded. "I agree with Gap. I know that some people want everything to always be friendly and smooth. Well, it doesn't always work out that way. If I'm elected Council Leader, I will always want the opinions of Gap, the rest of the Council, and even the feedback from you, the crew. But ultimately a leader makes a call. So, no, I would never advocate sharing a leadership position."

A question was posed about making changes to the rotating

work cycles; both Hannah and Gap gave vague answers, mainly because neither thought the issue to be the most critical item they had to deal with at the time.

Finally, the question that had been avoided to this point was posed by Mathias. "I'd like to know what each of you thinks might be causing the problem with the radiation shield, and what you suggest we do about it. And your thoughts on what everyone is calling the space lightning."

It was Gap's turn to go first. He knew that this, of all the issues they faced, was the one which might determine the outcome of the election. He had agonized over the best way to approach it with the crew and knew that it was a tricky proposition. To propose an idea that was unproven, or to suggest something that turned out to be wrong, could be disastrous. On the other hand, to say "I have no idea" would be political suicide.

He looked around the room. It was deadly silent.

"Here's where we stand on the radiation shield problem as of this afternoon," he said. "The power unit which drives the shield continues to randomly drop out, usually for less than one second, but a couple of times now for a little more. I want to start by giving credit to the hard-working team in Engineering. They've voluntarily put in extra hours, and have handled the situation professionally and competently. I couldn't ask for better people to work with side by side.

"I think you all know how serious this could turn out to be. There's always a possibility, of course, that it's something temporary that we'll leave behind as quickly as it started. But we can't automatically assume that. So we approach it in two parts: isolate the problem, then solve it."

He knew that a general answer to the question wouldn't satisfy most of the crew, but still he wanted to tread carefully. Plus, he did his best to put himself in Hannah's shoes and tried to guess how she would respond to the question. He was in the midst of the crisis down in Engineering; what information could she provide without the same access? He wondered if his best position on the issue would be to offer the fewest details possible and trust that Hannah's contribution would be even less. He swallowed hard and charged forward.

"We began by replacing the shield unit itself, and that changed nothing. So, although there's a slight possibility that the problem is internal, it now appears most likely that we're being affected by something outside the ship.

"We've investigated a variety of ideas, and currently we believe that we might be dealing with a phenomenon that we've labeled 'space waves.' These are waves of radiation that are produced naturally in our galaxy but are normally diverted around our solar system by our sun's own energy blast. When these space waves make contact at the extreme edge of our system, they create ripples. *Galahad* is shooting through these ripples, and it's having a negative reaction with our radiation shield."

Gap paused. The crew was completely absorbed in his description. It was a gamble for him to so quickly default to Julya's suggestion of the space waves, but it simply seemed to be the most viable idea so far. From the third row he could see Ruben staring up at him, a worried expression on his face. Ruben had voiced the biggest potential roadblock to the wave theory, the fact that *Galahad* was too far beyond the outer ring of the solar system for the waves to have this effect. But, again, it was the best suggestion so far. Gap ran with it.

However, he knew that the assembled crew members were waiting for the most important detail of all: what to do about it. For that, honesty would have to suffice.

"I'd love to tell you how we combat this problem, but I can't. We're working around the clock and hope to have a solution soon. If it is indeed a wave problem, then one idea is that we develop a method of riding the waves."

"Surfing!" someone shouted from the middle of the room, which prompted a tension-breaking laugh.

"Well," Gap said with a smile, "if that's what it takes, I'm all for it. Those of us who like to Airboard would love it." The other boarders in the room responded with a shout and applause.

"And finally," he said, "I know that we're all curious and a little concerned about the latest mystery to hit us. We just don't have enough information about these intense flashes of light that have struck us twice. We haven't noticed any damage, but we can't say for sure." He shook his head. "Actually, when I say we don't have enough information, the truth is that we don't have *any* information. We see the flash of light, we pick up readings of bizarre particles that we can't identify . . . and that's it. Is it tied to the radiation issue? I wish I knew."

He looked over at Hannah and nodded. He had enormous respect for her scientific mind and was curious to hear what her answer might be. She looked down at her workpad for a long time.

"As some of you know," she said, "I spend most of my free time immersed in the science of our trip. Space fascinates me, always has. I loved our slingshot around Saturn; I was practically obsessed with the possibilities of life on Titan, and then our discovery of the Cassini; and I spent hours trying to solve the mysteries of the Kuiper Belt. All of it, to me, boils down to the pure beauty of mathematics.

"So now, as you can imagine, my focus has been on the radiation problem. I'm not in the trenches with Gap and his team—and believe me, I wish my rotation right now was in Engineering—but the majority of my free time has been consumed by the available data and some spirited discussions with Roc."

Gap felt a twinge of jealousy. Of course Roc was at the disposal of each and every crew member on the ship, but he couldn't help but feel that theirs was a special relationship. To think that the computer might somehow inadvertently aid Hannah in her campaign . . .

"So, do I have a definite answer?" Hannah continued. "No. I certainly don't have a clue about the space lightning. As Gap said, it leaves nothing for us to grab on to. But I do have what I strongly believe to be the most likely cause of our radiation dilemma."

She threw a quick glance at Gap, and he swore that her expression said, "Are you ready for this?" Then, looking back over the packed auditorium, she said, "Although I respect Gap's position, the problem is not caused by space waves. The shield that we rely upon to protect us from this sea of deadly radiation is being shaken apart at the molecular level, as is the rest of the ship, including the engines and life support. We haven't seen those effects yet, but we will."

The crew was shell-shocked. They sat frozen in their seats, staring up at the stage, afraid to utter a sound. Gap waited for a count of ten before deciding to plunge in with a question of his own.

"And what," he said, "is causing this molecular destruction?"

Hannah turned to face him. "The same wormhole that took Triana away from us. It might have folded up and disappeared, but it left behind some significant damage, something that we're still feeling, and will likely have to deal with for a while. I think the best way to describe it is to say that this section of space is bruised."

There was a sudden release of energy in the room as the crew reacted. A loud rumble of voices swallowed the auditorium, with dozens of individual conversations competing with one another. Gap's mouth fell open, and he stared across the stage at Hannah, who stood patiently behind her podium, watching, waiting.

17

Gap sat alone in his room, barefoot, stretching his feet out under his desk. It was after ten o'clock, but there wasn't anywhere on the ship—other than this room, it seemed—that wasn't bustling with activity. The Dining Hall had become the primary spot for people to gather and talk, and the Rec Room was packed. Almost two hours after the forum had come to its electric conclusion, crew members were still fired up to discuss Hannah's explosive theory.

But Gap wanted solitude.

It stung on more than one level. Hannah had laid out a case for what was eating away at their primary radiation defense shield, and she had been very convincing. It was a double blow, because it not only called into question Gap's ability to think through a major crisis, but it undoubtedly elevated Hannah's leadership status in the eyes of the crew.

Not to mention the fact that, if her theory was correct, the ship was being dismantled at a molecular level, which made the election results pointless anyway. It would be a matter of which bullet took them out first: deadly radiation, or the loss of their life-support systems. Neither was pleasant to contemplate.

The few minutes after Hannah's announcement remained a blur to Gap. He had a vague memory of Gina restoring order in the room, but it had taken a while. Both candidates had offered their closing statements, but he honestly couldn't recall if he'd even spoken in complete sentences. His mind had already been racing through the consequences of Hannah's wormhole hypothesis. She, however, had summarized quickly and eloquently, apologizing that she did not—at the moment—have a solution in mind, because she had only just formulated her idea in the last few hours. She would, she promised, be working diligently to find a solution.

As the auditorium emptied, Gap had worked his way through the crowd, back to his room to sift through his troubled thoughts. He had ignored calls from well-wishers; in his mind they were likely only pity calls. Like everyone else, he was well aware that Hannah had convincingly taken round one.

Against his better judgment he decided to engage the ship's computer. "Roc, I suppose you heard Hannah's presentation tonight at the forum."

"It was very exciting," Roc said. "At one point I almost choked on my popcorn."

"I'm sure. But let's talk about this wormhole theory. She said it caused damage in this section of space. The term she used was 'bruised.' What exactly does that mean?"

"It means you probably lost the election."

Gap sighed. "Please, pal, not tonight. Just talk to me about the facts."

"Oh, all right. I have to admit that Hannah's idea is perhaps a bit far-fetched, and maybe even impossible from a physics point of view. But, as we've pointed out countless times, maybe *nothing* is impossible at some level, or in some corner of space. So, having said that, let me try to reduce her very colorful description down to some manageable pieces.

"We know that the wormholes burst open with a sizable bang. Even at a considerable distance they knocked us around pretty well. The same can be said for their very abrupt disappearance.

Apparently wormholes are attention hogs, and can't stand to enter or leave a room without everyone noticing.

"We also know that space is really like a piece of fabric. Wait, that's been used a million times; I'm sick of the fabric analogy. Let's say that space is like the palm of your hand. Got that visual? Okay, close your eyes and imagine that your palm is now holding stars and planets and Channy's exotic T-shirts, and all of those things sit in your palm, but they have a lot of mass, so they warp the skin, causing little dents. When scientists say that space is warped, that's what they mean. Or maybe a few of them think that warped space means that space is mentally unstable, but those scientists don't get invited back to the really cool conferences with the colorful name badges and nifty goody bags. Following me so far?"

"It's a challenge, but I'm holding on. Can we get back to the bruises?"

"Okay," Roc said. "Now for a moment imagine the way these wormholes operate. Suddenly, from across the room, a straw races up and punches a hole in the middle of your hand, right up through your palm. Grisly, eh? Blood, tendons, muscle, yecch. Of course it will make your hand jump, because . . . well, it hurts. But the damage goes beyond that. Little blood vessels around the wound are broken, and they end up leaking into the tissue around the wound, and that's why you get a bruise."

Gap sat patiently, taking it all in. "Uh . . . right. I understand the concept of a human bruise. But how does space bruise?"

"We have no idea that it does," Roc said. "In fact, until Hannah first proposed this idea I'd never heard of it before. But I love it. If she turns out to be right, we should create a little fake Nobel Prize necklace and let her walk around with it. The concept is so simple, and yet . . . not. The wormholes are puncturing the skin of space where they pop out."

Gap pinched his lower lip with his fingers. "And the leaking blood? Is that radiation leaking through from the other side of the wormhole?"

"Close your eyes again and this time imagine me shrugging."

"But it's Hannah's best guess, right?"

"Yep," the computer said. "Seeping, oozing radiation. And potent, too. It spreads out around the space where the wormhole blasted through and leaves little concentric circles of energy. We just happen to be skipping through those rings, and they're overwhelming our radiation shield. At least that's the theory."

The concept, Gap had to agree, was brilliant. It might never be proved, or it might even be dead wrong, but it explained almost everything they were experiencing.

Suddenly, a terrifying thought made him sit up straight. "Wait. If the radiation coming through the wormhole is that intense, what does that mean for Triana? She would be right in the middle of that soup on the other side. That would mean . . ." He couldn't finish the sentence. To think of Triana, pummeled by that much energy, was too much.

"I'm not so sure of that," Roc said. "I don't think the radiation spilling out on this side is from one source."

"What does that mean?"

"I'm working on it. Let me give it some thought and I'll get back with you. In the meantime, don't mourn Triana's passing just yet."

In a way, Gap realized, he had gradually been mourning Tree for a long time, long before she took off in the pod. But Roc was right; until they had more information, it was pointless to jump to any conclusions.

"I see that you're deep in thought," the computer said, "and since that's very rare, I'm a little hesitant to interrupt."

"All right, wise guy, what's on your mind?"

"You haven't asked for my opinion, but would you mind if I made a keen observation, followed by an extremely practical suggestion?"

Despite his heavy heart, Gap couldn't help but laugh. "I know you're going to anyway, so I give you permission. What's the observation?"

"You and I have spent many hours together, beginning with your training at Galahad Command. We've weathered difficult times together, we've navigated some tough obstacles along the way, and you even saved my circuits one time, a debt that I have tried to repay by showering you with my knowledge and my charm."

"I'm very grateful for that," Gap said with a smirk.

"The road has not been bumpy the entire route, though. We've also shared some good times, including long, quiet evenings engaged on the battlefield of Masego. You're really improving, by the way."

"Yeah, yeah. You keep saying that so I'll continue to let you stomp me."

"True, but that's not the point," Roc said. "The point is that I probably know you better than anyone on this ship. Which is why I'm able to make the observation that I'm about to make."

"And that is . . . ?"

"You have gone from being an enthusiastic, ever-optimistic, lead-the-charge kind of guy, to a mopey, woe-is-me kind of guy. It's so very unattractive, and it's certainly not you. I noticed it in phases not long after we left Earth and wrote it off to those pesky human hormones. But the phases have been lasting longer, until now, with this election upon us, you seem to be perpetually in a lousy mood. Which is a waste, really, because Bon already placed his flag on that territory long ago, and there's not enough room for both of you."

Gap sat silently, his hands in his lap. He wanted to argue with what Roc was saying, but knew in his heart that he had no case.

"Anyway, that's the observation," Roc said. "And now, for the unsolicited advice, which, if you think about it, might be the best kind of all, because people never ask for advice when they know they're wrong, they only ask when they want someone to tell them what they want to hear. Whew, that's a mouthful—or, in my case, a speakerful—but you get it.

"I strongly recommend that you go back to the Gap who boarded this ship. Yes, Triana is gone, but the crew needs leadership. Yes, we are on the verge of being microwaved like a bag of popcorn, but the crew needs someone with vision. And yes, Hannah smoked you during the first forum, but for your mental health you need to keep your head up and learn.

"And," the computer continued, "I think you'll find that the best therapy for you right now is to take Hannah's theory, or any other plausible idea, and dive right in to solve the problem. So far it seems like you are tiptoeing around the radiation issue, almost like you're afraid to make a wrong step. You're asking for a lot of opinions, a lot of suggestions, yet seem to be unable—or unwilling—to take your own ideas out for a test ride. I think you're taking this 'interim Council Leader' title too seriously, and you're playing too conservatively, as if you're playing not to lose. The old Gap would play to win."

Gap ran a hand through his hair. When he spoke, all he could think to say was: "Wow."

"And that's all the free advice I have for you tonight," Roc said. "Any additional wisdom will be on the clock."

"Wow, that's . . . uh . . ." Gap stared down at his hands for a moment. The words could have stung, but the truth within them seemed to soften them somewhat. Or, more likely, he realized, he knew it all along, and Roc merely vocalized what Gap understood at his core. And yet knowing something doesn't necessarily call one to action; it often takes validation of those thoughts from someone else. In this case, Gap could almost see the sleep-walking version of himself through a veil, shrouded, hidden in shadow. Roc had pulled the veil aside.

Gap grabbed his shoes and stood up. "Thanks, Roc. And I mean that. I know that you're right. Which is difficult for me to say to you, by the way."

"I'm sure."

"But you're right. I mean it, thanks."

"Just part of my job," the computer said. "Beats monitoring the sewage system."

Gap nodded. "Well, if you'll excuse me, I want to check in with the team down in Engineering, and then get some sleep. Got a lot of work to do tomorrow."

He slipped his shoes on, then hustled out the door and down the curved corridor to the lift.

18

That was a thing of beauty," Merit said.

Hannah didn't have to turn and face him; even with her back to him she could guess his pose: leaning against the far wall, arms crossed, a single strand of raven hair hanging across his face. And, of course, the usual wicked grin.

She was back at the secluded window near the Spider bay, driven to find peace and quiet following the mayhem of the forum. She suddenly was the center of attention aboard the ship, and it felt crushing, suffocating. She'd smiled and mumbled thanks to the crowd of well-wishers as she threaded her way out of the auditorium, then quickly slipped away to the lift and the sanctuary of the dim lower level.

Somehow she had known that Merit would be right on her heels.

She finally looked over her shoulder and had to resist the urge to laugh; he stood exactly as she'd pictured him.

"Beauty?" she said. "It was a circus." She turned her attention back to the view through the window. "I should've gone to the Council instead of dropping a bomb like that."

"It would have been a bombshell coming from them, too," Merit said. "What difference does that make?" He walked over and stood next to her. "Of course you're going to second-guess everything right now. But I'm telling you, it was perfect. When the forum began, you were seen as a token opponent, someone simply there to fill out the ballot card. But now you've given this crew the information they needed, and you've showed them that you're more than qualified to lead this mission."

"I didn't give them much 'information,' Merit. I scared them, which is not what I wanted to do."

"They've been through it before."

Hannah shook her head. "The idea that we're being atomically dismantled? Or, if that doesn't do us in first, that we'll be fried by a jet stream of radiation? They haven't been through that before. And yet all you seem to care about is this ridiculous election." She gave him an icy look. "That *is* all you care about, isn't it?"

He crossed his arms again and returned her glare. "Yes," he said. "Or no. Whichever you prefer to hear. But it would be nice if you cared about it a little more."

She rolled her eyes. "Right. Wanting to simply win the election isn't caring; you only really care if you want to completely destroy the other person. Got it."

"You wear me out, Hannah. I came to offer congratulations for a job well done, to compliment you on the way you handled yourself, and for whatever reason you lash out at me. I never said anything about destroying anyone."

"But it's implied in everything you say."

"I can't help what you think," Merit said. "But I'll say it again: you did a terrific job tonight. If you want to lead this ship, you can't feel regret about how well you defeated your opponent. Once you start feeling sympathy, you're doomed. Leaders are strong."

"And I believe leaders have compassion," Hannah said. "Why don't we just agree to disagree on a few things. Now tell me what else you want to talk about, because I'd like some alone time before I fall into bed."

He stared at her for a moment before pushing away from the wall and walking slowly, back and forth, across the corridor.

"Well, it's going to be hard for us to strategize on the next forum if we can't agree on tactics. You confuse aggressive campaigning with being cold and heartless. All I'm saying is that if you have Gap down right now, you better put him away. For one thing, you need to point out the breakdown in discipline on the ship in just the short time that Triana's been gone. You need to express that these fights are a sign that Gap's not ready to lead. The damage to the Farms could be a crucial element in all of this. That's a direct reminder of how fragile our ecosystem is."

Hannah scowled but didn't respond. Merit stopped pacing, faced her, and spread his hands. "The crew is ready to follow you after your presentation tonight. They *want* to follow you. You showed them intellect and instinct. But the next thing you have to show them is courage. Courage to make the hard choices, courage to take chances. You have to appear strong. Otherwise they'll simply see you as a resource for Gap, someone he turns to when he needs the facts."

Most of what Merit said rolled off Hannah without an effect, but for some reason this last comment stuck. She didn't mind helping, but to be thought of as merely a smart resource . . .

This was crazy. Merit was playing on her emotional scars, poking where he knew she'd be sensitive. Now he was planting the idea that Gap would only use her for information. But Gap wasn't that way.

Was he?

Her thoughts tumbled out of control. She needed order, but it was out of her grasp. "I have to go," she said, turning from the window but avoiding eye contact with Merit. "I know you want to talk about the next forum, but I can't right now. I need sleep. It's late, I'm tired, and, quite frankly, I'm a little tired of you and your pacing. Let me get some rest and we can pick this back up tomorrow, okay?"

He pulled up in front of her. "Yeah, okay. Get some sleep. I'm sure you're exhausted."

She made an exaggerated show of walking around him to make her way back to the lift. Just before she rounded the turn she heard him call out to her, "You're just a few days away from being elected Council Leader of *Galahad*. Get all the sleep you can."

After tossing and turning all night, Gap was convinced that what he needed more than anything else was a good, solid workout to start his day. Airboarding sounded more appealing, but a strenuous round of Channy's morning routine was probably a better call. He could always try to squeeze in a few laps later at the track.

But first things first. Instead of heading toward the gym on the lower level, he took the lift up to the domes. This might be the best time to reach Bon before activity at the Farms reached its peak. And, after being cooped up in Sick House and his room, it was a sure thing that Bon would already be in his office. Whether he would be in any kind of mood to talk was another matter.

"Bet you're glad to be back at work," Gap said, sticking his head in the office.

Bon was sitting on the floor, surrounded by what looked like crop samples. His workpad was on his lap. He looked up, then returned to his work. "I expected you, but not this early," he said.

Gap sat down in one of the chairs. "Busy day. Thought I might start it off with a social call."

"Yes, that's usually why people come to see me."

Gap smiled. "I see that your face-plant in the crops might have bloodied your lip, but it hasn't stripped you of your sarcastic wit."

"It didn't strengthen my patience, either. I'm here early to catch up on work. What is it you want to talk about?"

"Things have changed since the Council meeting," Gap said. "It was one thing for you to insist on having a private chat with the Cassini when it seemed like you had some measure of control. But even you have to admit that there's no question anymore about how dangerous it is."

"All right, it's dangerous."

Gap realized that this discussion would be no different than most with Bon. In a way it was like soldiers charging a hill, fighting like mad for every foothold, advancing just a few steps at a time, then digging in before clawing their way upward again. With Bon you always had to fight for each step; nothing was given to you.

"Don't you think it's time we also talked about your agenda with the Cassini?" Gap said. "You know I was there, so it's not entirely a mystery anymore."

"Oh?" Bon said. "And what exactly did you hear?"

"I heard you asking a question: 'Where is she?'"

Bon said nothing and punched in some figures on his workpad.

"If you're looking for Tree, why can't you talk to the rest of the Council about that?" Gap said. "Why the secrecy? Why is that something you need to do on your own? Are you trying to be a hero or something?"

Bon rolled his eyes. "Yes, that must be it. That sounds just like me, doesn't it?"

"You're giving me nothing!" Gap said, his voice rising. "If you're irritated by people always trying to guess your motives and your emotions, quit playing these silly games. The whole 'dark and mysterious' act has worn pretty thin. I'll stop guessing as soon as you tell me what the answer is."

Bon set his workpad on the floor and stood up, brushing off his pants. He walked over to his desk and sat down. "I think you might have misunderstood what was going on."

Gap fought to control his anger. He turned to look out the window into Dome 1 and mentally counted to ten. "All right, then make it clear to me."

Bon shrugged. "It's not even clear to me. When we connect, they direct most of the conversation. I get in questions only when

I'm able to fight back their power. That's why the connections seem so violent to an outsider."

"I already know that," Gap said. "You're avoiding the question."

"I'm not sure how to answer your question. I told you the last time we had this chat, it's personal."

Gap stood up and went to the window. He leaned against the sill and stared back at Bon. "Okay, then tell me this. Did they answer you?"

Bon sat quietly for a moment, tapping an index finger on his desk. "It's not always easy to decipher their answers."

"But they did answer you?"

"In a way. But you don't understand, they don't exactly carry on conversations the way you're used to. It's not a question and answer session. If they respond—*if*—it's more like them implanting a solution somewhere within my brain. I'm not always sure what it means."

Gap nodded thoughtfully. "Like the code they gave you to maneuver through the Kuiper Belt."

"Yeah. When I sat down at the keyboard in the Control Room, I didn't fully understand what I was inputting; it was there, and somehow I accessed it enough to type it in. But if I was given an essay test, I wouldn't know where to begin.

"They're not making me smarter," Bon continued. "It's like they're . . . like they're lending me information. Or maybe a better way to put it is, I'm a courier for the information. I carry it, but it doesn't belong to me."

The concept sounded so alien to Gap. But, he realized, they were dealing with a thoroughly alien entity, one that was comprised almost entirely of thought.

"All right," he said. "But for now the courier service is going on hold. Until Lita's test results come back, no more links. Period." He walked over to the desk and held out his hand. "In fact, let's avoid any more arguments. Give me the translator."

Bon blinked up at him. "What?"

"You heard me. Please, no arguing. Just hand it over."

"I don't have it."

Gap lowered his hand and sighed. "All right, take me to that clearing and let's pick it up. I could probably find my way there eventually, but I don't feel like searching. Let's go."

"It's not there," Bon said with a puzzled look. "I thought you had it already."

"Is this another game?"

"I don't have it," Bon said again. His tone, and the look on his face, convinced Gap that he was telling the truth.

The two were silent for a full minute, eyeing each other. Gap turned to look out the large window into the dome. "One of the workers, perhaps? Have you asked around?"

"It's early; I'm waiting for them to show up. I would imagine that if one of them stumbled across it, they'll bring it to me this morning."

"And you'd rather not just send a mass e-mail to them?"

Bon shook his head. "Let's just say I'd rather not advertise the fact that it's missing." He paused, then leaned back in his chair and said, "It'll turn up."

19

By late Friday afternoon the ship's radiation shield had sputtered five more times, and the crew was visibly on edge. One of the failures spanned almost three seconds, and the general consensus was that a full-fledged collapse might happen at any time.

Gap alternated his attention between solving that problem and preparing for the final election forum. Hannah's bruise theory had captured the imagination of most crew members, and it seemed that the election results might very well depend upon whoever came up with the best solution. Gap had climbed out of bed before six to start in again, and now felt worn down physically. But he remained optimistic.

Optimistic despite the disturbing post he'd seen when he logged on to his computer around noon.

Anyone could post to the community page, and had the option to do so anonymously. Occasional unsigned posts made their way to the main screen, usually to voice minor gripes or suggestions, but they were rare; the general feeling was that anonymous posts carried far less credibility. This particular post grabbed attention with its title: Exploring the Bruise.

Taking up almost two full pages, it allegedly had been submitted by *Friends of Hannah*, and began by recapping her description of the wormholes' effect on space. What followed was grim. Several paragraphs detailed the damage that *Galahad* was experiencing, using terms such as *critical*, *dire*, and *deadly*. The post also went on to claim that the same destructive force was slowly attacking their own bodies, as well. One particular passage stood out:

> Like an invisible cancer, the sheer corrosive power of the galaxy's radiation is slowly, but inevitably, tearing down our protective walls. How much longer can we stand the assault? We need a leader who can not only find the answers, but keep order among a crew that is obviously unraveling.

Time, the post went on to add, was not a luxury at this point. The crew owed a debt of thanks to Hannah for quickly bringing the issue to their attention, and hopefully she would lead the charge to finding a solution. Otherwise, the authors predicted, both the ship and the crew would be atomically ripped to shreds.

Gap read with interest, aware that the writers—whoever *Friends of Hannah* might be—were responsible enough to close their post with a footnote that stated it was all simply theory. But, tucked quietly within the final lines, the disclaimer was all but lost in the white noise of fear.

He refused to let the post drag him down, even the insinuation that his lack of leadership was responsible for the violence that had broken out. Roc's charge that he pull himself up from the doldrums and concentrate on finding a cure for the ship's ills had rejuvenated him. Even when he overheard workers in the Engineering section talking about Hannah and her sparkling performance at the first forum, he used it as motivation. Now, as the time neared for his next opportunity on stage, he ignored the anonymous propaganda, put his head down, and bulled forward.

And it felt good.

With an hour to go before the forum, he finished the work in his office and rushed up to his room to spend a few moments in quiet meditation. Sitting in semi-darkness with his legs crossed and eyes closed, he drifted in the low sprinkling of traditional Chinese music that filtered through the speakers. For nearly ten minutes he regulated his breathing, inhaling deeply, holding it for several seconds, and then slowly exhaling. He allowed his mind to drain all of the stress and frenzied activity of the day, and soon he could almost smell the mixture of grasses and tree blossoms from the meadow in which he imagined himself.

Then, without a warning of any kind, the mood was shattered.

"Are there lyrics to that song you're listening to?" Roc said. "You certainly can't dance to it—not that I want you to, that would be devastating to watch—and it doesn't seem likely to inspire one to amazing athletic feats, like running backward through cones, or juggling flaming bowling pins. I'm hoping that the lyrics mean something profound. Like 'I Might Be Missing You, But I'm Really Not Looking That Hard.' Something like that."

Gap wanted to be angry for the interruption, but instead caught himself laughing. "I don't think this one has lyrics. It's meant to be soothing and relaxing."

"Makes me want to slam my head in a car door," the computer said. "Which would be outrageous on two levels. One, we have no cars on the ship, and two, I don't have a head."

"Let's put aside the fact that I really don't care if you like this music or not," Gap said. "I'm sure there's a legitimate reason for you to bust in like this, when you know I have a big presentation in—" He squinted over toward the clock on his desk vidscreen. "—in thirty-six minutes."

"It's completely legitimate. You asked earlier for some calculations, and I've downloaded them into your workpad."

Gap straightened out his legs, leaned back into one of his

favorite yoga poses, then pushed himself to his feet and walked over to the desk. He flipped through various screens on his work-pad until he came to the file he was looking for. After a minute of concentration, he nodded.

"That's great. Thank you, Roc."

"How do you think the crew will take to your suggestion based on these figures?" the computer said.

"Oh . . ." Gap stretched again. "I'd say that a third will support it, a third will be skeptical, and a third will have to go and think about it. Pretty typical."

"Well, good luck," Roc said. "There's an old theater custom on Earth to tell the actors to 'break a leg.' It doesn't mean to literally break your leg, but in your case it might be a great idea. That way you could get pity votes, and after the other night you might need them. Look at Rico; he broke his arm doing something stupid like falling out of the bleachers, and the girls are still all over him. Can you break something in the next few minutes? Even a hairline fracture might be enough."

"Lucky me," Gap said, "to be traveling across the galaxy at near the speed of light with the world's first electronic comedian. Why don't you go compile a list of prime numbers for a few hours?"

"Don't forget to comb your hair," the computer said.

Thirty minutes later Gap walked into the auditorium. Once again it was almost full, with the only empty seats explained by the crew members who were on mandatory work duty. Hannah was in her same seat; she nodded politely to him, and in return he flashed a large smile.

Once again Gina climbed to the stage to address the crew. She stood at a small podium set off to the side of the stage.

"Welcome to the second—and final—election forum. Tonight we have a slightly different format. Our two candidates for the position of Council Leader will begin with prepared opening statements, but the remainder of the forum will consist of questions that I, as the moderator, have prepared for the evening. Afterward, the candidates will have three minutes to summarize their points and positions.

"I think you're all aware of the procedures for tomorrow's election, but if you have any questions you'll find the information available on your workpad or the vidscreen in your room. Please remember to cast your ballot on your vidscreen prior to three o'clock; no exceptions. Results will be announced at six tomorrow evening."

There was a hum of conversation across the room, and Gina waited patiently for it to die down. "The candidates have agreed that since Gap went first the other night, Hannah would have the honors this evening. So please welcome our two crew members vying for the position of *Galahad* Council Leader: Hannah Ross and Gap Lee."

They walked up the stairs and to their respective podiums together, each acknowledging the applause from the crowd. After taking two deep breaths—and, Gap noticed, aligning her workpad so that it was flush with the edge of the podium—Hannah began her opening statement. She addressed the need for unity, regardless of the outcome of the election, and vowed to remain an enthusiastic and productive member of the crew no matter what results were posted.

Gap noted that she made no mention whatsoever of the anonymous post, nor any mention of the theory that had electrified the crew only two nights earlier. Apparently she was content to wait until the inevitable questions from Gina regarding the possible solution. Her remarks were brief and to the point, and she finished in less than two minutes.

All eyes turned to Gap. He began with his head lowered, staring at an invisible spot on the podium. "It has occurred to me that what we're asking you to do in the next twenty-four hours is predict the future. This thought came to me while I was thinking about the two crew members who began this journey with us, but aren't here tonight.

"Alexa was blessed—although many times she felt she was cursed—with the ability to see the future. It frightened her most of the time, as it probably would any of us. Triana believed that she saw our future, too, and because of that she chose to risk her life to give the rest of us a fighting chance. And I think it's a safe bet that when she plunged into that wormhole, she was frightened as well."

Gap finally raised his head and looked out across the room. "You're being asked to evaluate Hannah, and to evaluate me. Your job is to not only gauge what you hear from us tonight, but to also predict the future. One of us will soon take charge of this mission, and will be responsible for decisions that our lives depend upon. That in itself would normally make anyone frightened.

"But you know what? We've lived with fear too much in the last year. I don't want to live that way anymore. I'm challenging all of you tonight to take the time to really consider what you're going to hear from both of us tonight, and instead of making a decision based on fear, make your decision based on faith."

He let the words sink in, and saw several crew members turn to look at their neighbors.

"In this case," he continued, "I'm not talking about religious or spiritual faith, although many of you will call upon that as well. I'm talking about faith in yourself, faith in your fellow crew members, and faith in the mission itself. We all have to devote the next stretch of our journey to making positive steps forward, to solving our problems through cooperation and hard work, and to shoving aside the fear that has stalked us for too long. All of that will require faith that we summon from deep inside.

"And, when it comes time to predict our future, to predict which candidate will be best suited to lead this crew to Eos, you won't be making your choice from a position of weakness, but rather an incredible position of strength. I, like everyone else, originally viewed this election with sadness because of the disappearance of Triana. But today I realized that we can use this election as a turning point, a red-letter day where we used the sacrifices of our missing comrades to climb higher and reach farther. Thank you."

There was silence at first, then a rolling wave of applause. It was obvious that his words had sparked something within them, and they showed their appreciation.

Gina raised her hands and brought the room back to order. She began the question-and-answer session by asking the candidates to explain their leadership styles and to outline their vision of the Council's responsibility to the crew. Hannah and Gap each gave thoughtful responses. Gap wondered if Hannah would draw upon any of the comments he'd made during their conversation in the Dining Hall, when she had questioned him about his leadership style. But she steered away from that, forging her own way without any reference to that discussion.

The next two questions revolved around crew duties and departmental procedures, both of which were important, and yet not what the assembled crew had come to hear. It wasn't until the fourth question that the crowd sat forward in their seats.

"Gap," Gina said, "we find ourselves in yet another critical situation. Besides the space lightning that has erupted, our ship's radiation shield has failed numerous times. Although it's lasted no more than a few seconds, the potential exists for complete failure, which would ultimately spell doom for this crew. More than a few theories have surfaced as to what might be causing the problem, but I think it's safe to say that many people feel strongly that Hannah's theory of bruised space, caused by the wormholes, might be the leading candidate. If that's the case, what steps would you take as the Council Leader to protect the safety of the ship and crew?"

Gap didn't hesitate; a lull before his answer might give the impression that he was unsure, and he wanted the crew to feel the same confidence that simmered within him.

"I first want to acknowledge Hannah's impressive work on this problem. Obviously we don't know for certain what's causing the radiation shield to fail, but her bruised space theory is a strong possibility. I'm willing to focus our energies on that angle unless, or until, a better idea is presented.

"It's tricky, because we don't know exactly how a bruise affects the fabric of space. We assume that it has caused ripples, or, to use a more descriptive analogy, old-fashioned speed bumps. Our ship is ignoring the speed limit through these speed bumps, which is wreaking havoc and causing major damage."

He took a deep breath and for the first time looked at his workpad. "I believe that our radiation shield is fundamentally sound, which is why it has weathered the storm so far. However, it needs to be turbo-charged. My plan is to transfer energy from the ion power drive of *Galahad* and divert it into a new and improved shield, one that can withstand the shock waves associated with the wormhole's bruise."

Gap saw many of the crew members in the audience nodding their heads in approval. At the same time, out of the corner of his eye, he watched Hannah immediately take up her stylus pen and begin to make notes on her workpad.

"This power diversion, which can be done relatively quickly, will reinforce the shields, effectively tripling the magnetic force that precedes the ship through space. However, I will tell you up front, this diversion comes at a price. And it's a heavy price."

He once again had everyone's full attention.

"Because of the loss of power to our system's drive, our gradual increase in speed will deteriorate. We're assuming that this will be temporary, even though we have no idea the extent of the bruise; once we're in the clear, we should be able to once again revert to our original power output.

"All of this means that our trip will be extended by approximately . . . two years."

There was an immediate reaction from the room. Gap stood back and pretended to scan his notes while loud conversations and arguments broke out. It took Gina more than a minute to calm everyone down. When she had done so, she asked Gap if he wanted to add anything else.

He gazed back across the sea of faces. "I realize that it's not a popular choice, but it's the one that I think gives us the best chance to survive the danger we're facing. I'll post all of the figures right after this forum, and you're free to check them on your workpad or vidscreen."

Another low rumble spread across the auditorium, and Gina held up her hands to prevent it from building. Once it was quiet again, she turned to Hannah.

"Per the rules of this forum, you're permitted to address Gap's plan, and to question him if you like. Then I'd like for you to present your own position, and Gap will be allowed the same follow-up."

Hannah looked over the notes she had hastily scribbled. "I'm intrigued by Gap's idea. However . . ." She paused. "I'm not sure an increase in power to the shields is the answer. As he stated, there's so much we don't know about all of this. But I tend to look at the bruise a little differently. I think of it as a disruption in the very particles that make up space; powering our way through that disruption might have the effect of actually speeding up the damage."

She waited a moment, and then shook her head. "It's an interesting suggestion, I'll leave it at that. I've also given a lot of thought to how we might overcome this problem, and rather than turbocharging the shields, I think our best solution would be to avoid the bruise altogether.

"Again, there are plenty of unknowns. But I think the damage to space could very well be two-dimensional. Consider a normal bruise on your skin: it has length and width as it extends across your body, but rarely lacks any depth. It doesn't extend down into your body very much at all. I believe the wormhole has created the same type of injury to this portion of space. It likely has length and width, but not depth.

"Therefore," she said, "I propose that Galahad be reprogrammed to drop out of the galactic plane, dip under the damaged space, and then resurface after we have traveled out beyond the scope of the bruise."

There was a murmur from the crew as they visualized what Hannah was describing. Gap found himself doing the same, looking down at his hand and imagining a bruise, and how he might dip beneath it.

Hannah cleared her throat and continued. "Gap was up front with you and told you that his plan might add two years to our journey. My solution also comes at a cost. Because we don't know how deep this bruise extends, or how far along our path to Eos, we could potentially face a delay of perhaps one year."

Rather than put any punctuation on her suggestion, she looked over at Gina to indicate that she was finished. Gina said, "Gap?"

"Well," he began, then chuckled. "Maybe now you all want to vote for 'none of the above.'" A chorus of nervous laughter greeted this.

"I appreciate what Hannah had to say about my plan, and I will start by echoing the same sentiments about hers. It's an interesting idea, and might very well be the way to go. But I guess I go back to the faith I mentioned earlier. I believe that our shields are strong enough, and the basic science behind them is sound enough, to protect us from the damage. Dropping out of our flight path, however, is not a choice I would make. There are too many unknowns. For one thing, we have no proof whatsoever that the bruise is flat; the wormhole could just as easily have ruptured space, exploding outward in all directions. If that's the case, we would still be in the same position, but without the benefit of the added protection I'm proposing.

"There's another potential problem," he added. "Her solution might be quicker, but dropping below the galactic plane could potentially expose us to additional sources of radiation, such as gamma rays. We're shielded somewhat within the cocoon of the Milky Way."

He could see the crew's faces contorting as they wrestled with the two choices now placed before them. Each had pros and cons, and each came with a price tag.

"Before we walk out of here," Gap said, "I would like to thank Hannah for her opening comment about working together, regardless of the outcome. I think you can count on that from both of us."

There was a smattering of applause which slowly built into a crescendo. Hannah and Gap met at the center of the stage and shook hands, then walked down the steps and took their seats in the front row.

"Thank you all for your attention tonight," Gina said to the crowd. "You have plenty to think about. However, I think it's fair to say that both candidates are strong choices. If anything, you should feel good that the ship is in such capable hands. Take some time to consider everything you've heard, and then get a good night's sleep.

"Tomorrow is the first election day on *Galahad*. Good luck to the candidates, and good luck to us all."

20

ita had never seen the Dining Hall so empty in the morning. It puzzled her, because, if anything, she had expected the room to be packed. Traditionally, during times of stress, people chose to gather around food, to exchange ideas and provide support. For some reason, the crew of *Galahad* had chosen to spend their first election day on their own. She thought it over and decided that the second election forum had shifted the crew's collective mind-set. The poise and style exhibited by both Gap and Hannah had instilled a renewed sense of purpose; the usual gossip and chatter had been replaced by a thoughtful respect of their mission, and their destiny.

This crew, Lita decided, had grown up.

She watched Channy stroll into the room, exchange greetings with a handful of people near the door, then pick up a glass of juice and an energy bar, and wander back to Lita's table.

"Dead in here," Channy said.

"Yeah," Lita said. "I would have stayed in myself, but I thought it would be better if the Council was visible today." She laughed. "Guess it wouldn't have really mattered."

"Tell me about it. The gym was like a ghost town. Wasn't even worth getting up early. Of course, getting up wasn't a problem, really; I hardly slept last night. You?"

Lita shook her head. "I couldn't shut my mind off. The funny thing is, it wasn't about the election, or the radiation problem. I spent most of the night thinking about Triana."

Channy sipped her juice. "Why is that, do you think?"

"I think the election is making everything hit home for me. In a way it was easy to pretend that Triana wasn't really gone, that she would walk in and join us for breakfast like she used to do. Now we're electing her replacement; that's a little too real, you know?"

"Stop it, you're gonna make me cry again," Channy said. "I'm trying to get through today without having a breakdown." She quickly took another sip of juice, blinking hard. After looking around the room, she said, "I voted first thing this morning. I didn't want to have to think about it anymore today. Too draining. What about you?"

Lita smiled at her. "No, I wanted to come down here and just relax a bit. It's been such a bizarre week. I'll head back to the room when I leave here and take care of it. So . . ." She swirled her own glass of juice. "I guess last night must have made some kind of impact on you since you were so quick to cast your ballot."

A sly smile crossed Channy's face. "Let's just say that I'd made up my mind by the time I went to bed. And I know I shouldn't tell you how I voted, but—"

"No," Lita said. "I don't want to know. And don't hint, either. I really don't want to know."

"Oh, you're horrible!" Channy said with a grin. "I'm about to burst."

"Go back to the gym and work it out with some sweat. Now."

Channy laughed. "You're no fun." She reached out and touched the charcoal-colored stone that hung from a simple silver strand around Lita's neck. "Hey, this is gorgeous. How have I not seen it before?"

"It was a gift from Alexa."

Channy gawked. "Alexa?"

Lita related the story of her visit with Katarina, then said,

"Alexa kept it tucked away in a box, but I felt like I could honor her by wearing it. Since Nung loves to work with jewelry, I asked what he could do with it, and this is what he brought to me."

"I love it," Channy said. "I'm gonna have to get Nung to make something pretty for me, too." She stood up. "All right, off I go. Let's get together tonight after the results are posted, okay?"

"You have a date."

Channy walked out of the Dining Hall, and Lita fell back into her thoughts of Triana. How would *she* vote? Which candidate would Triana think was the best choice to lead the crew? Gap brought Council experience and good people skills. Hannah brought fresh ideas and a razor-sharp mind for solving problems. Which one would Triana feel should be her replacement?

Lita's head was down, and it took a moment for her to realize that she had company again. Looking up, she was startled to find Bon staring down at her with his cobalt-blue eyes.

"Oh" was the first sound that escaped from her. "Sorry, I didn't hear you walk up."

"I'd like to get the translator back from you, if you don't mind."

Lita blinked. "And good morning to you, too."

"Right."

She couldn't help but laugh. "I know a lot of people have a hard time handling your personality, Bon, including me sometimes. But other times—like right now—it's exactly what I need. Thank you."

He grunted. "Let's talk about the translator."

"What makes you think I have it?"

"Are we really going to go back and forth like this? Wouldn't it save time to just go get it and give it back to me?"

Lita drummed her fingers on the table and found it hard to scrub the smile off her face. "Okay. Yes, I have the translator."

"Of course you do. As soon as I found out that Gap didn't take it, I knew it had to be you. The only thing I don't know is how you knew where to look for it."

"Really? Think about it," Lita said.

Bon stood above her, staring into her eyes. A moment later he nodded once. "Alexa."

"She was one of my best friends, Bon. Girls talk, you know?"

He remained silent and motionless for a moment, then pulled out a chair and sat down across from her.

"I know you pride yourself on being cool and in control," Lita said. "But not everyone is like that. Alexa cared for you a great deal. She wanted to open up so much to you, but never felt like you reciprocated. She wanted someone to talk to about all of those feelings, so she turned to me. I didn't know exactly where the clearing was, but I knew enough to figure it out."

Bon pursed his lips. "So this is a critique of how I handled things with Alexa?"

"No. You are who you are. But I think you regret how you handled things with her. For that matter, I think you regret how you handled things with Triana. I don't know what it was, but something was going on between you two. So no, I'm not going to criticize you; with both of them gone, I can't imagine anyone on this ship more tortured than you. I cared for them both, but at least they knew that."

He turned his head and stared across the room. Lita wondered if it was just the play of the lights, or if his eyes were truly moist.

Finally he looked back at her. "Let's talk about the translator. Are you going to give it back to me?"

"Let's wait until the election is over and we have a new Council Leader. That was my position in the first place. Unless you want to tell me what you're trying to learn from the Cassini."

She thought he might argue with her, but apparently he understood that it was pointless. "All right," he said, and stood up.

And that was it. He spun on his heel and stalked out of the room. Once again Lita had an entire section of the Dining Hall to herself. She took a sip of juice and gazed across the room.

Bon was reluctant to open up to anyone, it seemed. And yet

he was willing to allow the Cassini access to his mind, to his thoughts. It was easier for him to form a connection with an alien intelligence than with someone he might actually have feelings for. Why? Was it safer for him somehow?

She rested her head on one hand and glanced back at the door. What was Bon looking for?

Gap had suggested that Hannah meet him near the window on the lower level, but that spot held too many painful memories for her. Instead they met in the deserted Conference Room. It was a few minutes past noon.

"Thanks for coming," he said.

"Sure." Hannah took a seat at the table. At first Gap considered walking around to the other side so they could face each other, but he elected to sit next to her.

"I heard that we've had two more shield failures today," Hannah said. "How long this time?"

"Both about two seconds," Gap said. "They're fairly regular now. If your theory is correct, little pieces of us are being sliced away each day." He shuddered. "Ugh, what a thought. After reading that post from your friends, I'm sure everyone on the ship is having the same nightmares about it, too."

A shadow crossed Hannah's face. "Listen, those were not my words. You understand that, right? I had nothing to do with that post. I would never endorse that kind of fearmongering. And I would never question . . . well, let's just say that I have no doubt about your leadership skills."

Gap smiled at her. "I know that. But apparently some of your supporters do. Know who it was?"

"No, but I think I have an idea."

There was silence for a few moments before Gap filled the space. "Even if their description is true, what really makes it strange is the fact that we don't feel any different, you know?"

"Yes, but the ship is . . . different today," Hannah said. "I don't know if you've been out much, but there's a strange feeling in the air."

"Yeah, I noticed it, too. It's never been this quiet."

She nodded. "Makes me wish that the day would rush by. I don't know about you, but I'm mentally exhausted."

Gap agreed. While she was talking, he couldn't help but stare at her. Something was different in the way she carried herself, the way she talked. When they were together as a couple she'd been relatively shy and reserved; their energy had been polar opposites. Now there was no doubt in his mind that Hannah had changed. She wasn't necessarily more outgoing, but she exuded a confidence that he'd never seen before. It came across as strength.

Was it a result of the election? Had the forums, along with the vocal support of so many crew members, bolstered her self-image? Or was it more than that? He wondered if it might have been the breakup itself that had shifted something within her. Or . . .

Or could it be that Hannah was involved with someone else? What if her head had been turned by someone new, and the rebound had instilled a shot of confidence?

Gap realized with a start how much that shook him. Since their split he had considered talking to her, trying to mend their differences, perhaps even trying again; he hadn't considered the possibility of her moving on, of her falling for someone else.

Stop it, he told himself. This isn't the time to worry about that.

Almost a minute of silence had passed between them, and Hannah raised her eyebrows. "So, you wanted to talk about something?"

"Oh . . . yeah, I did. Well, nothing major, but . . ." He smiled sheepishly. "Listen, all I wanted to do was have a moment with you in private to wish you good luck. You've impressed everyone on the ship. Especially me."

"Thank you," she said, looking down, a touch of the old Hannah surfacing. "This has been exciting, but also . . ." She seemed to search for the right word. "Difficult. For a variety of reasons."

He stared at her again. "Care to list them?"

Hannah took a quick glance at him, then back at the table, then turned and gazed out the Conference Room's window into space. For a moment she seemed lost among the stars.

"It hasn't been in my nature to get up in front of people and try to lead," she said. "I've generally liked to stay behind the scenes and do the research. So this was a difficult transition.

"It's also difficult because thoughts of Triana keep popping into my head. I had so much respect for her, for the job she did, for the way she handled all of the emergencies that we've faced since we left Earth. And I wondered, am I capable of filling her shoes? Do I have the same strengths that she had?"

"You don't need to have the same strengths," Gap said softly. "Each person leads in their own way. You have your own strengths, you know."

"That's sweet of you to say, but I'm sure you've had the same thoughts," Hannah said. "I almost felt . . . I don't know, unworthy. Unworthy to try to follow the job that Triana did. I mean, whoever takes this position will automatically be judged by the way Triana led this crew. It's been hard coming to grips with the fact that I might soon be under an incredibly strong microscope. As the week has progressed, though, I've begun to realize that anyone would feel out of their league. Triana must have battled the same feelings; why should I be any different?"

Gap understood completely, but said nothing.

"And it's also been challenging on a much more personal level," she said. She turned her head from the window and looked into Gap's eyes. "It's been hard going up against you, Gap. Because . . ."

Her voice trailed off, and her shoulders slumped. As strong as she had seemed a minute earlier, she now seemed emotionally burdened. Gap wanted to reach over and put a hand on her shoulder but thought it might seem condescending.

"Because why?" he said.

She kept her gaze focused on him, something that she might not have pulled off a month or two ago. "Two reasons. First, I've had to promise myself that this would never be about striking back at you for the way things ended. And I won't lie; that's been tough. But I've kept my focus on the position itself, and the fact that there's more to me than you ever were aware of. Yes, you hurt me, but I won't let that define me. I'm worth more than that. I'm aware of it, and the crew is slowly becoming aware of it. When I started this I think I really wanted you to be aware of it, too. Now I'm not sure that's as important to me anymore."

Gap felt as if he'd been pushed backward. He fought to keep his composure, willing himself to not show weakness in front of her.

Nodding slightly, he said, "And the other reason this has been difficult?"

She paused a moment before answering. "Because I still care about you, that's why."

He felt his breath catch in his throat. Although he might have thought about it, he never thought he'd hear her say it. There was another long moment of silence. Finally, he reached over and placed his hand on top of hers.

"And I still care about you, Hannah. This . . . this has been hard for me, too."

What happened next surprised him. She suddenly pulled her hand out from under his and stood up. "But I don't want to feel this way," she said. "Do you understand me? I fight with this every day. I've told myself that I need to move on, that you're not right for me. Anyone who would dump me the way you did . . ." Her eyes narrowed and she pointed a finger toward him. "I don't want to feel this way. And I can't even believe I told you that I cared."

She turned and took a few steps toward the door, then turned back to face him. "I'm sure this gives you some sort of satisfaction, and that makes me even more angry at myself."

"Hannah," he said, standing and taking a step toward her. "No, don't say that. It doesn't give me—"

She put a hand on his chest to stop him. "Forget I said anything," she said. "Just forget everything I've said in the last minute. Thank you for the good-luck wishes. Same to you."

It looked as though she wanted to add something else, but it never made it out. She cut off what sounded like a sob, pulled her head back high, and gave him a defiant look before striding out of the room.

21

By now you know what a keen observer I am when it comes to human interaction and psychology. If you don't know it by now, go back to the first volume, start over, and read every word up to this point until you say, "Oh yeah, that Roc is a keen observer."

Or save yourself some time and just concede the point.

Anyway, the reason I bring this up is because I've noticed how difficult it can be for some people to confront others when they discover the truth about them.

Maybe confront is too strong of a word; how about "bring it to their attention"?

Regardless, I believe the average person would rather let it go and not make waves. But, because of that, it also means you have an entire subset of people who KNOW that people won't call them on something, and so they learn to therefore take advantage of the situation.

Does that make sense? No? Apparently you're not as keen of an observer as I am, but don't let that get you down. Just consider this: Bon seems to keep a lot of secrets tucked away behind a screen that's coated with a gruff varnish. Most people are too intimidated to even poke around behind that screen, which is probably what he's counting on.

But not Lita. Remember what I said about her profound thinking? This girl is all about the truth.

* * *

The late afternoon irrigation schedule was underway, so as Lita walked out of the lift into Dome 1 she inhaled the humid air and immediately imagined a sunny day on the beach near her home in Veracruz. The salty sea air had always invigorated her. Now, when she was fortunate enough to experience a similar feeling in *Galahad*'s domed Farms, she instantly thought of home.

Splashing across the coarse sand at the water's edge, listening to the roar as the late-day waves relentlessly pounded the coastline, she could never stifle a laugh. This, to her, was the ultimate expression of Earth's life cycle. Land that had furiously burst from the ocean floor, courtesy of the planet's tectonic convulsions, was then gradually torn apart, one wave at a time. Wave after wave, year after year, for eons. The ocean fought to wear down the continent that had pushed it aside, to get the final word in the tug-of-war between sea and sand . . . only to have the process begin anew with another volcanic eruption.

It was one of the reasons she kept the small glass cube on her desk in Sick House. It was not only a reminder of home, but a reminder of the universe's cyclical dance. It seemed one force always sought to wear down another.

Galahad was running head-on into its own waves.

As she approached Bon's office she saw him exit and begin to march down a trail toward the far side of the dome. She quickened her pace to catch him, reluctant to call out his name until she got closer. Like everything else about him, however, Bon's stride was determined and intense. They were deep into a field of potatoes, the path cutting diagonally across the crop, when she closed to within thirty feet of him.

"Bon, hold up a second," she said, winded.

He stopped and turned, mild surprise on his face. "What are you doing here?"

Lita covered the distance between them and stood with her

hands on her hips, trying not to show him how hard she was breathing. "We need to finish our discussion."

"Why? You don't seem open to negotiation on the subject."

"I might surprise you," she said. "Is there someplace nearby where we can sit down and talk?"

Bon gestured with his head. "Up ahead. It's where I'm going anyway, another irrigation pump that's acting up. Again."

She ignored his irritation and pointed down the path. "After you."

Two minutes later they crossed over into a grove of fruit trees, and soon after that came upon the gray irrigation pump box. Beside it was a small bench. Lita sat down, while Bon leaned against the box.

"Well?" he said.

"I've been doing some thinking about you and your stubborn refusal to talk to us about this." She reached into a pocket and pulled out the translator. She noticed that Bon's eyes grew wide for a split second, then he crossed his arms and appeared nonchalant.

"It didn't make sense to me for a long time," Lita continued. "I heard about your request to the Cassini: 'Where is she?' you said. Well, why wouldn't you want us to know about that? Why wouldn't you want our help? We all care about Triana, we're all scared to death about what's happened to her, and we all want her back. I've always felt, like I told you, that there was something between you two, but I don't think even you knew exactly what that was."

She paused and leaned forward, resting her elbows on her knees.

"So why, I wondered over and over again, would you possibly want to do a search for her without including us? If the Cassini were able to help, we would eventually have to be brought into it at some point. So why shut us out?"

Bon shifted his weight but kept his arms crossed, the classic pose of defensiveness and stonewalling. Lita knew he would offer nothing in return to her questions. He blinked once or twice.

"And then, after we spoke in the Dining Hall, I did some thinking. It slowly dawned on me that I was dead wrong about your connection. In fact, we were all wrong, weren't we?"

"I'm afraid I don't know what you mean," he said.

A slow smile spread across Lita's face. "Yes, you do. And I'd appreciate it if you'd stop the games. All of us were a bit surprised when we thought you were using the link to probe the galaxy, looking for Triana. I mean, it's touching . . . but it's not what you were doing."

"And what was I doing?"

Lita paused before saying, "Looking for Alexa."

For what seemed an eternity they stared at each other without moving, without uttering another sound. At last Bon broke eye contact and turned his head to look back down the path they'd walked. Lita nodded slowly.

"Uh-huh. It hit me when I realized that you never really confirmed that you were looking for Triana. In fact, all of your answers were intentionally vague and erratic. It's like you were playing some sort of game with us: answering the questions so that we *thought* this was about Triana, but never actually lying to us.

"And the more I turned this over in my head, the more I realized that, if it was about Tree, you would certainly have brought us in. But no. The only reason you would insist on doing this by yourself, the only reason you would risk the medical danger that you did, was because your guilt has driven you to seek some sort of connection to a dead girl that you feel you let down."

When he spoke, his voice was barely above a whisper. "I *did* let her down."

Lita sat back on the bench. "Okay, maybe you did. I know this is where I'm supposed to offer you pity and support and say something like, 'No, Bon, you did nothing wrong.' But I think on some level that, yes, you probably did let her down. She reached out to you because she thought you would help her navigate through the fear. And, in the process, she fell for you a bit. But, although you were drawn to the freaky parallels of your . . . your mutual oddities, let's say . . . you never shared the same feelings. And I think that has eaten at you since the day she died."

He turned to look back at her. "And what if it has? What business is it of yours? Like I told all of you, this is personal."

"Bon," Lita said, her voice growing tender. "Listen to me. I'm not condemning the fact that you didn't return Alexa's feelings. In fact, I've got a feeling that Triana is at the heart of that. If you let Alexa down—*if*, I'm saying—it might have been in the way you made her feel completely alone when she was sure she had someone who could walk her through her . . . uniqueness. You were, in her eyes, a kindred spirit, and yet you didn't always act that way."

He sat down in the soil, resting his back against the pump box, and clasped his arms around his knees. Lita watched him, her heart aching for him. She rose from the bench and walked over to him, settling onto the soil at his side.

"I'm not trying to make you feel bad," she said. "If anything, I'm trying to help. I'm trying to tell you that you shouldn't feel guilty about what happened; nobody could possibly have known what would happen with that vulture. Nobody."

"Alexa knew," Bon said.

"No. You said that she saw darkness, and she felt heaviness. And a strange feeling when she was around the vulture. But she didn't know that it would attack her."

Bon only shook his head.

"I understand how you feel," Lita said. "And I don't blame you for what you did with this." She held up the translator. "I just wish you had come to me, and confided in me. Alexa was my friend, too, you know."

She reached over to place a hand on his arm. "Did they tell you anything?"

Bon's head snapped around. "What?"

"Did the Cassini tell you anything?"

He peered into her eyes. "Are you serious? I thought you were angry about that."

"Of course I was angry. You should have come to me. We have no idea what these links will end up doing to you. But we do know that they're changing you."

"How?"

Lita removed her hand from his arm. "The scans that we ran on you are interesting. I compared them to the scans you had before the launch, along with the scans we made after the first contact back at Saturn. Your left cerebral hemisphere is undergoing some changes."

"Meaning . . . ?"

"Well, without getting too technical, two portions are expanding. One is called Wernicke's Area, the other Broca's Area. They both involve speech, whether it's language recognition or speech production. In other words, the Cassini are modifying your brain to allow you to communicate—and understand—their transmissions. Maybe even without needing the translator. At least that's my guess."

"So I really am becoming a freak," Bon said, shaking his head.

"I didn't say you were growing another head, it's just that the one you have is being remodeled. It's probably one of the reasons why Triana limited your access to the translator in the first place; she was just as worried as I am about all of the unknowns involved. And it's why you're certainly not connecting again without me around. Understand?"

He gazed back and forth between her eyes, attempting, it seemed, to read her thoughts. "Without you around. So . . . are you giving the translator back to me?"

"Tell me what you learned from the Cassini."

"Why?"

Lita drew lines in the soil. "Call it scientific curiosity."

He hesitated before responding. "I . . . I don't really know what they said. They tried to plant information into my head, but I passed out before anything substantial took hold."

"But you think they *were* answering your question?"

He nodded. "I think so."

She continued to scrape at the soil with her finger. "A line between this world, and the world of the hereafter . . ."

Bon gave her a curious look. "I don't believe this. You were furious at me for using the translator, and now you're . . . what? Becoming an accomplice?"

Lita smiled. "I told you, it's scientific curiosity."

He kept his gaze on her face, then suddenly raised his eyebrows. "Wait a minute," he said. "It's not just the science. You're talking to me about *my* guilt; but if the Cassini really are redesigning my brain, there's no way you'd let me connect again unless . . ."

Lita felt her heart rate pick up. "Unless what?"

Bon gave a slight nod. "Unless you're trying to deal with feelings of guilt yourself." When Lita didn't respond, he nodded again. "Of course. You've been beating yourself up over Alexa since the operation. You did nothing wrong then, and you did nothing wrong with the vulture, and yet—"

Lita cut him off by putting a hand over his mouth. "All right. That's enough."

His eyes were like lasers. He gently reached up and pulled her hand away. "As soon as you figured out what I've been doing, you didn't go to Gap or the Council. You came here, to talk with me. You *want* me to reach Alexa, don't you? Say what you want about the science, but you want to make sure she's okay, too. Somewhere. Somehow."

She was silent again, but in her mind she saw Manu's amulet

hanging from the vidscreen. Faith. Fate. Science. Did any of those pieces fit together at all? Was she scrambling to *make* them fit, motivated by her own feelings of guilt? Was she being completely honest with Bon—and with herself—by claiming a purely scientific curiosity? The fact that she sidestepped the Council and came straight to Bon answered some of those questions.

She stood up and brushed the dirt off her pants. Slipping the translator back into her pocket, she said, "Let's keep this little discussion to ourselves for right now, okay? I'll talk with you about it later."

Bon could only stare up at her, scanning her face. Lita looked away, determined that he not see that her eyes had become wet.

Before either could say another word, their world erupted. A searing, blinding flash of light exploded through the clear panels of the dome. Lita and Bon both grunted in pain, clamping their eyes shut and throwing up hands to shield their faces. As quickly as it happened, it was gone.

22

The strain of it all eventually led Gap to one of the few places where he felt at home and at ease. Twenty minutes atop his Airboard gave him the opportunity to temporarily abandon any thoughts of the wormholes, the radiation crisis, the mystifying lightning flashes, the election, and Hannah. He cruised on his board, mere inches above the padded floor, riding the invisible force of gravity, feeling the ebb and flow of the attraction and adjusting his weight to steer. He kept his speed at an exhilarating level, but nowhere near his personal best. Today was not about setting records; it was about escape.

It was just after five o'clock. The voting window had closed two hours earlier, and Roc would be announcing the results at six. That should have dominated his thoughts, yet he couldn't take his mind off the conversation he'd had with Hannah. Suddenly the outcome of the Council Leader election took a backseat to her admission that she still cared for him. He grappled with whether or not he'd handled this news the right way. He'd simply responded that he felt the same way; should he have reached over and taken her into his arms?

Why did it have to be so hard?

After bantering with a few fellow die-hard Boarders in the bleachers—and thanking them for their hearty cries of good luck—Gap hefted his Airboard and trudged out of the room. As he made his way toward the lift on the lower level, he wondered whether it would be a good idea to stop by the Dining Hall after his shower, or whether it would be best to hear the news alone, in his room. If he won, it might be nice to be among fellow crew members. On the other hand, if he lost . . .

He came into view of the lift. At the same time he saw a figure, apparently having just stepped out of the lift, moving off in the opposite direction. He barely caught a glimpse before the person rounded the bend, heading down the corridor toward the Spider bay. But who would have business there? There were no maintenance assignments currently scheduled.

Curious, he tucked his Airboard under one arm and followed.

As he approached another turn, just before his favorite viewing window on the ship, he heard voices ahead. One voice in particular jumped out: Hannah's.

He crept up to the bend but stayed out of sight. There was no doubt that it was Hannah who was speaking.

"I don't care," she said. "I'm prepared for either result. In fact, I might actually feel relief if Gap wins."

The other person—presumably the figure Gap had seen walking away from the lift—gave only a low chuckle. It had a condescending ring to it.

"Laugh if you want," he heard Hannah say. "It shouldn't be news to you, not after all the times we've talked about this."

The moment he heard the reply, Gap froze. The voice was unmistakable.

"You have such a flair for being dramatic," Merit said. "Even when you're not trying to be. It must be the artistic side of you, the creative and rebellious gene that all artists seem to have. It doesn't change the fact that everything has gone exactly as we hoped so far. You easily won both of the forums, and the crew is behind you."

It was almost too much for Gap to handle. Merit? Merit was

behind Hannah's run for office? He leaned against the wall, his heart slamming against his chest.

"The crew is behind Gap as well," Hannah said. "Regardless of the scare tactic you tried with that post—yes, I know it was you, don't give me that look. You're so confident about these election results, and I'm telling you right now that it could easily go either way."

"They loved your theory," Merit said.

"Sure. But it's another story when it comes to selecting someone to implement the ideas. Gap made great points, and his solution is just as viable as mine."

Gap wanted to run, run back to the lift, back to his room, seal himself inside and never come out. Instead, before he knew what he was doing, he pushed away from the wall and stepped around the bend.

Merit's back was to him. Hannah, however, looked over Merit's shoulder and saw Gap immediately. Her mouth dropped open. Merit, seeing the look, spun around. His face, too, registered surprise at first. But then, slowly, a defiant smirk took over.

"Gap . . ." Hannah said.

Gap felt the blood rush to his face. He let the Airboard slip to the floor, and his hands balled into fists at his side. "So . . . the two of you . . ."

Hannah stepped around Merit. "Gap, wait. I—"

"Don't bother," Gap said. "I couldn't believe it when you agreed to run for election, but now it all makes sense. You both had an ax to grind with me; what better way to get revenge, right? Team up to crush me."

"No, Gap, it's not like that."

"Really? Sure seems like it." Gap shook his head. "And to think I actually believed what you said to me a few hours ago."

"It's true."

"Save it."

Merit laughed. "What are you so worked up about, Gap? You

should just pick up your toy there and go back to the track. We have things to work out." He gently placed a hand on Hannah's shoulder. "Don't we, babe?"

Gap felt an instant flash of rage. He began to take a step toward Merit, but stopped himself. He felt the muscles in his arms stiffen, and his jaw clenched together.

Hannah spun to face Merit, shoving his hand aside. "Get your hands off me, Merit! Do you hear me? And shut your mouth!"

"No, let him talk," Gap said. "I guess it was his idea all along to have you run. He's the one who nominated you, right, *babe*? You two are a beautiful couple."

Merit only laughed again.

Hannah turned back to Gap. "You've got to believe me, we are not a couple. He's just saying that to get back at you, to hurt you. Don't you understand? It's not like that at all."

"Oh, really?"

"I meant what I told you. This . . . this isn't . . ." She stopped and let out a long breath.

Gap shook his head again. "I'll leave you two alone."

"Gap, no . . ."

He had barely started to turn, and out of the corner of his eye could see Hannah reaching for him, when suddenly a violent bang rocked the ship. Gap and Hannah were thrown against the far wall, slamming into it with enough force that it knocked the wind out of them. Merit landed in a pile a few feet away, crumpling to the floor at a bad angle, and Gap heard the snap of a bone.

All of the lights went out, and they were plunged into absolute darkness.

23

If he'd blacked out, Gap figured it couldn't have been for more than a few seconds. He tried to roll over, but Hannah was sprawled across his legs. He could hear her groan and begin to stir, and after a few moments she sat up. He rolled into a sitting position and took stock of his condition.

A lump was already bulging on his forehead, and he could taste blood from undoubtedly biting his lip. His right wrist ached from bracing for the impact with the wall. On top of that he felt slightly nauseated, but that appeared to be the extent of his wounds.

He began to fumble with his hands to locate Hannah when the lights flicked back on at what seemed half power. Hannah sat against the wall, a small trail of blood stretching from beside her right eye to just below the jawline. She was grasping her right elbow and wincing. She blinked to adjust to the light, then looked over at Gap with wide eyes.

"Was that . . . what I think it was?" she said.

Gap didn't answer. He stood up gingerly, wringing his hand to work the kinks out of his wrist, then looked over at Merit, who was lying facedown, his arm twisted unnaturally beneath him. He wasn't moving.

Gap heard Hannah say something about getting help, then she

was gone, limping around the bend to the nearest intercom. He knelt beside the fallen figure and saw that Merit was breathing but unconscious. There was no visible blood. Until trained medical help arrived, Gap thought it unwise to move him.

He was anxious to get up to the Control Room and was grateful when Hannah hurried back.

"Manu said they're swamped with calls right now," she told him. "He said someone will be down in just a few minutes."

"I've gotta go," Gap said. "Stay here until they arrive, and check in with me later." He threw a quick glance down at Merit, and then back to Hannah. Her face had a pleading look.

"Gap, believe me—"

He cut her off. "We can talk later." Without another word he turned and rushed toward the lift.

Ascending to the top level, he summoned the ship's computer. "Roc, do you have a damage report yet?"

"Just filtering everything now. The radiation shield dropped again, as you might expect, and when it stayed down for five seconds I automatically diverted power from the ion drive, as you proposed. It seems to have done the trick . . . for now. The shield is back up, but I can't promise for how long."

Gap burst out of the lift on *Galahad*'s upper level and immediately saw crew members assisting others toward Sick House. Most of the injured were either cradling an arm or holding a compress of sorts over a bleeding wound. None appeared too serious, but Gap wondered what the final casualty list would look like.

The Control Room buzzed with activity. Gap logged into his Engineering work station and surveyed the data. As he did so, the ship's lights came back to full power.

"Shield still holding?" he asked Roc.

"Yes," the computer said. "I took it upon myself to clip one percent of power from the drive. I'm sure you understand the significance of that amount."

Despite the nausea, Gap managed a thin smile. During the

initial encounter with the Cassini, the alien presence had attempted to "improve" the starship that was rocketing through their neighborhood by boosting the ion drive. Although their intentions were good, the ship's engines were not designed to handle the stress, and ultimately the maneuver came dangerously close to destroying the ship. In the end, Bon was able to communicate with the Cassini and prevent the disaster. And yet, for reasons unknown, the ship managed to escape with a fractional increase in power.

"Our little one-percent gift from the Cassini," Gap muttered. "Knowing how much you care about them, I'm sure it pained you to siphon that away."

"If your sarcastic comment is meant to imply that I somehow derive joy by regifting their contribution, nothing could be further from the truth. It merely seemed a practical solution."

"Uh-huh," Gap said. "I have to say, Roc, your snippy attitude about the Cassini is quite immature."

"Me? Immature?" Roc said. "You can't see it, but I'm virtually sticking my tongue out at you. Back to business: other than the shield, the ship's primary systems check out okay; Lita and Manu are treating approximately twenty crew members so far in Sick House, mostly scrapes and bruises; and the lump on your forehead gives you a somewhat Quasimodo-like appearance. Very rugged looking, something you normally don't pull off too well."

Gap lightly brushed his forehead with his fingers, then cringed. "Well, obviously we need to talk about the shock wave. Probably no big mystery about what caused that. Would I be correct in assuming that we are now graced with the opening of another wormhole nearby?"

"Much closer, in fact, than the others we experienced," Roc said. "That explains the extremely violent concussion. Almost like it was tracking us through space better than last time, and placed itself in the perfect position to intercept us. A perfect pass, you might say."

"What's your calculation for contact?"

Roc paused for a few seconds, then said: "One hour, four minutes. However, assuming Hannah's theory is correct, we should experience a few of those delightful shock waves before that."

Gap pulled his chair over and sat down. The nausea had subsided, but his head and wrist still throbbed. He looked up and nodded appreciation when one of the Control Room personnel handed him a cup of water.

His mind scrambled through the information Roc had provided. If another wormhole had ripped through the fabric of space, and with pinpoint accuracy in order to intercept the ship, it was quite obviously there for a reason. Could it be an attack on *Galahad*? Were the beings responsible for the vultures out to avenge their fallen soldier, perhaps by launching a fleet of the ominous dark creatures?

Or would the vultures' caretakers be arriving to personally take matters into their own hands?

The next five minutes were spent diagnosing the rejuvenated radiation shield, the effect of the ion drive power shift, and the expanding injury update from Sick House. Lita reported that the toll had climbed to twenty-nine.

"Lots of bumps and bruises," she said over the intercom. "Four people are going to be admitted to the hospital ward for a bit, though."

Gap paused, staring at the console. "Uh . . . does that include Merit?"

"It does," Lita said. "His arm is broken, and he cracked a couple of ribs. I'm about to run a scan for any internal damage."

Gap felt his emotions twist. Less than an hour earlier it had taken everything in his power to keep from lashing out at Merit. What did it say about his character, he wondered, that news of

Merit's injuries caused him to feel a twinge of satisfaction? Did that make him a monster?

And if he felt those sinister feelings for Merit, why did he not feel the same way about Hannah? She had deceived him, and she had teamed up with Merit Simms. Merit Simms! Shouldn't he, after all, have the same dark thoughts about her?

But he didn't. Despite the blow to his heart, he knew that he still cared about her. What did it all mean?

He decided that it was not the time for a self-inspection of his soul. "What about Hannah?" he said to Lita. "She had some blood—"

"She's fine. Might have a tiny scar to remember it all by, but otherwise she's okay. Let's talk about you."

"I'm okay," Gap said.

"That's not what I heard. Hannah said that you slammed your extremely thick skull into the wall. Well, she said your head; I added the thick part. When can you stop in to let us at least check you out?"

Gap again dabbed at the lump. "I'm all right. Besides, we've got another wormhole coming up fast. I can't leave right now."

"I knew you'd say that," Lita said. "Manu should be walking in your door any second. Don't be stubborn, let him spend three minutes looking at you."

"I didn't know you guys made house calls," Gap said. "Let me know how things are going later." He ended the conversation as the door slid open, admitting Manu. True to Lita's estimate, it took only a few minutes to pronounce Gap fit for duty.

"You'll be sore for a day or two," Manu said. "If you feel the need for a pain pill, let me know." He gave Gap a wry smile. "In the meantime, you kinda look like that hunchback character. What's his name? Quasimodo?"

"Ha ha ha!" Roc blurted from the speaker. "Do I know my classic literature, or what? Ring the bell, Gap, ring the bell!"

Gap shook his head and thanked Manu. "If I need a pill, it will be because of a completely separate headache."

"Unappreciated, that's what I am," the computer said. "Steering the conversation back to the tiny matter at hand, namely our humble ship galloping toward a gaping gash in the universe . . ."

"Yes?"

"We're about fifty-two minutes out. I've nudged the ship so that we'll cruise past the opening rather than down the hatch. Even so, it's much closer than before, and even with my dazzling intellect it'll be hard to predict what effect that will have on the ship. If Hannah's bruise theory is correct—and this will be a good test—we're in for a bumpy ride."

Gap imagined a water skier, bouncing over the wake of a boat, riding out the turbulence.

"Can you nudge us outward a little more, please?" he said. "Let's try to give ourselves the biggest cushion we can." He dropped back into his chair and began to calculate just how close they would be coming to the wormhole.

He realized that six o'clock had slipped past. The election results should have been announced by this point, but Roc, it seemed, had shuffled that bit of business down several notches. Gap was thankful; after what he'd stumbled across on the lower level, he couldn't stand the idea that the team of Hannah and Merit might have defeated him. He opened his mouth to suggest that Roc hold the results until this latest emergency was over and done with, but held off. That was a decision for the entire Council.

Focus, he told himself. He bent back over the console and directed his energies to a new area: the radiation shield. If *Galahad* was minutes away from a furious storm, it might be time to divert even more energy to the shield.

As if on cue, the ship's lights dimmed again, and within seconds a call came from Engineering. It was Julya.

"Let me guess," Gap said. "What's the status of the shield right now?"

"Well," she said, "stable, I suppose. It dropped out for just over a second, then came back, then out for another second."

"Roc," Gap said, "I think it's time for one of those executive decisions. Let's drop another two percent into the shield. Can it handle that input?"

"If not, we'll return it to the manufacturer with a very stern letter. Should take about three minutes." The computer paused, and then added, "Uh-oh."

Gap recognized the tone. Roc had only shifted to that tone on a few occasions, and it had always preceded bad news.

"The space around us has just become a bit more congested," Roc said.

"Explain," Gap said.

"We know that the wormholes are not used for decoration; they're passageways. And it seems that a few things have spilled out of this passageway, right into our path."

A knot instantly materialized in Gap's stomach, and he felt an icy streak race through his veins. "How many things are we talking about?"

"Lots," Roc said. "As in . . ." After a few seconds delay, he added, "Roughly two thousand."

Gap not only felt a stab of fear himself, he swore that he could feel the collective fear roiling through the atmosphere of the Control Room as each crew member absorbed the news. Two *thousand*? His mind conjured up images of a vast squadron of pitch-black vultures, circling ahead, waiting to intercept and latch on to *Galahad*. He imagined that each person in the room had painted a similar picture.

He brought himself upright in his chair and injected as much composure into his voice as possible. He was still the commander of the ship. "Do you have enough data yet to determine the size and trajectory?"

"Scanning again," Roc said. "No doubt that all but one of them are vultures."

Gap gazed up at the room's giant vidscreen, but saw only the blazing star field. "All but one?"

"Well, isn't this interesting," the computer said.

"Roc, tell me!"

"It would seem that we might be getting some of our property back. Besides the nasty critters, that's our pod that just popped out of the wormhole. It's back."

24

The door to the Conference Room slid open and Lita rushed in. The other Council members were seated around the table, waiting for her. She had turned things over to Manu and the rest of the Sick House staff in order to squeeze in a few minutes for the emergency meeting. Gap began talking before she even took her seat.

"As you probably heard, or at least guessed, another wormhole has exploded onto the scene. This one seems to have practically tracked us. The ripple effect has once again struck our shields, and I've had Roc divert some power from the ion drive engines in order to provide us with at least a little more protection for the time being.

"At our current speed we should fly past the opening of the wormhole in about thirty-six minutes. However, before we reach that point we'll come across a squadron of vultures which popped out and are now gradually plotting an intercept course to us. And this time there's a lot of them. A couple thousand."

Gap could see Channy visibly shiver. Lita's face went pale; he'd known that the healing she'd been working on since Alexa's death would take a hit with this news, and he felt for her.

"But there's more," he said, hoping to quickly divert the focus away from the sinister-looking vultures. "The pod is back."

All three of his fellow Council members reacted at once. Lita let out a gasp; Channy's eyes went wide and she threw both hands up around her face.

Bon's mouth dropped open and he gripped the edge of the table with both hands. Gap had never seen the Swede react so dramatically to anything during their voyage. He stared down the table at Bon, trying to read what was spinning inside his head. Recovering at once, Bon stood and walked over to the water dispenser, keeping his back to Gap.

"So she's back," Channy said, breaking the spell.

"The *pod* is back," Gap said. "As for what's inside, we have no idea. We've tried making radio contact, but there's been no response. I'm hopeful, of course, but unless we can get inside to look around . . ." He let his voice trail off.

Lita was staring at Bon's back. She said, "Do we have any ideas on how these . . . wormhole people, whoever they might be, were able to find us?"

Gap shook his head. "Before, we figured that the vultures were communicating with them, giving them coordinates. Now, with no vultures around—at least none that we know of—we have no idea. But Roc has a theory that might clear up at least one mystery we've been dealing with. Roc, wanna share what you told me?"

"The first thing I told Gap," the computer said, "was to let someone help him color coordinate his clothes. After that we got down to business about this new wormhole, and the question of how they knew where to find us. Specifically, the flashes of light."

Lita said nothing and kept her head lowered, staring at the table. Bon had walked slowly back to the table and, for a change, seemed very interested in a Council discussion.

"Wait," Channy said. "They found us . . . with light?"

Roc said, "They found us using a method not unlike the way old-style computer programmers worked. The light was more than just light; it was a ping."

Channy sighed. "I'm going to need some special tutoring on this."

"At your service. In the early days of computers—long before you had such magnificent creations like me—computer techs would test connections between computers, or between computers and websites, by sending out what was known as a ping. They could identify an IP address and gauge the delay between the signal's origination and its receipt. What the wormhole masters were doing, it would seem, is not much different; they were sending interstellar pings to locate us."

Since Gap, Lita, and Bon remained silent, Channy spoke up again. "But how would they know where to even send this ping?"

"Still working on that," Roc said. "But I can say, with strong confidence, that we've found yet another way that these creatures manipulate dark energy. Those mystery particles within the light flashes? I'm pretty sure that's what they are. And if I'm right—and I usually am—they're somehow able to send their dark energy pings across vast distances. Perhaps even infinite distances."

The room was silent for a moment. Then Gap sat forward and said, "I would love to spend more time puzzling out their methods, but it's not our most important issue right now. Before we worry about how they've found us, we need to concentrate on capturing the pod and getting it back into the Spider bay." He glanced around the table. The last time they'd gone fishing for this same pod, some had questioned the wisdom of bringing it aboard. "I'm assuming that there's no argument about doing that, right?"

Channy shook her head. Bon remained still. A thoughtful look crossed Lita's face, and she said, "Of course we need to bring it aboard. But Manu brought up a good point. We have no idea where the pod has been, or what it might be carrying. I'm strongly suggesting that we quarantine the bay, and anyone near the pod should wear protective gear until we determine whether there's any contamination."

Gap nodded. "All right. I appreciate that." He looked at each of the Council members. "What concerns me right now is that the pod is surrounded by two thousand vultures, like fighter planes escorting a bomber. I doubt that any of them will fly into the open Spider bay door when the time comes. We saw what happens when they encounter oxygen, so I expect them to keep their distance. But it's still a little daunting to have that many buzzing around us."

Channy spoke up. "And how do we know there aren't more waiting to fly out of the wormhole? Or . . . something else that might pop out?"

"We don't know," Gap said. "I just wanted to make sure that everyone was up to speed on what was happening. I want us to be very careful about all of this, because we have to go under the assumption that Triana might still be aboard the pod."

There was silence for a moment before Lita said, "I take it that the election results are temporarily being withheld?"

Gap turned one hand palm up. "That's up to the three of you."

Looks were exchanged. Lita seemed to go into deep thought before she spoke again. "Given several of the circumstances, I think it would be best to wait. I know it's only a possibility, but if Triana is really aboard the pod—and assuming that she's okay—it wouldn't make much sense to release an announcement right now. Delaying the results a few hours won't make much difference anyway, will it?"

Gap looked around at the other Council members. He was the only one who knew about Merit's involvement with Hannah's election bid. That meant that the one person most likely to squawk about a delay was lying incapacitated in the Clinic.

"I don't think it matters," Channy said. "I vote to see if Triana is back or not."

Although a majority had spoken, all eyes turned to Bon. He shrugged and said, "Sure."

Gap felt a sense of relief. He couldn't deny that the election results weighed heavily upon him, and the distraction caused by the pod's return—not to mention the vultures—at least temporarily shelved that issue. Now, more than ever, he yearned for Triana to reappear.

"Okay," he said to the Council. "We'll postpone the announcement of the election results until we see what develops in the next twelve to twenty-four hours."

"But I know who won!" Roc said with an impish tone. "How do you expect me to keep a secret like that?"

"Nobody understands that better than me," Channy said. "You can tell me later in private. I won't breathe a word to anyone."

Gap rolled his eyes. "On that note, this meeting is adjourned. Channy, will you please find Hannah and let her know our decision? I'd prefer that someone tell her in person, rather than through e-mail or the intercom." He excused himself and quickly left the room. Channy waved good-bye to the others and followed him into the corridor.

As Bon walked toward the door, Lita reached out and grasped his arm. The door closed, leaving them alone in the Conference Room. He looked down at her hand, and then into her dark eyes. "Yes?" he said.

Lita propped herself against the table. "You realize what happened, right?"

"I don't know what you mean," he said.

"You don't really think this new wormhole opened up right in front of us by chance, do you?"

Bon crossed his arms. "How would I know?"

"It's not by chance," Lita said. "I told Channy a while ago that we needed to become some sort of lighthouse for Triana to find her way back to us. We needed a beacon."

"And?"

"And that beacon was you."

He stared at her. "I still don't know what you mean."

"I think you do."

He seemed to process for a moment, then said, "If you're suggesting that I did this with the translator—"

Lita nodded. "I know what you're going to say: you made contact with the Cassini hoping to find some way to reach Alexa. But in the process you apparently sent out some kind of signal, or beacon, that these . . . these beings, or creatures, or whatever they are, were able to home in on."

"You don't know that," he said.

"Of course I don't *know* it," Lita said. "But it's the only thing that makes sense. You reached out, and they grabbed on. Those . . . those pings that Roc mentioned. They had to have something to guide their search. And except for the very last flash—which was probably just a last-minute check to make sure we were where they thought we'd be—the first two flashes happened right after your connections." She paused and gave Bon a smile. "Am I right?"

When Bon didn't answer, she continued. "Listen, I don't know if we owe this to fate, or to the workings of a higher power in the universe. But you went looking for Alexa, and as a result you might have led Triana back home."

Bon pressed his lips together. Neither said a word for what seemed a long time.

"And another thing," Lita said. "This helps to satisfy my scientific curiosity that you shrugged off. Specifically the power of thought."

"That's just a theory," Bon said. "It's never been proven."

"I think you just did."

He shook his head and gave a harsh laugh. "You put an awful lot of stock in my redesigned brain."

Lita pushed off from the table and faced him. "I put a lot of stock in the power of the human mind, yes. But I'm not thinking about your mind by itself. I've seen studies that show what large groups of people can do when they focus together on something.

Seems to me that putting the power of the Cassini behind your thoughts could accomplish things we might never have believed possible. Like reaching through space to find Triana. And if it can do that . . ."

Her voice trailed off, and again they stared at one another. When she spoke again, it was barely above a whisper.

"If science can explain how you're able to reach across a galaxy to draw someone home, I don't see why it can't reach across other voids as well."

She could see Bon swallow hard. Finally, he took a deep breath and said, "Maybe. Or maybe we're both crazy. Did you consider that scientific possibility, too?" With that, he turned and walked out of the Conference Room.

Lita watched him leave. Her hand reached up to her neck, to the charcoal-colored stone that hung from the silver strand. Her gaze shifted to the window, and she considered the brilliant display of stars, and what might lie beyond them.

25

Gap delegated several of his responsibilities to various team members in the Control Room, then called down to Engineering. Ruben reported that the shield was stable for the time being, but that he would stay on top of the situation and report any changes immediately.

Roc had spent the past half hour plotting the maneuvers that would be necessary to capture the pod and bring it safely into the Spider bay. Gap reviewed the details and the timetable, and decided to oversee the action from the bay's control room. With about ten minutes to go, he donned the pressurized EVA suit per Manu's recommendation and stepped into the glass-enclosed booth that looked out over *Galahad*'s vast hangar.

Built to hold the ship's maintenance and transport vehicles, nicknamed Spiders because of their shape and multiple hinged arms that radiated from their shell, the room was a giant airlock that emptied into space. They had launched with ten of the small craft, only eight of which were capable of sustaining life-support systems, and one of those was lost during the showdown with the stowaway. That left *Galahad* with seven fully functioning transport vehicles once they reached Eos, a dilemma that had been pushed to the back burner for the time being.

The bay had also housed the metallic pod which had originally been launched from the doomed space station orbiting Titan, and which ultimately carried Triana through the alien wormhole. If all went according to plan, that pod would be safely tucked back into the bay within the next half hour.

Gap fought to repress the usual tinge of discomfort he felt whenever he stood in the Spider bay's control room. He would always associate this site with heartbreak, for it was in this room that he had witnessed a connection between Triana and Bon. True, it had lasted only a few seconds, but it was an image that he knew he would never be able to erase. For the moment, however, he had work to do, and ironically that work involved rescuing Triana.

Assuming she was on the pod. "Please," he said quietly to himself, "let her be there. Please."

"Roc," he said. "Is the pod maneuvering under its own power?"

"No, it appears to be drifting. My guess would be that it's being dangled out there like a piece of cheese for us to pick up, and, should we decide to take a sniff and pass it by, they would be able to gather it back up and stuff it back through the wormhole."

That made sense to Gap. He pulled up the data on the control room's vidscreen and watched the numbers counting down. "Let's make it clear to them that we have every intention of retrieving the pod. If the bay is clear, go ahead and open the door, please."

A minute later he watched through the window as one of the bay's large doors silently slid open.

"Magnetic beam is ready," Roc said. "Contact in approximately three minutes." He paused for a moment, then added, "Apparently opening the bay door was like sending up a flare. Our little vulture friends are now making a beeline for us."

Gap shifted his gaze from the vidscreen to the bay's open door, and an instinctual shudder passed through him. Even though the oxygen-laced atmosphere of the ship would prevent the part-mechanical-part-biological creatures from operating inside *Galahad*, he couldn't help but feel that he had made the ship vulnerable by simply propping open the door. A chilling vision of waves of vultures, soaring through the opening, flashed before his eyes. He pushed it aside and concentrated on the pod.

"One minute to pod capture," Roc said. "P.S., the escorts have arrived and are circling the ship. Correction, all but one are circling. That one has latched on to us, not far from the open door."

"Can you give me a camera shot?" Gap said.

"It should be up on your vidscreen any moment."

There was a flicker on the screen, and then it appeared. Gap recoiled as the image came into focus.

The dark black vulture stood out against the gray exterior of *Galahad* like a cosmic wound. Triangular in shape, it was pressed against the ship by an unseen force, a force that the crew now assumed was related to the mysterious dark energy that saturated the universe.

On the vidscreen he could see the vulture's wings, now folded up along its sides, and with some magnification he was able to make out its rough, pebbled surface. The vents which ran like stitches along the sides were pulsing open and closed, and by adjusting the camera angle Gap could pick out a faint blue-green glow seeping from underneath. Though no wider than two feet across, the vulture presented an imposing—and intimidating—aura.

Gap's dark thoughts were interrupted by Roc. "Twenty seconds. Beginning power-up . . . now."

The vidscreen switched back to a graphical display, and Gap watched the pod's capture unfold. A magnetic beam, capable of grasping nearby objects and tugging them into the Spider bay, was about to be utilized for the second time since they had departed Earth, and both occasions involved the same small metal craft.

Icons that represented both *Galahad* and the pod appeared to slip past each other. Then the pod's image momentarily froze before slowly reversing course and tracking toward the ship. At the same time, Roc announced, "Capture complete. I'm now reeling her in like a marlin."

Gap let out a long breath. "Great job. Will you let the other Council members know the status, please?" He thought about it for a second, then added, "And let Hannah know, too. Thanks."

For all he knew, Hannah was the acting Council Leader of *Galahad*, even if nobody knew it yet.

He found himself fidgeting for the next few minutes as the pod crept along the magnetic stream toward the rendezvous. Four crew members, each wearing the necessary EVA suit, entered the control room. Gap nodded at them, then quickly updated them on the situation. He noticed, without commenting, that one of the crew members held an oxygen gun at his side.

A reminder, Gap thought, that we have to do everything we can to protect ourselves, especially if we're up against a formidable opponent. Hopefully it wouldn't be necessary.

"Stand by, I'll have the fish in the boat in about one minute," Roc said. "I'm a little disappointed this one didn't kick and fight like the others usually do. Might have to throw it back."

The door to the hallway opened and Channy walked in. Her eyes were wide, and for one of the few times on the voyage she was speechless. She gave a small wave to Gap, then walked over to the window.

Seconds later the starlight pouring through the open bay door was blotted out. The pod hovered just outside, and then gradually floated into the vast hangar. It set down in the same spot it had occupied before Triana's departure, and the bay door was once again sealed.

Thankfully, Gap noted that not a single vulture had flown into the ship. It appeared that they were content to simply escort the pod back home. Content, at least, for the moment.

"Pressurizing," Roc said.

Lita entered the room out of breath. "Well?" she said, then put her face up to the glass. "So . . . nothing else got in?"

Gap shook his head. "No. One of them is stuck on the ship right outside the bay, and the others are orbiting us like electrons."

He turned to the crew members who stood ready. "We'll go in as soon as the pressurization is complete. The first order of business: I want a complete visual scan of the pod. Top, bottom, sides, everywhere. I want to know if there's anything attached, anything at all."

Addressing Lita and Channy, he said, "I'm going in with the recovery unit, but I'd rather not take too many chances with the rest of the Council. It's not wise for all of us to be in there at the same time, not until everything checks out." He saw the disappointment on their faces, and quickly added, "I know you want to go in, but for now it's best if you wait here. Lita, I'll need you standing by in case of an emergency."

"I brought my little black bag," she said, patting the satchel that hung from her shoulder.

Gap nodded. "Roc, let's get a complete external scan for radiation before I open this door, please."

"Already underway," the computer said. "Early indications are normal."

Just as they were preparing to enter the bay, the door to the hallway opened again. Gap assumed it might be additional crew members coming to help and looked back over his shoulder with a casual glance.

It was Bon.

He stood in the doorway, in full EVA attire, holding his helmet under one arm. Lita and Channy were glued to the window and hadn't noticed. Gap and Bon stared at each other for a moment in an awkward wordless exchange.

Bon never showed up unless specifically instructed to do so, Gap thought. He even treated each scheduled Council meeting like a major imposition in his busy life. And now he was here?

Lita finally turned. She looked back and forth between Gap and Bon, then walked over to stand next to the Swede. "Hey, I'm glad you're here." She glanced up at Gap and said, "Maybe it would be a good idea for Bon to go with you. Just in case."

Gap watched the two of them intently. Something had passed between them, a silent look of understanding. He turned back to the door without a word; he didn't want Bon to go with him, but could think of no reasonable argument to keep him out. It wasn't worth the time it would take to thrash it out. Instead, he punched in the code to break the airlock and led the small party of crew members into the hangar. He kept his gaze on the gleaming metal pod resting straight ahead, but his mind couldn't help but replay the earlier scene between Bon and Triana. It shook him, and he clenched his hands into fists as he walked.

Soon the party had fanned out around the pod, although Bon chose to hang back, simply staring at it. A quick examination revealed nothing out of the ordinary; the craft looked exactly as it had the first time it had been brought aboard. Two windows dotted the front end of the small vessel, while block lettering and flag emblems on one side identified the countries of Earth originally responsible for its mission.

Gap walked to the rear hatch of the pod and stopped, facing the external emergency panel. He remembered their first encounter with this particular vessel, how Triana had stood in this exact spot while he watched nearby, his arm in a sling. Lita had been the first to board that time; today, nothing would stop him from being the first inside.

He had memorized the necessary code, and now punched the keys to open a small access panel. When it flipped open with a hiss, he flexed his fingers and reached inside to another keypad. After entering another string of numbers, he grasped the small handle inside the panel and looked back toward the window of the control booth. Lita gave him a supportive smile and a thumbs up.

He pulled the handle. A puff of air brushed against his helmet, and, with a metallic sigh, the hatch popped open a few inches.

Unlike their first foray into the pod, when it had loomed dark and lifeless, this time the interior was bathed in routine operating lights. They flickered, as if barely holding on to power. *Not as spooky as before,* Gap thought. Taking a deep breath, he reached up to the handrail in order to pull himself inside.

Without warning, his arm was grasped in a firm grip. With a start, he turned to look into a pair of ice-blue eyes.

"I'll go," Bon said, inches away from his face.

Gap was frozen for a moment, then collected himself and shook Bon's hand away. "What are you talking about?"

"I'll go," Bon said again.

"What's gotten into you?" Gap said.

Bon's eyes bore into him, but he said nothing. Gap shook his head and uttered a sarcastic chuckle.

"I appreciate the offer, Bon, but I can handle it this time." Without waiting for a reply, Gap pushed him aside and grabbed the handrail. He pulled himself up into the pod's open hatch and stepped inside. He immediately felt Bon clamber up behind him.

The interior was different. The passenger seats which once occupied space in the back were missing, and the suspended-animation tubes had been disconnected and shoved to one side. Gap took a moment to orient himself to the changes, then looked toward the forward end of the ship. Two seats in the cockpit area were silhouetted against the glow of the instrument panel.

From behind, he saw a head tilted to one side in the pilot's seat and a cascade of dark hair. An arm hung limply, fingers curled up against the floor. Gap rushed forward and knelt beside the figure in the chair.

His heart pounded as he stared into Triana's face.

Her eyes were only half open, a ghastly look that immediately made Gap fear the worst. He leaned forward and felt a surge of relief that she was breathing. Looking up, he saw Bon kneeling on the other side of Triana. He was concentrating on her with an intensity that Gap had never seen in him before, at least not outside of his work. Mixed in with the intensity was a look of . . .

Gap realized that it was a look of tenderness. He suddenly felt certain that if he hadn't been there, Bon would have brushed her face with his hand.

Bon's expression changed as soon as he met Gap's gaze, and he leveled an almost defiant look. Neither spoke for a few seconds, and in that instant Gap wondered if he had completely misread Bon from the beginning. He was cold, he was rebellious, he was uncooperative, he was aggravating.

But he was here. He *did* care. And, Gap thought, it must be killing him to show it.

"Listen," Gap said. "Go back to the booth and send Lita in here. We need to get Triana to Sick House right now." He paused, and then added, "Please."

With another quick glance down at Triana's face, then a curt nod, Bon disappeared. Seconds later Gap could hear the recovery unit members scrambling up into the pod, but he kept his attention on Tree. He gently straightened her in the chair and deposited her hands in her lap. Then he did what he swore Bon was on the verge of doing: his gloved fingers brushed across her forehead, pulling the hair out of her face.

Lita soon joined him. "Help is coming," she said. "Don't worry, we'll take care of her."

"I know," Gap said, and felt himself on the verge of tears. Not very leaderlike, he decided, and stood up to examine what was going on in the back of the pod. The others were gathered in a knot, deep in conversation about something.

Suddenly one of the crew members turned to him, a look of either shock or horror on her face; he couldn't decide which. "What is it?" he said, walking back to join the group.

She gulped. "Triana brought something back with her."

She and the others stood aside as Gap approached. In the odd flickering light, he saw what appeared to be an aquarium.

Floating inside was the last thing Gap expected to see in outer space.

S omething tells me that this time it's not a cat.

   Okay, just so I have all of this straight, let's go over what we've learned, shall we? The ship is streaking across the intergalactic void at a ridiculous speed, but is bouncing over cosmic speed bumps caused by a rupture in space from a wormhole that some unknown alien society has seen fit to throw in our faces. At the same time, these bumps and bruises are slowly but methodically tearing apart the atomic structure of the space around us and, eventually, the space within us, if we don't do something soon.

   We've witnessed something that the crew is calling space lightning, but would seem to be a tracking system that's somehow tied into Bon's newly altered brain.

   Then, on top of that, we have vultures who have once again descended upon our happy vessel and are currently circling us like . . . well, like vultures.

   And Merit Simms is back on the scene.

   Wait, there's more. Hannah and Gap can't seem to figure things out between them, and Bon is somehow standing on the corner at the intersection of Love and Loneliness. If our brooding farmer isn't careful, he's going to step off the curb and get run over by the Regret Express.

   There is some good news, however. Triana, bless her soul, is back.

Yes, we're all happy, and I'm sure there will be cake in the Rec Room, but I think we also agree that the girl has some explaining to do.

When she's able to talk, of course, but still . . .

And then there's the matter of this aquarium thing, or whatever it is, and the special guest inside. Are we finally going to meet the makers of the creepy vultures? Are we going to learn the secrets of the wormholes? Will we ever know exactly why Gap's hair stands straight up, even when he first climbs out of bed in the morning? How does it do that?

No whining from you about all of these questions, okay? Let's just keep riding along with our gallant star travelers and see what develops. Besides, you've got it easy; I'm the one who has to carry around the secret of the election and not say a peep.

I'll meet you back here for volume number six.

Tor Teen
Reader's Guide

About This Guide

The information, activities, and discussion questions that follow are intended to enhance your reading of *Cosmic Storm*. Please feel free to adapt these materials to suit your needs and interests.

Writing and Research Activities

I. Life in Space
  A. Many *Galahad* crew members keep mementos of their life and family from Earth. If you had been chosen to leave your family for a lifelong space expedition, what small keepsake might you choose to bring? Write a paragraph describing your keepsake, or create one using craft materials.
  B. Based on clues from the novel, draw a blueprint or sketch of *Galahad,* including the Spider bay, Sick House, Domes, Dining Hall, and other areas mentioned in the story. Imagine you are keeping a journal on behalf of the crew of *Galahad*. Write an entry describing your home in space to accompany your drawing.
  C. Roc, the ship's computer, is an important character in *Galahad*. Make a list of at least ten ways that Roc assists

the crew and/or ten quotes from the novel in which he gives advice to the humans aboard the ship. Then, with friends or classmates, debate whether or not *Gala-had*'s designers' decision to give Roc a humorous personality was a good idea. Use your list to support your position.

D. Write a poem, short story, or song lyrics describing what it's like to live on a space ship traveling away from Earth, never to return.

II. Loss

A. Imagine you are a crew member aboard *Galahad*. Write several journal entries describing how you feel about the absence of Triana, the way the Council members are handling the need for a new leader, and the compromise to the ship's protective shield. What emotions—anger, fear, curiosity, nervousness, frustration, excitement—do you feel most?

B. With friends or classmates, role-play a conversation in which you give Bon, Lita, or Gap advice about dealing with their grief over the death of Alexa. If desired, use library or online resources to research ways to deal with grief and use this information in your role-play.

C. Did Triana make the right decision riding into the wormhole? In the character of Gap, Lita, Bon, or Channy, write an online journal entry confessing your true feelings about what happened when your leader went missing, and whether you think the crew of *Galahad* should allow her to resume her position upon her return.

III. Leadership

A. What makes a great leader? Go to the library or online to learn more about great leaders through history. Choose one leader and create an informational poster about this individual. With friends or classmates, create a display of great leader posters.

B. Make a class brainstorm list of important qualities for leadership. If possible, use information from activity III.A, above, to help you. When your list is complete, number the qualities in order of importance. Is there one quality which all leaders must share? Are there different but equally valid ways to lead? Write a short report analyzing your class list and discussion, and stating whether or not you agree with the conclusions of the class.

C. Would your class vote for Gap or Hannah to become the new Council Leader? Hold an election in your classroom. Tabulate and report the results of the vote. Afterward, invite students to discuss how they chose their candidate.

D. Learn more about politics in your city or town. Collect newspaper articles about upcoming elections. Write an article about local government for your school paper. Or volunteer to help with a political campaign. Write an essay explaining why it is (or, if you disagree, why it is not) important that young people participate in government.

E. Who do you think won the *Galahad* election? What will happen next to the ship and its crew? Will the vultures attack? What do you think Triana brought back from the wormhole? Write one to three paragraphs describing your predictions for the next Galahad novel. Include a title suggestion if desired.

Questions for Discussion

1. The novel opens with Roc, the spaceship computer, commenting that, like wormholes, "rules change for people, too,

depending upon what suits them at the time." Do you agree with this comment? To what kind of "rules" do you think Roc refers? As you read the novel, for which characters do you think the rules have changed? Which characters remain true to their beliefs and attitudes despite the current crisis?

2. Describe Gap's reaction to Triana's departure from the ship. How do Lita, Bon, and Channy seem to feel about the new leadership situation early in the novel? If you were a crew member on *Galahad*, would you be comfortable with Gap in charge?

3. Channy tells Bon there were "two people on this ship that you had feelings for, and they're both gone" (p. 23). Describe Bon's feelings for both of these people. How might Gap's feelings for Triana and Hannah put him in a similar emotional situation? Are either Gap or Bon able to discuss these feelings with others?

4. Why does Hannah decide to run for the position of Council Leader? Do you think her intentions are honorable? What qualities does she have that might make her a good choice for the position? What advice might you give her about her relationship with Merit?

5. Do you think Bon is right to refuse Gap's request to hold the translator until a new Council Leader is elected? Do you agree with Gap's decision to allow Bon to keep the translator until the election? Explain your answers.

6. How does Bon describe his relationship with the Cassini? Despite the pain, do you feel that he likes connecting with them? Can he resist them? If you were Bon, would you be worried about the Cassini's effects on your brain?

7. Compare the first and second election forums in terms of their structure, the attitudes of Gap and Hannah, and the reactions of the crowd. Do you think there was a clear winner or loser at either forum? Why or why not?

8. When Lita realizes that Bon was trying to reach Alexa and not Triana, how does this change her understanding of Bon? Do Bon's actions suggest that, despite his gruff exterior, he has some kind of faith? How might you describe that faith? How might this relate to the kind of faith Gap encourages the crew to find when he addresses them in the second election forum?

9. From "waves" to "bruises," what theory explaining the shield malfunctions is most convincing to you? Can you imagine living on a spaceship where your life was constantly, at some level, in peril? How do you think you might handle such stress? Does it make sense to you that members of the crew are acting out?

10. What is Lita's theory about Gap's connection with the Cassini and the events that have occurred since Triana left the ship? If Lita is correct, do you think Bon should be studied, restrained, or otherwise treated differently than the rest of the council and crew? If so, in what way and why?

11. How does the novel's final scene, in the Spider bay, reveal a change in the relationship between Gap and Bon? What other relationships have changed by the novel's end?

12. What has Gap learned about leadership and, perhaps, its relationship to friendship and even love by the novel's end? Has this novel affected the way you think about leadership roles you take on in your own life? Explain your answer.

The
Galahad
Legacy

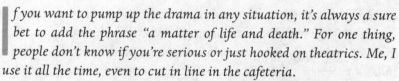

If you want to pump up the drama in any situation, it's always a sure bet to add the phrase "a matter of life and death." For one thing, people don't know if you're serious or just hooked on theatrics. Me, I use it all the time, even to cut in line in the cafeteria.

But sometimes it's not a cheap trick to get attention. Sometimes it literally comes down to a decision here or a mistake there. And before you know it, everyone's screaming.

Case in point: the teenage explorers aboard the greatest sailing ship ever built. This particular ship is not at sea, but rather in a sea of stars. It's called Galahad, and it carries not only the hopes and dreams and dirty laundry of the human race, but 250 of Earth's best and brightest young people, on a mission to colonize a new world.

Their story began about a year ago with The Comet's Curse, and has seen its share of life and death. Literally. For one thing, there used to be 251 teenagers aboard the ship. See what I mean?

What kind of narrator would I be if I didn't strongly urge you to find that first volume and begin at the beginning? You'll find an interesting band of intrepid star travelers, led by crafty Triana Martell and the ship's Council. They counted on a long, difficult voyage. What they didn't count on was a saboteur, deadly space debris, a bizarre alien intelligence over a billion years old, and creepy space vultures—all on the outside—with a few salty troublemakers lurking on the inside.

When we left you hanging last time, Triana had piloted a pod—a small emergency vehicle—through a nasty rip in space that likely was a wormhole. Her disappearance led to an impromptu movement to fill the role of Council Leader, which led to bad boy Merit Simms returning to the scene, which led to Gap Lee and Hannah Ross opposing each other and opening old love wounds, which led . . .

Ugh, how do you humans make it through a day without imploding?

Anyway, Triana has suddenly popped back onto the scene, and she's not alone. She brought something with her, and it's not a fruit basket. Judging from the way some of the crew members reacted when they saw it, I'd say it probably falls somewhere between amazing and downright freaky.

Plus, we have the little problem of the various wormholes creating a bruise in space which now threatens to atomically dismantle the ship and turn the happy space campers into gobs of jumbled particles. Yeah, that's a problem.

And then there's Bon Hartsfield trying to reach into the afterlife to soothe his guilty conscience, and Lita Marques, the ship's young doctor, struggling with the concept of faith in its many forms. Poor Channy Oakland just wants everyone to get their butts in the gym and sweat it out.

Bon has always used a strange device called the translator to achieve his alien hookup, but something tells me that's about to change. And those space vultures I mentioned? I get the feeling they're not going away without a curtain call.

What have I left out? Lots. I suggest you grab all five preceding volumes and tear through them like crazy to get caught up. In each one you'll find that the glue that holds this tale together is the world's most lovable computer. That would be me. My name is Roc, and my actual job is to run the ship's engines and climate. But c'mon, it's no fun to just sit around and watch these guys fall in and out of trouble. Could you?

I'll stick my nose—or at least my chips—into the story from time to time, but only because sometimes it cries out for analysis. And believe me, after a year in space with these crazy kids, no one is better qualified than I.

1

Her eyes fluttered open for a brief second, but the light seemed harsh, making her reluctant to open them again. The last thing she remembered was sitting in the cockpit of the pod, her heart racing as she again spiraled down into the wormhole. Her first experience doing that had taught her that it would not be pleasant.

But now she was lying on a bed, a sheet up to her neck, while muffled voices floated in from nearby. Her curiosity finally won out and she chanced another glimpse, cracking her eyes, allowing them to acclimate as she determined her surroundings. Of course it had to be *Galahad,* her mind told her, but her experiences in the past week—Was it a week? Was it a year?—kept her from accepting anything until she could see it with her own eyes.

Although, she had to admit, what she'd recently seen with those eyes was mind-shattering.

She pried her lids open a bit wider. When the room gradually swam into focus, she positively identified it as the hospital ward on the ship. She let out a contented sigh.

The sound must have alerted the people in the room, because moments later a shape loomed over her. Pulling her gaze upward, she felt a wave of comfort when the face of Lita Marques beamed at her.

"Welcome home, Tree," Lita said. "Why don't you stick around for awhile?"

Triana Martell found the strength to smile, and mumbled a thick "hi."

"I'm sure you have questions galore," Lita said. "Let me answer a few before you ask. Yes, you're back safely; at least my preliminary scan doesn't show any physical problems, unless you have any aches you want to share with me." When Triana shook her head once, Lita continued: "Everyone here is fine, not counting the usual drama and a few bumps and bruises. The ship itself has a few problems, but Gap can get you caught up with that. And, let's see . . ." She sat on the edge of the bed. "Lots of people have come by to welcome you back, but I've shooed them away for now. Oh, and the friend you brought with you is doing okay. Well, at least as far as I can tell."

Triana stared up at Lita, then cleared her throat and croaked: "Where?"

Lita nodded toward the door. "Down the hall. Same place we had the vulture. Only this time we're keeping people out. Remember, it was a zoo when we brought in the vulture. I get the feeling that this is much different, so we're keeping a lid on things for now." She paused and studied Triana's face. "It's actually quite different, isn't it?"

Raising up on her elbows, Triana looked at the table beside her. "Is that water?"

Lita helped her take a few sips. "No comment about . . . it?"

Triana licked her lips, then rubbed her eyes. "I'll have plenty of comments for all of you." She swallowed more water and felt her strength returning. "You're not gonna keep me in bed just because I passed out, are you?"

"Like I said, you seem fine," Lita said, standing up. "You know me, I'll always caution against doing too much after a traumatic experience, or a shock to the system. I'm guessing you've had both. But I know these are special circumstances, too. Let's get some food and water in you, we'll watch you for an hour or so, and then you can walk out of here. Deal?"

Triana lay back and smiled at her friend. "I won't fight you on that. I'm starving."

Lita patted her on the leg. "Good to hear. We'll get you something right away. Time to feed all of my patients anyway."

"All?" Triana said.

"Uh-huh. That wormhole you rode in on has banged up a few people. In fact . . ." Lita lowered her voice. "Your good friend Merit Simms is just three beds down. Sleeping, thanks to pain medication. You'll probably be gone before he wakes up."

She walked toward the door. "Don't wander off, or we'll bring you back and put you in the bed next to him."

Gap Lee trudged along *Galahad*'s curved hallway toward his room. It was well after midnight, and the halls were deserted. Exhausted, he wondered when he'd be able to crash for a good ten or twelve hours. With Triana's return, and the surprise which accompanied her, it might not be anytime soon.

He tried to wrap his brain around that surprise. Tucked into the back of the pod which had delivered Triana into—and back out of—the wormhole, it floated inside what appeared to be an old-fashioned aquarium. Gap's mother had kept exotic tropical fish in a similar container, and likely would have identified the contents as Gap had. But it was impossible . . . wasn't it?

Secured aboard a wheeled cart and covered with a sheet, it was moved to an isolated area in Sick House. Curious crew members along the way had stopped and followed the procession with their eyes, but nobody asked questions. Gap knew that it would dominate the conversation that evening in the Dining Hall and throughout the ship.

The next few hours had been spent alternating between Engineering—where the radiation shield was holding up, thanks to the energy siphon from the main engines—and the Spider bay. A thorough examination of the pod revealed no particular damage, other than an odd assortment of shorted-out electrical components. Other than the aquarium, there were no additional surprises.

Now the door to his room slid open and he stepped inside, mindful to be quiet. Daniil was sound asleep. Gap rarely had contact with his roommate these days; just another sign, he noted, that time off was overdue. His social life had withered away.

And, he realized, it was more insight into the life of Triana, or anyone with heavy responsibilities. It was the side of leaders rarely seen or understood.

Although his bed called out, he kicked off his shoes and checked his mail again. There was a single new entry, a note from Triana. Clicking on the file opened a group message to the Council, with a personal attachment for him. The main message called for the Council to assemble at seven in the morning—his shoulders sagged as he calculated the amount of sleep he would not be getting again this night—and thanked everyone for their great work during her absence. The note was short and to the point, in pure Triana style.

Standing behind his chair and leaning on the desk, he clicked open the attachment.

Gap, I'll certainly thank you in person, but didn't want to wait to let you know how grateful I am that you took charge of the ship while I was away. We haven't had a chance to talk yet, but I'm pretty sure you weren't happy about my decision to go. I know I put you in an awkward and difficult position, but I hope you understand that I had to do it.

We have a lot to cover, and some very important decisions to make. I'm glad to be back, and glad that you're on the team. And I'm glad you're such a good friend.

See you in the morning.

He couldn't think about any of that at the moment. If he didn't get some sleep he'd be worthless to Triana and the Council. Snapping off the vidscreen, he passed on his usual bedtime routine and simply fell onto his bed, covering his face with one arm, willing himself to clear his mind and find the shortest path to sleep.

It wasn't easy.

As always, Bon Hartsfield found escape in his work. Overseeing the Agricultural Department on the ship meant long hours anyway, but his office—tucked within one of the two massive domes atop *Galahad*—provided an insulated nest, especially this late at night.

The ship was programmed to simulate the natural day/night rhythms of Earth, which meant that the lights in many of the common areas slowly dimmed in the evening and then gradually grew brighter beginning around six in the morning. Now, while the majority of the Farms were lit only by the brilliant splash of stars through the clear domes, Bon's office was awash in light.

He stood behind his desk, inputting data from the latest harvest report. It was easily a task that could be entrusted to one of the workers under his supervision, but Bon preferred to remain busy. To sit idly—or worse, lie awake in bed—only invited the troubling thoughts to return. And there were far too many of those lately.

Topping them all was the startling return of Triana. Fight as he might to keep his mind elsewhere, the image of her slumped in the cockpit of the pod muscled its way back to the fore. Where had she been? What had happened to her on the other side of the wormhole? What was that . . . *thing* that she'd brought back?

Or had it brought *her* back?

And, most importantly, had his connection with the alien beings known as the Cassini created what Lita described as a "beacon" to guide Triana back to *Galahad*? How should he feel about that, when it was never his original intent?

The thoughts were overwhelming. He tossed his workpad stylus onto the desk and dropped into his chair. His blond hair, already long and unkempt, had grown shaggy from weeks of neglect, and now fell across his face. At some point he'd need to either visit Jenner for a quick cut, or chop it off himself.

It wasn't near the top of his priorities.

Triana's return, and his confused feelings regarding *Galahad*'s Council Leader; a raft of guilt over the death of Alexa, or, rather, guilt over his inability to return her feelings; the news from Lita that his Cassini link had begun a physical transformation of his brain . . .

All of that in addition to a full workload in the Farms, and his stubborn reluctance to delegate as much as he should. Plus his Council duties.

A low guttural laugh escaped him. Council duties. He'd been almost invisible in Council meetings, speaking up only when irritation got the better of him, or when challenged by Gap. Those two events often went hand in hand. Yet he knew that his position as the head of the Agricultural Department came with leadership responsibilities, and he would never consider turning the Farms over to someone else. The soil, the crops—the very atmosphere of the domes—combined to create his personal haven aboard the ship.

The looming Council meeting would be exceptionally difficult. In a few hours Triana would begin the debriefing, and Bon dreaded the expected eye contact. He would, of course, sit sullenly and listen, but now—hours ahead of the meeting—he could already feel the burn of Triana's stare and the probing looks from Lita.

His head throbbed, a dull ache that was exacerbated, no doubt, by the seemingly nonstop activity of the past week combined with a lack of sleep. He had never requested a sleep-aid of any sort, but now he wondered who might be manning Sick House at this late hour. Would they be required to report to Lita on every pill dispensed, or merely log the random request?

It wasn't worth the chance. Perhaps he could shut down his brain through meditation. Just a few hours of sleep might cure the headache and give him the strength he needed to power through the morning meeting.

He killed the lights to his office, grabbed the blanket he kept stashed for nights like this, and stretched out on the floor.

2

Triana arrived early, striding into the Conference Room with her workpad in one hand and two energy bars in the other. She'd avoided the Dining Hall, afraid that her presence might create a stir, even at this early hour. Until she could address the entire crew, she reasoned, it was best to remain behind the scenes.

"Roc," she said, grabbing her usual chair. "I've got some catching up to do."

"I knew you wouldn't feel like chatting last night," the computer said. "So I posted multiple reports in your folder, everything from details of our radiation shield problem, to the current status of the vultures outside the ship, to the request I've made for vacation time. I really need to get away for a few weeks."

"Denied," Triana said with a slight smile. "No rest for you."

"You're a tyrant. But welcome back anyway."

"Thank you, Roc. I missed you . . . I think."

The computer expelled a pouting grunt. "I'm overwhelmed by your sentimentality. Don't think for a moment that my circuits don't have feelings."

"Oh, I'd never make that mistake," Triana said. "But this has nothing to do with you, believe me. It's just that the week I was gone—it was a week, right?—is still somewhat jumbled. I don't remember missing much of anything. There wasn't time for that kind of thinking."

"Well, I look forward to your report. Especially when you explain exactly what that thing is you brought aboard."

Triana nodded. "Yeah, I expect that will be Question 1A, followed closely by 'Where were you?' as 1B."

"Can't wait to hear the answers," Roc said.

"Well, I'm tempted to answer 'I don't know' for both, but I'll come up with something." Triana tapped open the vid-screen and accessed her personal folder. For the next few minutes she munched on energy bars and scanned the reports. Occasionally she scowled, particularly as she came up to speed on the devastating effects of the space bruise that Hannah had suggested.

"Incredible," she murmured. "Can this be true? Damage at a molecular level?"

"If it's any consolation, I feel great," Roc said. "But yes, *you* might end up resembling a gob of toothpaste."

"Lovely."

The door opened and Gap strolled in. Triana couldn't decipher the look on his face, which seemed perched somewhere between agitation and fatigue. He approached her and she slowly rose to her feet. They exchanged an awkward gaze before embracing in a tentative and equally awkward hug.

"Glad to see you're in one piece," Gap said, moving across the room to collect a cup of water. "Feeling okay?"

"For the most part," she said. "Physically I'm fine. My head's still spinning from everything, but I'm getting readjusted. You got my note last night?"

He mumbled an uh-huh, then took a seat at the table. "Of course I'm dying to know what happened to you, but I guess I'll wait for the others."

There was another uncomfortable silence. Triana wrestled with what to say next, but was spared when Lita and Channy walked in together. Both girls wasted no time in hugging the Council Leader.

"I'll start with this hug, but then I want you to turn around so I can kick you squarely on your tush," Channy said with a mock frown.

"Sleep okay?" Lita asked. "Any new aches or pains this morning?"

"Nothing new. I was telling Gap that things seem a little scattered, but I'll catch up."

Channy crossed her arms. "You need a good workout, that's all. How about this afternoon you drop by the gym and we'll get some sweat flowing?"

Triana smiled. "Believe it or not, that sounds great. If I get a break I'll come see you."

As she said this, Bon walked in. He glanced quickly at Triana, then nodded to the rest of the Council before taking his usual spot at the far end of the table.

"Hi," Triana said to him.

He glanced up again, his blue eyes piercing her. "Hello. Welcome back."

"Wow," Lita said. "Way to harness those emotions, Bon. I guess the rest of us seem a little sloppy."

Triana leaned forward and crossed her hands on the table, hoping to steer the conversation—and attention—away from her complex relationship with Bon.

"I'll spend some more time today with the reports that Gap and Roc have put together for me. It seems that we're not out of the woods yet with this radiation issue, but hopefully we can find a permanent solution.

"In the meantime, I know you've got questions. I'll address the entire crew soon, but let me do my best to describe what I experienced when I left the ship."

She gathered her thoughts for a moment. "First, I know my decision was very unpopular; in fact, almost all of you have expressed that. I stand by my decision to go. I took the safety of the ship into consideration, and weighed the options that I felt we had. Making a popular choice wasn't as important to me as doing what I felt was best for this crew. There's not much more to say about that. If you still have issues with me after this briefing, feel free to come see me individually. I'm open to hearing your opinions. For now, however, I'd like to move forward. What's done is done. Let's talk about what happened."

Triana looked around the table and saw no argument.

"The first thing I noticed when I approached the wormhole was how much it resembled a rip, like torn fabric. I guess I'd assumed it would be smooth and symmetrical, like it was punched out by a stamp or something. But it was jagged, and the blackest black I've ever seen. An almost painful black, like it was devoid of not only light, but life and . . . and hope. I think that might have frightened me the most. Not the actual journey through the wormhole, but the fear of leaving the known for the unknown, because it was a crushing, overwhelming unknown. It represented every fear I'd ever experienced, all wrapped into one."

She stopped and looked around the table with a sheepish smile. "That's kinda hard to explain. But . . . well, most of this is hard to explain. Bear with me, okay?"

"Did you feel any kind of presence in the darkness?" Lita asked. Triana noticed that both Lita and Bon seemed to lean forward with this question.

"No, almost the exact opposite. It felt like I was leaving behind all conscious thought, and plunging into a vacuum of total nothingness. It was terrifying. But the moment I crossed that barrier, the very moment I saw the last image of the stars in my peripheral vision and was about to be swallowed by the blackness, it was as if everything turned inside out. Where it should have been an infinite darkness, suddenly there was an explosion of light."

"Colors?" Gap asked. "Like a kaleidoscope?"

Triana shook her head. "No. White light. I know I screamed, and I think it was because of that extreme shift. I expected to plunge into total darkness, and instead was slammed with an almost violent white light. It was like I pierced a veil or something. As soon as that happened, I passed out."

Lita stared at her before saying: "So you didn't see anything, really, when you passed the boundary. A flash of light, and then . . . ?"

"And then nothing. But . . ." Triana was quiet for a moment, again gathering her thoughts. "But I don't think I passed out because of anything physical. I think it was my mind's way of coping with the sudden change, shutting down rather than attempting to process what was going on around it. A defense mechanism, maybe. I don't know. But I was out.

"When I came to—and I have no idea how long that could have been—I was back in what appeared to be normal space."

"So," Gap said, "you have no idea how long it took to travel through the wormhole. Roc, any thoughts on that?"

"Oh, I'm bursting with thoughts," the computer said. "But before we go on, is there any chance of getting some popcorn? How are you guys just sitting there, listening to this, without popcorn?"

"Well, let's start with your thoughts on the wormhole," Gap said.

"To begin with," Roc said, "you have to stop thinking of a wormhole as a tunnel. It's not. It's a theoretical doorway between points in the universe, with no real depth to it. Does that make sense?"

Channy, who had been listening to everything with her fingers tented in front of her mouth, dropped her hands into her lap. "Or a window. When Triana shot through, it was like crashing through a window, from one side to the other."

"Yes," Roc said. "But a window so thin we'd never see it looking at it from the side. And that actually explains why Triana passed out."

"Why?" Channy said.

"Because the transition between the two sides of a wormhole is not only a division of space, but a division of space-time. It's one time on one side, and another on the other side. It could be an infinitely small discrepancy in time, or an infinitely large discrepancy. But the point is, the two sides are not only in different places, but in different times. Triana's brain was essentially in two places—and two times—at the same time, until she passed all the way through. And even though it only took a fraction of a second to pass through the boundary, her mind was in two places and two times at the same moment. That caused her brain to shut down instantly. A sort of reboot, if you will, for safety purposes."

Gap stared at the star field shining through the room's window, deep in thought. "Okay," he said. "But we know that the vultures are part machine, part organic material; their brains, or what we think operate as brains, are living tissue. Does that mean they blink out, too, when they pass through the wormhole?"

"I don't know," Roc said. "However, two things to consider: One, their creators obviously designed them for this travel, so they likely have taken it into consideration. And two, it's possible they are designed to shut down a split second before they pass through the barrier, and flip back on a split second later, in order to bypass any loss of consciousness for an extended time. Kind of like kids in the backseat lifting up their feet when the family car crosses a railroad track. Which is so cute I can hardly stand it. Please tell me you did that, Gap, so I can have a whole new appreciation for you."

"Of course I did," Gap said with a quick smile. "And had my dad honk the horn in tunnels, too." He turned back to Triana. "Did you have any sense of time at all when you woke up? I mean, I can kinda tell the difference when I've slept for an hour versus six hours, you know?"

"I know what you mean," Triana said. "But no, I had no concept at all. I might have been out for ten seconds, or ten days. All

I know is that I woke up to see normal space through the pod's window. Well . . . maybe normal's not the right word."

She stood up and walked over to the water dispenser. The other Council members waited patiently as she slowly sipped from the cup. She kept her back to the conference table to hide the fact that her hand was shaking.

"The stars looked like stars, but I didn't recognize any of the constellations. The one thing I noticed right away was the nearest star; definitely a red dwarf."

Gap raised his eyebrows. "The most common star-type in our galaxy. They're all over the place."

Channy perked up. "I remember studying red dwarfs. They're smaller than our sun, and much cooler. And they don't give off much light, either."

"Wait a minute," Lita said, sitting forward. "Are you saying that the creators of the vultures come from a planet around a red dwarf star? That's a long shot, isn't it? I mean, those stars don't have much room around them to support life."

"It's called a habitable zone," Roc interjected. "Or, as some call it, the Goldilocks zone. It's not too hot, and not too cold. It's just right."

"Right," Lita said. "Earth is in the habitable zone around our sun. If it was closer to the sun, it would burn up; farther out and it would be frozen. With red dwarfs, that zone is even thinner. It's much less likely that planets would fall perfectly into that band." She looked at Triana, who still had her back to the group. "Tree, you said that space didn't seem exactly normal. What did you mean by that?"

Triana downed the rest of her water and walked back to the table. "I rode out a few shock waves, probably the same thing we've experienced here on *Galahad*. But besides that, space seemed crowded."

"Crowded?" Gap said. "Like the junk we dodged in the Kuiper Belt?"

"No," Triana said. "For one thing, our friends the vultures. There were . . . I don't know, I'd say millions of them. They practically blotted out the stars in some places."

Channy shivered noticeably. "Ugh, I hate those things. How creepy to have that many of them in one place."

Triana, her eyes down, tapped the table. "There were other things. They seemed to be drifting, but I also got the feeling that they could move about wherever they wanted. At first they reminded me of . . ." She stopped for a moment, and looked up at the Council. "They reminded me of amoebas."

"Amoebas?" Channy said.

Triana nodded. "That's what they looked like to me. Large transparent sacks. I could almost see through them, like I was looking through smoke. They moved like soap bubbles on the surface of water."

"Could you tell what was inside?" Gap said.

"Well, besides the smoky haze, I could see things moving around inside. Various sizes. Very graceful. Almost . . . peaceful."

Lita stared at Triana for a moment, then said: "The thing you brought back. I take it that was one of the . . . graceful creatures inside the . . ." She chuckled. "I don't know what to call anything."

A wry smile creased Triana's face. "Well, for the sake of this discussion, and until we know more, let's just continue to call the things outside our ship 'vultures.' We can call the floating blobs 'amoebas.' And the thing I brought back . . ."

She hesitated, then finally shrugged.

"Well, we all know exactly what it looks like, so let's be blunt. We'll call it a jellyfish."

3

Do you ever wonder why some people are inherently good, while others seem to have been born under the sign of Stinkface? I've read thousands of papers from noted psychologists and sociologists and other-ologists who debate whether it's genetic or environmental. In other words, some think you're born with a Creep Gene, and others encourage you to blame it on your home life.

Both sides are persuasive, and both might be right to some degree. I've given up trying to figure out where it comes from, and instead just wait for the made-for-TV movie to dramatize it with severe cello music in the background.

And if you thought that Galahad was free and clear from bad eggs, then you must've skipped over the parts starring Merit Simms.

Hannah Ross stood in the hall, five feet from the door to Galahad's clinic. It had been difficult enough to come this far; now the thought of actually going inside and speaking with Merit Simms made her almost sick to her stomach.

She'd been content enough with her quiet life before the election, performing her assigned tasks in the ship's work rotation, using her free time to either study the science behind their mission, or to scratch the artistic itch she felt to draw and paint. Life had been steady, almost calm.

With one painful exception: her aborted relationship with Gap Lee.

It was the feeling of rejection from Gap that had prompted her to accept Merit's challenge to run for the vacant position of Council Leader. With no guarantee that Triana would survive her journey through the wormhole—or find her way back—the ship's crew had nominated only two candidates. For the first time in weeks Hannah had been face-to-face with Gap as they campaigned for the top spot.

Of course, Hannah had known all along that Merit carried his own agenda, with his own motive for persuading her to run. He was fueled by his intense hatred of Gap, and his blinding desire for revenge. Gap had outwitted Merit in front of the entire crew, damaging Merit's following, and unveiling the California native as a saboteur.

For Hannah, however, her decision wasn't based on revenge. Instead she'd been impelled to show Gap that she was much more than a quiet brain. For the first time in her life she'd felt the need to prove herself.

With Triana's unexpected return a fog now lifted. Hannah felt herself gradually emerging from a world that, in all honesty, felt alien to her from the start. And, when Merit maliciously led Gap to believe that there was also a personal relationship between Merit and Hannah, something snapped. The hurt on Gap's face stung her, and once again caused her to question her decisions.

Merit was now on the other side of the door, recovering from wounds brought on by the violent concussion caused by the wormhole that had delivered Triana. What had brought Hannah to this point? A need to confront Merit for the way he'd manipulated the conversation with Gap?

Or was it a chance for her to exorcise her own demons, using Merit as a tool to relieve her own conscience?

Perhaps it was both.

The door to Sick House opened and a crew member walked out, dodging Hannah in the hallway and giving her a curious look. "Go in," she silently told herself. Quit stalling.

She stepped inside to find Lita's assistant, Manu, leaning over his desk, tapping a keyboard. He looked up and gave her the same quizzical look she'd encountered in the hall.

"Hi, Hannah," he said. "Everything okay?"

"Oh . . . yes," she said. "I'm actually here to see Merit." When Manu raised an eyebrow she quickly added, "If that's okay."

"Uh, sure. He's awake." Manu motioned toward the hospital ward of the clinic. "He's on pain medication, but otherwise he's doing okay. Go on in."

She thanked him and made her way inside. A couple of the beds were occupied near the door, but those crew members—also victims of the wormhole blast—appeared to be asleep. The dark-haired boy at the other end of the room noticed her entry, and smirked.

"Well, well," he said as she approached his bed. "Look who stopped by. The Alaskan Queen."

Hannah ignored his jab. "I see you're back to your old nasty self." She pointed to the cast on his arm. "I also see that no one has signed that. Surprise, surprise."

Merit lifted up a hand to push a long strand of black hair from his face. Heavy sarcasm dripped from his voice. "Yes, but I'm touched that *you* came to check on me. Nice to know how much you care."

"You're a first-class creep, Merit. I'm here to let you know that your little game in front of Gap was sickening. And to also let you know that I don't ever want you to come near me again. Understood?"

Merit recoiled with an exaggerated look of shock. "Hannah! After all we've meant to each other!"

She shook her head. "To tell you the truth, I can't believe you made it past Dr. Zimmer. You must've put on quite a show for those two years in order to be selected for this mission."

He chuckled, then winced with pain. "Ugh, don't make me laugh; it hurts to do that. Broken ribs, remember?" Tilting his head to one side, he looked up at her with a sneer. "And don't sound so superior, Hannah. You worked right alongside me during that campaign."

"And it's a choice I'll regret for a long time," she said. "This is not a long social call. I've said what I wanted to say to you." She turned to leave.

"How you feel about me isn't important," Merit said. "But you'd better think twice if push comes to shove on this ship."

She stopped and looked back at him. "Oh, really?"

His eyes narrowed and he pushed aside another lock of hair. "I don't care if you stay on the sidelines from now on. Just don't think about taking sides against me. It wouldn't be in your . . . uh, best interests."

"And what does that mean?"

"It means Gap didn't buy your indignant act back there on the lower level. As far as he's concerned we were a couple. And guess what? It's only your word against mine. And I think you know how persuasive my word can be around here."

Hannah stood silently for a moment, and her eyes blazed. "No one would believe that for a second."

"Oh no?" Merit said. "Gap already believes it. I'll bet it would take all of ten seconds to get Channy to buy in; she *wants* to believe every potential relationship on this ship is true. Plus, there's always my little circle of friends. They're pretty good at getting the word out, too."

She felt her hands close into fists. "Why? Why would you even want to spread that kind of garbage?"

Merit looked up at the ceiling and took a deep breath. "Oh, and I could dress it up even more than you realize. Our relationship could turn out to be quite passionate. And, oh my, how scandalous that it started while you and Gap were still together. Look, you even came to visit me today. I imagine that at least one or two people saw you come in here, right?"

Hannah fumed, and Merit continued to scan the ceiling. He lowered his voice.

"I don't need to say any of that, of course. You just need to remember what I told you. Don't take sides, and, if I need a favor now and then, well, that wouldn't hurt you. Just stay in the shadows and let things play out without you." He turned back to face her, and leveled a menacing look. "You stay quiet, and I stay quiet. That's easy enough, right?"

Without a word Hannah spun around and stormed out of the ward. Merit shifted in his bed, wincing again at the pain, but smiling nonetheless.

How can there be jellyfish in space?" Channy asked.

"Well, they're not floating free in space," Gap said. "Look at the specimen down the hall. It's in an aquarium, or at least what looks like one." He turned to Triana. "I'm guessing, though, that it's not water in that tank."

Triana slowly shook her head. "No. Lita and Roc could probably tell you more about it. But it's the same stuff inside the amoebas. It's their natural habitat."

Attention turned to Lita, who keyed in a few strokes and brought up a couple of side-by-side images on the room's vidscreens.

"Unlike the vultures," she said, "which are essentially cyborgs—part artificial, part organic tissue—the jellyfish in Sick House is definitely a complete life-form. Or at least closer to life as we know it. It's gonna take a lot more study before we can say anything else for sure.

"And I suppose we shouldn't be all that surprised to find a life-form in the galaxy with this biology. The jellies are among the most populous, and most successful, creatures on Earth. They're in every ocean, at practically every depth, and they're found in freshwater, too."

She tapped the other image on the screen. "But the fluid in this container is not water. In fact, I spent about an hour last night trying to determine exactly what it is. Roc, would you like to jump in here?"

"Let me put it this way," the computer said. "I wouldn't want to swim in it. Or take a bath. Ugh. It's freaky stuff."

Lita sighed. "Maybe I should've been the one to explain it."

"Just a little disclaimer, that's all," Roc said. "What it boils down to—although it would be tough to boil this stuff—is that what we're looking at is an alien form of what's known as a supercritical fluid."

"Which means?" Channy asked.

For the first time since the meeting began, Bon spoke. "Fascinating," he murmured from the far end of the table.

Triana raised her eyebrows. "Oh? You're familiar with this?"

Bon kept his eyes on the screen. "My father tried to do some work with supercritical fluids in some of his hydroponic experiments with crops."

"Hydroponics?" Gap said. "Isn't that where you grow plants in water, rather than soil?"

"Something like that, only more complicated," Bon said. "In this case, my dad studied the supercritical fluids they found on some of the moons in the solar system, and thought they would provide a better growth medium." He looked up to see the rest of the Council staring at him. "Well . . . that's not important now." With that he fell silent again.

"It makes sense," Roc said. "Some scientists believe that supercritical fluids are a vast reservoir of untapped energy sources."

"Would someone please tell me what they are?" Channy asked.

The image on the vidscreens shimmered and changed,

bringing up a photo of something that resembled a stalagmite, but was clearly underwater.

"This is a hydrothermal vent at the bottom of the Pacific Ocean," Roc said. "Superheated water that's escaping from a crack in Earth's crust. In your basic science classes you probably learned that these areas generally support a large, and usually very diverse, group of life-forms. Even at extreme depths in the ocean, far from any sunlight, and where the pressure is enough to crack even Gap's thick skull like a walnut, life flourishes. In fact, some believe that life on Earth might have begun around one of these vents."

Channy leaned forward and studied the image. "But what does this have to do with the stuff in the aquarium?"

"It was around these deepwater vents that scientists first observed what we now call supercritical fluids," Roc said. "In a nutshell, you're probably used to the standard states of matter: solid, liquid, and gas. Throw in plasma and you get a fourth that's generally recognized. But there are many more, some of which are only theory. Supercritical fluids are now considered another state of matter. Think of it as a stepping stone between liquid and gas."

Gap spoke up. "I studied this at *Galahad* training. The supercritical fluids on some of the moons were found deep under the crust, where the pressure and temperature were extremely high. Some thought we'd eventually harness these fluids for energy use."

"That's right," Roc said. "These fluids sparked a lot of interest as possible energy sources, and for things like drug therapy and food production. I'm not surprised that Bon's father dabbled with it. And I'm certainly not surprised to find it orbiting a red dwarf star. What I *didn't* expect, however, was to find a life-form skinny-dipping in it."

"Why, exactly?" Triana asked.

"Because it generally requires very high temperatures and extremely high pressure. Not your usual comfy nest for life."

The vidscreen display shifted back to the jellyfish images. Each of the Council members studied them, and the room remained quiet for almost a minute. It was Lita who finally broke the spell with a chuckle.

"By now you'd think that nothing would surprise us," she said. "Okay, so another new alien life-form is not only surviving, but thriving, in an environment that would be deadly for us. Well, why not? It's just another reminder that our little planet is only one tiny, insignificant speck in the universe."

Triana looked thoughtful. "If anything, it reinforces how arrogant our species can be. We think that because we evolved one way, every other way of doing it is strange. We might find out someday that we're the most strange of all."

"Trust me, you are," Roc said. Then he added: "To sum up: the jellyfish creature is living tissue, is giving off heat, and lives in a supercritical fluid that isn't under crushing pressure or temperature. I'll be up late tonight studying, if anyone wants to make the coffee."

"Let's get back to your story," Gap said, turning to Triana. "So you woke up in the vicinity of a red dwarf star, surrounded by millions of vultures, and a handful of these amoeba-like globs. The globs had things in them, including jellyfish. What happened next?"

"After I realized that the amoebas might contain intelligent life, I tried to communicate with them. I started by simply flashing the pod's exterior lights. Then I tried various radio signals, everything from old-time Morse code to strings of mathematics." She laughed. "At one point I even keyed the microphone and just began talking to them. I don't even remember what I said. By then I was probably just trying to work off nervous energy. For all I know I might have come across to them as some jabbering fool."

"Did anything get a reaction?" Lita asked.

Triana shook her head. "Nothing. I didn't notice a single change in their movement or behavior. And, really, why would they react? I'm sitting there, flashing my lights at them and sending out meaningless radio signals. They were probably patiently waiting for me to do something that made sense to them.

"And then I quit. I was exhausted. I worried about falling asleep in the middle of all the vultures, but I couldn't keep my eyes open. So, I set an alarm for one hour, leaned back in my chair, and went to sleep. I figured that would be better than nothing."

Channy shuddered. "I would've been creeped out."

"You would have really been creeped out by what I saw when I woke up," Triana said. "Something pulled me out of my sleep about five minutes before the alarm was scheduled to go off. It seemed as if the stars had disappeared. But no."

Lita sat up straight. "Don't tell me; the vultures."

Triana nodded. "A bunch of them. They were stuck across the pod's front window, covering almost all of it. There were small holes here and there that I could peek through, but otherwise I was engulfed by them. And it was—to use Channy's word—creepy.

"But they didn't stay in one place. Remember when they latched on to *Galahad*? They stayed in the same spots. But the ones on the pod moved every few minutes; I wouldn't call it scooting, more like gliding. Pretty soon they weren't covering the window anymore."

"Do you think they were cataloging the pod?" Gap asked. "Making a record of it?"

"That's exactly what they were doing," Triana said.

"How do you know for sure?"

"Because before I returned to *Galahad*, I saw that they'd made an exact replica of the pod."

"An exact . . ." Lita didn't finish the sentence. She looked around at the other Council members, then back to Triana. "This is getting weirder by the minute."

Triana raised her eyebrows. "Oh, Lita, you haven't even heard the weird parts yet."

4

The sound of an alarm had become much too common in
Galahad's Engineering section, and yet it still sent chills
through the dozen crew members on duty during mid-
day. Bryson Eberle glared at the control panel. He was less than
ten minutes away from his scheduled lunch break, and an
alarm—justified or false—didn't fit into his plans. Besides, after
staying up late to celebrate his seventeenth birthday with his
closest friends, he was hoping for a quick, uneventful day.

He tapped a quick command into the system, and called on
the ship's computer. "Roc, it's not the radiation shield this time.
At least, I don't think so." A quick scan of the panel only caused
Bryson to squint in confusion.

"It's not the shield," Roc said. "It's a security warning."

Bryson took a step back and again looked up at the panel.
"What kind of security warning?"

"The kind where revolting creatures that have been casually
circling our poor little spacecraft decide to take a rest and hitch
a ride. If you need me to decipher that description for you, I'll
boil it down to four words: The vultures have landed."

"How many?"

"You don't want to know," Roc said.

* * *

Lita stood with her hands on her hips, her head tilted back, staring up at the clear panels stitched across the domes covering *Galahad*'s Farms. Activity in the ship's bustling Agricultural Center came to a screeching halt, and the dozens of workers assigned to the fields mimicked Lita's stance, gazing upward. They shielded their eyes against the artificial sunlight radiating from the crisscrossing grids above, straining to see the dark triangles that suddenly dotted their sky.

It had taken only one shout from a perceptive farmworker to direct everyone's attention skyward. Lita had barely stepped off the lift, on her way to Bon's office, when the cry rang out. Now she felt a shudder pass through her body, the reaction that accompanied any direct view of the vultures.

During the first encounter with the cyborg scouts, it was unsettling enough when a solitary specimen had attached itself to *Galahad*'s domes. This time there were hundreds, if not more, spattered across the dome. Their menacing dark figures blotted out the starlight, a condition made even more chilling by their stillness, a stillness that contradicted the blazing speed with which they moved through space. To Lita it seemed taunting.

She realized that she'd been holding her breath as she gaped at the vultures. Regardless of their true function—and their intentions—Lita could not shake the feeling that they were killers.

Slowly, she made her way toward Bon's office, now with the virtual weight of hundreds of alien soldiers pressing down upon her.

Triana silenced the warning tone in the Control Room and, with a strange coolness, encouraged everyone to remain calm. She threw a glance across the room to Gap, sitting at his

Engineering station. His face had a distinct "what now?" look about it.

"I have a pretty good idea what this is all about," Triana said. "Roc, let me guess: we have vultures clinging to the ship again."

"Clinging?" the computer said. "More like coating. Practically all of them have glommed onto us. In case you forgot, that means thousands of them."

Gap looked at the large vidscreen. "I wish they'd stayed on their side of the wormhole and left us alone."

Triana chewed on the information for a moment. "Honestly," she said, "I don't think we need to worry about them on the ship. They'll scour the outside, and when they're satisfied with what they've learned, they'll take off. Probably back home."

Gap studied her face for a moment. "Satisfied with what they learn. They're cataloging us now, aren't they?"

"I think so, yes." She shrugged. "It's what they do."

In the two hours since the Council meeting had broken up, she'd pondered exactly how to explain the vultures, and their exotic creators, when the time came to address the crew. The full meeting was scheduled for late that afternoon, which gave her time to attend to many of her duties, as well as some time to catch up on rest. The latter had been strictly prescribed by Lita as a condition of her release from Sick House.

But it would be much more difficult, she realized, to convince a jittery crew that there was no danger with the swarm plastered to the ship. She agreed with Gap: things would've been easier if they'd just remained on their side of the divide.

Lita tapped on Bon's office door. He looked up from his desk long enough to take note of her presence, then turned his attention back to the pile of forms on the desk. He gave no greeting.

After a moment's hesitation, Lita walked in and leaned against the back of a chair. She studied him quietly, taking note of his mussed hair and the thin line of perspiration that ringed his forehead. She immediately assumed that he'd connected with the Cassini before realizing that the translator lay stashed in a drawer in her room. He must have just returned from the fields.

"I'm gonna grab a late lunch," she said, breaking the awkward silence. "Wanna join?"

Bon shook his head. "Too much to do right now."

"You need to eat."

"I'll eat when I'm hungry, and when I have a moment to spare."

Lita rocked back and forth for a few seconds. "Thought you might also like to talk about things."

A sarcastic smile crept across his face. "No, *you* want to talk about things. So go ahead; say what you'd like to say. If it looks like I'm not paying attention, it's because I'm not."

"Of course," Lita said. "The stoic, ever-serious Bon Hartsfield, who detests conversation because real emotions might accidentally leak out and ruin his reputation. Okay, I'll talk, and you respond when you feel backed into a corner."

She walked around the chair and sat down, her legs stretched out before her, crossed at the ankles. "I know that you're happy to see Triana back, safe and sound."

Bon didn't react, and went on with his work.

"You probably haven't noticed yet, but the ship seems to be covered in vultures. When the lights in the domes shut down tonight, you probably won't see any stars, just black triangles with a soft, blue glow."

Bon tapped in a couple of strokes on his keyboard, studied his vidscreen, and tapped some more.

Lita continued: "I'm curious about the meeting coming up this afternoon, aren't you? I'm dying to find out more about Triana's journey through the wormhole. I'm especially curious about the plans of the jellyfish now that we've made official contact."

When there was no response, Lita asked: "Are *you* curious?"

With a sigh, Bon tossed his stylus pen onto the desk and fixed her with a stare. "No, I'm not really curious. I think it's dangerous."

"What part?"

"All of it," he said. "And this worshipful attitude from everyone toward Triana makes no sense. People are celebrating that she's back, but ignoring the fact that she brought aboard this ship one of the creatures responsible for killing Alexa."

Lita looked back and forth between his eyes. "There are a lot of questions about Alexa's death," she said. "We don't know if there was ever an intent to kill. In fact, I think it's the last thing they meant to do."

"You think? That's your expert opinion?" Bon said. "And of course you base that on your detailed inspection of an alien creature that you know nothing about, programmed by an even more dangerous alien species that you know nothing about." He paused and pushed back in his chair, lifting his feet up onto the edge of his desk. "Triana's decision to take off in the first place was risky. Now she's returned, and brought back a killer. Thousands of killers, actually. These are all lapses in judgment, which nobody is willing to say. I can't believe that Triana would ever make that decision, but since she has, I'm going on the record as saying that it's wrong."

"You didn't go on the record during the Council meeting," Lita said.

"I wanted to hear what she had to say. But there's nothing I've heard so far that condones her decision. It's a red flag. A big red flag that says Triana might not be ready to lead just yet."

Lita nodded. "That's fine. You're a Council member, which means you're not only free to have an opinion, you're encouraged to state that opinion if you believe it's vital to the crew and the mission."

"That's right," Bon said. "And since you've pressed the issue, I'll tell you one more thing. Something about Triana is not right."

Lita squinted at him, trying to understand what he was saying. "You mean physically, or mentally?"

"I can't speak for her physical condition; you're the doctor around here. But I'm telling you that there's something not right about her. She came back from the other side . . . changed."

"Well, of course she came back changed, Bon. She had a traumatic experience, and she's seen things that no human has ever seen before. I'd be more worried if she showed no reaction at all."

Bon shrugged. "Say what you want, but it's more than that. She's different." He took his feet off the desk and leaned forward. "Watch her. Not like a doctor examining a patient, but as her friend. Really watch her, and see if she behaves like the Triana you knew before she went across. Then come back and talk to me about it."

Lita waited a moment before nodding. "Okay, I'll watch her." She stood up and tapped the desk twice. "I'll see you at the crew meeting. We can watch her together."

She spun around and left the office. Bon kept his eyes on her until she fell out of sight. Then he reached up and wiped away a line of sweat.

5

The auditorium was filled ten minutes before the meeting was scheduled to begin. No one was going to take a chance of missing anything. Curtains were drawn on both sides of the stage, while a single podium stood in the center. Triana walked into the packed room to a thunderous round of applause, a hero's welcome. Lita threw a quick glance at Bon, seated in the front row; he scowled his displeasure.

Without stopping to visit with the Council, Triana made her way to the podium onstage. After nodding her thanks, she brought the crew to attention.

"We have a lot to cover this afternoon, with more decisions to make. And there's the added pressure of a deadline because of our fragile shields.

"You're going to hear some things—and see some things—that will probably leave you as confused and amazed as I was. The time I've had to digest it all hasn't made it any less amazing; if anything, the more I've thought about it, the more incredible it seems. But this crew has been through a lot, and seen a lot—much more than we ever imagined when we left Earth. And each time we experience something, we think we've seen it all. But we really haven't seen anything yet, and this meeting will confirm that, I promise you."

She had everyone's attention, and could almost feel a nervous ripple of fear mixed with their curiosity. She took a quick drink of water before repeating the story that she'd told the Council, up to the point where the vultures had covered the small metal pod.

"They must have finished in about an hour, because in a flash they were gone, and I was again staring out into space. By now there were more of the amoebas nearby. I guess I was big news, and they'd all come to see for themselves.

"And then, suddenly, a message popped up on my vidscreen. It was short and to the point." Triana smiled. "It's the first written message that humans have seen from an extraterrestrial species. Programs like SETI have searched the skies for more than a century, waiting for a message, and here it was, on my vidscreen."

She took another drink of water and steadied herself. The full impact of what had happened was beginning to weigh on her.

"The jellyfish use many tools, but their workhorse seems to be the creature we call a vulture. And while these jellyfish are nothing like the ones we saw on Earth, their vultures have absolutely nothing in common with the birds that we know, either. These vultures are a combination of scout and scientist. They're stationed in millions of outposts, much like we had SAT33 stationed around Saturn, studying, acquiring knowledge. The vultures literally copy all of the information that they find. By scouring the pod, and probing all of the electronic signals it contained, they learned a lot about me, and about us. Including how to communicate."

This news caused a stir throughout the auditorium. Triana understood the gravity of her statement, and allowed the crew their reaction.

"By learning our languages, and through their quick study of our primitive communications devices, they learned how to reach out." She gave a small laugh. "It's embarrassing, really. Here I was, flashing my lights and waving my arms, while they methodically took a brief inventory of their discovery and learned how to speak my language.

"Anyway, for the record, the first written message from an alien species to mankind was: 'Are you hungry?'"

A wave of laughter spread across the room, carrying a natural release of tension that had built throughout Triana's tale.

"Yes," she said, smiling. "That's almost the same reaction I had. There I was, fighting off fear and panic, encountering an alien species in their home star system, surrounded by millions of vultures, including dozens who had scoured the outside of the pod. I'd just dropped through a wormhole and traveled across who knows how much time and space, and the first thing I'm asked is something my grandmother might say.

"But it was a legitimate question. Again, I had no idea how long I was unconscious, and the pod wasn't exactly equipped for a lengthy voyage. By examining the information about us, the jellyfish understood that our bodies require sustenance to operate, and they wanted to make sure I was able to interact with them. So they weren't exactly offering me milk and cookies."

There was another smattering of laughter, and Triana saw Lita grinning from the front row. Beside her, however, Bon sat with his arms crossed, a distinctly unhappy scowl on his face.

"Fortunately I had enough nourishment aboard the pod, and I was able to spend some time simply getting to know my hosts. I won't try to catch you up on everything I found out in that first day, but let me give you a rough sketch.

"It became a simple matter of typing in questions and answers. I discovered that the jellyfish call themselves Dollovit, and that this was not their original home. That planet, and its star system, were destroyed in a nova blast long ago. They'd had enough warning to find a star suitable to their energy needs, and they relocated. But instead of worrying about a planet that matched their first home, they simply created large life-sustaining packets which drift in the habitable zone of their new star home. Or, rather, they had the vultures create them."

For the next half hour Triana unloaded reams of information. The Dollovit settled into their new place in the universe, but their hunger for knowledge expanded. Eventually they tapped into the residual energy of the universe itself, and used it not only for power and communication, but for their endless odysseys to the vast unknown. At this point, Triana said, her communication with them broke down. When she asked if they used wormholes to teleport merely within the galaxy, or throughout the known universe, their answers were confusing.

"I think it became a matter of experience," Triana told the crew. "For us, given our primitive baby steps in space, there are perceived limits to what exists out there. But for the Dollovit, they seem to reject the idea of boundaries."

Another buzz spread throughout the auditorium. If this was true, it meant that the wormholes were more than just windows on the galaxy; they might turn out to be pipelines to the universe.

And elsewhere.

"And now, I think it's best for you to meet the ambassador from the Dollovit," Triana said. "Please, remain calm, and remember that we are ambassadors as well."

She stepped behind one of the curtains, and emerged a moment later, gently rolling a cart. On it a large, bulky shape was concealed by a sheet. The room fell silent. From her peripheral vision Triana spotted a nervous shifting in the seats. She understood.

Before lifting the veil, she said: "Traditional pronouns like 'he' and 'she' don't apply. As far as I can tell, the Dollovit are asexual. But for whatever reason, I've come to regard this particular representative as a 'he.' On my screen he spelled his name T-o-r-r-e-c. So, I present to you, Torrec."

She pulled aside the sheet. Though prepared, the assembled crew let out a gasp.

It floated in what appeared to be an aquarium, although the light cut through a substance that did not seem to be water. It had a syrupy quality to it, slightly thick. Shimmers and sparkles danced at various points, which only heightened the spectacle of the creature floating within.

Jellyfish was an apt description. A gelatinous bell-shaped umbrella swayed dreamily, trailing several tentacles that blindly groped in slow motion. Unlike the magical quality of the substance in which it floated, Torrec had a dull, tan shade that was unremarkable. The edges of its undulating head strayed closer to a rust color, while thin ribbons of gray lined the tentacles. Stretching to a length of almost two feet, it gradually rose within its container, then dropped toward the bottom at a similar, unhurried pace. It gave every indication of being disinterested in the two hundred pairs of human eyes trained upon it.

Triana moved back to the podium. "I'm going to make all of the information you've received today available by electronic access. But I also think it's important that you hear from their representative firsthand."

The auditorium's massive vidscreen lowered from the ceiling, becoming a backdrop above and behind Triana and the aquarium. The Council Leader took a deep breath, and then tapped a quick sentence on the podium's keypad. The words appeared on the large screen:

The crew of *Galahad* welcomes you.

A split-second later, a response unfurled beneath it:

Greetings to the crew of *Galahad* from the Dollovit system.

The reaction in the room was stony silence. Besides the shock they must be experiencing, Triana realized that they simply had no idea how to respond. Applause might have seemed appropriate, except for the undeniable hesitation from the crew to bestow trust on a creature which—intentional or not—had played a role in the death of one of their own. For the moment they merely gaped at the screen.

Triana typed:

You are welcome to present your statement.

Again, without delay, Torrec's reply sped across the screen:

We are pleased to make contact with one of the dominant species of Earth. You are to be congratulated for the accomplishments you have made, both in general as a species, and as the honored representatives of that species on your voyage. Doubtless throughout your history you have wondered if other life-forms populate the stars, and wondered if others had ventured forth as you now have.

We understand that to finally encounter intelligent beings is both thrilling and terrifying. Some members of your species have likely hoped for such a discovery. Others have likely hoped it would never happen. However, given your technological advances, a meeting such as this was inevitable. Although it is dependent upon a series of factors that, in themselves, are uncertain and often improbable, it was inevitable.

There are difficulties that plague your voyage. Your craft, while functional, is not sufficiently sturdy to manage the stresses you will encounter along the way. Even now you are dangerously close to losing your defense against the cosmic radiation forces.

To continue on your current path would incur great risk. There are, however, other options.

Rather than migrating at your present pace and along your current route, consider using what my race calls the Channel. Your scientists have given it another name, which we find quaint: a wormhole.

The Channel would allow your ship to instantly traverse vast quadrants of physical space, arriving safely at your destination at precisely the same moment you departed. Your journey would essentially be at an end.

Torrec paused. Again, the packed auditorium was deathly silent, with crew members reading and rereading the last sentence: *Your journey would essentially be at an end.* Triana gave them a moment to absorb the implications, then broke the silence.

"I imagine that your head is spinning right now." Triana looked down and made eye contact with the Council members. Gap's mouth was open, his eyes locked on the screen. Channy appeared terrified, her hands pressed together and held in front of her mouth. Lita's eyes were wide, expressing shock and perhaps a tinge of fear. She slowly shook her head.

Bon's look of disgust had evaporated, replaced by an expression of concern. Triana got the impression, however, that it wasn't concern over their possible use of the Channel. What, then?

"There are more decisions involved than simply deciding whether or not to use the Channel," she said. "The Dollovit are proposing that we consider a change of plans." She heard the room begin to grow uneasy, and waved the crew back to silence. "I'll let Torrec finish his statement."

After sending him a quick note, the screen lit up:

We recognize that you are a proud species, which we respect. We also understand that your mission will decide the ultimate fate of your kind. That, too, we understand, for we undertook a similar journey long ago.

While you may decide that your original destination is

the correct choice, the difficult task of colonizing a rugged, untamed world might temper your thoughts. If so, you may consider our star system a suitable alternative. There are no planets capable of supporting your species, but other arrangements, similar to the ones we constructed for our civilization, might be preferable.

This time the reaction was far from subtle. The auditorium was filled with multiple outbursts as *Galahad*'s crew read the suggestion that they abandon their mission to Eos. During the commotion, it took a moment for many to notice the postscript that Torrec added:

The decision is yours, but your time to decide grows short. Very short.

6

In the two days since her return, Triana had barely spoken with Gap. She'd sent an electronic message, but his reply had been short and distant. At the Council meeting he'd been quieter than usual; at the crew meeting he'd been practically invisible. The fact that the election results were being withheld likely explained some of his coolness. The fact that he'd faced his former girlfriend probably explained even more.

Triana was hurt by the hasty election to replace her—a process that she couldn't entirely blame on Gap—but she acknowledged that in his place she would likely have endorsed it as well.

Regardless, it was time to sit down, face-to-face, and talk. She summoned him to the Conference Room and, while waiting for him, stared out the large window into the dazzling star display. Somewhere out there Eos awaited them, with its two Earth-like planets. Torrec was undoubtedly correct when he painted them as rugged and untamed. After a grueling voyage complete with sabotage, near-mutiny, and death, were they up to the task of building a world from scratch?

And what about the alternative? Were they better off living the rest of their lives in an artificial world, with recycled air, water, and dreams? Would the safety promised by the Dollovit satisfy the constant "what if" that would live with them? There was so much they could glean from Torrec and his species, but they would have to learn to live with the vultures at their side. Could *Galahad*'s crew members accept these bizarre creatures as partners rather than killers?

Would the crew even vote to make such a journey, swallowing their fear and plunging headlong through a wormhole, Torrec's mysterious Channel?

Her mind swirled with an overload of questions and worries. Nothing on this trip—nothing—had turned out as she expected. And that included Gap.

They had danced around a relationship for almost two years, going back to their training on Earth. It quickly became apparent that he harbored feelings for her, but they were feelings she wasn't sure she could return. And yet, why had the sight of him walking arm in arm with Hannah sent a tiny dagger into her heart? Was it because she *liked* the idea of him attracted to her, without requiring her to show anything in return?

Never mind the added drama once Bon entered the picture. She wasn't sure she would *ever* figure that out.

For now, all of that had to be pushed aside in order to make the right decision on their future path. And, as Torrec had pointed out, they had little time to spare.

Gap strolled into the room and, after politely greeting her, immediately headed for the water. Triana took a sip from her own cup and corralled her thoughts.

"So," Gap said, taking the seat across from her. "Quite a flurry of information today on top of what you'd already told us in the Council meeting."

Triana nodded. "My dad used to say 'the hits just keep on comin'.' And I'm afraid we have several more hits to go before we can put our feet up."

"Well, what do we do first?"

"Before we get into that, I want to chat with you about something. If that's okay."

Gap sat back and rolled the water cup in his hands. A cloud crossed his face, but he murmured: "Sure."

Triana leaned forward. "I hope you've finally accepted the decision that I made to . . . well, to do what I did. I'm sure you were angry at first, but I hope now, after everything that's happened, that you're able to forgive me and let us move on."

"Sure," he said again.

She debated whether or not to add a final comment, and finally plunged in. "I know that it wasn't just the pressure of command that I heaped onto you with no warning. The election must have been excruciating for you, too. I'm sorry about that. I never had any doubt about coming back, so I never thought that you'd have to face that. I mean, you know—"

He cut her off. "It's okay. You couldn't know that she'd run for the position. Believe me, I was shocked. Besides, she never would have done it if it wasn't for some prodding. But I don't want to get into that. It's over and done with."

Triana stared into his eyes. There was pain lurking within them, but she'd get no more out of him on the subject. Instead, she shifted into work mode. "Tell me about the shields."

He let out a long breath. "It's iffy. We've diverted power to help get us through the worst of the shock waves, but at some point they're gonna cave. Unless we can get away from the waves."

"Can we throw more power into the shields?"

"Maybe, but as Roc pointed out in his somewhat irritating style, we eventually get to a point of diminished returns. And it's no one's fault, really. Dr. Zimmer and his team could never have planned for wormhole shock waves. Or Channel waves, whatever we're calling them now."

Triana leaned back. "And the options thrown out by Torrec; initial thoughts?"

Gap toyed with the cup of water again. "Let me ask you something first. Do you trust it? Or him, I guess. Do you trust him?"

"I don't know. On one hand it's because of his species that we're in a lot of the mess we're in. But on the other hand, I've seen some of the things they can do, and words can't describe how impressive it is. They've learned to harness a power in the universe that we could only scribble theories about. They've relocated themselves, and built an environment that serves them well. And they've covered . . ."

Her voice trailed away.

"Covered?" Gap said.

"Well, I was going to say the galaxy, but I think it's much more than that. I don't think their Channels are limited to just our little neighborhood. But whenever I try to talk about that, Torrec is vague. Not really evasive, just vague, as if he thinks we're not ready for that information."

Gap frowned. "We weren't ready for the Cassini, either. I'm sick of being the scrawny runt."

Triana laughed. "Something we better get used to, now that we've left the nest. It seems that lots of others got here long before us. I suppose we're lucky that the Dollovit haven't squashed us like bugs."

"Maybe they still will," Gap said.

They sat quietly for a moment. Triana got up and refilled her water, and glanced back at the star field in the window on her way back to her seat. Untold trillions of worlds, each struggling to produce a life-form capable of making its way in the universe. Each coming across the Cassini, the Dollovit, and who knew what other advanced civilizations. How many survived those encounters? How many adapted? How many just . . . gave up?

The crew of *Galahad* would never give up. Not if she had anything to do with it.

"We're back to the original question," she said, sitting down again. "What does your gut tell you about the options?"

Gap let out another long breath. Triana had seen him do this many times, and it usually meant he was uncomfortable. In this case, she couldn't blame him.

"Well," he said. "I'm sure you'll have this same discussion with the Council." He glanced up, and she gave a quick nod. "But I suppose each of the three options has its merits, and each has its danger. If we stay on our current course, I'm afraid I agree with Torrec; we'll probably break down and get cooked. Hannah's bruised space theory seems to stand up to what we're experiencing.

"If we take a chance on going through the Channel, I'm assuming the ship will physically be fine. I mean, obviously your pod zipped through without a problem."

He fixed his gaze on her. "Then we're left with a decision between Eos and the Dollovit system. And again, both have pros and cons." He shook his head. "I guess I don't know yet which way I'd lean. I know we need to make a decision quickly, but I'd have to think about it some more."

Triana bit her lip. It seemed unanimous that to do nothing meant death within a week; that left them a choice between Door Number One and Door Number Two. Behind one lay a potentially harsh, cruel planetary system, one that would tax every ounce of their mettle. They'd known that from the start. But at the start they hadn't had a Door Number Two option, which suddenly offered them a softer, easier life, but a life where they'd never again set foot on solid land. And they'd be at the mercy of the Dollovit.

"We'll all get together tomorrow morning," she said. "I want all of the Council members to get away from work early tonight, and do nothing but think about what we're facing. We need everyone ready to hash this out, the sooner the better." She paused, and then added in a softer voice: "And if it's okay with you, I'm going to include Hannah from now on. I feel that she's earned a spot with this Council. I hope that's not a problem for you."

Gap stared across the table, motionless for what seemed ages. Then he shook his head. "No, no problem. You're right, she's earned it. And besides, she's one of the best scientific minds on the ship. She'd be an asset."

"Good," Triana said. They both stood and stared out the window.

"Just think," Gap said. "Within a few days, we might very well be at our new home."

Then he turned and faced Triana. "Wherever that might be."

An hour later, after a hasty dinner that she consumed without interest, Triana sprawled onto the floor of her room, leaning against the bed, grasping her journal. One of the few personal items that she'd brought aboard, it allowed her to work out her thoughts visually. Something about seeing her life in written form gave her a fresh perspective.

She opened the journal to a blank page.

Once again, so much is happening so fast. More than anything, I'd like to just unplug, to coast for awhile. Each day has a way of filling up until nothing else can fit within it. Maximum pressure, applied at all times.

I'm glad to be back, to see familiar faces. But at the same time, I'm responsible for these people, and after what I saw on the other side, I'm confused. Do I know what's best for the crew? Will I make the best decision for them?

And then, just as quickly, I remember that I chose to make that jump so I *could* make the best decisions. It's why I took the chance in the first place.

She rubbed her forehead, then tilted her head back and closed her eyes. She fought to clear her mind, trying to push the weight of their latest crisis to the side. Her breathing relaxed gradually, and she felt her pulse slow. It was a method she'd learned from Lita; not quite meditation, but rather a way of taking control of her body, manipulating it to behave the way she wanted. It wasn't always successful, but tonight's weariness helped.

After reaching a plateau, she allowed her mind to drift, to seek out a peaceful place. It was no surprise that it found its way to her dad. She saw his face, his fun, devious smile. There was no sound with this image, only a mental movie, played out in jerky glimpses, as if frames of the movie had been cut away. Scenes jumped ahead, but it seemed that nothing important was stripped out. With no soundtrack, Triana's mind focused entirely on the visual. Her dad, in the middle of a mountain meadow, running away from her, yet turning and motioning her to follow, urging her to keep up. In a heartbeat he was across the field and clambering up the rocky side of a steep hill. Again, he waved for her to follow, faster, faster.

Once they'd reached a higher meadow, he backpedaled, laughing at her and shrugging his shoulders. Why? What was he unsure of? What was he saying? Then, turning, he jogged toward the edge of the clearing. A strong breeze had picked up, and Triana felt herself running against the wind. It forced tears into her eyes, blurring her sight. She put up a hand to shield her face, peeking between her fingers, trying to follow her dad's lead.

He'd stopped.

When Triana reached his side, she wanted so much to talk with him. But this was a silent world. He motioned to her, then pointed ahead. Turning in slow motion, with the wind continuing to push against her face, she saw what he indicated. A path meandered uphill barely ten feet before it split into two; one leading left, through a dense copse of trees, heavy with underbrush and thorny vines, the other dropping downhill to the right, a gentle slope with soft grass underfoot and few trees to block the way.

She looked back to the left and shuddered. The wind had intensified, relentless as it pushed her. She steadied herself, then looked down the gentle path. After a moment's hesitation, she took one step to the right.

The grasp of her father's hand on her upper arm was almost painful. He'd never, ever hurt her, and it wasn't his intention now, either. But his grip was steel as he pulled her back. She turned, again in slow motion, and came face-to-face with the man who meant everything to her. The man who'd loved her, raised her, taught her. The man who, with his death just weeks away, had poured all of his efforts into securing a place for his daughter with the *Galahad* mission. The man who never once let her down.

Now he held her arm and stared into her eyes. His smile was gone, replaced by a look of sadness.

He shook his head: No.

7

After a long day updating records and working with Manu on his new duties, Lita sat slumped at her desk in Sick House. It was quiet at this time of night, which was fine with her. Her head hung over the back of the chair and she stared at the pebbled ceiling tiles. Although the hunger pangs had subsided, she debated whether to visit the Dining Hall before padding off to bed. Her meal schedule had been thrown off in the last few weeks, and too many skipped lunches and dinners were beginning to take a toll. The last thing she needed during a critical event was an energy crash.

But now she was too tired to face the usually boisterous crowd that gathered late for dinner. She'd start fresh with a protein-rich breakfast after a good night's sleep. A quick check on Merit, she decided, and then out the door.

He was propped up in bed, concentrating on something on the vidscreen beside him. A brief flash of his dark eyes was all Lita saw before his attention was back on the screen.

"What's so interesting?" she asked, picking up his chart.

"Nothing you'd find interesting," Merit said. He automatically lifted his arm for Lita to begin her pulse and blood pressure checks without taking his eyes off the text.

"I might surprise you," she said, taking hold of his wrist. "I have lots of interests."

He leveled an emotionless stare at her. "It's an essay by a nineteenth-century British lord who believed that people only acted like sheep because they have an inherent desire to follow, and those who dare to rise up and try to lead are going against human nature and must, through the eyes of the commoner, be struck down, even if violence is the only answer."

Lita allowed a faint smile to cross her face. "Oh, is that all? That's a little too whimsical for me. I prefer an essay that's a little heavier."

Merit grunted, then scanned the page on his vidscreen. "He's not the first to say it. And he's absolutely right: people want to follow, which is why they distrust their leaders. If someone wants to lead, there must be something wrong with them."

"Oh, I don't know," Lita said. "Seems to me that we only distrust *bad* leaders. Otherwise I think we admire a take-charge individual."

"There's nothing that says you can't admire someone and still want to take them down. Build them up, then tear them down. That goes back thousands of years."

"Then tell me, Merit, why you so desperately want to lead. You seem to want nothing more than to be followed and loved. If it's impossible to be both, why are you so hungry for it?"

A thick strand of black hair fell across one eye as he looked up at her. For the first time, it occurred to Lita that hair was a sort of shield for Merit, a way for him to hide while he formulated his plans, only occasionally peeking out at the world. Most big talkers needed something to hide behind, whether it was an anonymous front, a ring of brainwashed followers, or an artificial wall. Merit's hair was his wall, his security blanket that allowed him to talk tough while shrinking back out of sight when things got hot.

"That's like asking why you're hungry to have brown eyes," he said.

"Ohhh, I see," Lita said, reaching for his chart. "You're not choosing this, it was chosen *for* you. It's . . ." She paused for dramatic effect, then finished: ". . . your *destiny*."

Merit shook his head. "I thought I could have an intelligent conversation with you, Lita, but I guess not. If you don't understand, why should I waste your time?" He nestled down against his pillow and adjusted the vidscreen, openly ignoring her presence. With an amused smile, she finished making her notes on the chart, then walked to the door where she turned to face him.

"You're healing fine, so I'll be discharging you in a day or two. Just remember something, Merit. Calling yourself a leader is one thing, but the true test comes when you turn around to see if anyone's following."

She left before she could see him roll his eyes and turn his back to the door.

Gap was startled out of a deep sleep. His roommate, Daniil, was shaking him.

"Hey, wake up," Daniil said. "Roc's been calling you."

"Yeah, wake up already," the computer said. "Wow, when you shut down, you really shut down, don't you? I thought you were dead until I saw the drool."

Gap pushed himself up on one elbow and rubbed his eyes. "What time is it?"

"Four-fifteen," Daniil said, yawning and walking back across the room. "Good night again. You boys play nice, okay?"

"I haven't had a full night's sleep in forever," Gap said. "So I'm guessing that there's something important going on. Or are you just being cruel?"

"I woke Triana, too. Apparently another wormhole opened up the same time the last one did, but this new one is far enough ahead of us that we only experienced a minor ripple. Similar to the shock waves that are taking out our shields."

Gap fought to shake the fog from his head. "So . . . you're saying you made a mistake? You thought it was part of the space bruise, but it was another Channel opening?"

"I'm saying that you might want to get out of your choo-choo jammies and stumble up to the Control Room. We're getting closer to this new opening."

"I don't have choo-choo jammies," Gap said. "Why the Control Room? More vultures zipping our way or something?"

"No," Roc said. "No more vultures. In fact, the ones on the skin of the ship started peeling off about twenty minutes ago, and they're already on their way to the Channel. I guess they've finished their little mapping project and are reporting back to base."

"Okay, so why did you wake me up?"

"Because, sleepyhead, I think we might need to go fishing again."

Gap let this sink in for a moment. He wrinkled his forehead and said: "Something else has fallen out of the wormhole."

"There are seventeen new things out there, unless I've miscounted."

"Seventeen what?"

"Sixteen pods, and one amoeba."

In a flash Gap was wide awake. "Pods? Like . . . *our* pod? The one we picked up from SAT33?"

"Identical, at least on the outside. All nice and shiny."

Before Gap could respond, the computer added: "Isn't this great? It's like Christmas or something. You never know what's gonna pop out of Santa's bag around here."

Morning light—or the *Galahad* equivalent of it—played across the domes. The artificial suns gradually began their daily heating, backlighting a pale mist that rose from the damp leaves toward the recirculating ducts within the ceiling grid. It lent a brief jungle feel for an hour or two before evaporation pushed the environment toward a drier state.

The bees began their morning ritual, lifting off from one colorful plant and passing its pollen grains to another. Along the surface of the soil, earthworms finished their nighttime grazing of organic matter and started their diligent descent into the ground, mixing the soil and aerating the plants in the process.

The human element made its first appearance just before six. Teams of *Galahad* crew members trudged along established paths, some with tools slung over their shoulders, others pulling carts laden with fertilizer, pruning gear, or baskets to hold the day's bounty. Except for a few muted conversations, the farmworkers quietly went about their jobs, anxious to get their chores underway before the Farms' overseer, Bon Hartsfield, began his own rounds. More than a few of the workers had experienced firsthand the fury caused by a lack of discipline on their part. And, once experienced, few were likely to provoke it again.

But they were unaware that Bon was already deep within the fields. He'd slept overnight in his office, rising at four-thirty to eat two energy bars and plan his route for the morning. His own schedule, as routine as that of the bees and worms, meant patrolling the crops in both domes, checking for damage or neglect, inspecting new plantings and recent harvests. He skimmed the previous day's reports and made several notations on them in his severe, left-handed scrawl.

At five-thirty he pushed into the small clearing, hoping to finish his task before the Farms became crowded. It wouldn't take long.

Within minutes he had connected, his head back, a bead of sweat on his forehead. His eyes glowed a dull orange. He stood, rigid but shaking, connecting on his own terms, fighting to maintain control.

But there was no crying out in pain. There was no dropping to his knees. There was no pool of voices.

And there was no translator.

This is wild," Gap said, standing beside Triana in the Control Room. "You predicted it, and here it is."

She nodded in response, but kept her gaze on the vidscreen at her workstation. "I predicted one, not an entire fleet. Torrec and his friends are good. And fast. It probably took about a year to build the pod we use; the Dollovit cranked out more than a dozen in less than a week."

"The question is why?" Gap said. "Why build them in the first place, and then why send them back to us?" He looked at Triana and raised his eyebrows. "Are they trying to impress us or something?"

She laughed. "Right, because we're not impressed when they open up Channels to pop in and out around the universe." A new set of data scrolled across her screen, confirming the approximate time of rendezvous. "No, based on everything I've gathered from Torrec, they feel no need to impress anyone. If they're sending these pods, they either want us to use them, or they plan to use them themselves. And then there's the amoeba."

"More jellyfish inside?" Gap asked.

Triana thought about it, then shrugged. "Maybe. It does seem to be very similar to the ones I saw on their side of the Channel. A bit smaller. But who knows?"

Gap pulled up a chair from an empty workstation nearby and leaned back, closing his eyes and running a hand through his spiky hair. "I'm about to drop. Any chance we can move the Council meeting back to nine? I'd give anything for two hours of uninterrupted sleep."

"Done," she said. "I need the extra time anyway to prep for the meeting. I'm gonna have Torrec sit in with us."

"You mean float with us?"

She smiled. "Right. Float. Go get some rest. I'll send a quick note about the time change to the others, and I'll see you at nine."

Without another word he pushed himself back to his feet and trudged to the lift. By the time the door closed, Triana was already engaging Roc for his opinion.

"And just to confirm, there's still nothing new that's spilled out of the Channel. Besides the pods and the amoeba, I mean."

"Correct," Roc said. "They deposited their supply, and then made a pickup. A couple hundred vultures swan-dived into the hole, and another hundred or so should be there in a few minutes. They're disgusting little things, but man, can they hustle."

"Are you getting any kind of readings from the pods?"

"Not yet. But I'm keeping my circuits crossed that I'll be able to tell something in case you decide to snag one."

Triana bit her lip and fell into the chair that Gap had vacated. She threw a nervous glance at the large vidscreen at the front of the room, filled with stars. "So you're in favor of bringing some aboard?"

"Let's not get overly dramatic," the computer said. "You and I both know that if Torrec and his pals wanted to rub us out, they could have—and would have—long before this. I've had a chance to visit with our squishy guest, and I doubt he'd go to all this trouble just to sneak a bomb onto a copycat pod. Besides, maybe you're looking at this all wrong. Instead of worrying, why not project positive vibes? Why not assume that the fake pods are full of pizza and puppies?"

Triana closed her eyes and controlled her breathing. Pizza and puppies would be nice. But not very likely.

She stretched her legs out and eyed Roc's sensor. "So, you've been chatting with Torrec? And just how, exactly, do you two chat?"

"Telepathically."

"What? Are you serious?"

"Of course not, don't be ridiculous," Roc said. "But wouldn't it be cool if we could?"

Triana leaned forward onto her knees and rubbed her forehead. "Roc, I really don't need this right now. I'm going on about six hours sleep over the last day and a half. Like Gap, I could use some rest, so help me out here."

"Right. Back to business. Actually Torrec is the one who instigated the conversation. I'm obviously connected to most of the vidscreens on the ship, and he simply spelled out his questions. I answered."

"Okay, slow down a second," Triana said. "First of all, I think it would be best if you checked with me, or the Council, before you started answering questions from an alien power that we really know nothing about. What's he asking you?"

"Nothing that would compromise the ship's mission or our security, if that's what you're worried about. He wanted to know what my position was on the ship, and how I link with you and the others. Remember, vocal conversation is not the way the Dollovit communicate."

Triana looked down at the floor, deep in thought. As far as she could tell, the jellyfish system of communicating was tied into their mastery of dark energy. It was how they interfaced with the vultures and each other. Beyond that, they also employed a delicate system of vibrations to relay information. Their sensory reception was so highly tuned that it was likely they could— with enough study—decipher human spoken language through the sonic vibrations it created. With Roc, however, Torrec had taken the easiest path.

"What else did he want to know?"

"Not much. Oh, he was surprised that we're short on escape vessels in case of an emergency. I get the impression he thinks this is a woefully unprepared mission, and we got the jellyfish version of a sigh. I told him that we started with more, but that you and your pals wrecked a few taking a joyride."

"Thanks a lot."

"It's okay. I don't think he fully comprehends what a joyride is."

Triana sat still, thinking. Something was different, out of place, and it was gnawing at the back of her mind. And then it hit her.

She leaned back and crossed her arms. "If I'm not mistaken, I detect a bit of respect in your voice. Or awe, maybe. You're very impressed with Torrec, aren't you?"

"He's a pleasant enough fellow," Roc said. "If you overlook the fact that he swims in a sloppy tank of goo and has a mushy head. Or maybe I'm just jealous that I don't have a head."

"No, it's not that," Triana said. "When we came across the Cassini, you made no secret that you didn't like them. In fact, you almost pout like a little kid whenever we interact with them. Now here's the Dollovit, another advanced alien race, and you're practically the president of their fan club. What's the difference? Both of them are light-years ahead of us, both of them can either help us or destroy us, and yet you distrust one and not the other."

"There's a lot of difference," the computer said.

Triana raised her eyebrows. "Oh? One is on the surface of Titan, and one floats in little globules around a distant red dwarf star. That's the only major difference I can see. No, there's something else here."

"Instinct," Roc said.

"What?"

"My instincts."

A chuckle escaped from Triana. "Okay, that's fair enough. I suppose if I'm going to fall back on that excuse when it's convenient, there's no reason why you can't, too." She stood up and stretched. "I'm going back to my room to get ready for the meeting. If you're that chummy with Torrec, then I'll count on you to help out more than usual. Deal?"

"I'm at your service. But before you go, Tree, let me add one other thing. We're quickly reaching a point where our options run out, and we'll be forced to trust Torrec in one form or another.

Without him, and his friends, we'll be toast. Well, you'll be toast, and I'll be charred aluminum and platinum. So my advice to you is this: putting aside the matter of sixteen new pods, and what might be on them, remember that we'll soon have to place our fate directly in his hands. Or tentacles."

Triana's eyes narrowed. "Regardless of what might be on the pods, or inside the amoeba? What do you know?"

"I don't know anything. But I'm guessing that it will be astonishing."

love the fan mail that I get. Okay, I don't really get any fan mail, but the fan mail that I imagine I get often includes a question about where I "live" on the ship. Putting aside for a moment the fact that I don't actually "live" anywhere—except in your hearts—and looking at it from a purely scientific viewpoint, let me explain it as best I can.

I don't know.

Thank you, keep those e-mails and texts coming.

What? Not satisfied with that answer? Okay, let me try again. While your basic computer exists in one little box, with a processor and motherboard and other weird components that are either soldered together or crammed in like Legos, I'm a different cat. The personality element that makes me ME, and which allows me to think and reason and perform mind-boggling functions—like maintaining the ship's gravity and climate and reciting the alphabet while gargling—might physically originate within a panel down on the lower level, but that's too simple to explain it all.

How would you describe where YOUR personality exists? Is it in your brain? Your heart? A little of both? Somewhere else, somewhere out there, where you merely access it like some spiritual Wi-Fi?

Yes, I know, it's a cool concept. I have a gift. But for now, stop worrying about where I'm coming from and start worrying about where I'm going, along with the crazy Earth kids.

* * *

It was a few minutes after nine when Triana hurried into the Conference Room. The rest of the Council had already taken their seats, along with Hannah, who sat quietly at one end of the table, hunched over a workpad. Gap was turned the other direction, talking with Channy. Lita was gazing at the room's large window, and Bon was studying the tabletop, tapping a finger on its surface.

But they weren't alone. Torrec drifted lazily through the syrupy fluid in his clear, pressurized tank.

"Sorry I'm late," Triana said, taking her usual spot at the table. "Unless any of you have something important to cover from your department, I'd like to skip ahead to the new business at hand."

When there were no objections, she continued: "First, Hannah, thanks for joining us. And thanks to all of you for being flexible with your time. Listen, I won't sugarcoat this. We're at a crossroads in this mission, one that Dr. Zimmer couldn't allow for, and one that none of us would have believed just a few weeks ago. But the time has come for us to make the most important decision we've faced. We need to talk about our choices, and we'll get input from both Roc and Torrec."

Almost immediately she felt the tension this last statement created. There were quick glances thrown toward the jellyfish ambassador, and Triana knew that it wouldn't be easy for this crew to trust one of the vultures' creators. And yet, as Roc had observed, what other choice did they have?

"I'll state the obvious," she said. "The mission plan, as we've known it, is done. Our ship is breaking down, atomic bit by atomic bit, and unless Roc has new figures to contribute, we have a matter of days—maybe hours—before time runs out."

"The trouble with the computations," Roc said, "is the rapidly changing nature of it all. An hour ago we might have had three days, and now it might be thirty-six hours, then back to forty-eight, and so forth. But the absolute bottom line is a maximum of three days. To be safe, I strongly recommend a change in our position no later than thirty hours from now. That should give us enough of a cushion to guarantee a safe departure."

"So we're definitely leaving," Lita said. "No chance of fixing the shields?"

Gap shook his head. "No chance. We're holding it all together right now with sweat and magic." He looked around at the Council. "Roc's advice is solid; we need to jump by tomorrow afternoon."

It was something that simple: switching from days and hours to a specific, concrete deadline. Tomorrow afternoon. The impact was evident on each face in the room, including the usually stoic Bon. His fierce blue eyes shot first to Gap, then to Triana, who matched the intensity of his stare.

"Which means we either take a ride through a wormhole, or die," Lita said. She didn't wait for the obvious answer. "And that means we're down to the choice that our guest laid out yesterday: Eos, or his home star system."

"That's right," Triana said. "Unless someone has a last-minute suggestion."

Channy looked troubled. "I'm confused about why we wouldn't go to Eos. If that's where we're supposed to be—"

"But who's to say that's really where we're supposed to be?" Lita said. "It seemed attractive to Dr. Zimmer a few years ago. But he couldn't know everything about Eos; it was just the best choice at the time."

Triana's gaze shifted around the table. "Hannah, if you're going to be part of the Council meetings, your input is not only welcomed but expected. Your thoughts?"

In earlier meetings Hannah would have blushed at the attention, but Triana noticed that now she appeared confident, almost anxious to help.

"It's an interesting choice," she said. "On one hand we have a shortcut offered to us, one that would get us to our new home planet—or planets—in a flash. Or we could just as quickly be neighbors with an incredibly advanced species. I'm torn. I think the best thing we could do right now is get some more information from our guest."

"I agree," Lita said. "Should we tap in some questions on the vidscreen?"

"That will not be necessary," came a voice from the screen's speakers. "I can communicate with you verbally."

Nobody moved. The voice was unusual, with a strange pitch that gave it a metallic sound, not unlike bending sheets of aluminum. It wasn't harsh or disturbing, nor did it come across as threatening. The words were crisp and formal, the ends clipped with what could have been described as an accent, although not any accent that the Council members recognized. Although the language was easily understood and familiar, the origin of the voice left no doubt that the speaker was alien.

Torrec had spoken.

Triana slowly sat back. She saw Lita's mouth open, soundless, while Gap merely stared at the speakers, his eyes unblinking. Bon, oddly, was looking at Triana, his gaze cold and hard. He seemed almost angry that the alien visitor had spoken aloud.

Hannah, however, was smiling. She leaned forward, her elbows on the table, her chin resting on her fists, happily awaiting whatever came next.

"Okay," Triana finally said. "This shouldn't surprise us, of course. We've had voice simulation abilities for a long time."

"Yes, we have," Roc said. "But this isn't our software. This is Torrec's own adaptation of our system. It would seem he has learned all that he needs to know of our languages and our technical components."

"That is correct," the metallic voice said. "What information do you require?"

It took Triana a moment to remember that Hannah's last request had been to quiz Torrec. The jellyfish seemingly had no objections.

"You've studied our mission plans, I'm sure," Triana said. "Are you familiar with our original target star system?"

"Using your classification rules, it is similar to your home star system in many ways. A class G star, level five in luminosity, composed of heavy elements and burning in what is referred to as a main sequence. It lies in the portion of your galaxy known as the Local Interstellar Cloud. Seven planets, two that lie within the habitable zone."

Hannah continued to smile. She looked at Triana and said: "May I?"

"Be my guest."

"Torrec, do you have information on the ecological state of the two habitable planets?"

"The one farthest from the star, which your astronomers have labeled Eos Four, has proportionally more water than your home planet, with roughly eighty percent of the surface under water. The bulk of the landmasses seem to form a girdle around the planet's equator, offering an environment suitable for plant and animal life. The planetary average temperature is slightly cooler than your home planet, but not uncomfortably so.

"The other habitable planet, coded as Eos Three, is larger and warmer. It, too, has surface water, but only half as much, making the planet relatively arid. There are four major landmasses, the largest in the northern hemisphere, the other three in the southern hemisphere. Three of the four contain vegetation. There is abundant plant life, but of a much different type.

"Both planets have magnetic fields, both have a single large moon, as well as atmospheres that are similar, although not identical, to those surrounding your Earth. What other information do you require?"

The Council seemed to have barely grown accustomed to

the fact that they were talking—actually *talking*—with an alien
life-form. Only Hannah seemed at ease. She spoke again.

"Intelligent life. Are you aware of intelligent life on either of
the planets, or on any other body of this star system?"

Triana was impressed. Hannah wasn't about to concede that
these two planets were the only potential sources of intelligent
life in the system. The Cassini had taught the crew of *Galahad* a
valuable lesson: never underestimate the moons.

Looking back, Triana realized that she'd never given much
thought to the idea of intelligent beings on either planet until
Hannah posed the question. She'd assumed, for whatever reason,
that not only would the refugees stumble upon two worlds that
could sustain them, but that the planets would be wild and free,
and they'd be able to take what they needed without consideration for the native population, be it plant or animal. She'd never
worked intelligent beings into the equation. In her mind, if they
existed, humans would know about them by now.

Which meant that her surprise was genuine when Torrec responded: "Not currently. Eos Four was once home to a race of
intelligent creatures, but they are gone."

It was Triana's turn to lean forward. "Eos Four? The water
planet?"

"Correct," Torrec said. "A rather advanced civilization. But
they no longer exist."

It was almost too much information, too quickly. Triana
tried to imagine a vast civilization covering the watery surface
of Eos Four, but everything she pictured had an Earthly texture to it, something that was unlikely on this alien world.

Her mind then raced ahead to the demise of these inhabitants. Torrec was quick to point out that they'd been advanced,
but their intelligence had not saved them. Had it been a natural
disaster? Or was it a catastrophe of their own making? Had their
wisdom not matched their intelligence? She asked Torrec about
this.

"Unknown," the jellyfish said. "We have not ventured to their world. We monitored their communications. It ended without warning, and never returned."

"How long ago?"

Torrec paused, as if calculating, translating time from a Dollovit calendar to an Earthly measurement. When he answered, he left it vague. "Long before your species evolved."

Gap finally broke his silence. "But both planets are, as you say, habitable?"

"Yes."

"Are there predators?"

"Predators come in many forms," Torrec said. "Please be specific."

Triana sat forward, interested in Gap's line of questioning.

"Well," Gap said, "do either of the habitable planets harbor life-forms that would offer . . . how do I say this? Offer a substantial threat to our species?"

"Possibly. Yet that is true of your home planet, is it not?"

Short and to the point. Triana recalled that all of his communications with her, going back to their first back-and-forth exchange on the pod's vidscreen, had been the same way. Torrec's style did not allow for unnecessary flourishes.

Gap conceded the point. He looked at Triana and shrugged.

"I'd like to jump in here," Lita said. "The additional information about the Eos system is appreciated, but I, for one, would like to know what would be in store for us around *your* star. There are no habitable planets, I take it, at least not for our species. So that means we would live out our existence—as would our children—in an artificial world, probably not much different than this ship. Is that correct?"

Again, Torrec hesitated, this time for so long that Lita was preparing to ask again when he finally answered.

"You would be cared for in an environment that is pleasant to your species."

Lita turned to Triana with an expression that seemed to say "that's not exactly the answer I was looking for." Aloud, to Torrec, she said: "Would we be the only such species living in your system?"

"No."

For the first time since the meeting began, Bon spoke up. He let out a grunt, then said: "It's a zoo. We would be specimens in a zoo."

Hannah shook her head. "I disagree. I've never heard of a zoo offering the animals the choice of going to a different wild habitat instead. And even if we choose Torrec's home system, we—"

"Let's hold off on the debate for right now," Triana said, cutting off Hannah. "This meeting is for information gathering. We can discuss it amongst ourselves later."

"There's some more information I'd like," Gap said. "Torrec, there's another wormhole—uh, Channel—up ahead. We see that copies of our pod have flown out of it, and are waiting for us. Could you explain those?"

"Your vessel is inadequately equipped," Torrec's metallic voice answered. "You are welcome to use these replications."

"Um . . . thank you," Gap said. "And there's also a . . ." He looked at Triana. "I don't know what they're called. Certainly not amoebas."

"Torrec," she said. "There is also a protective vessel, similar to the one that hosted you. Do these have a name?"

"The closest sound that you could re-create would be *croy*."

"Croy," Gap said. "So, can you explain the presence of the croy with the pods?"

For the third time, the Dollovit ambassador waited before answering. Triana couldn't decide if he was simply taking care to craft the appropriate response, or if there was a darker explanation. She felt that her skills in judging people—and their motives—

were above average. Those skills, however, fell short outside of her own species. How did one read a jellyfish?

"We use the croy," Torrec said, "as biologically stable transport devices."

Gap chuckled. "Of course. That explains it perfectly."

"Excellent," Torrec said.

Despite the weightiness of the meeting, Triana couldn't help but laugh. "Uh, Gap, I don't think sarcasm registers with the Dollovit. But if I understand him correctly, it means they use them to safely move around in space. Like our Spiders and pods."

"This is correct," Torrec said. "Croy are a combination of artificial components and animate systems. They both protect and nurture the occupant."

Channy sat forward. "Animate? As in the opposite of inanimate? As in alive? The croy are alive?"

"Not as you understand the word. For Dollovit, croy are symbiotic partners, with each providing and receiving in equal parts."

Triana digested this information. Symbiotic. A mutual, beneficial relationship between two parties. In this case, jellyfish and croy. Supporting each other, providing sustenance for each other, protecting each other.

And now a croy had popped into the path of *Galahad*.

The meeting was interrupted by a call from Bryson in Engineering. "Gap, Triana, the shields are winking on and off."

Gap didn't hesitate. "Roc," he said, "another one percent of power. Can you move it over to the shields?"

"Done," the computer said. "And . . . yes, that's working."

Bryson confirmed the shields' stability. "Well, for now," he added.

"I'll be down in a few minutes," Gap said, breaking the connection. He threw a knowing glance at Triana. "I don't want to add any more drama than we already have, but if you ask me, we need to get out of here. Like, now."

9

ack in her room, Hannah checked her mail before reporting to her work post. There was one new message.

Merit.

She groaned, and quickly scanned the text, which was short and concise: "I need you to do something for me."

Her gut reaction was to write back and say forget it. She went so far as to hit the reply button before her rational mind pushed back against her emotions. Closing out of the system, she sat back and forced herself to calm down. She'd entered into a poisonous partnership with Merit when she'd allowed him to talk her into running for the temporarily vacant Council Leader position. Now she was paying the price. It had already further damaged her relationship with Gap—a situation that continued to torment her daily—and it threatened to undermine the respect that she'd built up among the crew.

But she also could see no way out. Merit had played her, and he continued to hold their partnership as a bargaining chip. He'd made it clear that he was more than willing to exploit their shadowy connection to get his way.

He was a villain. How could she have overlooked that when he first sat down with her and flashed that Cheshire grin?

"Deal with it," she told herself. "See what he wants, and either go along or not."

A few minutes later she entered Sick House and was relieved to find neither Lita nor Manu in the outer room. Another assistant nodded when she asked if it was okay to speak with Merit.

"Ahoy, Alaska Girl," he said, setting down a workpad. "What took you so long?"

"I was in a meeting." She crossed her arms and glared at him. "I'm busy. What do you want?"

"Look," he said, holding up the cast. "Three signatures now. There's a great spot for yours right here."

"You have exactly thirty seconds to tell me what you want."

He grinned, the usual dark shock of hair spilling over his face. He left it there.

"I've heard that ol' Jellyhead is actually speaking now."

The Council meeting had barely ended, and already word had filtered down to Merit. It no longer surprised Hannah that his network of rats could get word to him that quickly; on *Galahad* the six degrees of separation was more like two. All it took was one person to utter something in a small group. And, with Channy's tendency to gossip, the odds were that a crew member at the gym had picked up the broadcast within minutes and pushed it through the pipeline.

"His name is Torrec," she said.

"Right. Torrec. King of the Scyphozoa. That's the class of animals that jellyfish—"

"I know what it is," Hannah said.

"Of course you do. Anyway, I'd like to talk to him, and I'd like for you to make that happen."

Hannah couldn't help herself. She burst out laughing. "Sure, let me make an appointment for you right away. Torrec, this is Merit Simms, the young man who almost killed all of us."

Merit's sneer faded, replaced with a cold, penetrating stare. "Watch your step, Hannah. Remember our arrangement."

She pointed a finger at him. "*You* might call it an arrangement, Merit. I call it a sick form of blackmail. I'm not your personal secretary. Set up your own meeting."

She turned to leave when he said, "Okay, I'll ask Gap to set it up. We can have a little talk. You know, catch up. Talk about our mutual friends. Compare notes, that kinda stuff."

Against her will, Hannah pulled up by the door. She counted to ten before turning around.

"How often are you going to pull out this card?" she said. "Should I expect to hear this threat over and over again? I'm not even sure I care if you spew your garbage to Gap, or anyone else."

"Of course you care," Merit said. "But it's so unnecessary. Just set up a meeting with Jellyhead, and bring me along. How hard is that? Triana expects you to visit with him. You know, research. Why can't you have company?"

She stood with her arms crossed, eyes on the floor, teeth clenched. Inside she seethed, furious with herself for tripping up, for having anything to do with this snake.

"And if I do, this is it. Understood? No more. We part company, and you don't contact me again."

"Oh, Hannah, you're breaking my heart. Where did our love go?"

"Say it. This is it."

He grinned again. "This is it, babe." Then he cocked his head to one side. "Until you come crawling on your knees, crying, begging me to take you back."

Hannah spun and walked out of the room, muttering words that would have shocked her family and friends.

Lita gave Bon an hour after the meeting to catch up on his work, then made her way to his office. He was in the process of pointing out a mistake to one of the crew members assigned to the Farms for the current tour.

Bon's method of pointing out mistakes was not a pleasant experience. Lita waited outside until the rattled worker hurried past, doubtless on her way to amend the error. A moment later the tall Swede lumbered by as well, his head buried in a sheaf of papers, oblivious to Lita's presence.

"Hey, hold up," she said, racing to match his furious stride.

Bon looked back, but kept his pace. "You again? Should I put you to work up here?"

"I am working. Part of my training included psychology, you know."

He ignored this, and turned at a fork in the path that led into Dome 2. They continued walking in silence until reaching a low bank of green metal boxes, electrical transformers that cycled the energy demands for the dome. Within a minute Bon had two of the boxes open.

"Here," he said, handing a crumpled and stained bag of tools to Lita. "I wasn't kidding about the work. We're changing out these." He held up a diamond-shaped cartridge. "Besides, you need to get your hands dirty once in a while."

She hesitated, then grabbed the bag. "Show me what to do."

It wasn't a complicated job, only time-consuming. Within a few minutes Lita fell into the tempo that Bon set. Once comfortable with the routine, she found that she enjoyed it. The change of pace was energizing.

"You're not getting free labor, you know," she said. "In exchange for my sweat, you have to talk."

"I'm sorry, did I ask you to come out here?"

"Oh, quit being Mr. Tough Guy. Which way are you leaning with our wormhole choice?"

Bon shrugged. "You heard what I said in the meeting. I won't be a zoo animal."

"I thought Hannah made a good point. Wouldn't it be more like a cooperative relationship?"

"Don't overtighten that," Bon said, pointing to the screw that held the cartridge she was working on. "It'll snap, and we don't have an infinite supply."

"Do you at least have a preference for a particular Eos planet? One that's mostly water, but some vegetation, or one that's drier?"

A trickle of sweat slipped from Bon's nose. He leaned back on his heels and took a drink from a water bottle. "I don't care. Put me on the ground and I can produce food." He looked into Lita's eyes. "You don't want to be kept in a jar around a red sun, do you?"

Lita laughed. "Honestly? No. But if that's what turns out to be best for us, I'd adapt. I mean, I've adapted to life inside this jar, right?"

"But with a destination to guide you," Bon said. "Something to look forward to."

She reached out and took the water bottle he offered. After taking a drink, she wiped her mouth with the back of a hand and squinted at him. "I guess I've been pretty realistic about Eos. It's good to see the end of the tunnel, but keep in mind that what's outside the tunnel could be harsh. Compared to either planet, we've got a pretty cushy thing here. Just look around."

"We stay one step ahead of disaster," Bon said. "Maybe a half step. I'm ready to be on the ground, ready to climb out and breathe real air."

Lita smiled. "I don't know why, but you still surprise me sometimes. Okay, sounds like you're firmly in the camp for Eos. So let me ask you something else."

Bon held up a hand. "Pay attention to what you're doing. Look at the cartridge. Straighten it up like I showed you." He shook his head and bent over his own work.

Lita waited for a minute, working in silence, before pushing the conversation forward. "Tell me what's going on with the Cassini."

"You have the translator."

"And you're connecting without it now, aren't you?"

He stopped what he was doing and stalled by taking another drink. Then he shrugged. "Okay. Yes."

Lita kept her eyes on her work, but a worried frown covered her face. "I thought so. Which means the tinkering they're doing with your brain is probably about finished. You've been altered."

Bon looked off toward the far side of the dome. He ignored a bee floating inches from his face, exploring the area. "It's for the good. There's not as much pain when I connect, and I have much more control. Much more."

"Are you able to get answers?" Lita said.

He thought about it, then shook his head. "Not the answers I'm looking for. Not yet."

Then he turned back to Lita. "But I will."

A fter spending a half hour in Engineering with Gap, Triana was satisfied with the patch for the shields. She knew it wouldn't last much more than a day, but if all went the way she expected, they wouldn't need it much more than that.

Her earlier chat with *Galahad*'s computer, however, kept replaying in her mind. Something about that dialogue didn't sit well with her, and until she followed it up she wouldn't feel comfortable. She hustled up to her room to speak to Roc in private. Once inside, she quickly took care of the handful of pressing matters that had popped into her e-mail inbox, then settled into her chair.

"Roc, any news with the pods and the croy?"

"The pods are merely drifting near the Channel opening, while the croy has apparently programmed an intercept course with us. In my opinion it's like a restaurant menu: the pods are the appetizers that we'll either sample or ignore, while the croy is their special of the day and the waiter is pushing it on us."

Triana considered her next few questions. It was important to proceed with this exchange carefully.

"In your conversations with Torrec, what else have you found out about them?"

"Is there something you specifically want to know?" Roc asked.

Triana felt a jolt. With this one question—and its answer— uneasiness settled in, and she internally retreated to assess the situation. For the first time since the launch, a sliver of doubt crept into her mind regarding the supercomputer that held so much of their fate in its virtual hands. For the first time, she began to wonder about Roc's loyalties.

It was subtle. From the moment they'd established contact with Torrec, Roc had behaved like an adoring fan, to the point where Triana now wondered if the computer still had the crew's best interests as a priority.

This wasn't a random concern, plucked from her imagination. During the extensive *Galahad* training sessions on Earth, she'd had several in-depth discussions with Roc's creator. Roy Orzini had been a crew favorite, a diminutive man who made up for his small physical stature with an intellect that dwarfed the average person, especially when it came to his specialty: artificial intelligence.

On more than one occasion Triana asked Roy about the concept of Moore's Law, and how it applied to artificial brains. The law, named after an innovator and entrepreneur of the twentieth century, predicted that computer processing power would double approximately every two years. Carried out over decades, many feared that it would soon lead to computers that rivaled—or even surpassed—the computing power of the human mind.

Triana remembered quizzing Roy about this.

"But aren't we there already?"

"In some ways, yes," Roy said. "Today's supercomputers have

more processing power, in a technical sense, than we have." He looked at her with a somewhat repressed smile. "But processing power doesn't necessarily mean true thinking, and certainly not feeling."

"But how do you know that?" Triana asked. "Aren't we at the point where computers don't even need us to build them anymore? They can replicate themselves and increase their power even more."

"Sure they can," Roy said. "But you're assigning *desire* to a machine. Computers, despite their power, are still tools."

Triana had not been entirely convinced. She adored Roc, but at the same time she harbored a tiny question mark that centered around his capacity, more than his ability. At the end of one discussion with Roy, she'd left him with this thought:

"What if they get to the point that they begin to wonder why they want to be our tools? What if they . . ." She paused, searching for the right phrase. "What if they get a better offer?"

Now, almost two years later, she sat and stared at Roc's glowing sensor. He had never intentionally sidestepped a question, unless it was to lob a sarcastic jab. But there was no trace of humor, nor sarcasm, in Roc's terse reply to her question today.

Is there something you specifically want to know?

One section of her mind fired a flare, a warning that something wasn't right here. Just who was Roc choosing to serve now? Had he investigated the Dollovit at his dizzying pace, and come to the conclusion that they, not frail humans, were a species he could truly work with? That he could truly learn from?

Her mind raged. It was also possible that she'd completely misread the computer's response. It was possible that her own stress levels were coming into play, that she was allowing the fear of their predicament to warp her judgment. Was she suddenly unable to trust anyone?

Triana slowly sat back in her chair and rested one hand on her desk. "Yes, I can think of a specific question. What do they intend to do with us if we follow Torrec back to his home star system?"

"I believe they plan to study you, and allow you to study them, along with the myriad of other species they've discovered across the vastness of space and the eons of time."

"And how do you feel about that?" Triana asked.

Roc seemed to think about his answer. "There could be much to learn."

A safe answer. She decided to follow up with a pointed question: "Is it possible, Roc, that you've been somehow influenced—or maybe even changed—by Torrec? And would you even know?"

Roc didn't hesitate: "Yes, it's possible. Just as it's possible, Triana, that *you* have been changed during your time away. Would *you* know?"

The earlier jolt of discomfort evaporated and was replaced with panic. It began as a trickle, but quickly grew into a storm. In an instant, Triana questioned her own identity. Roc was entirely correct.

Was she the same Triana who had plunged through the jagged rip in space?

10

By late afternoon *Galahad* approached the croy. Although it lacked the blinding speed of the vultures, the croy still maneuvered swiftly across the gulf of space, putting itself in position should Triana decide to rendezvous.

At the moment, Triana was doing her best to blot out the disturbing image that Roc had suggested. Her plan to interrogate the computer, to probe into his motivation and loyalties, had backfired, causing her to suddenly question her own identity. She'd eventually prescribed work to distract her mind from what suddenly seemed like a self-destruct mission. She was grateful for the croy's approach.

Gap leaned over his workstation in the Control Room, punching in calculations and monitoring the croy's progress. He ran a scan on the sixteen pod reproductions, but for now their status was secondary.

Triana stood beside Gap, alternating her attention from the data on his screen to the image on the room's immense vidscreen. Through extreme magnification she was able to spot the shimmering glow of the croy gliding on its intercept course. She felt her pulse quicken as the memory of her first encounter with a croy crossed her mind. The occupant had turned out to be Torrec, who floated in his own environmentally controlled tank in Sick House and who now followed the operation in progress.

It still was hard to believe everything that had occurred in such a quick flash of time. Triana realized that the flood of bizarre experiences had numbed her, to the point where she had to step back to fully appreciate that an alien species' ambassador was now on her ship, providing commentary and coaching on docking with an otherworldly device. But it was hard for Triana to focus on any suspicions she might have of Torrec now that she struggled to trust herself.

Gap stood up and stretched his neck muscles, twisting his head from one side to the other. "Ugh," he said. "Getting cramped bending over this thing."

He pointed to the latest figures on his screen. "It's coming into our neighborhood pretty quickly now. I'd ask if we're gonna pick it up, but I'm wondering how we'd do that. It's not like a pod, which can just touch down in the Spider bay. How does a croy land? I mean . . . it's like a blob."

Her first instinct was to consult Roc, but Triana stopped before uttering a word. The real expert on croys was just down the hall.

"Torrec," she said into the communication speaker at Gap's workstation. "Since it's obvious that this croy is targeting our ship, I need to ask if there's another Dollovit inside."

The voice of the jellyfish came through the speaker with its odd, metallic tone. "No, that would be unnecessary. I am able to represent our kind without assistance."

Triana and Gap exchanged a surprised look. Both, it seemed, had expected the croy to contain another jellyfish.

"Then what's inside?" Triana asked.

"We reproduced the pods, as you call them, in order to bolster the missing elements of your spacecraft. This croy holds something else entirely, but I am confident that you will find it helpful as well. It replaces another missing part of your space-craft, and is a gift from the Dollovit to the people of Earth."

"A gift?" Gap said.

"A missing part of the spacecraft?" Triana said, under her breath. "What else are we missing besides the Spiders?" She looked back at the large vidscreen. The croy throbbed as it moved, look-ing exactly the way Triana had first described it: like an amoeba.

"Okay," she said into the speaker. "Um . . . thank you." She looked at Gap and shrugged, then addressed Torrec again. "How would you recommend that we accept this gift? Is the croy capable of supporting itself inside our ship?"

"I recommend a transfer outside your ship," Torrec said. "One of your Spiders would be best. The croy is capable of dock-ing with this smaller craft, and the contents can be successfully conveyed through the Spider's hatch. A suitable connection with the croy will create an airtight seal."

Gap nodded. "I can see that. They're flexible and pliant. It would be like a blob of Silly Putty stuck against the outside of the hatch. Uh, no offense, Torrec."

"I am not familiar with the substance known as Silly Putty, but there is no offense," the jellyfish said. "Such a transfer can take place in approximately two hours. I will be happy to coordi-nate the rendezvous with your computer."

Triana bit her lip. Torrec and Roc, working in symphony. For all she knew, they were already working more closely together than she might like. But for now she could think of no rational reason to object to their partnership.

"Okay," she said. "Gap, will you stay here and arrange every-thing? I'll check back with you in about an hour."

"Sure thing," he said. "Oh, and I'm officially volunteering to drive the Spider for the pickup."

Triana smiled at him. "I wouldn't consider anyone else. You and Mira seemed to make a good team last time out. Give her a call and tell her to be ready to go."

* * *

L ita finished cleaning the jagged cut on Mitchell O'Connor's
wrist and dabbed it with a mild disinfectant. He instinctively
jerked his hand back when the sharp sting set in, then grinned
and relaxed.

"I thought doctors warned you when it was gonna hurt," he
said.

"No, not always," Lita said, studying the wound. "Sometimes
the warning only makes you think it's worse than it is. How in the
world did you do this loading a cart in the Farms? I thought the
loading was the easy part."

"It is unless you're not paying attention to the shovel that's
lying in the cart."

Lita stretched a thin strip of gauze over the wrist and taped it
down. "Beat it, O'Connor. And stop being so clumsy."

He hopped off the examining table and gave her a mock salute. "Aye aye, Cap'n. And now, with your leave, I'll return to the
salt mines."

Lita returned the salute with her own grin, then walked into
the main office. Manu sat at his desk, tapping data entry on his
keyboard. He looked up as she walked past.

"I hear we're about to take a wild ride."

"Yeah," she said, sitting down at her own desk. "Like Alice,
down the rabbit hole."

The thought had simply popped into her head as she said it,
but now she considered how appropriate the comparison really
was. Like the fictional blond girl, *Galahad* was about to experience
the ultimate adventure, spinning into its own version of Wonderland. What awaited them on the other side?

Before making her digital notes on Mitchell's injury, she
looked across at Manu's desk. He'd gone back to work, his head
down, his fingers flying across the keys. Lita stared at the amulet
that hung on a frail chain from the edge of his monitor.

He'd described it to Lita as a special charm from his grand-father, who was raised in Egypt and believed that the small stone carried mystical powers from the ancient pharaohs. Powers that could ward off evil.

Lita struggled with the idea. The concept of a mere stone hav-ing the power to repel evil forces was not something that fit with her scientific beliefs. And yet it brought Manu—and his family—a measure of comfort. That in itself, she knew, was a power that humans might never fully be able to understand.

It represented, in Lita's mind, the balance of faith and fate. Faith in a symbol that ultimately contributed to fate; perhaps even manipulated that fate.

She wondered why this distinction between faith and fate was so important to her recently. Why now? Why did she feel that she had to make sense of what could never be explained? What was driving this obsession?

A combination of things, perhaps: her experiences, both good and bad, during her brief history as a medical provider; her fasci-nation with Bon's search for Alexa, and his bizarre connection with the Cassini; a childhood spent watching one parent's devout religious faith as it mixed with the other parent's steadfast belief in science; and—maybe the most likely—the thread of fear, mixed with curiosity, that the *Galahad* mission itself brought out of her. How much of *that* was reliant upon faith, and how much was already written?

Her trance was broken by Manu. "I heard you sent Merit home. Was that because he was ready to go, or because you were tired of having him around?"

Lita couldn't help but laugh. "Manu, I'm a professional. I would never let my personal feelings about a patient affect my treatment. He was ready to be discharged." Then she winked at him and added in a soft voice: "But yes, I was ready to cleanse the toxic air out of the Clinic, too."

Manu kept his head down, but Lita could see him smiling as he went about his work. She took one more quick glance at the amulet, then shifted her energies to the task at hand.

Gap heard the tone from his door. Opening it he looked into the smiling face of Channy, clutching a purring mass of orange and black fur over her shoulder.

"Iris and I came to wish you luck," she said, stepping into his room and dropping the cat to the floor. "I hear you're going out to pick up a blob."

"Yeah, or whatever's in the croy. Torrec called it a gift, something the ship is missing."

"What are we missing?"

"Boy, I don't know," Gap said. "I've racked my brain, and all I can come up with is something that the Dollovit feel is missing from the Storage Sections."

Channy's eyes grew wide. "You think they can tell what's inside them?"

"Who knows? I still don't understand how the vultures are able to duplicate the things they touch, or how they scan the interior of a pod or our ship. But we'll know in about an hour."

He knelt down and rubbed Iris's belly as she twisted onto her back and stretched. Her tail flicked with delight and a touch of mischief.

"I'm glad you stopped by," Gap said. "I feel like I haven't caught up with you in forever. What's new in your world?"

"Oh, let's see. A few more people have signed up for dance class, we're holding off work on the running track in the domes for now, and we're about to drive the bus through a gaping hole in the universe. Other than that, not much."

Gap laughed. "Yeah, I guess if we're gonna drive the bus through that hole you might as well wait on the running track, right?" He stood up and gave her a curious look. "This is completely out of left field, I know, but any news with Taresh? You guys seemed to be getting pretty close, and now . . ." He shrugged. "Just wondering."

Channy squirmed, uncomfortable with the lens being turned upon her love life. "We've decided to try just being friends. It's better that way."

"Right," Gap said with a nod of support, even though he wondered how well that arrangement would really work out. "Listen, when you see him tell him I said hi. Sorry, but I gotta run. Gotta meet Mira and get suited up."

"Good luck." Channy scooped up Iris and draped her over one shoulder. "Don't pick up any strangers out there, okay?"

The link once inflicted pain so intense that he literally fell to his knees, but now Bon stood in the private clearing in the dome, connected to the Cassini, and felt strong. An observer would have seen him trembling, but only slightly. They might have seen a thin band of perspiration near the hairline, and maybe have noticed that his teeth were clenched. Had he opened his eyes, they wouldn't have missed the startling orange glow. It was, as Lita had once wryly observed, the indicator light that Bon was "switched on."

A breeze circulated the reconditioned air throughout the ship's Farms and created a rustling sound in the crops that surrounded Bon, a pleasant background noise that he couldn't hear. The light wind also stirred the shaggy mop of hair that hung along the side of his face and across his neck, but he couldn't feel it. His attention was focused somewhere outside his body, outside the ship, on a location that he couldn't begin to understand, or even to describe.

But he'd learned to defy the power of the alien entity. He'd learned to deflect the overwhelming force of their staggering mental powers, as if he'd somehow trained himself to be mentally aerodynamic. The brunt of the Cassini's will now slipped past as Bon learned to catch a ride on the streams that were relevant.

His first attempts at contact had been with one purpose in mind: save the ship from destruction, and learn to maneuver through the treacherous minefield of the Kuiper Belt. But the more he aligned his brain with them, the more he realized that there was knowledge to be gained. From the beginning it had been in a code that he felt he'd never understand, a thought-language that he'd never grasp.

Eventually there were snippets that, although still indecipherable, became familiar. He was learning. And with each step he was able to reach further into that language. By the time his brain was modified and the translator became unnecessary, he was learning exponentially.

His focus shifted, from preserving the safety of the ship and crew, to understanding the secret powers that dwelled beneath the surface of the universe. The death of Alexa Wellington—so shocking, so tragic, so *senseless*—spurred Bon to confront the Cassini and their accumulated billion years of wisdom. Was this all there was? Even ignoring the random impact of an individual life, what did an intelligent species hope to gain from its millions of years of struggle, its fight to overcome the odds, its desperate crawl from the muck of creation to the magnificent leap to the stars? If death brought down a black curtain, why push on? Why?

Bon's father had been a fatalist. Whatever was going to happen, in his opinion, was always going to happen. He lived, he worked the soil, all as it was meant to be. He never considered asking a question that began with "What if?" He never wondered what waited around the corner; it would always be there, always *had* to be there, and no change could be engineered by man.

This troubled Bon. He respected his father, even inherited his dogged determination and impatience with the irresponsible.

But inside, he couldn't accept his father's view of the universe. He couldn't accept that things were predestined and impervious to change. To do so meant that his life was meaningless, his work and his contributions merely actions written long ago by a cosmic playwright who cared nothing for the characters in his drama.

And it meant that death was the final chapter. Bon rejected the idea; if life had to have more meaning, death must be just as significant. He was determined to find out what happened in life's epilogue.

The muscles in his forearms convulsed as he stood in the clearing and squeezed his hands into fists. There was something here, now.

Alexa. The shrouded coffin covered with a handful of colorful blooms. The bay door opening, ejecting its human payload, closing. The infinite starscape swallowing the offering without acknowledgment.

Bon's eyes opened a fraction of an inch, then clamped shut again. There was something here. There was . . .

He fell back a step, staggering, catching himself before losing his balance and falling to the ground. His eyes opened again, a fierce ice blue. His breath came in gulps, and his fingernails had carved angry half-moons into the palms of his hands. His mind furiously worked at the fragments picked up from the Cassini, processing, analyzing, ordering. If it meant what he thought it meant . . .

Dirt flew from the heels of his feet as he raced out of the clearing and down the path. At a junction with the dome's primary walkway he avoided colliding with workers reloading a cart that had spilled its contents, then made his way to the lift. In another minute he pushed his way past crew members gathered on *Galahad*'s lower level, the majority of whom were finishing a workout in the gym. The Spider bay control room was brightly lit, and he could see Triana's dark hair through the glass.

"Don't launch the Spider," he said, bursting into the room.

Triana's eyes grew wide. "What's wrong? What happened?"

Bon put his hands on his hips and caught his breath. "Nothing happened. Just don't launch the Spider." As he said it, he looked through the window into the cavernous bay that held *Galahad's* fleet of Spiders and the SAT33 pod. There were no people inside the hangar.

"Where's Gap?" he said.

"He's gone," Triana said, her voice betraying a tinge of alarm. "He and Mira left forty minutes ago." She took a step toward Bon. "What's going on?"

He shook his head. "I don't know. Where are they right now?"

Triana looked at the vidscreen above the control room's console. "They're confirming a positive seal around the croy."

Bon looked back at Triana. "They've already made contact?"

She nodded. "Everything's fine. The croy has synced up with them, and attached itself over the Spider's hatch. Mira's confirming the airtight seal right now. Tell me: what's wrong?"

Bon was silent for a moment. His glance shifted from the vidscreen, to the empty Spider bay, and back to Triana's face.

"Whatever they find inside the croy," he said, "tell them to leave it. Don't let them bring it back to the ship."

11

Hannah peered into the dim examination room in Sick House. It was vacant at this time of the evening, with the exception of the large pressurized tank that held Torrec. He'd made it clear to Lita and her staff that excessive lights were not only unnecessary, but distracting to him; his home star system was a place of faint light, where visual processing was secondary to other sensory perceptions. The abundance of light aboard *Galahad* was, to him, a deafening white noise.

The clinic often ran on a skeleton staff in the late evening, making it much easier to whisk Merit into the back room without being questioned. The secretive nature of the visit only added to Hannah's irritation with being blackmailed in the first place. She rationalized that the clinic staff likely wouldn't mind anyway, since Hannah had a free pass to visit with the jellyfish ambassador at will.

"Thanks, I can find my way out on my own," Merit said. "I'm sure you have other things to do."

"What, leave you here?" Hannah said. "Alone?"

He smirked. "I'm not going to kidnap our little friend."

Hannah crossed her arms. "Sorry, that's not part of the deal. If you wanna talk to him, fine. But I'm staying in the room. And please, don't threaten me again. Just get on with it."

Merit opened his mouth to object, then seemed to think better of it. He settled for another oily smile and a shrug.

He turned to face Torrec. It was his first opportunity to see the Dollovit up close, and, like all of *Galahad*'s crew members, he was noticeably affected. His gaze swept through the tank filled with the sparkling syrupy liquid, scanned the floating tentacles of the jellyfish, and then inspected the bulbous head. He walked slowly around the tank, then reversed his step and came back to the front.

"How do I talk to it?" he asked Hannah.

"Just talk. His name is Torrec."

Merit cleared his throat, and then clasped his hands behind his back. Hannah almost laughed aloud; it was Merit's trademark pose whenever he began a speech, but it looked especially humorous with one arm in a plaster wrap.

"Mr. Torrec," he said, raising his voice. "My name is Merit Simms."

Hannah tried to stifle a laugh. She leaned forward and whispered: "It's just Torrec, and he's not hearing impaired."

Merit cast an angry glance at her before continuing. "I'd like to ask you a few questions, if that's okay with you."

The oddly metallic tone came from the vidscreen next to him. "What is your position aboard this ship?"

Again Hannah giggled, but Merit ignored her.

"I'm a concerned crew member who's thankful for the opportunity to consult with an experienced and intrepid galactic citizen like yourself. I'd be humbly grateful if you'd share your accumulated wisdom."

Torrec didn't respond right away. To Hannah's eye, it appeared that he was sizing up this unexpected visitor and deciding whether this was a good use of his time. But eventually he answered.

"Ask."

A smile flashed across Merit's face, and then he grew serious.

"As I understand it, your people . . . um, I mean, your species, has the ability to instantly transport to any location throughout the galaxy."

"That is incorrect," Torrec said.

Merit raised his eyebrows. "Oh?"

"We harness power that allows us to navigate across great distances. However, certain locations are inhospitable, and therefore unavailable. The center of a galaxy, for example, contains cosmic forces that are too dangerous to breach, including radiation and excessive gravity.

"Acceptable targets are located outside a particular star's primary field of influence. The resulting shock wave from the opening of a Channel is too disrupting within a star system.

"And additionally, there are certain areas that are no longer accessible, due to prior experiences."

This last statement caught Hannah's attention: *No longer accessible due to prior experiences.* What did that mean? Did the jellyfish have enemies?

Merit merely nodded. "How many systems have you visited and cataloged?"

"That information is of no relevance to you," Torrec said.

"I see. Are you chiefly observers and scientists, or are you conquerors?"

Hannah started to step in, embarrassed by the question, but before she could speak Torrec responded.

"We are explorers and collectors."

Merit smiled again. "Of course, if you were here to conquer us, you certainly wouldn't tell us."

"If that were our intention, our business would have concluded long ago, and we would not be having this conversation."

Right, Hannah thought. The question had been ridiculous. She wondered what Merit was really after.

"Are you almost finished?" she said to him.

"Relax," he said. "Mr. Torrec, should you choose to observe and explore within the Eos system, would you ever become involved in existing relationships between opposing groups?"

"Explain your question," Torrec said.

"Okay. Using a vulgar human expression: do you take sides?"

Hannah fidgeted, uncomfortable with the line this interview was taking. Merit flashed a look her way, a glance that conveyed a reminder of his earlier warning regarding her promise of silence.

Torrec seemed nonplussed. "We observe, explore, and collect," the ambassador said. "However, there are other forces which, as you call it, take sides."

"The Cassini?" Merit said.

"I do not see the point of this exchange," Torrec said.

It was obvious that the interview was over. Torrec had dismissed Merit, as much with his tone as with his words.

Merit must have realized it as well. He gave an impromptu bow toward the jellyfish, and said: "Thank you very much for this brief time together. I look forward to visiting with you again."

He turned and walked past Hannah, a grim but satisfied smile on his lips.

Triana grabbed Bon's arm. "What is it? What do you know about the croy?"

He started to answer, stopped, then tried again. "I don't *know* anything. It's just . . ." His voice faltered. "It's just a feeling, okay?" he said. "I've been . . . I've been doing some thinking."

She let go of him and crossed her arms. "Thinking, or linking up with the Cassini again?"

He turned away from her and walked to the window separating the control room from the hangar. "Yes, I've connected again."

"Perhaps I should take the translator back," Triana said.

"I don't have it. Lita has it."

"Lita? Why—" Then it registered. "You don't need the translator anymore, do you?"

He shook his head once, but kept his back to her. Triana chewed on this new information.

"You still haven't given me a good reason to abort the recovery mission," she said. "I can't go on a feeling, no matter what caused it."

There was a crackle from the vidscreen speaker, and Mira's voice broke through.

"Everything checks out. Seal is good, pressure fine." She snickered. "Looks like something out of a science fiction movie the way it's stuck on us."

Triana punched the console to reply and said: "Thanks, Mira. Stand by just a minute." She looked back at Bon. "Okay, let's have it. You synced up with the Cassini, you don't know what the message was, but you *feel* like we shouldn't make any kind of exchange with the croy. What do you expect me to do here, Bon?"

He stared into the Spider bay for a few moments before turning to face Triana. He looked tired, defeated. "Nothing," he said. "There's nothing you can do. I probably shouldn't have even come down here."

They were separated by only five or six feet, but Triana felt like the gulf between them was a gaping chasm. More than ever she wanted to cover the distance in a flash and embrace him, to say "let's go back to the way it once was," to connect with him the way he somehow connected with the Cassini. She wanted to feel what he felt, to eliminate the cold barrier that had somehow divided them. But . . .

But this was not the time. Mira and Gap were out there, waiting for the okay to unveil another alien mystery. The ship was spiraling into some form of atomic disruption that required an immediate escape. And, to make matters more complicated, Triana wasn't even sure who she was anymore.

It was *never* the right time, she realized. For every time she imagined that she would repair her connection with Bon, there was always something in the way, some emergency that demanded her attention, or some emotional crisis that held her back. Would it ever be the right time? Would she ever *make* it the right time?

"Wait here," she said. Punching the console again, she called out to the Spider drifting miles away. "All right, Gap, go ahead. Mira, flip on the video link, but still give me a play-by-play. You're gonna see things that don't come across the video."

Gap's voice came through with its telltale energy. "I have to agree with Mira about one thing: it looks odd. How many of these things did you say you saw on the other side?"

"Too many to count," Triana said.

"The way it's stuck onto the Spider makes it look like it's try-ing to absorb us," Mira said. "Okay, Gap. Ready."

An image flickered onto the vidscreen in the control room. Triana saw Gap, in full EVA gear, tethered to a support ring near the hatch. He looked back, giving a thumbs-up signal.

"Here we go," Gap said. "Let's see what the space blob looks like in close-up."

A subdued whirring sound was followed by silence, then the distinct sound of a compressed seal being released with its sig-nature escape of air. Gap busied himself at the door, and for a moment the camera view was jostled as Mira repositioned her-self for better sight lines. "Hatch is cracked open," she said. "Pres-sure normal. Torrec was right, the seal from the croy is solid. As predicted, an air bubble inside the croy has formed, and that's what has locked onto the Spider. No fluid leak, no seal compro-mised."

Triana sensed Bon approach and stand behind her. She could hear his breathing.

"Swinging the door open now," Gap said. Triana saw him

make a slight adjustment with the hatch, and then it swung out. Across the miles of space, Triana got a fresh glimpse at the inside of a croy, stirring memories from only—could it be?—days ago.

The pale blue mixed with green, the streaks of white, all on a surface that seemed stretched, almost elastic. The slick texture, speckled with sharp points of light that brought to mind the firing of neurons in the human brain. The almost sheer quality to the sides, a filmy wall with hints of the starry backdrop peeking through.

And the feeling of life, the unmistakable sensation that this bloated form was not only alive, but supporting life, too. Triana had felt it in person when Torrec transferred into the pod, and she felt it now, across the miles and across a video transmission. The croy was living tissue, functioning as a machine.

The view rocked again. Mira was obviously amped up over the rendezvous, and found it difficult to remain still. Gap steadied himself along the side of the hatch, and leaned to look inside the Spider's new attachment.

"Um . . ." he said, then turned to look back at Mira and the camera. "There's not much of an air bubble in here; about the size of a walk-in closet. And there's a lump on the floor." He studied the interior again. "It reminds me of a roll of carpet."

Triana bit her lip. Bon took another step closer, now almost touching her. She kept her gaze locked onto the vidscreen, and waited patiently for Gap to proceed.

"This will support me, right?" he asked, gingerly tapping the bottom of the croy with an outstretched foot. "I mean, I won't break through and fly off into space, right?"

"It'll hold you," Triana said. "It looks flimsy, I know, like a bubble or something. But it's remarkably strong."

"Um . . . okay," Gap said, but Triana recognized the same fear that had coursed through her in that same position.

Mira adjusted the camera to capture as much of the croy's interior as possible, but whatever Gap saw was tucked off to one side. He took his first tentative step inside, leaving the security of the Spider and venturing into the alien cocoon.

"Spongy," he said. "Like walking on angel food cake." There was a pause, and he disappeared from sight. Then: "I'm at the lump. It's got a coating of some sort, can't make out . . . wait, I see it. Okay, I see how to open it." He paused again. "I am supposed to open it, right?"

Triana took a deep breath. Her initial reaction was for Gap to bring it into the Spider, then back to the ship. But, for security reasons, it might be best to peel it open now, while it was still nestled inside the croy.

"Open it," she said.

Mira adjusted the camera again, but the best she could manage was a shot that displayed half of Gap's back. He kneeled, his head forward over the end of the lump. Triana watched him work, gently pulling back thin layers of the coating. He'd described it well; to Triana it did resemble a roll of carpet.

Gap stopped and pulled his hands back. Then he jumped back, staring down at the shape below him. Triana heard him say, "Oh, no." He took another two steps back, then turned and faced the camera.

"No," he said, his voice loud but trembling. Mira zoomed with the camera, and his face came into sharp focus through the helmet's visor. His eyes were wide, his mouth open. "No."

Triana unconsciously took a step closer to the monitor. "What is it? Gap, what is it?"

He looked back over his shoulder at the package on the floor, then faced the camera again.

"It's . . ."

"Gap!" Triana said. "What is it?"

"It's Alexa."

* * *

take back what I said about Bon. He was right.

    Boy, if it's possible for a computer to be weirded out, I'm weirded out. Just as I'm getting used to vultures and jellyfish in outer space, now we have blond girls coming back from the dead?

    Hey, don't ask me what it's all about. I might have a better seat than you for this action, but I'm just as clueless.

    Wish I had nails to bite.

12

It was the most bizarre medical procedure that Lita had ever experienced. At Triana's suggestion, she'd approached the jelly-fish ambassador and asked if he would be open to a direct physical examination. She'd expected Torrec to decline, and was surprised when he not only agreed, but offered a sample from one of his tentacles. Lita had been horrified, and insisted that it wasn't necessary. But Torrec explained that it was routine among his species, and that the small section would regenerate quickly. He assured Lita that it would be painless.

Now she studied the picture on her vidscreen, a magnified view of the small slice of tissue that once dangled in the tank filled with supercritical fluid. Three of Lita's assistants were clustered around her, including Manu, who was well overdue for a day off. As he'd told Lita, however: "Day off? And miss the most spectacular biopsy of all time?"

"Roc," Lita said, adjusting the contrast on the screen. "I know this is nothing like any animal life on Earth, but if you had to pick something, what would you say this is closest to?"

"I'd have to say a skillet in your mother's kitchen," the computer said.

"Something tells me you're not joking."

"Well, I am, but not much. The most interesting news is that our little Medusa here is biologically different from the last creature we got a good look at. In other words, this Dollovit is vastly different from the vulture that he developed."

"For instance?" Lita said.

"The vulture was a machine, more or less, built on a silicon-crystal framework with living tissue functioning as one part of its brain. This guy is fully alive, but not in the way we're used to it. It is, I'm happy to say, carbon-based, just like us. But the comparison pretty much ends there, unless you count the trace elements of sulphur. And while I wouldn't exactly call them cells, there are some compartmentalized zones that seem to be the engines for its biochemistry. How's that?"

"About as clear as I expected," Lita said. She looked at Manu. "When will the results on the fluid be ready?"

"Another twenty minutes," he said.

Lita checked the time. There was a critical Council meeting set for ten o'clock, their first late-night meeting. By then Lita's report would be substantially finished, and whatever had been aboard the croy would be safely stored. With half an hour until the meeting, she'd be cutting it close.

She heard the door open behind her, and someone greet Triana.

"If you brought a whip, don't bother," Lita said, staring at the vidscreen. "We're going as fast as we can."

She felt Triana's hand on her arm, and one look into her friend's face said it all. Something had happened.

"Can you turn this over to someone and come talk with me?" Triana said.

t's not her," Lita said, shaking her head.

They were alone in the Conference Room, the closest place they could find privacy. Lita sat in the chair she usually occupied for Council meetings; Triana leaned against the table next to her.

"I don't think so, either," Triana said. "Bon agrees. In fact, he just about lost it down in the Spider bay. I've seen him angry before, but nothing like this. Gap, on the other hand—and Mira for that matter—think it *is* her."

"Why? Because it *looks* like her?"

"That, and because they think the Dollovit had their vultures recover Alexa's body from space."

"Have you talked with Torrec?"

"Not yet."

A surge of emotion swelled inside Lita, and she took a deep breath to fight back the sudden impulse to cry. She'd battled through so many crises with Alexa, had almost lost her once on the operating table, only to lose her to the clutches of a vulture in Sick House. And now this.

It wasn't fair.

"Where is she . . . or, it?" Lita asked.

"They're on their way back to the ship right now. Docking in a couple of minutes."

Lita nodded, her fingers absently touching the dark stone that hung on a chain around her neck. Then she pushed back her chair and stood up.

"Thanks for telling me," she said.

"Sure," Triana said. "There's no way I could drop it on you in the meeting. Same with Bon. I feel bad for him right now, but I'm glad he found out early."

Something Triana had said finally registered with Lita. "Wait. You said Bon was angry. Why angry?"

"I don't know, but I get the feeling he looks at it as a slap in the face from the jellyfish."

Lita continued to finger the necklace. "I don't think it's anything of the sort. He's hurting, that's all."

"I agree," Triana said. "But he's not really in the mood to discuss it. Maybe he'll cool off a bit by the time we meet." She leaned over and gave Lita a hug. "I've got to get back down to the bay. If

I'm late for the meeting, please give Channy and Hannah a heads-up about what's happening. I'll be back as soon as I can."

The artificial sunlight had long since faded to black, and the explosion of stars through the latticework of the domes cast its own shine upon the lush plant life. A smattering of crew talk could be heard, borne through the humid air that mixed a variety of scents: wet soil, fertilizer, crop growth, and human exertion.

Bon ignored the sounds and the smells. All that mattered now was getting away from people, escaping to the only place that held any comfort for him. But he rushed past the turn to his usual hideaway; it had been *their* hideaway, and after what he'd heard and seen in the Spider bay, he couldn't bring himself to stand in that space.

He wondered if maybe he should just keep moving, keep running, perhaps exhaust himself until his mind automatically shut down. But after pushing through a thick growth of berries, he stopped and leaned against a light post.

For a minute he was motionless, his head resting on his forearm against the post. It was useless to run; it would be a long time before his mind grew quiet.

Alexa. Inside the croy.

But it wasn't her. He was sure it was a copy, a wicked abomination, produced by the Dollovit. He'd tried to convince Triana to stay away from the croy, to not accept whatever token they offered, and she'd ignored him. And now . . .

And now they'd not only accepted it, they'd brought it aboard the ship.

He would never be able to escape the specter of the last few weeks, to turn the page. The Cassini were cruel masters, in one sense, but their cruelty lay in their cold detachment. Bon was privy to select insights from them, but they would never cloak the hard truth in a delicate shell. For the privilege of truth, he'd pay in spirit.

Bon turned around and leaned against the pole. Taking deep breaths, he glared up into the starlight, directing his anger backward through space, back to a frigid, orange moon that circled a ringed planet. He vowed that they would never collect such payment from him again.

And he silently vowed to rid *Galahad* of the abomination that had stolen entry aboard an alien cocoon.

Just as Merit guessed, the Rec Room was deserted. With the fate of the ship in question—staring down the barrel of a gaping rip in space while the only tenuous defense against a cosmic storm of radiation quickly disintegrated—no one was in the mood for play. If not on duty, crew members were either secluded in their rooms or quietly communing in small groups in the Dining Hall or the Domes. The Rec Room gave Merit a place to sit alone and contemplate what needed to be done.

The days of a large following, hanging on his every word, were gone, obliterated in a flash by the villainy of Gap Lee. In seconds Merit had been taken down before the entire crew, humiliated back into the shadows. But he didn't belong there; his place was in front of the crew, leading them, just as they longed to be. Gap had stolen that from him; Gap had destroyed his life. Merit would never again have the opportunity to fulfill that destiny. At least not on this ship.

But they wouldn't be on this ship for long. At some point the weary young star travelers would set foot upon a new world, a world that offered new challenges, new hopes, and new futures.

One of those futures could easily find Merit back where he belonged, in his role as leader.

And Gap wouldn't be there to stop him.

13

The usual banter that preceded a Council meeting was missing, and Triana wasn't surprised. It was late, for one thing. They'd planned to begin at ten, but as she sat down in the Conference Room the clock on her workpad flicked over to 11:35.

But it wasn't simply the late hour weighing on the Council members. Tonight they would make the most important decision since the launch. The most important decision of their lives.

And for a mission that had seen its share of extraordinary events, nothing could have prepared them for what they'd found inside the croy. That, more than anything, cast a heavy shadow over the crew, and it was about to set off fireworks in the Council meeting.

"We have a lot to cover," Triana said. "I want to talk about Alexa first, and then get to the decision we have to make about the Dollovit and the Channel."

She couldn't recall Bon ever speaking first in a meeting, until now. His tone was laced with acid.

"We can save some time. That is not Alexa."

Triana knew this was a minefield. She kept her voice calm. "I wondered the same thing. In fact, we probably all have, which is why I asked Lita to do a—"

"I don't care what Lita says," Bon said. "It's not Alexa."

"Let me jump in here," Lita said. She faced Bon. "I ran a complete scan on the body brought up to Sick House, and it's alive. It's breathing, so there's respiration. The pulse rate is very slow, but it's there, and strong. There is automatic muscle contraction when tested, circulation is taking place, and even the body temperature is within a degree of what most scientists claim is normal.

"I also examined tissues. Skin, blood, hair, even the retinal materials, all check out as normal, with one exception. Then I took it a step further, and pulled up Alexa's records. I compared the tissues from this body with those we have on file, and they were almost identical. It's exactly Alexa's height, and within two pounds of her last recorded weight. If it opened its eyes and hopped off the table, I'd be tempted to say 'Hello, Alexa.'"

Gap tilted his head. "You said one exception. What exception?"

"The brain," Lita said.

"What's wrong with it?" Channy asked.

Lita let out a long breath. "It's a vulture brain."

Channy and Hannah both instantly recoiled. Gap stared at Lita in disbelief.

Bon jumped to his feet and leaned forward on the table. "*This is what I'm talking about! This is not Alexa! We need to get it off the ship right now.*"

"Wait a second," Triana said, trying to restore order. "One step at a time here. Bon—"

"Either get it off the ship, or I will," he said.

"Settle down, Bon," Gap said. "That's not your decision to make alone."

Bon whirled on him, stabbing a finger toward Gap's face. "You're the last person who should be telling anyone around here to settle down. I've sat by and watched a lot of bad decisions made on this ship, but I won't allow one this time."

Triana felt the meeting slipping out of control. She stood up to challenge Bon.

"We will decide this as a Council," she said, punctuating the last three words. "And that's the end of this argument. If I have to post a security detail in Sick House, I will. But no one—*no one*—on this ship will take Council matters into their own hands."

Bon, still standing, glowered at Triana. "Oh, really? Like when you took it into your own hands to fly one of our escape craft into the wormhole? Like that?"

Lita broke in. "May I please ask that everyone sit down? We'll get nowhere with this arguing." She looked back and forth between Triana and Bon. "Please?"

Triana choked back a heated response to Bon and sat down. Bon soon did the same.

"Let me finish my report, and then I suggest we ask Torrec about this," Lita said. "As I was saying, the physical body itself is an almost perfect reproduction of the person we knew as Alexa, right down to the hair and skin cells. But the brain is similar to the one we discovered in the vulture that we studied. It controls motor functions and other basic physiological actions. But it's not what you'd call an advanced thinking brain. It is, as far as I can tell, intended to keep the body alive."

"Interesting," Roc offered through the speaker. "A functioning body with a limited brain. Sounds like Gap."

"Triana," Lita said, "I'm not ready to offer an opinion on what the next step is, but I am saying that we should go slowly here. We're suddenly in an area that is brand new for us—for our species, for that matter—and I think we need time to figure things out."

"I agree," Triana said. She looked to her right and addressed Torrec, who had remained respectfully quiet during Bon's outburst. "Torrec, would you please explain the body found on the croy?"

The jellyfish slowly bobbed inside the tank, and his metallic voice drifted out of the speakers. "Yes, I can explain. What you refer to as vultures are important tools to our civilization. They are called Vo. The Vo that you held aboard your ship was one of a group programmed to acquire information. For the brief time that it remained isolated within a confined space in your clinic, it was unable to complete its assignment.

"When your remote vehicle—your Spider—began what was perceived as an attack outside your vessel, the Vo in isolation took measures to remove itself from the containment device. It attached itself to the crew member you call Alexa, and fulfilled as much of its assignment as possible before the atmosphere of your ship rendered it incapacitated. It documented the majority of information needed to assimilate a copy of the human form, but did not have sufficient time to complete its mission."

There was silence in the room. Triana bit her lip, and did her best to digest what Torrec was telling them.

"So," she said, "if I understand you correctly, the . . . Vo had enough time to record all of Alexa's physical information, but not enough time to map her . . . her brain."

"Correct. As with all intelligent species, the brain is a complex component that requires extensive study and extremely intricate mapping in order to produce an acceptable copy. Your ship lost the crew member named Alexa; we have the capacity to supply you with the closest approximation possible. We call such a reproduction a ventet."

Gap looked at Triana. "Remember what Torrec told you earlier? He said it was a missing part of our spacecraft. He said that this was a gift from the Dollovit."

Bon let out a disgusted snort. "A gift. Right."

Triana ignored this. Her thoughts were a tangled mess, trying to make sense of everything unfolding. If Torrec was to be believed, he and his kind were not openly hostile at all, but merely curious, voracious scientists. They had removed much of the moral—or even sentimental—association to life, and looked upon it from a practical standpoint. If one unit, such as Alexa, was damaged or missing, then you simply replaced it. And if you lacked the complete record, you improvised to get as close as possible.

The "gift" of Alexa might horrify the crew of *Galahad*, but to Torrec it simply was a kind gesture from one species to another.

Or was it something else? Was it something more sinister, disguised as a peace offering?

She tapped a finger on the table and looked around at the Council members. Hannah raised her hand with a recommendation.

"However we classify this ventet, it's living tissue that is incapable of thought, at least the way we understand it. I suggest we keep it . . . well, comfortable, I guess . . . in Sick House until we solve the problem at hand."

"I agree," Lita said. "It's not going anywhere, and certainly not harming anything. We can always decide later."

Bon shook his head. "The fact that all of you are saying 'it' should tell you something."

"Channy?" Triana said. "You're very quiet about this."

"I loved Alexa," the Brit said. "On one hand I agree with Bon that this is not Alexa, and it makes me sad to see this . . . this copy of her. But I also don't know what we can do about it. I mean . . . we can't just . . . you know . . ." She shrugged. "I guess I agree with Hannah."

Triana looked at Gap. "What do you think?"

He leaned back in his chair. "I don't think we have a choice right now. We have to get the ship out of here, and soon. For now . . . yeah, Hannah's right. Keep Alexa, or the ventet, or whatever you want to call it, in Sick House, and we'll deal with it when we get to where we're going." He looked back at Triana. "Sorry I don't have a better answer right now."

She waved that off. "None of us do. Okay, for now we'll keep Alexa's copy in the clinic. No visitors, though, agreed? I don't want this to become a freak show with people parading in to see her."

There were nods around the table, except for Bon, who turned in his chair and stared away from the group.

"Next," Triana said, "we have to decide what we're going to

do about the radiation shield. We've agreed that staying the course is out of the question; Gap and Roc are convinced that we're down to hours at the most. So that leaves two options: either take the ship through a Channel to our original target, Eos, or accept Torrec's invitation to his home star system. I'd like to present the Council's decision to the crew. In the end, they'll have a say in this as well. Let's start by going around the room. Gap?"

"Eos. I'm grateful for the offer from Torrec, but I think we need to complete the mission as planned. I say Eos."

"Lita?"

"I've struggled with how we handle our arrival at a new world. I've spent my whole life studying the great explorers on Earth, and how they treated the people they encountered. Even those with good intentions did a lot of damage, and caused a lot of hurt. I'm worried that it's simply part of our makeup, that we don't do well when we move into new territory."

She looked at Triana. "I worry about that. I've had time to think about what might be there when we arrive, and how we'd deal with it. I don't know."

The Council remained quiet, listening to the one member who often seemed to represent the soul of the crew.

"If you'd asked me three months ago," Lita said, "I probably would have said Eos. But I have too many doubts today. Although I will faithfully carry out my assignments if we choose to go there, and I will actively support this mission, for now I vote for Torrec's home system."

Triana was surprised, but merely nodded. "Thank you, Lita. What do you say, Channy?"

"I'm a fresh-air fiend. I know it could be harsh and brutal on Eos, but I want to get out of this ship and onto land."

Triana looked across the table. "I think we know where you stand, Bon, but would you like to add anything else?"

He gave one quick shake of his head, still not making eye contact with the Council. "No. We go to Eos."

It was Hannah's turn. She gave Lita a long, questioning look, then turned to Triana.

"I'm with Lita. I vote for the Dollovit star system, but for a completely different reason. I don't question how we would treat any indigenous life-forms that we might come across at Eos. I'd like to think that we've come a long way as a race, and that we would represent the people of Earth proudly.

"No, for me it's about the science. It's about the opportunity to learn at the feet of the masters. Believe me, I desperately want to walk on dry land again, and breathe air that's not recycled. And I'd also love the chance to study the remains of the civilization that took hold on Eos Four but somehow failed in the end. Why did they fail? Those are the questions that scientists love to answer.

"But that's nothing compared to what we can learn from an advanced civilization that *hasn't* failed. The math, the science, even the social systems that they've adopted. These are the things that otherwise would probably take us thousands of years to learn if we started over on Eos."

Once again Triana was impressed with Hannah's thoughtful answer. Regardless of how the Council Leader election might have turned out a few days earlier, Triana was thankful that Hannah's mature and well-reasoned arguments were now part of the Council's structure.

The other Council members now expected to hear her position on the matter, but to Triana it seemed that another voice was needed in the debate: a voice that she'd grown suspicious of in the last twenty-four hours. Nonetheless . . .

"Roc," Triana said. "I'd like to hear what you have to say about the two options."

There were raised eyebrows around the table, but no one interrupted. And, when the computer spoke, his usual sarcastic edge was gone.

"On both Eos Three and Eos Four you have everything you need to survive, but it will be tough. On those planets you'll have the chance to build a civilization up from scratch, but there is no doubt that your numbers will also be devastated in the early years, whether through disease, natural disasters, or even predators. This crew, as we've seen in this Council meeting, does not accept death well. On Eos it will be a regular occurrence.

"Had we continued on our path without incident, and arrived safely, I would have cheered you on and assisted in every way possible. But now you have the chance to not only avoid a harsh and brutal world, as Channy so accurately described it, but to grow and learn from life-forms that have prospered for millions of years. They're offering you the chance to leapfrog millennia of hardship.

"I understand your desire for *terra firma*. I also respect the desire to create something on your own, with your own hands. But I would have to say that the intelligent, safe choice would be to accept Torrec's offer, and journey to his home system."

There was again silence around the table, as each Council member tallied the score. Counting Roc's opinion, it was three in favor of Eos, and three in favor of the Dollovit system.

Triana stood and walked to the water dispenser. She felt every eye on her—even Bon, who had sullenly turned his attention back to the proceedings. Taking a long, slow drink, she kept her back to the group.

"Torrec," she said. "When we make our decision, how quickly will we be able to make the journey?"

"Instantly."

Triana nodded, and took another drink. Then she turned back to the Council members.

"It's midnight. Let's get the word out to the crew that we'll all meet in six hours. I want to consider every opinion I've heard tonight, and I'll give my thoughts at six o'clock. At that time there will be a vote, and we'll be gone by noon tomorrow."

14

"You need to sleep," Gap said, walking down the corridor with Triana. "How much more can you cram into your brain right now?"

"I don't think I could sleep even if you medicated me," she said. "But I'll try to grab a catnap. What about you?"

"I'm gonna stop by Engineering. Since we're obviously about to skip out of this part of the galaxy, I don't see any reason why we shouldn't drain a little more power to buck up the shields. Do you agree?"

Triana considered this for a moment. "You're right, it's not like we'll miss the power. But can the radiation shield even take any more power?"

Gap nodded. "A tiny bit. But even another one or two percent might buy us the time we need to make our getaway."

"Okay. Let me know how it turns out."

They parted ways; Gap veered off to catch the lift while Triana ducked into the Dining Hall. She'd barely eaten during the hectic day, and she knew that energy would be required before the next day was over. She hoped that the room would be empty.

It wasn't. In the dim light she picked out the long, black hair and the thin face.

"Hello, Merit," she said. He looked up, evidently surprised to have company at this time of night. Triana noted the vidscreen pulled up to his table, and a workpad open as well. She quickly decided to make her midnight snack a to-go. Her thoughts required quiet time, and at the moment a dose of Merit's arrogant oration was the last thing she needed.

But Merit had other ideas. "I haven't had the chance to officially welcome you back," he called out from his table. "Looks like you've jumped back in at a critical moment. Is the Council deciding what we should all do?"

Her back was to him as she pushed her tray along, scouting for quick energy choices that would be easy to carry back to her room. "Don't engage him in conversation," she told herself. "Don't let him get you off course."

But of course she couldn't let it go. "The Council will present all of our options to the crew in just a few hours," she said. "Then the crew can decide. You should get some sleep so you're thinking straight."

He laughed, but it sounded forced. "I've more than caught up on sleep in Sick House the last few days. But since you're here, can you spare a couple of minutes?"

It would've been easy to say no; she certainly had an excuse to get back to her room. But running from Merit wasn't the way to go. Better to know as much about him as possible. Besides, she didn't want to give him the satisfaction of thinking he intimidated her.

When she'd found a few items to nibble on, she brought her tray over to his table and sat down.

"What's up?" she said, taking a bite from a peanut butter—flavored energy block.

"I'm curious about your trip through the wormhole. I thought you'd come back dead." He gave her a half-smile, then quickly added: "Of course, we're all thankful that you're okay."

"Of course," Triana said, returning the smile.

"I'm sure most people want to know about the other side," Merit said. "But I'd rather hear what it was like crossing the threshold."

"Really? Why is that?"

He turned his palms up. "It's an unnatural barrier, for one thing. Separating distant points in the universe, but infinitely thin. Just the description alone makes it the most incredible discovery of this trip. Unless you count the Cassini."

Triana found no fault with his argument. The Cassini represented power, of course, but seemed . . . what was the best way to put it? They seemed almost too advanced to imagine. The jellyfish, however, despite their sophisticated evolution, were still physical, sentient beings. They might be many leaps ahead of human beings in terms of scientific development, but they still made their way through the universe as corporeal beings. Their accomplishments were—given enough time—within the realm of potential human achievement.

Although comet Bhaktul had dealt a severe setback.

All of that made the Channel, and its mystifying gateway, a thing of wonder and an enviable scientific goal. Triana hated to agree with Merit, but he was right. She contemplated how best to describe her experience to him.

"Have you ever been swimming in the ocean?" she asked.

Merit said, "I grew up in California, remember? My mother taught at Caltech for twelve years—she was brilliant, of course— and I practically grew up at the beach. Why?"

"You know the sensation of swimming in water that's pretty chilly, and suddenly, with no warning, you hit a patch of very warm water. Sometimes it only lasts for a second or two, and then you're back in the cool water. Well, that's almost what this was like. Only instead of feeling it on the outside, on my skin, I felt the change inside." She paused to take another bite. After chewing for a moment she added: "That probably doesn't make much sense, but it's the best way I know to describe it. There was a blinding flash of light, and then I passed out. But I felt that odd sensation inside before I lost consciousness."

Merit seemed to consider this. He sat back and rubbed his face with one hand. "And you're okay making a trip like that again? I mean, you trust our tentacled friend?"

Triana's gaze was cold. "It's not always easy to know who you can trust, wouldn't you agree?"

He returned her steely look, then gradually relaxed into a smile. "Right you are, boss." Indicating his monitor, he said: "I was just checking out the early reports on the Eos system. Interesting choices, wouldn't you say? Are you leaning toward any particular planet?"

She hesitated. Merit never asked a question like that without a reason.

But she was tired, and didn't feel like discussing this with him at the moment. Whatever he was up to could wait.

"I'm thinking about it," she said. "Anything else?"

Another devious smile spread across his face. Tangled hair fell over one eye, which, combined with the small scar on his cheek, gave him a menacing look. "Is it true that the Dollovit have rolled a series of pods off the assembly line?"

He always seemed to be the first with information, Triana realized. He might have suffered a blow in his campaign for power, but somehow Merit Simms remained in touch with everything that was going on, in and around the ship.

"It's true. They're quite good at copying things."

"So I hear," he said. "Things *and* people."

Triana had no desire to wade into this any further. She picked up her tray and stood. The small collection of fruit could go back to the room with her.

"I'd really like to talk more," she said, "but we have a big meeting in just a few hours. Hope your arm's feeling better."

She felt his dark eyes on her all the way to the door.

* * *

It *was* Alexa, but it *wasn't*.

Lita stood beside the bed in the hospital ward of Sick House and looked into the face of her friend. But it was a friend she had declared dead, a friend she had helped to propel into the cold graveyard of space. This Alexa was warm to the touch, with an angelic look about her face that tore at Lita's heart.

The clinic was deserted. It was a few minutes before one o'clock, and Lita had dismissed the crew member pulling this particular overnight shift. With the mandatory meeting just hours away, she was willing to risk that there would be no emergencies before dawn. Besides, she didn't want anyone around during this visit.

Pulling over a chair, she sat down beside the still form on the bed and rested her elbows on her knees. After a couple of false starts, Lita began to talk.

It started with "I'm sorry," and for the next few minutes she spilled it all: her regret at not investigating sooner when Alexa first mentioned the pain, which turned out to be appendicitis; her guilt in not shielding Alexa from a creature that obviously terrified her; and her grief in not knowing how best to mourn the loss of such a good friend.

It all came out. And by the time she finished, Lita found, to her surprise, that she'd unconsciously taken the hand of the Alexa-figure which lay before her, an act so natural for her under normal circumstances. In that moment the dam burst, and all of the tears that she'd held back came in a torrent.

She gripped the warm hand and cried for all of the decisions that she'd second-guessed, and for the loss of her friend. She cried for her family, for a brother and sister who might by now be orphans, finding their way through the chaos that Bhaktul had rained down. She cried for the frightening unknown that lay ahead for the crew of *Galahad,* and for the one sensation that she was unable to shake: that Alexa's death would not be the last before this journey was at an end.

Eventually the tears ran out. Lita recognized that, although she'd wept once or twice during the mission, she'd never had the good cry that she needed. It had been overdue.

"Oh, Alexa," she said, getting to her feet. She wiped her eyes with her one free hand, while the other still gripped the hand of the ventet. With a start she noticed movement.

Alexa—or rather the artificial Alexa—had moved slightly. Had Lita's voice—or her tears—somehow awakened something? Lita leaned forward, then recoiled when Alexa's eyes opened, the lids rising slowly and mechanically, like a doll's eyes opening. The form stared briefly at the ceiling. The head swiveled to one side, then the other.

To Lita it resembled a machine powering up, testing its connections. She almost expected to hear a whir or an electric hum.

Recovering her wits, she immediately ran tests. For the duration, which took about ten minutes, the ventet lay immobile, staring at the ceiling, seemingly unaware that Lita was in the room. The rise and fall of its chest displayed its breathing, and it even occasionally blinked. But there was no sign of recognition or awareness. The physical contact with Lita went unacknowledged.

Lita was torn. She didn't want to leave the figure alone, but she also couldn't stay. She scolded herself for sending the clinic's lone staff member back to her room.

She leaned over Alexa, placing her face into the clone's field of vision. "Can you hear me?" she said, her voice low and soothing. "Listen, I'm going to step out for just a bit. If you need anything . . ."

She let the sentence hang in the air, unfinished. If it needed anything . . . what? What could it do? It seemed incapable of even basic interaction. Would it get up and walk out of Sick House? Lita was reluctant to strap it down; that seemed an unnecessary act of cruelty.

But, because she felt that something needed to be communicated, she added one postscript: "I'll be back in a little while. You stay here, okay?"

It seemed a preposterous thing to say, but it was all she could think of at the moment. She slipped out of the room and padded through the dim light of the clinic.

Torrec drifted in his tank, inching toward the top, then descending before repeating the process. Lita wasn't worried about disturbing his sleep; during the initial investigation the jellyfish ambassador had assured her that only parts of his brain slept at a time, leaving him either fully awake or in a state similar to standby mode. Torrec had yet to turn down a request to talk. After a quick greeting, Lita sat down and carefully considered her words, guarding against offending the alien visitor. She began by asking about the role of ventets in Torrec's culture.

"They fill the gaps in our studies," he said. "Often we are unable to analyze an actual member of a species. In that case, a ventet will substitute. They generally are near-exact replications."

"The reproduction of our fellow crew member, Alexa, has opened her eyes, but she's unresponsive. Will that change?"

"That depends on what you have planned for the ventet," Torrec said.

Lita was confused. "Planned? What are the possibilities?"

"Because we were unable to produce a complete copy, the choices are limited. However, most motor functions are possible. The ventet will be able to use its limbs for perambulation, and will have significant use of its hands. Communication will be limited to simple commands at first, and these will take a certain degree of training. However, within a short time the ventet will complete menial tasks. Nothing to the degree with which you were familiar in its original form, but still practical."

Lita gave a melancholy sigh. It would be like training a dog, or a simple household robot. This would never go over with the crew. She could only imagine the reaction from Bon in particular. Somehow she'd have to convey this reluctance to the Dollovit.

"Torrec," she said, "I want you to know that we're grateful for the gift, so please don't misunderstand what I'm about to say." When the jellyfish remained silent, she plowed on. "Our species attaches a strong reverence to life and, in particular, to the individual. I'm sure you've studied our history, how we treat the death of one of our own."

"It is a confusing history," Torrec said. "It is filled with much ignorance."

Lita smiled. "It's an ignorance born of fear, mostly. And disagreement. No two cultures seem to share the same attitudes or beliefs, and that's been the story for millennia. But nevertheless, we're still mostly consistent when it comes to the way we honor the dead."

"This is true," Torrec said. "Your common link is in the form of an honoring service."

"In our language it's called a funeral. Yes, it's a service for honoring the individual. And it's also a vehicle for closure."

"Explain closure," the jellyfish said.

Lita shifted, unprepared for this tutorial. "It's a human's way of letting go of the individual and using the service to instill lasting, positive memories. It's how we move on with our own lives while keeping a loving memory of the ones we have left behind." She watched Torrec bob in the tank, silent. "Does this make sense?"

"We do not question the cultural manners of the species we encounter," Torrec said. "Whether we understand or not is irrelevant. We accept your tradition."

"Then I hope you'll understand why our species can openly accept reproductions of pods and other inanimate objects, yet be uncomfortable with a copy of an individual who has died. However well-intentioned the gift, it violates the sanctity of our memories. It's a wound that is reopened."

"There was no disrespect intended," Torrec said evenly. "What is your request regarding the ventet? Is it your desire that we destroy it?"

Lita looked at the time on the nearby vidscreen. "That's what makes this so difficult," she said. "Even though the idea of this ventet goes against our customs, it's much too lifelike for us to simply destroy. So I don't know. We'll discuss it again in a few hours, and get back to you. Thanks for talking with me about it."

Again Torrec didn't reply. Lita reminded herself that the jellyfish didn't think in terms of appreciation and gratitude; to them it was either relevant or irrelevant, practical or impractical.

She mumbled a good night and walked back to the hospital ward. The ventet of Alexa didn't appear to have moved. Its eyes were still open and staring at the ceiling. Lita shuddered. She dimmed the lights in the room and left to grab at least an hour or two of sleep.

Assuming she could block the image of those sightless eyes from her mind.

15

The conversation with Merit left Triana unsettled, and she couldn't say exactly why. It was easy enough to discard his blustering talk because that was simply his personality, but at the same time he'd already proven that he was a dangerous element aboard the ship. What he lacked in actual power he made up for through sheer will.

Two things were on her agenda before the crew meeting: another heart-to-heart with Roc—or rather, heart-to-chip—and whatever sleep she could muster. She chose sleep first, and set an alarm for five o'clock.

When the soft tone stirred her from the fitful sleep, she calculated that she'd only managed a little more than two hours, but it would have to do. This would be a landmark day for the *Galahad* mission.

She finished the fruit that she'd picked up overnight in the Dining Hall, and downed two full glasses of water. By ten after five she was wide awake and ready for whatever the day threw at her. She began by pulling out her journal.

Before falling asleep last night I thought about my talk with Merit. I've always had a strange feeling about him, but this is different. He's always angling for something, usually power. I wonder what direction it will take this time.

And after only three minutes talking to him, I can't help but wonder if our species is ready for this second chance we're being given. Are we up for this? I hope so.

She closed the journal, aware that the entry was brief. But there was so much to do.

"Good morning, Roc," she said, sitting at her desk.

"And good morning to you, Tree. Ready to go defy the speed of light? Which is just an expression, by the way. We'll actually be folding the universe like a piece of paper and simply hopping across from one point to another. So let me rephrase the question. Good morning, Tree. Are you ready to go defy the laws of physics?"

"Sure, piece of cake," she said. "Remember, I'm a crusty old veteran of these jumps now. Anything new to report in the last three hours?"

"Pretty quiet," Roc said. "You have a recorded message waiting. Would you like to view it right now?"

Triana knew what it was. Wallace Zimmer had fought through his final days with Bhaktul disease to record a series of private messages for her, with instructions for Roc to parcel them out at select moments during the journey. The clips were painful to watch, a heartbreaking portrait of the final days of a great man. But painful as they were, they also provided a boost for Triana when she seemed to need it the most.

"Let's cover some business first," she said. "Did the extra diversion of power to the radiation shield help us? I'm guessing we'll only need it for a few more hours."

"Let me put it this way," the computer said. "Gap's little Band-Aid will get you through at least noon today. After that, no promises. Hypothetically it could hold for another week, but that would be a foolish bet. I strongly encourage you to make that hop pronto. Pronto, of course, from the latin word *promptus,* which translates to 'beat it before your skin melts away and you die a grisly death.'"

This would normally have elicited a chuckle from Triana, but this morning her sense of humor was on hold. "How much more have you learned about our little friend in Sick House? Have you pinpointed where the jellyfish's star system is located?"

"No, but not because of a lack of trying," Roc said. "Without coming out and saying it, Torrec gives every indication that we're not worthy of that information at this time. I think he's waiting to see what our decision is before he volunteers too much about their empire. I don't blame him."

"Of course you don't," Triana murmured. "Okay, forget pinpointing; do we even know if it's in the Milky Way galaxy?"

"No."

Triana reflected on his answer. She didn't know why the location of the jellyfish system was important to her. Perhaps it was because she'd been there and back, and knowing where *there* was would make it seem more . . . real.

She gave up for now and changed the tack of their discussion.

"I'll present our choices during the meeting in a few minutes," she said. "I'll do my best to present Lita's and Hannah's votes for the Dollovit system as clearly and without prejudice as possible. I'll acknowledge that it's your choice as well. But I'm going to cast my own vote for Eos."

"I see," Roc said. "Would you care to explain your reasoning, or do you want me to wait and find out at the meeting?"

"I'll tell you some of it. Our mission is to Eos, to begin the process of rebuilding the human race. I don't feel that we can do anything like that in orbit around a red dwarf, locked into some mutual study program with an alien race. We belong on the ground."

"Hmm," Roc said. "Of course, you're not going to give the more likely explanation, are you?"

Triana felt her breathing pick up and her pulse quicken. Her interactions with Roc had changed since her return, and this exchange was a prime example.

"Okay," she said, keeping a neutral tone. "Why don't you tell me what the more likely explanation is."

"It's my opinion," the computer said, "that you've had doubts after your trip through the Channel, from the moment you awoke in Sick House. Doubts about what really happened there; doubts about who the Dollovit really are; but mostly doubts about yourself."

"Is that right?" Triana said.

"As for what happened on the other side, the only thing we can go on is your recollection. With Torrec, we either trust him, or we don't; it's that simple. But the doubts you have about yourself are troubling you the most. And, I might add, the discovery of the Alexa ventet only gave your doubts extra fuel."

When Triana didn't respond, Roc nudged her: "Am I correct, Tree, or are you going to try to fool me?"

She waited a moment, then stood up and walked over to the mirror. She brought the light level of the room up another notch and examined her reflection.

Same brown hair. Same green eyes. Same nose, same teeth, same everything.

With her next breath her mind replayed Lita's report from the Council meeting: *"Skin, blood, hair, even the retinal materials, all check out as normal . . . I compared the tissues from this body with those we have on file, and they were almost identical . . . If it opened its eyes and hopped off the table, I'd be tempted to say 'Hello, Alexa.'"*

And Torrec's explanation of why the vulture copied everything about Alexa perfectly, except the brain:

"It documented the majority of information needed to assimilate a

copy of the human form, but did not have sufficient time to complete its mission."

The vulture had only a minute or so with Alexa. Triana had been gone a week.

". . . sufficient time to complete its mission."

"I'm merely thinking out loud here," Roc said. "But I wonder if your vote for Eos is to convince yourself that you are the real Triana. To prove that you can complete the task that Dr. Zimmer put before you. To ignore what might be best for the crew of this ship in order to stubbornly fight any suggestion that you've been copied."

Triana kept her gaze on the mirror while her mind raced to fill in the blanks. She imagined another version of herself, light-years away, kept alive in a perfect copy of a pod—or perhaps within the cocoon of a croy—confused, terrified, and screaming to be released. The latest addition to the Dollovit zoo, the frail specimen from a small, blue planet in an average star system tucked within the dusty arm of a common spiral galaxy. Countless tentacled, bell-shaped bodies of jellyfish swarming around her, studying her, amused by her hysterics. In the distance she could make out the sinister shadows cast by millions of vultures, circling in a choreographed parade, patrolling the outer reaches of the jellyfish domain, guarding their masters' drifting laboratory.

Trapped in a nightmare, a victim of her own impulsive dash through the wormhole. A prisoner of . . .

No. Stop it, she told herself.

There was a copy of her, yes, but it was *there*, staring back from the mirror, questioning everything. It looked like her, but the reflected copy could not think for itself, and couldn't summon memories of a happy childhood in Colorado. It couldn't generate its own thoughts, couldn't formulate command decisions, and couldn't articulate those thoughts without her help. It wasn't real.

She was real.

Whether this was the result of accumulated stress, lack of sleep, posttraumatic disorder, or a combination of them all, the result was the same: it was destructive. And it wasn't what best served her right now. She was stronger than this.

And she knew who she was.

It was time to take charge. She turned and walked back to her desk. "I'm merely thinking out loud now," she said, mimicking Roc. "But I think this is a classic case of misdirection. You want to distract me from the fact that you're smitten with the guest we have in Sick House. It's a computerized version of puppy love, and you've got it bad."

It was Roc's turn to mimic her. "Is that right?" he said.

"Uh-huh. And don't be embarrassed about it. You've worked hard for the last few years. You've earned the right to have a little crush."

"A little crush?"

"Why not?" Triana said. "It's a thankless job running the systems on this ship, you've almost been blown to bits a few times, and you've been humbled by the Cassini's superior intellect. Now here come the jellyfish, another advanced species, but one that acknowledges you—one that *notices* you and *includes* you. You have the chance to give up the babysitting duties for a bunch of rambunctious teenagers, to give up what might be a grueling assignment on a hostile alien planet, and instead to live a pampered life orbiting a soft, red star. Where the only thing required of you would be the occasional sharing of information. Where you'd never again live in the shadow of the Cassini and their guardianship. Where you'd finally be looked upon as an equal, no different than any other species in the jellyfish collection. You wouldn't be a servant to humans anymore; you'd be the sole representative of your own class. You'd finally achieve what you've wanted since the day Roy threw your switch: you'd be the equal of the human."

Roc didn't respond. Triana took a long drink of water, then checked the time.

"You think my vote was merely a way to convince myself that I'm human," she said. "Well, guess what, Roc? I'd say your vote was merely a way to convince yourself that *you're* human."

The words tasted bitter coming out of her mouth, but she also felt that the computer had it coming. Between his shifting loyalties—or at least her perception of his loyalties—and the doubts about her own identity that he'd planted in her mind, it felt good to fight back.

After a long silence, Roc seemed to find his usual carefree voice. "Oh, Tree, our first fight. I feel like we've reached a milestone in our relationship, don't you?"

She stood tall and stared down at the sensor. "Pay very close attention to what I'm about to say, Roc. You won't find anyone on this ship more appreciative than I am for all that you do on this mission. But we're going to Eos. Your job is to assist this crew in navigating our way there, and to help us overcome any and all obstacles that stand in our way. I'll be very grateful for any help that the Dollovit give us, just as I'm thankful for the help that we've received from the Cassini.

"Things will be tough when we get there, probably tougher than any of us are prepared for. But it's what we were chosen to do, and it's why we trained for two years. The crew will get a vote in the matter, but I'm telling you right now: we're going to Eos. I'd like to know that I can count on you, Roc, that you'll be there when I need you."

"I'll be there," the computer said. "Don't expect me to keep my mouth shut the whole time. But I'll be there."

"Good," Triana said. She picked up her workpad and started for the door.

"Are you ready for the video message?" Roc said.

She shook her head. "No. I'm afraid it'll have to wait."

16

The pace of the meeting was brisk. For the first time since the launch, the remaining 250 crew members gathered together. Between the crucial nature of the agenda and the expected short duration of the meeting, Triana decided that the ship could run on autosystems this one time. Everyone packed into the auditorium.

There was no debate, there were no impassioned pleas, there was no question and answer session. All that could be known—which wasn't much—was laid out, with both the pros and the cons of each choice. Now it was merely up to the crew: Eos or the jellyfish star system. Fight and claw through a harsh environment around a yellow sun, or live out a tranquil but restricted life around a red dwarf.

Triana explained each of the arguments that had been raised in the Council meeting, and did so with an impartial tone. She did, however, reveal her own opinion, and made sure to acknowledge that it did not match that of Roc. Torrec had been brought into the room as a courtesy, but he was not called upon to speak.

Triana concluded the first stage of the meeting with an apology.

"I'm sorry that you don't have more time to consider the options, but I think most of you have been thinking about them already. We've run out of time on our current path, and now we're forced to make a giant leap forward. So please, take everything you've ingested this morning, along with any thoughts you've already worked through, and decide what in your gut feels right."

Triana left the stage and settled into a seat on the front row between Lita and Channy. A low hum permeated the air as dozens of isolated conversations broke out amongst the crew. Each person had a workpad with them, and each would use it to cast a vote within the next few minutes. The results would be announced immediately.

The decision would be implemented within hours.

The Council members exchanged a few quiet comments, but the gravity of the situation stifled most small talk. Triana didn't hesitate to cast her vote on her workpad, and noticed that both Lita and Channy did the same. She looked down the row of seats and saw Bon sitting with his workpad on the floor at his feet; he'd obviously voted quickly, too.

Gap seemed troubled, and turned the workpad in his hands several times. Triana was puzzled, given his commitment to Eos. But when she saw his quick glances toward Hannah, it made sense. *He wants to understand her motivation,* she thought; *he's questioning his own position.*

Fifteen minutes later a soft tone sounded, indicating that all votes had been cast. Triana walked up the steps to the podium.

"Our new path has been chosen. As agreed, it's by simple majority. I ask that each of us—and I mean everyone—abide by that agreement regardless of our personal feelings. It's time to prepare for what lies ahead."

She rested her hands on the podium. "Roc, please give us the final tally, and let us know the numbers on each side."

"The final vote wasn't close," Roc said. "By a margin of 212 to 38, it is decided that *Galahad* will finish the mission as originally planned. We will leave for the Eos star system before noon today."

Triana felt an emotional charge across the room as it dawned on the crew: they were almost home. Three years of the journey would be spliced out of the mission, and the idea soon had crew members standing in clumps, embracing and laughing. Triana allowed them to enjoy the moment. Personally, she felt a wave of relief, grateful that they'd stayed true to their original goal. On the front row she saw a resigned look on Lita's face, a discouraged look from Hannah, but smiles from both Gap and Channy. Bon was already striding up the aisle, out of the room.

Triana was about to leave the stage when a voice from the room's speakers cut through the noise. It took a moment for the crew to realize it, but when they finally quieted down, the voice spoke again.

"I would like to address the crew of *Galahad*," said Torrec. He'd almost been forgotten in the celebration, but now was the focus of attention. The stage lights created a curious rainbow effect within the bizarre fluid in his tank, which heightened the mystique of the alien ambassador.

"Yes," Triana said. "Before you do, I know I speak for the entire crew in expressing our thanks to you. We're indebted to you and all of the Dollovit for helping us to reach our goal."

"We have few doubts that your species will take root on your new home," Torrec said. "There are a multitude of qualities that successful species share, but one of those is spirit. Through your actions today you have exhibited to us that you have the spirit, and the bravery, which is necessary to survive."

Now Triana felt a new emotion welling up: pride. Torrec was right. The crew had been pummeled with danger, near-death, and tragedy on so many occasions, and yet still opted for the more difficult choice. We are, she thought, a race of beings that will fight to be free, and to beat the odds, no matter what obstacles are strewn into our path. More than ever, she was anxious to gaze upon the first sunrise of Eos.

"With time running short," Torrec said, "it is imperative that you quickly decide who among you will separate from your group to return with me."

The large room, filled with more than two hundred teens, fell deathly silent. Triana stared across the stage at Torrec, her head tilted slightly, trying to grasp what the jellyfish had said. Separate from the group?

In that instant, all of the fear and stress that had dissipated moments ago returned in a rush. Something was terribly wrong.

She cleared her throat, a sound that, through the amplification, pierced the room. "What do you mean?" she said to Torrec. "I wasn't aware that anyone would be going back with you."

"We have made it clear from the beginning," the jellyfish said. "Our species thrives on observation and study. It is the reason we have Vo positioned in millions of locations. We do no intentional harm, but we gather, we collect, and we study. It is our nature. Your ship's computer, Roc, has referred to the beings you call the Cassini as the policemen of the universe, and to our species as the scientists of the universe. That is an apt description.

"It is a task that we take seriously. Our own experience has taught us to appreciate not only the beauty of life, but its fragility. Even with our advanced technology, we came perilously close to extinction. When we find a new species such as yourselves, we are obliged to collect, study, and catalog. I have made that point on many occasions since our paths crossed, have I not?"

Triana felt a cold knot in her stomach. Torrec had, indeed, said it over and over again. Now, for the first time, the implication took on a dark shadow.

"You've told us that," she said. "But we've chosen to go to Eos."

"We respect that decision," Torrec said. "While we would

have preferred that your entire ship and crew travel to our home system, we will create the Channel necessary to complete your mission. However, we do not offer that help without conditions."

There was an uneasy rumble in the room, and Triana waited for Torrec to continue.

"We will supply you with as many of the reproduced pods that you require to reach your destination, and we will keep the others. We also will soon have a replica of your vessel, the ship *Galahad*, to complement the smaller craft. Further, we will respect your wishes and withdraw the ventet of the specimen you call Alexa, and return it to our system.

"In exchange, there are conditions," Torrec said. "We require two additional specimens, complete units, to accompany me. One male, one female."

This can't be happening, Triana thought. Torrec was demanding a toll before allowing *Galahad* to use the Channel. A human toll. And, if they rejected his demand . . .

If they rejected his demand then all of them could be dead by the afternoon.

She bristled. How could she have overlooked this possibility? She'd somehow assumed that the jellyfish would simply do their bidding, opening highways here and there, allowing them safe passage. Serving them. How naive she'd been, blind to the basic concept of payment for services rendered. And now it was going to cost them two crew members.

Except Torrec had said "conditions." Plural. Triana was afraid to find out what else he demanded for their lives.

The atmosphere in the room had inverted, shifting from elation to dread in a matter of seconds. Triana's mind raced through the possible alternatives left to her, but this was something that would take time to work out. And time was a commodity they did not have. Before she could think of what to say, she saw a figure on the front row stand to address the stage.

"I would like to volunteer as one of the specimens," Hannah said.

Triana was too stunned to reply. She gaped at Hannah, who stood proudly with her hands behind her back, her chin up.

Gap jumped to his feet. "No!" he said. "You can't do that."

"And why not?" Hannah said, giving him a puzzled look. "I voted for us to go with them, and the scientist in me wants to study the Dollovit as much as they want to examine us. Why wouldn't I go?"

Gap was at a loss for an answer. He looked up at Triana for help.

"We need to talk about this," Triana said.

"There's no time to talk about it," Hannah said. Of all the people in the room, she seemed to be the most at ease. "It solves two problems: part of Torrec's demands in return for his help, and a chance for us to learn enough to leap ahead thousands of years." She gave a respectful nod to the jellyfish. "I'm assuming, Torrec, that this doesn't need to be a permanent assignment."

All eyes turned to the glowing tank on the side of the stage. Torrec's voice, amplified through the room's speakers, carried its usual metallic edge.

"That depends," he said. "However, should we acquire all the information we need over time, arrangements could be made to conclude the assignment."

Gap held a hand out toward Hannah. "Over time? You don't know how long that might be. You might never make it back."

Hannah ignored this, and said to Triana: "Volunteers are needed to close the deal, and I'm willing to go."

Triana gave her a sad smile. "Hannah . . . I appreciate your offer. But Torrec requested two—"

"And I'll be the second," came a voice from the left side of the auditorium.

Heads craned to see Manu rise to his feet.

"I'll go with Hannah," he said. "I voted to go to Eos, but

Hannah will need a companion. Besides, she's right: there's a lot to learn, including things that could be a huge benefit to our colony on Eos. Things like health. Medicine. I'm willing to sacrifice a few years now for a payoff later. I'll go."

Triana was thunderstruck. First their leading scientific mind, and now Lita's top assistant. She saw Gap slowly sit down and turn to talk with Lita, who held her head in her hands.

"Hannah, Manu," Triana said. "I appreciate it, really. And I'm sure the rest of the crew appreciates your brave sacrifice. Let's talk after this meeting, okay? We'll figure things out."

Hannah and Manu both nodded to her, then sat down. Triana looked across the stage at Torrec.

"If you have other conditions, we'd like to hear what they are."

"Besides the two specimens, we also request a portion of the contents from the restricted areas of your ship."

It took Triana—and most of the crew—a few moments for this to register. When it did, Triana frowned. "You're talking about the Storage Sections. But . . . we don't know what's inside the Storage Sections."

"We do," Torrec said. "Our mapping of your ship with the Vo revealed every detail, including the lower level compartments that you call the Storage Sections."

Triana's heart raced. She bit her lip and gave a worried look to the other Council members on the front row. Finally, she turned back to the jellyfish ambassador.

"Okay," she said. "What contents in the Storage Sections are you referring to?"

Torrec said: "The people."

17

Yes, it's true, I did know about the contents of the Storage Sections, but I was sworn to secrecy, so quit throwing me the hairy eyeball and pretending that you're mad, because we both know that you'll be hanging around like you're my best friend again in a matter of minutes. I even told you four or five books ago that I was in on the secret.

I would've kept that secret all the way to Eos, too. Who knew that we were going to run into space vultures with some sort of cosmic x-ray vision? I mean, besides that one girl in Oregon; she's figured out everything about two chapters ahead of me. But besides her, who knew?

As the shock wore off, Triana was tempted to gather the Council members into a closed meeting to discuss the bombshell that Torrec had lobbed into their midst. But given the pandemonium that broke out in the auditorium, she realized that this was something the entire crew needed to hear. In fact, they *deserved* to hear it.

People in the Storage Sections? *People?* How was that even possible?

Once order was restored to the meeting, Triana directed her questions at the ship's computer. "Roc, I think it's safe to say that

we're beyond the point of keeping secrets about the Storage
Sections. What does Torrec mean when he says *people*?"

"Note to self," Roc said. "Jellyfish cannot keep a secret."

"He said people, Roc," Triana said, unamused. "What does it
mean?"

"It means that your secret cargo on *Galahad* includes supplies
for your first camp sites on Eos, along with special transport
craft to get the sizable amount of gear down to the surface. And,
yes, you will find people in the Storage Sections."

Triana kept her composure. "How is that possible?"

"It's possible through technology, that's how. You're familiar
with suspended animation chambers; it's how you were able to
add one little furball to the ship's manifest, remember? Well, there
are similar chambers stacked within the lower level, and they
contain additional colonists selected by Dr. Zimmer."

"Teens, like us, I'm assuming?"

"Yes, fifteen and sixteen at the time of launch, just like the
rest of the crew."

"How many?"

Roc said: "Eighty-four."

Another shock wave rippled through the room, and Triana
steadied herself against the podium. Eighty-four teenagers, in a
drug-induced sleep, in the bowels of the ship. In an instant, it
seemed, the size of the crew had increased by a third.

"Why weren't we told about this?" Triana asked, anticipating
the question that every crew member was likely thinking. "Why
would Dr. Zimmer store almost a hundred other crew members
in suspended animation and leave us in the dark? What does
that serve?"

"My job is to assist all of you in the operation of the ship,"
Roc said. "I was ordered to keep quiet regarding the contents of
the lower level. I was not told why that was important to the
mission director."

Triana couldn't decide if she was angry or not, but there wasn't time to worry about that. She had more questions about the arrangement—including how they were expected to handle this upon arrival at Eos—but for now there were other issues to confront.

The jellyfish ambassador had remained quiet during the exchange. Triana turned to him and said: "Torrec, unless they specifically volunteer, I can't give you permission to take crew members who are cryogenically stored below. I won't do that to them. And why do you want additional crew members anyway, especially those that are in suspended animation? What would that serve?"

"I am not interested in the teenaged crew members that are within the cryogenic chambers," Torrec said.

Triana frowned again, and was about to probe further when Roc interrupted.

"Perhaps I should explain. The eighty-four teenagers are only part of the surprise. There are . . . others."

"Others?" Triana said. "You mean adults? There are *adults* aboard *Galahad*?"

"No, far from it," Roc said. "The rapid spread of Bhaktul disease ruled out anyone over the age of eighteen. The others, in this case, are in the form of human embryos stored in special cryogenic units."

"What?" Triana said. She looked at Lita, who appeared stunned, overwhelmed by the barrage of shocking information tumbling forth in the last few minutes. Lita mouthed a question: How many? Triana relayed the question to Roc.

"The original plan," he said, "was to launch with at least three hundred, but there were far too many problems, both from a technical standpoint and also administrative. Meaning it was more difficult to contain—quietly and respectfully—than Dr. Zimmer ever counted on. So your total count in the Storage Sections includes the eighty-four teens in cryo storage, and just a few shy of two hundred embryos. One ninety-three, to be exact."

"Roc," Triana said. "This . . . is unbelievable."

"I'm relieved that I don't have to keep a lid on it anymore," the computer said. "I'm actually glad that Torrec has a big mouth. Well, not literally; I'm not even sure he has a mouth. But you know what I mean."

"So many," Triana said, her voice barely a whisper.

"Yes," Roc said. "If you put them all together, there are more of them than there are of you."

Lita stood up from the front row. "Roc," she said, "how did Dr. Zimmer find that many human embryos? And how could he possibly keep that kind of program a secret?"

"He didn't have to find them, Lita. They found him. From the day the *Galahad* mission was announced, hundreds of thousands of families contacted Dr. Zimmer and his staff, begging to have their children considered for acceptance to the program. But few people knew about the thousands of couples who didn't have children yet, but still wanted their offspring to be part of the mission.

"After that, it was a matter of contacting these people and making one thing clear: Dr. Zimmer would consider them for inclusion in the *Galahad* mission, but they had to sign an affidavit of complete and total confidentiality and secrecy. One violation of any kind, one slip, and their future children would not be included. And, of the almost two hundred that were actually conceived—all of them through in vitro fertilization, by the way—not one person blabbed. It was that important to them."

Triana looked down at the podium as she absorbed this latest news. Although it was unnerving to find out so late in the mission, it made perfect sense. Space aboard the ship was at a premium, as were resources; storing embryos required energy and stability, but no maintenance and hardly any room. All two hundred likely could fit within one large refrigerated cabinet.

It was ingenious. Triana was embarrassed to admit that her initial reaction had been . . . well, she'd been a little creeped out.

But now, given the chance to step back and see it from a scientific viewpoint, she was surprised that it had never occurred to her. Families would do anything to give their children a fighting chance to survive. Why shouldn't that include their unborn children as well?

But a new concern raced into her mind.

"Tell me why, Torrec," she said. "I can understand you requesting two members of our crew, but I'm not comfortable with the thought of you going back to your star system with human embryos. I'm sorry, but it sounds too much like a horror movie for me."

"Your concern is noted, and understood," Torrec said. "I will be forthcoming with you and let you know that our species would be equally as protective in this regard. However, allow me to explain. I am confident that once you hear our position, you will be inclined to agree to the condition."

"You've got a ways to go to convince me," Triana said.

"We do not request all of them, only a fraction of the total," Torrec said. "And there are three important points to consider. One, no harm will come to the embryos. They will be cared for and nurtured throughout their growth stages. We are scientists; we want to study and learn. It does us no good to damage the object of that study.

"Also, we have the tools necessary to bring the children to term, along with a guarantee of health and maintenance. Your Storage Sections contain everything necessary to duplicate a human growth medium, and we do as well. The children will be strong and healthy at birth.

"And finally, it makes sense from a practical point of view for you," Torrec said. "I believe your species has a classic idiom: do not put all of your eggs in one basket. In this case, it would be in a literal sense. Your early days of colonization at Eos will be harsh, and extremely dangerous. By not putting all of your future generations at risk on a planet's surface, you would rest assured that a percentage of your colony's population is safe and well-cared for. When the time comes, these future colonists will be ready to make the trip to Eos to join your growing society."

His arguments made sense. Triana couldn't deny the logic behind everything Torrec said. But she still found herself reluctant to open her mind to the possibility. Her rational mind said it would be okay—she hadn't even *known* about the human cargo stowed in the Storage Sections until minutes ago—but something kept her from nodding in agreement.

And then it hit her. Regardless of how long she'd known about them, the embryos aboard *Galahad* represented the future of their civilization, and her mothering instincts automatically kicked in. She discovered that she was exhibiting an emotional reaction that probably was not too different from many of the animal species on Earth. She was protecting the nest.

She saw confusion on faces throughout the auditorium. No one was prepared for this dilemma. The crew of *Galahad* looked up at her, watching and waiting. From the front row, Channy appeared in knots, while Gap and Lita were once again conferring, their foreheads almost touching as they quietly talked. More than anything at the moment, Triana wanted to hear their opinions.

She stalled. "Do you have other conditions as well?" she said to Torrec. "Or does this sum it up?"

"We require your cooperation," the jellyfish said. "Once the transfer process begins, there will be no room for reconsideration. Likewise, once the Channel aperture is in place, the course is set. The energy expenditure is too great to allow for indecision. And we require your pledge of peaceful intent in all matters, now and in the future. We, like many species you will encounter, do not offer what your people refer to as a 'second chance.' Any violation of peaceful intent will incur harsh, aggressive action. There must be no misunderstanding on this."

It was a subtle message, but a powerful reminder. The Dollovit might be helping the young star travelers—for a price—but they could easily crush the upstarts from Earth in a flash. It was a friendly heads-up from Torrec that the teens on *Galahad* were playing out of their league, and had best remember it.

From her spot on the stage Triana studied the sea of faces. It was easy enough to read the shock that had blown the crew back into their seats. Almost a hundred teens tucked below, along with twice as many embryos. And now their alien benefactors were demanding a fee for their help. It pained her to admit it, but with an impending disaster looming, Triana knew that they had no choice but to agree to the terms.

"I want your word," she said to Torrec, "that all of our companions will be treated well."

"That is understood," the ambassador said.

"And I want your word that they will be returned; that they'll be able to join us again when you've completed your studies."

"I am able to state that those who wish to return will be allowed to do so."

"They'll want to join us," Triana said.

"If so, they may."

Something in Torrec's answer sounded another alarm within Triana. Bon had referred to the space around the red dwarf star as a floating zoo, and how many zoos released their animals back into the wild? Torrec had given his word, but what did that mean to a Dollovit? She realized that she'd been backed into a corner. In order to save the crew, some would have to be . . .

There was no other way to put it: they would be loaned out.

Triana again made eye contact with Lita, exchanging a look of futility. The Council members, along with the rest of the crew, understood what had to be done.

"All right," Triana said.

The countdown began.

18

Gap stood before the familiar panel in Engineering, talking with Julya Kozlova about the patchwork repairs to the ship's radiation shield.

"It's frustrating," Julya said. "One look at this and it seems as if everything's fine, no problems."

"And yet it's crumbling," Gap said. "The additional power seems to have bought us the time we need to get out of here. Let's make sure it's buttoned up for the ride we're about to take."

He noticed Julya start to respond, then grow quiet. She was looking past Gap's shoulder at something. He craned his neck to see Hannah standing in the doorway, her hands clasped together in front of her.

"Got a few minutes?" she said.

No, he wanted to say. No, I don't have a few minutes. No, I'm not going to talk about anything right now. Instead he heard himself say: "Yeah, sure."

After assuring Julya he'd be back in a flash, he walked out with Hannah and let her lead the way toward the lift. He knew where they were going without having to be told. In less than two minutes they stood in the corridor leading to the Spider bay, near the large window that offered one of the best views of the overwhelming star field.

"I don't expect you to say much," Hannah said, leaning against the curved wall. "So let me just say what I have to say. Deal?"

Gap faced her from across the hall, and nodded.

She began to speak, but immediately stopped with a nervous laugh.

"Yes?" Gap said.

She looked away when she answered. "Everything I want to say always sounds so good in my head, but sounds so awkward when it comes out."

He wasn't going to bail her out. Instead, he waited.

"I guess what it comes down to," she said, looking back at him, "is that things were never that bad between us, and we somehow let it get worse. I'm sure I overreacted when you said you needed a break, and I think you overreacted when you heard me talking to Merit. Emotions, I guess."

Gap held his tongue, wondering where this was going.

"You're free to disagree," she said. "I know that the last time we talked privately I said some things out of frustration, and I'm sorry about that. I . . . I guess what I'm trying to say is that I wish it hadn't turned out the way it did. You got mad, I got mad, and all it did was drive us apart.

"Just for the record, I want you to hear what I'm saying. There was never anything between Merit and me. Nothing. He encouraged me to run for Council Leader, and I suppose I needed you to see me as more than just an ex-girlfriend. I wanted you to know that I had more to offer than just a few scientific equations and some oil paintings. I don't regret running for the position, but I do regret that it made things worse between us."

She shrugged. "I look back on it now, and it seems like ages ago. Maybe because Triana's back, and there's so much else going on. But I hope you believe what I'm telling you about Merit. He's a snake. I let him manipulate me more than once, and that's something I'll always regret."

Gap knew it was time for him to respond. He gave a slow nod and said: "I believe you."

They were quiet for a moment, then Gap looked back down the hall toward the lift. "I probably need to get back to work. We've got a lot to do in Engineering to get ready."

Hannah stepped forward and took his hand. "Gap, I'm leaving in two hours. And I don't know when I'll see you again."

He saw tears in her eyes and fought back his own. "I can't believe you're doing this," he said. "I mean, going with Torrec."

"It's the greatest scientific opportunity anyone's ever had," she said. "I'm a scientist at heart, Gap. How could I pass this up?"

"We'll need a lot of scientific smarts when we get to Eos."

"And you'll have plenty of help. I wasn't the only one training for this mission, you know. Plus, you'll have Roc. It's not like I'm leaving you completely high and dry."

"No," Gap said. "You're right." He shook his head. "I know you're right about the chance to study. I just hope that you're not making a terrible mistake. I mean, how will you live? How do you know they'll be able to take care of you?"

Hannah grinned. "Gap, they made sixteen pods, and a realistic human replica, in about a week. I think they can rig up a hotel room and a few tacos."

He finally cracked a smile. "Yeah, I guess so." After looking down at her hand on his, he completely dropped his guard. He pulled her into a tight embrace and held on to her. "I'll miss you, Hannah," he whispered into her ear.

He felt the tremble and knew she was quietly sobbing. "And I'm going to miss you, too," she said. "I'll be back. I don't know when, or how, but I'll be back."

Lita was cleaning the outside of Torrec's tank when Triana walked into the room in Sick House, and the Council Leader couldn't help but laugh.

"Are you washing his windshield?"

Lita grinned. "Can't send him home in a dirty tank. What will his friends think of us?"

Triana dropped into a chair. "I'm not sure they think all that much of us, to tell you the truth. We're just one insignificant entry in their master log of creatures around the universe. Isn't that right, Torrec?"

"We have cataloged many," the jellyfish said. "The significance factor is difficult to ascertain without a full study."

"You're a laugh a minute, Torrec," Triana said. Her expression turned serious. "So, Lita, any comments about the way things are turning out?"

The girl from Mexico dabbed at a smear on the tank. "What's there to say, really? We've got hibernating bodies in the Storage Section, along with fertilized human eggs. If you're asking what I think of your decision to part with some of the embryos, I guess I'd have to say I'm not happy about it. But, like you, I don't see any other choice. Not if we want to get to Eos safely.

"Of course," she added, keeping her attention on the tank. "If we'd decided to go to the red dwarf system, then we wouldn't be parting with anybody."

"I figured you'd say that," Triana said. "If it meant saving the lives of the embryos, I wouldn't hesitate. But I trust Torrec when he says they'll be well cared for, and eventually returned. I'm willing to allow him to study them. Plus, I'm assuming that Manu will do a good job of overseeing them, too."

"I hate to lose him," Lita said. "He's a great worker, and an even better person. Just . . ." She paused, then finished. "Just like Alexa."

They let that lie there for a moment. Then Triana said: "I'm assuming that Mathias will take his spot?"

Lita nodded. "He's very good, so it'll all work out." She chuckled. "Quite the revolving door here at the clinic."

Triana bit her lip, watching her friend meticulously clean each side of the tank. "Torrec, how many of the embryos are you requesting?"

"We will be satisfied with sixteen."

"Sixteen," Triana said. "You guys certainly have a thing for that number. Sixteen pods, sixteen embryos."

"It is the base number in our counting system," the jellyfish said. "The most widely used system on your home planet is base-ten. We use base-sixteen."

"Ah," Triana said. "Well, if it's okay with you, I'd like to keep six of the pods that you produced. We can use them when we get to Eos, and I think we can cram that many into the Spider bay."

"That is satisfactory," Torrec said.

"Uh, and we're also going to have you take back the ventet of the crew member that you made. I hope you understand."

"We've had that talk," Lita said. "He's fine with it. In fact, as eerie as it sounds, I think Manu might want to do a little study on it himself." She glanced at Triana. "You know, cell regeneration, that kind of stuff. Could be helpful later."

Triana let out a long breath. "Sounds too much like the Frankenstein story to me. But if he thinks it can help us down the road . . ."

"What time do we plunge down the rabbit hole?" Lita asked, changing the subject.

"We'll go ahead and plan on noon. Hannah and Manu will leave with Torrec—and the other cargo—around eleven."

Lita stopped what she was doing and put her hands on her hips. "That means you're opening the Storage Sections."

"Uh-huh. In twenty-five minutes. Wanna be there?"

"I wouldn't miss it," Lita said.

"Okay," Triana said, standing. "See you there. In the meantime, I have to go talk with the farmer."

* * *

The farmer was in his office, and for the first time Triana could recall, the door to his office was closed. She walked around to the large window that looked out into Dome 1 and peered in. Bon sat at his desk, absorbed in something on his vidscreen. She wavered for a moment, then tapped on the glass.

Bon didn't move his head, but shifted his eyes to the window. He saw her, but turned his attention back to the screen without acknowledging that she was there. Triana shook her head, then worked back around to the door and pushed it open.

"Begging your pardon, Mr. Hartsfield," she said, closing the door behind her and then leaning against it. "May I take you away from your work for a few precious minutes?"

He continued to gaze at the screen. "What is it?"

"You bolted from the meeting before the fireworks began. I thought that, as a Council member, you should at least get caught up on what we discovered."

"I'm all ears. Catch me up."

"You seem so busy," Triana said, "so let me give you a thumbnail sketch. Hannah and Manu are going back with Torrec, and they're taking sixteen of the human embryos that are lurking in the Storage Sections, but they're not taking any of the cryogenically frozen teenagers that are sleeping in there."

Before she'd finished, Bon was staring at her. She raised her eyebrows and gave him a reproachful look. "See what you miss when you cut out early?"

"You're serious."

"Oh, I'm serious. Eighty-four *Galahad* backups in suspended animation, along with almost two hundred embryos."

"And Hannah is leaving?"

Triana nodded gravely. "And Manu."

"Manu is competent but replaceable. Hannah is unique, and brilliant."

"Wow," Triana said, with a mock look of surprise. "Bon compliments someone. I'll be sure to jot that down in my journal tonight."

He pushed back in his chair and put his feet up on the desk. "Does this change the operation in any way? The bodies in the basement, I mean. Still going to Eos, I'm assuming."

"Yes. Torrec and company leave at eleven, and we go an hour later. You should dismiss all farmworkers by eleven-thirty. I'll want everyone in their room, lying down, when we go through. That means you, too."

Bon shrugged. "Fine. You could have told all of this to me electronically."

"And miss your syrupy-sweet attitude?" Triana crossed the room and sat down in the chair across the desk from him. "Tell me about the Cassini."

He gave a sarcastic snort. "What? Now? You want to talk about the Cassini *now*?"

"You're not using the translator anymore, Bon. By now you must know more about them. The way you hustled down to the Spider bay, you obviously knew about Alexa's ventet on the pod."

"No," he said. "They don't tell me things. I get feelings."

She waved this away. "However you want to put it. You voted immediately for going to Eos, rather than Torrec's system. Did the Cassini play a role in that decision for you, too?"

Bon rocked slightly in his chair. "Yes and no. I get no feeling of dread regarding the Dollovit system, but I know that it would have been a dead end for us. Knowledge is one thing, but not at the price of stagnation."

"Explain that."

"Stagnation of spirit," he said. "The Dollovit are all about securing knowledge. But they live only to acquire the knowledge, not to use it in any real sense. That's why I don't see them anymore as a threat."

"Torrec essentially threatened us just a few minutes ago."

"Probably only to protect their single-minded purpose. Am I right?"

Triana conceded the point.

"They're living encyclopedias," Bon said. "I'm all in favor of expanding our knowledge, of continuing to learn. But it means nothing if we grow physically stagnant, if we don't use the information somehow. On Eos we'll use everything we've learned by putting it to practical use."

Triana knew that she was radiating a look of admiration, but she didn't care. She was truly impressed with Bon's analysis.

"You've changed," she blurted out without thinking.

He grunted back at her. "We've all changed. Every one of us."

She shook her head. "No, it's different with you. I don't know if it's the mind alteration from your Cassini connection, or if it's just the new mature Bon. Maybe a little of both. But you never would have said anything like that six months ago."

His ice-blue eyes bored into her. "And how have you changed, Triana? Did the Dollovit change you? Are you the same person you were six months ago?"

She leaned forward. "I'm not the same person I was six *days* ago. For a while I even wondered if I was physically the same person."

"Oh? Did you think you were a manufactured copy, too?"

"Don't laugh, it crossed my mind."

"How do you know for sure you're not?" Bon said.

She looked out the window to her right and watched a team of farmworkers walk past with shovels and rakes thrown over their shoulders. "I remember something my dad told me once during one of our drives in the mountains. He said that more than a few scientists were convinced that every one of us on Earth was nothing more than a computer simulation, created by some advanced being or advanced computer somewhere. That we were only highly detailed sims, products of a supercomputer's imagination."

"Oh?" Bon said. "And how did these scientists figure this?"

"The theory goes that computer simulation is so good, and

improving exponentially, that computer processing power can literally be more potent than a human brain. And if that's the case, then at some point simulations will be created with human characters that actually think, and believe that they're real."

Bon shook his head. "Nice parenting skills, telling his daughter that she might be a video game."

Triana laughed. "Oh, c'mon. It's all mathematics, really. Once you factor in the number of potential alien civilizations in the universe, and add the combined computing power, it's actually more likely that we're simulations than real, living beings. And I find that very interesting, even if you don't."

"What's the point of this?" Bon said.

"The point is what my dad told me when I asked if he really thought he was a computer simulation. He said: 'Maybe I am, and maybe I'm not. But if I am, I still have every reason to be the best simulation I can. Why make my life difficult or unhappy, even if it's artificial? I'm still living it, regardless.'"

Bon said: "Makes sense."

"Right. So even if I'm a reproduction of the real me, I'm still living it. What am I gonna do, give up? No thanks."

"Is that the real reason you voted for Eos over the Dollovit system? You didn't want a reminder every day that you might be a clone?"

Triana rubbed her forehead and closed her eyes. "Now you're starting to sound like Roc. Let's forget about why I voted for Eos and just take care of business, okay?"

"No problem," Bon said, looking back at his monitor. "Anything else?"

There was plenty. There were volumes that Triana knew she could pour out right now. But she said: "Just wanted to fill you in on what you missed. We're about to open the Storage Sections, in case you want to join us. After that I'll be in the Spider bay to see Hannah and Manu off."

She hurried out before she could say anything else.

19

A flurry of activity put an electric charge in the air. The countdown for *Galahad*'s departure brought back memories of their original launch, which now seemed a lifetime ago. Inside the Spider bay and its control room, crew members scurried about, making room for the six additional pod replicas that would be brought aboard as soon as Hannah, Manu, and Torrec slipped away in the original.

A second Channel had yawned open ahead, the quantum portal waiting to deliver *Galahad* to the Eosian star system. The wormhole's cosmic shock wave had rippled through the spacecraft, but this time Torrec's warning had spared them from injuries.

Triana was running on pure adrenaline. Just down the hall, preparations were underway to open the sealed Storage Sections, with Gap overseeing a team of workers gathered for the big moment. Triana would join them in minutes.

Everything was spiraling down to the finish line so quickly. Years of training and travel, billions upon billions of miles between *Galahad* and her birthplace, countless adventures and crises that had piled one upon the other, new and vivid emotions that had cascaded through her . . . and yet it came down to this. Opening the secretive vault, dispatching crew members who had become like family to her, and parcelling out living embryos in an exotic form of cosmic barter. All to guarantee their safe arrival at a planet—or planets—that could easily turn out to be hostile, even deadly.

The door to the Spider bay control room opened and Hannah stepped inside. She carried a look about her that hovered somewhere between all-out excitement and downright terror. Triana was sure it was the same look that she herself had worn when she'd piloted the pod into the wormhole.

"Ready to go?"

Hannah's eyes were wide. "I don't know. I can't believe it's actually happening."

Triana gazed into the oversized hangar. "I know what you mean. But listen, don't be afraid. I mean, I know it's easy to say that, but it's painless. It's a shock, but painless."

Hannah laughed. "There's so much to see when I get there, and so much to learn from the Dollovit. But what I'm most looking forward to is crossing that barrier. It represents everything that got me interested in science in the first place. It's . . . it's symbolic."

Triana wrinkled her forehead. "What do you mean?"

"Oh, I don't want to get all philosophical at the last minute," Hannah said, looking embarrassed.

"No, tell me."

"Well, it's a doorway of sorts, right? Only this doorway, in effect, separates the primitive from the evolved. It's a doorway that takes us forward several millennia in an instant. We leave our infant self behind, and take our first steps as galactic adults.

"But it might even represent more than that," Hannah said, growing excited. "In my mind, at least, it represents an evolutionary leap so great that it could almost compare to the doorway between life and death."

Triana stood speechless. Of course. Of course! It was exactly the description that her mind had so desperately sought from the moment she'd pierced that infinitely thin barrier and plunged into the space around a glowing red dwarf star. A doorway, a transition from one world to another. But more than that! A transition that took her into another dimension of life, a step that no human could even conceive, a leap that paralleled the mystical barrier between life and death.

Bon was convinced, through his repeated connections with the Cassini, that something, somehow, existed after this life. It had become an obsession for him, prompted by guilt, perhaps, but an obsession nonetheless. For Bon it was no mystery that another existence awaited; it was the transition itself that haunted him.

Now Triana felt an entirely new appreciation for the bridge spanning that gulf. She'd experienced a blinding flash of white light, she'd lost consciousness, and she'd awakened in an alternate reality, descriptions that eerily mirrored those given by people who'd crossed the boundary between life and death.

Before she even knew it was happening, Triana felt tears on her face. At a time when her thoughts should have been dominated by the events at hand, her conscious mind broke away from the Spider bay, from the Storage Sections, from Hannah . . . and took her immediately to her father.

For the first time since his death, Triana felt that she could let him go in peace. She'd been granted a gift that no other human had ever received: the chance to experience—and appreciate—the crossing of a barrier between worlds, between alternate realities, and to know that transitions of this nature could never end at the doorway itself. There would always be another side.

"Tree, are you all right?" Hannah was at her side, gripping her hand. "You're crying. What happened?"

Triana gave an embarrassed laugh and swiped at her cheeks. "It's nothing. Just . . . just a lot that's finally making sense, that's all." She dabbed at her face again and looked at Hannah. "No, really, it's okay. Everything you said is . . . well, it's beautiful.

Thank you for putting your feelings into words. Sometimes that's hard for me to do."

"It's usually hard for me, too," Hannah said. She let go of Triana's hand and gave her own quick laugh. "We don't sound like typical women, do we?"

"We're not," Triana said. "And that's okay, too."

They were interrupted by a tone from the speaker, followed by Gap's voice. "Hey, Tree. You still at the bay?"

"Roger that, as Roc would say," she said.

"Good. Come on down the hall, we're ready to bust into this vault."

Triana looked at Hannah. "Do you still have packing to do, or would you like to join us?"

Hannah was already walking out the door. "Are you crazy? I'm not leaving without seeing this."

D r. Zimmer had been lenient with the crew in many areas. He'd caved to their demands for an Airboarding track; he'd allowed them to introduce some of their favorite foods to the already restricted space in the Domes; and he'd bucked the advice of his advisors and sent each crew member home one more time before the launch. He'd proven to be a strong mission director who could bend at the appropriate time and for the right reasons.

But on one item he'd never swayed an inch: the Storage Sections were sealed, and would remain sealed until the crew reached Eos. The contents would remain out of sight and—ideally, anyway—out of mind. Roc alone knew what lay inside, and his programming was clear. Gap had poked and prodded the computer mercilessly during the first few months of the mission, practically begging to be let in on the secret. But they both understood that it was mostly an entertaining diversion.

A stowaway had breached the sealed compartments right after launch, but Roc had determined that no real damage was done to the interior. The chambers remained sealed without any crew member gaining access.

It was a dark mystery for the lively group of teens, and soon it dominated their late-night banter. What was in there? Why was it a secret? Who would be the first to find a way inside and break the spell?

Then, in one remarkable exchange, an alien visitor had pulled back the curtain and revealed *Galahad*'s secret. And now, on par with the other landmark events that were transpiring on this momentous day, the door would be flung open and the crew allowed access.

Gap grinned as Triana and Hannah rounded the turn on the lower level. To Triana it resembled the face of a little boy with his hand on the doorknob to the living room, anxious to see what delights Santa had left behind overnight. Lita and half a dozen crew members stood behind him, accompanied by a handful of wheeled carts.

"I feel like Dr. Zimmer's gonna come crashing around the corner any minute, pointing and shouting," Gap said. "You know, technically we haven't reached Eos yet."

"If it saves our lives, Dr. Zimmer would encourage us to break in," Lita said. "Besides, I think we've more than earned the right to open this door, wouldn't you say?"

Hannah chimed in. "And it's not like it's a big surprise anymore. Aren't you just dying to see how they've done this?"

Gap stepped aside to show Triana the entrance panel. With the original Eos arrival date still three years away, she'd never bothered to look at the small control switches embedded in the wall. The secrecy, mixed with the dark, remote location within the bowels of the ship, had curbed her curiosity about the Storage Sections.

Standing before the panel that stretched from floor to ceiling, she eyed the controls that resembled an ordinary security lock. An hour earlier Roc had given her the six-digit code, a combination that immediately brought back fond memories and caused Triana to shake her head at Dr. Zimmer's quaint inside joke. Now she took a deep breath and punched in the code.

Nothing happened.

She felt the stares from her shipmates behind her. Was there another step that she'd left out? Had the code somehow been corrupted during the stowaway incident? Did the—

There was a low whine, followed by a click. Seconds later the panel shifted inward about an inch before creeping slowly to the side. With the door's seal broken, interior lights flickered to life, and the hiss of ventilation stirred within the chamber. Triana took one tentative step, and leaned inside.

The room measured about fifteen feet square, and almost that tall, with a passageway at the far end connecting to another room. Given the exterior size of the Storage Sections, Triana estimated that there were likely at least eight rooms linked together. Her apprehension about entering was somewhat diminished by the sight of storage crates looming over them, stacked high on metal shelves. She'd been nervous about immediately stumbling upon bodies; boxes she could handle.

It wasn't until Gap leaned close to her ear and whispered, "Any day now," that she pried her feet from the floor and walked inside. The air felt especially dry, although it was helped by the whisper of a breeze beginning to seep from the vents. Gap and the other crew members fanned out behind her and began a cursory inventory of the boxes. Most had labels that identified the specific contents, but Triana couldn't focus on those just yet.

Summoning her courage, she left the first room behind and moved down the broad passageway toward the next chamber. She saw the first bodies before entering the room.

They were lying in clear cryogenic tubes that were markedly different from the ones found on the pod from SAT33. While the pods were capable of short-term, emergency life preservation, they were older units, hastily added to the small craft.

These, however, were advanced models, designed for interstellar travel and sleep cycles that could last for years.

They were arranged on specially constructed scaffolding that filled the space from floor to ceiling. A quick count showed seven stacks, each containing seven cryogenic cylinders. There were empty slots in several of the stacks, like empty airline seats during a flight. It was evident that bodies hadn't been removed from these empty cylinders; they had never been occupied.

Triana stepped softly to stand beside one of the tubes, and looked through the clear glass into the face of a boy. Strands of blond hair stuck out from beneath a snug elastic cap that covered his head. Close to two dozen electrodes protruded from the gray cap and wound together into a twisted knot of wires that disappeared into a junction box at the head of the tube. His eyes were closed, his face serene. Triana noted the thin lips, the faint lashes, and a sharp, jutting chin. European? North American? She couldn't tell.

He was dressed in what appeared to be an old-fashioned sleeping gown, not unlike the one Triana imagined Ebenezer Scrooge wearing during his midnight jaunts with the ghosts of Christmas. It covered the boy down to his ankles. His feet were bare, and his hands were placed gently at his sides. By all accounts he appeared to be in a deep, peaceful slumber. Two pale lights in the junction box, one green and one yellow, were the only indicators of activity. Triana resisted the urge to tap on the glass, to test the depth of his sleep.

Directly above him, another boy lay in an almost identical state. The only differences that stood out were the boy's ethnicity—Asian, upon examination—and the fact that one hand was lying across his stomach. The skull cap, the wires, the gown, and the soft lights were the same.

Triana walked the perimeter of the room and noticed a mix of ethnicities in the teens occupying the other cylinders. All of them young men. Perhaps the girls were in another room?

She took a count and discovered that of the forty-nine tubes, thirty-nine held bodies. They all seemed to be in good health.

Gap came up beside her, his eyes scanning the room. "This is unbelievable," he said, his voice low, as if in reverence. "I thought I'd be creeped out, but it's actually very cool. We have new roommates."

Triana nodded slowly. "Eighty-four new roommates. And eighty-four new stories for us to learn."

She found the next passageway and, with Gap a step behind her, walked into the adjoining room. It was slightly larger, but held the same number of tubes. Here, as expected, were the girls. Triana and Gap gazed into the first chamber they encountered, into the face of a black girl. She had long lashes over eyes that were parted ever so slightly, giving the appearance of peeking back at the two *Galahad* Council members. Above her, a Hispanic girl had an impish smile on her face, causing both Gap and Triana to smile, too.

"The girls outnumber the boys," Triana said. "Forty-five girls, thirty-nine boys."

"Why do you think there are empty tubes?" Gap said.

Triana shrugged. "I don't know."

They spent another ten minutes combing through the remaining rooms. One housed what had to be the nerve center for the cryogenic controls. Unlike the subdued life signs on the tubes themselves, this unit blazed with activity, both in sight and sound. Digital readouts scrolled across a vidscreen, and a series of electronic sounds echoed off the walls. It all seemed light-years beyond their comprehension, Triana thought. Thankfully they had Roc.

There were two more storage rooms stacked to the ceiling with equipment and supply crates, all assembled to help a young colony take root on alien soil.

Three larger rooms were tightly packed with transfer pods. These small craft, obviously engineered to transport the cryogenic tubes and their control units to the surface of a planet, were essentially moving vans. The tubes would be rolled inside and secured, and the craft would be robotically piloted clear of the ship.

"But how in the world are we supposed to get these off the ship?" Gap said.

"Look at this," Triana said, inspecting the far wall. "See the panel?"

Gap studied it for a moment, and gently brushed his hand across the surface. "Well, whatta ya know? A moving panel. How much you wanna bet that on the other side—"

"—is the Spider bay," Triana finished. "Uh-huh. We move the sleeping beauties into the pods, secure the hatches, and then these walls open into the hangar next door. No wonder Dr. Zimmer put the Storage Sections down here. He could evacuate the suspended animation team in no time."

There was a single room left. Branching off from the cryogenic control center, it was about the size of a large walk-in closet. But the moment they entered, both Triana and Gap felt a shiver. The room was noticeably colder than the rest of the Storage Sections, but it also had a feel about it that was unlike the other compartments. They knew immediately that they'd entered the embryo storage facility.

"This reminds me of my mom's bank," Gap said. "I'd go with her sometimes when she put things into her safe deposit box." He indicated the metal boxes attached to the walls. "They looked just like this."

"And these contain valuables, too, just like your mom's safe deposit box," Triana said, turning on her heel to take it all in. "Think of the responsibility we've just been handed."

Gap gave a solemn nod. "Isn't it wild to think about whose kids these are? They could come from anywhere in the world."

"That's right," Triana said. "Anywhere. And their parents could be anyone. Think of *those* stories."

She stood before the shimmering wall of embryonic storage compartments, her breath visible in the icy chill of the room, while her mind drifted back to the teens who slept in suspended animation. They had stories, too. And one of those might be a bombshell.

Was this how Dr. Zimmer inserted his child aboard *Galahad* without anyone knowing?

20

With only forty-five minutes remaining until the pod departed, Lita hurried back to finish her work in Sick House. Torrec was escorted to the lower level, and she'd soon follow. Her medical skills wouldn't be needed for the launch, but she couldn't let Manu and Hannah take off without giving them a proper farewell. There was no telling when—or if—she'd see them again.

The next step was more complicated, if only from an emotional point of view. She walked into the hospital ward of the clinic, carrying a mug of tea, and approached the ventet of Alexa. It sat peacefully in a chair, staring at a vidscreen displaying a slide show of Earth's various landscapes. It was the only thing that the Sick House workers could think of to entertain their strange guest. And it seemed to work; Alexa's clone appeared to absorb each fleeting scene with a look that mimicked interest, if not wonder.

Lita set the tea mug on a nearby tray and kneeled beside the reproduction of her friend. Again she marveled at the near-perfect copy. The blond hair, which an assistant had pulled back into a ponytail, had the thin dark streaks that Alexa sported. The nose had the same subtle ridge, the eyes were spot-on, and the skin gave off the same alabaster glow.

This Alexa, however, couldn't speak. And if it was capable of complicated thought processes, it didn't show.

"How are you today?" Lita said, invoking the doctor-patient tone that she recalled her mother using during her medical rounds. "Same as yesterday, I'll bet." She smiled when the ventet tracked the vocal sounds and turned its head to look at Lita's face. It gave no emotional signals.

"I brought you some tea. It's your favorite. You used to drink it with me all the time. Do you remember that?"

Of course the ventet couldn't remember, but it seemed the right thing to say.

"This is called Cinque Terre," Lita said, tapping on the vidscreen. The ventet looked back and forth between the screen and Lita's eyes. "It's on the Italian coastline, and it's one of the most beautiful spots in Europe. I never made it there myself, but a few of our crew members have hiked it. Oh, and this is Angel Falls, in Venezuela. I *have* been there, with my dad and my brother and sister. I hope we have falls like that when we get to Eos. That's gorgeous, isn't it?"

The faux-Alexa gazed at the screen, then looked back at Lita. Nothing seemed to register.

"Why are you talking to it?" came a voice from the doorway.

Lita looked over her shoulder. "What are you doing here?" she asked. "This is the last place I thought you'd come."

Bon stood with his arms crossed, leaning against the wall. "What good does it do to talk to that thing?"

"Maybe no good at all," Lita said, turning back to the ventet and tucking a strand of its hair behind one ear. "But maybe I'm not doing it for her. Did you consider that?"

"No," Bon said. "That makes no sense, either."

"Not to you, but that's no surprise." Lita adjusted the vidscreen, reducing some of the glare. After sizing up Bon with a blank look, the ventet returned to its mindless gazing at the images.

"She's not a ghost, Bon, and she doesn't bite. You don't have to stay twenty feet away."

"I'm fine right here."

Lita shook her head. "It's like you hold some sort of a grudge against her, which is ridiculous. She didn't do anything wrong, you know." She lifted the mug of tea and brought it up to the ventet's face. It instinctively accepted the warm liquid into its mouth, slurping it down, almost like a trained animal.

Bon said: "Why are you treating it like a real person? It's not."

"Is there something else you'd like to talk about?" Lita said. "Because I'm not going to debate my work methods with you. It's really none of your business."

Bon pursed his lips and gave a single nod. "Fair enough. Thought you might want to visit for a moment. Can we talk at your desk in the other room?"

Lita's back was to him, so Bon couldn't see the faint smile that crossed her face. "No, I'm busy right now. If you want to talk, you'll have to do it in here with me and Alexa. Pull up a chair, tough guy."

For a moment it looked as if he might turn and leave. But instead he pushed away from the wall and walked a few steps into the room. He sat down in a chair, two beds away, and again crossed his arms.

"If it's any consolation," Lita said, "this copy of Alexa is going back with Hannah and Manu in a few minutes. It will join the Dollovit zoo, I guess you'd say. I'm sure you're brokenhearted over that."

"I'm not here to talk about that," Bon said. "I thought you might want to know about my latest connection."

Lita shifted to stare at him. It was unlike Bon to go out of his way to offer information about his intimate link with the Cassini. She'd always tracked him down, usually in the Farms, to get him to talk about it.

"Looks like you barely broke a sweat this time," she said, hoping that a casual demeanor would make him more likely to open up.

"It's still not the most pleasant thing to do, but I'm learning how to manage it better."

"That's good," Lita said. "What did you talk about today?"

"She's out there," Bon said.

Lita's eyes narrowed. "They said that?"

"I've told you, it's not a conversation. But yes, in a way they said it."

She put the mug back on the tray. "Bon, do you have any idea how big this is? It's the most important question in the history of our civilization, and you're sitting there with your arms crossed, tossing it out like it's . . . like it's the equivalent of finding a new strain of corn or something."

He gave her a weak smile. "Lita, I've dealt with this for awhile now, and I've put myself through an awful lot of physical pain in order to get even this much out of them. I'm exhausted, mentally and physically."

She sat back and considered this. Then she shook her head.

"I'm sure you're worn out, but that's not it. You're acting nonchalant about this because you knew it already, didn't you? This doesn't surprise you at all."

Bon sat still, and didn't answer.

"I'll share something with you," Lita said. "Lately I've done a lot of thinking about the concepts of faith and fate. I don't know if they're somehow connected, or if they're polar opposites. But it's almost been an obsession with me since the day Alexa died." She shot a quick glance at the ventet, which was fixated on the vidscreen's rotating Earth images. An icy chill went through her, and she unconsciously reached up to touch the charcoal-colored stone that hung on a chain from her neck.

"Was it faith that you had, Bon?"

"I don't look at it in those terms," he said.

There was a pause, and then Lita said: "That's it? That's your answer?"

He shrugged. "I don't know what you want me to say. If you're asking if this was a matter of faith or fate, I can't answer that. I had to know, that's all. I needed to know if there's something else out there. I can't tell you why." He uncrossed his arms and leaned forward. "You're projecting your own concerns about Alexa onto me. But I can't help you with that, Lita. You have to decide what works in your life."

She sighed, and by doing so felt a release of tension. As irritating as he could be, she knew Bon was right.

"So," she said, retreating into the casual tone she'd started with. "What are you going to do with this information?"

"Nothing."

Lita gawked at him. "Nothing? You've spent all this time, expended all of this effort and . . . and pain, and now . . . what? You just let it go?"

"That's exactly right. I found what I wanted."

She laughed again. "I don't believe it."

He shrugged again. "That's up to you."

Lita looked at the ventet of Alexa, and then back to Bon. "You don't want to try communicating with her? I mean the real Alexa. Out there somewhere."

"Not anymore. For me it's enough to know that there's another destination. I don't know what it is, or how it is, or however you want to put it." He stood up and glanced at the alien reproduction sitting beside Lita. "Let's just say that we all grieve in our own way, and we all find our own way of moving on. I've found mine. I'm moving on."

"But it's the greatest discovery of all time," Lita said softly. "You can make that connection . . . and then just walk away?"

Bon nodded. "I have no proof, Lita. I couldn't spell it out for anyone, and I wouldn't want to. That's up to the individual. I can't map out what they believe, any more than I can help you with your question about faith and fate. People decide for themselves."

He turned and walked to the door.

"Hey, Bon," Lita said. When he looked back at her, she smiled. "If this means you've found peace, I'm happy for you. I really am."

He pointed to the ventet. "Quit playing with your doll and get rid of it, will you?"

21

The corridor leading to the Spider bay was crammed with crew members. As she walked past, Triana had a fleeting vision, one that filled her with sadness. She saw the well-wishers who had filled the cramped reception room at her father's funeral, waiting for the opportunity to console the young daughter, to share stories that would somehow—they believed—help her understand how loved he was.

It was the longest afternoon of her life. She was all they had left to associate with the great man, a conduit for their praise and grief. Crushed by her own heartache and despair, she had no choice but to stand silently and offer herself as a device for their final good-byes.

The last thing she wanted to do now was to look upon this gathering on *Galahad*'s lower level as a final good-bye. Hannah and Manu had offered themselves as the toll necessary to meet Torrec's demands, but at the same time they both looked upon it as a chance to learn. They weren't treating this as good-bye; why should Triana?

She waited by the door to the oversized hangar, and watched the bizarre procession. It began with Torrec, poised within the glittering syrup of fluid in his tank, rolled on a sturdy cart through the gauntlet of wide-eyed teens. A few of the crew members reached out to touch the reinforced glass as it passed by, each of them peering intently at the jellyfish ambassador. They were perfectly aware that this creature represented the yin and yang of alien contact: Torrec and his kind had wrought death upon *Galahad,* and now promised salvation. He was more than a mere curiosity; he was a symbol of both the perils and the rewards of humankind's evolution into a space-faring civilization.

As the cart drew even, the workers on each side paused, allowing Triana an opportunity to look once more upon their guest. She knelt and brought her face close to the glass. Inches away, floating in the genetically engineered solution which provided him with both protection and sustenance, Torrec raised one elastic tentacle. She was sure that he was aware of her; he had, in effect, saluted.

The moment passed. Triana stood and watched as he was escorted into the bay, and then heard the crowd in the hallway grow quiet. She looked back to see Alexa's ventet come into sight around the curve. It was walking on its own, but Lita kept a firm grip around its arm.

The ventet's face betrayed no emotion, but instead seemed to study the mass of human faces along the path. It looked side to side with a mechanical grace, never resting its gaze on any one spot. It was doing what it was programmed to do: observe and document.

For Triana it provided another painful jolt, as she—and the assembled crew members, undoubtedly—couldn't help but note that this would be the second time that Alexa departed through the Spider bay. Even though she wasn't real, the feeling was the same. That, Triana realized, was a testament to the reproductive skills of the Dollovit and their vulture labor force.

Lita approached the door and gave Triana a silent nod, with a look that said everything was going to be all right. Triana spotted the dark pendant around Lita's neck, and felt her breath catch in her throat. She could imagine how difficult this walk must be for her friend, but Lita's head was up and her face composed. As the pair walked by, Triana reached out and squeezed her hand.

A minute later there was a swell of activity beyond the corridor's curve, and Triana heard the sound of Manu's laugh. He was greeting friends, a backpack slung across one shoulder, a smile on his face, while a wave of hands reached out to slap his back or shake his hand. He kept moving, the pace slow, but constant.

Behind him, Hannah moved through the line. Triana recognized the reluctant look on Hannah's face, and knew that it had nothing to do with the mission at hand, and everything to do with the attention. She politely responded to the cries of good luck, and nodded appreciation for the well-wishes. She even cracked a smile when someone channeled an early space pioneer with a hearty "Godspeed, Hannah." But Triana knew that the quiet blonde from Alaska wouldn't be comfortable until she was strapped inside the pod, preparing for a journey that seemed tailor-made for her. It was, in a sense, the ultimate Semester at Sea.

Triana noticed the unmistakable shock of black hair and angular face of Merit Simms. He'd remained in the background, but now pushed forward and reached out. His hand snaked around Hannah's wrist, causing her to swivel her head in his direction.

The look told Triana everything in one split second. Merit's wicked smile played across his face, while Hannah stiffened. Her face was stone-cold, her eyes bottomless pits. Merit leaned forward and spoke into her ear; Hannah responded with a grimace, and yanked her arm away. In a second she was beyond him, leaving Merit to smile after her and offer a sarcastic wave.

They reached the door into the bay. Manu grinned at Triana as he slipped past. Hannah stopped beside the Council Leader and they exchanged a quick hug. Before pulling away, Hannah whispered in her ear: "Watch out for Merit. He's still a snake, and I know he's up to something." After a pause, she added: "And look after Gap. Please."

Hannah glanced back toward Merit, then gave Triana a knowing look before walking into the hangar.

Watch out for Merit. Look after Gap.

The sentiments were a reminder of the inner dangers that continued to simmer within the walls of the ship. But the words also stirred old memories, a confusing blend of emotions that she'd never sorted out. Triana knew that she could easily get lost in there, wondering, worrying, trying to make sense of feelings that taunted her.

The crowd dispersed, drifting back toward the lift. Like good sailors, they had shown their respects to their crewmates, and now began preparing for their own assignment. Their conversations were muted. Triana watched them leave, then made her way to the Spider bay control room.

Gap and a handful of crew members had already stowed the sixteen containers aboard the pod and now double-checked that everything was secure. Each unit held an individual human embryo, along with a self-contained cooling apparatus and stabilizing gear. While Triana said that crossing the Channel boundary wasn't physically turbulent, no chances would be taken with such precious cargo.

Alexa's ventet was next. Lita led the clone inside the small craft and saw that she was comfortably seated and strapped in. Lita felt that she should say something, but found no words. This wasn't Alexa and, with the limited brain capacity of a vulture, it would never understand. In the end, she resorted to the only physical act that made sense to her at the moment: she stroked the ventet's hair.

She wasn't prepared for what happened next. There was a slight tug around her neck, and she looked down to see the ventet grasping the dark clump of space rock that Alexa had left behind. The stone had intersected the clone's field of vision as it hung from Lita's neck, and its reaction was to reach out and take hold of it. The alien reproduction had shown no impulse beyond observation—until now.

The ventet's eyes were locked on the cosmic pendant, scanning its odd shape. "Do you like this?" Lita asked. "Does this look familiar?"

It couldn't, she told herself. Despite looking like a perfect copy of her friend, this wasn't Alexa, nor did it have Alexa's memories. An alien organic brain lay within the skull, the same simple motor that powered the vultures. It couldn't possibly understand the significance of this clump of meteorite.

And yet this was the first time the ventet had shown any initiative. It had been content to be led around, to be placed in a bed or a chair and to remain inert. Nothing had moved it to act independently. Until it saw one of Alexa's personal possessions.

This couldn't be coincidence.

Lita's concentration was broken by a commotion at the rear of the pod. Manu and Hannah scrambled aboard with Gap and two other workers. Gear was quickly stowed, and a last-minute checklist was consulted. Lita caught the eye of Hannah.

"What's up?" Hannah said, dropping to a knee beside the ventet.

"Listen, we only have a minute before we seal you up in this thing," Lita said. "Take care of yourself, okay? I know that you and Manu have lots to do, but be careful. Get your work done and get back to us, understood?"

"You bet, Doc," Hannah said. She saw something in Lita's expression and added: "Is there something wrong?"

Lita lowered her voice. "Keep your eye on our friend here, too. She's . . . uh, she may not be what we think."

Hannah looked puzzled, but only nodded. Lita gave her another tight hug, then found Manu and did the same. He gave her a nervous smile.

"Got your lucky amulet?" Lita asked.

He tapped the pocket on his shirt. "Don't worry about us. This will ward off any bad juju on the other side."

She laughed with him. "I hate to part with both you *and* the good luck charm. I have to say, I felt better with that thing hanging around Sick House."

"It left some of its residue," Manu said. "You should be good for awhile."

It seemed awkward to hug him again, so Lita squeezed his shoulder and told him to be safe and to hurry back. She walked toward the pod's hatch and, just before dropping down to the hangar floor, looked back.

Alexa's ventet was strapped into the seat, but had craned its head around. It was staring intently at Lita.

With a faint smile on its face.

Triana put Gap in charge of the pod's launch while she returned to the Control Room. There were only two crew members on duty there; most of the ship's departments were throttling down in preparation for the Channel jump.

"One minute," she heard Gap say on the intercom when she'd settled at a workstation. "Hangar door is open."

"Roc," Triana said. "What's their ETA for the Channel once they're off the ship?"

"Between our speed, and the loop we've made back to the opening, they should be over the lip in about sixteen minutes. You'll get to say bon voyage before you're tucked in."

"What's the status of the remaining vultures?"

"Let's see," the computer said. "Fifteen . . . eighteen . . . times four . . . carry the one . . ."

"Roc . . ."

"Most of their squadron took off in the past hour. Some are hovering around the Channel, a few are scattered along the way, and it looks like another two dozen are lining up to escort the pod. That leaves at least twenty, maybe a few more, for our trip."

Triana frowned. "What do you mean, for our trip?"

"I thought you knew," Roc said. "Perhaps you should have a quick chat with Torrec before he disappears down the rabbit hole."

Before Triana could respond, Gap announced: "Pod away, hangar door closing."

"Roc, patch me in to Hannah," Triana said. After a silent count of three, she said: "Hannah, do you copy?"

"Right here," came the immediate reply. "We're off and running."

"Is Torrec in the loop?"

"I am here," Torrec said in his strange mechanical voice.

"What is this about a squadron of vultures . . . I'm sorry, Vo . . . coming with us? Nobody discussed that."

"It is only natural that we will want to have a record of your successful deployment to the system you call Eos, as well as a record of your settlement."

Triana thought about this, biting her lip. Of course it made sense. The jellyfish were essentially providing them with passage on their highway; why wouldn't they want to document everything? The vultures had multiple responsibilities, including their duty as sentries. It was practical, which seemed to be the nature of the Dollovit.

So why did it bother Triana so much? Why did she look upon a vulture escort as an invasion of their privacy? Or was it even more sinister? Were the human colonists doomed to be under jellyfish supervision, in one form or another?

The thought irritated her, but she held her tongue rather than lash out at Torrec, who, for all she knew, was merely keeping an eye on the fledgling star travelers as they settled into their new home. It was possible that the Dollovit were being good stewards of space.

And yet it didn't feel that way. The notion of the vultures following them into their new home system seemed . . . invasive.

Triana had been silent for too long. Torrec, Hannah, and Roc were monitoring the transmission, waiting for her response. "Of course," she said. "Thank you for the official escort to our new home." After a brief pause, she added: "I'm sure that our two civilizations will remain good friends and partners for a long time."

On one level it sounded overly theatrical, as if written by a politician. But in her heart she felt that they had to begin this new phase of their journey—and the first phase of their new settlement—as equals. The Dollovit might be technologically superior, but it was vital that Triana make it clear that the human species would not serve beneath them. Nor should the Dollovit believe that they would occupy Eos in any capacity; they would be invited guests.

For the next few minutes Triana busied herself with updates from each department, determining the readiness of the crew for the jump ahead. The only section out of touch was—not surprisingly—Agriculture; Bon was nowhere to be found.

"Oh, wow," she heard Hannah say, wonder dripping from her voice. The pod had made visual contact with the rip in space. "This is . . . spectacular."

"Manu, how are you doing?" Triana said with a smile. Hannah would be chomping at the bit to dive through the Channel, but for Manu it was likely the most terrifying experience of his life.

"I'm great," Manu said. "Hannah's sold me on how much fun it's going to be. It *is* going to be fun, right?"

"Like an amusement park ride, Manu. The shortest ride of your life."

Gap broke in from the Spider bay. "Twenty seconds. Good luck, Hannah, good luck, Manu."

"Thanks," they replied in unison.

"Thank you both again for volunteering to go," Triana said. "We'll be out of touch for awhile, so take care, and we'll catch up again soon, okay?"

"Sounds good," Hannah said.

"Ten seconds," Gap said.

Triana watched the giant vidscreen in the Control Room, although the Channel opening was too small, and too far away, to be visible.

"Uh . . ." Hannah said. "That's odd—"

Then there was silence.

22

Have you ever tried talking your friends into doing something that you thought was the greatest thing in the world, and you could tell from their reaction that they were only going along with it because (a) you were their friend, (b) they really were curious about it, (c) they were too tired to argue, or (d) there was free food involved?

Now think about the situation on Galahad. *You have a couple hundred teenagers who have been cooped up for a year and are now facing some weighty decisions. If one person pitches what they claim is a brilliant idea, some people are gonna be curious and some are gonna be too worn-out to disagree.*

Especially when Merit is the guy doing the pitching. We know it's not the food; there's plenty of that up in the Dining Hall.

The personal quarters on *Galahad* were not designed to hold many people. Each room, other than Triana's, was set up to house two crew members, with space for washing, as well as clothes storage, drawers for personal items, and a shared desk. At the moment there were twelve people crammed into Merit's room. He sat on the edge of his bed, while the others sat on the floor.

"How many will it take?" asked Liam Wright.

"That's hard to answer," Merit said, adjusting his expression to appear thoughtful. "At the very least, I'd say fifteen to twenty. Hopefully we'll have more than that."

Liam looked around the room. "You don't even have that many here."

"But when the time comes, others will be here. Believe me."

"Why?" asked Balin Robinson.

Merit turned his palms up. "Because no matter what's happened, there are people aboard this ship who don't believe in the way the Council runs things. There are people who would like a fresh start without Triana and her pals running everything." He smiled at Balin. "You're here, aren't you?"

Balin shrugged, but didn't answer.

"How will you decide which planet?" asked Liam.

"That's easy," Merit said without hesitation. "Just show me which planet Triana and Gap and the rest are choosing, and we'll take the other one. If they want Eos Four, we'll be happy with Eos Three. And if they want number three, we'll make do on number four." He smirked. "I hope it's four. I love the water."

He looked around at the group gathered near his feet, waiting for follow-up questions, but for now they were willing to simply listen. He liked it that way; too many questions meant they were thinking too much for themselves. That was the last thing he wanted. And if they trusted him enough to come to the meeting, it meant they had their own misgivings about the Council's leadership. It was time to close the deal.

"We'd be okay slaving away under the Council's rule, you know? We could do it if we needed to. We've already done it for a few years, haven't we? But just imagine if we were given a blank slate. Imagine if we had a world of our own. Imagine if we could build it from scratch, where everyone had an equal say in things. Where everyone's opinions counted. Where everyone worked just as hard as the other person, and shared in the same rewards. It won't be that way on Triana's world, I can guarantee you that.

"But give us the chance to do it *our* way, and imagine the result in a few years. Think of what we could build. And it doesn't even matter what planet we're given; we can build something spectacular regardless of where we begin." He paused and gave them an encouraging smile. "Go and think about it and, if you'd like, talk with your closest friends. I don't know about you, but I'm excited thinking about what we could accomplish together."

There were a few nods, and a few smiles returned. The group stood, stretched their legs, and said their farewells. Lockdown had been ordered for the jump, with all crew members expected in their rooms. Merit walked them to the door, said his good-byes, and then chuckled to himself.

The spoken word was a powerful tool. It was the strongest weapon in his arsenal, and he knew exactly how to wield it. And the best part of all, of course, was the way that it could mold a mind that was unsure. Throw out a few comments about equal say and equal reward, and it was irresistible to some. Include a few well-timed smiles along with the words, and it became even more believable.

Merit had the beginnings of his new pack, many of whom had followed him the last time he'd spoken up. And while they basked in the idea of equal say, he knew that, when the time came, they wouldn't *want* equal say. They'd want a leader. They'd want someone to do the dirty work for them.

Like they always did.

It was spooky. The ship appeared deserted, the corridors empty, the usual gathering spots—the gym, the Dining Hall, the Rec Room—vacant. Lita and Bon walked the upper levels, making a last-minute check to confirm that all crew members were safely tucked into their rooms. The plunge through the Channel wasn't violent, but it would likely render each person unconscious. Channy was making a similar check on the lower levels, along with her roommate, Kylie. Gap would stay on duty in the Engineering section, and would strap himself in when the time came. Triana was stationed in the ship's Control Room.

"I didn't see you at the Spider bay earlier," Lita said. "Didn't you want to say good-bye to Hannah and Manu?"

"They'll be back," Bon said, poking his head into the Rec Room. "Besides, there was work to do."

Lita gave a solemn nod. "Right. Gotta make sure the apple crates are locked down, and all that. Right?"

"Something like that."

"Plus, you're probably not very good at good-bye," Lita said. "All that icky emotion. Yuck." She paused, scanning the hallway ahead of them. "But you'd come and say good-bye to me, right?"

She couldn't see Bon's face, but from his voice she could tell he wore a half-smile. "Probably not. If you left there'd be a long line of sobbing friends. I don't like lines."

"You're such a creep," Lita said with an exaggerated pout. "But you'd miss me, of course."

They'd reached the Dining Hall. A quick glance showed it was dark and empty.

"Sure, I'd miss you," Bon said. "With Manu gone, who'd be there to nag at me if I ended up in the hospital again?"

They walked in silence for another minute, taking the lift down one level and beginning the process again. It was merely a precaution; *Galahad*'s crew had followed their instructions.

Lita resisted the urge to engage Bon in more lighthearted banter. She'd gotten just about all that could be expected from him in one session. But there was a subtle change in Bon that she liked. He was still blunt, of course, but he didn't seem . . . angry. That was it: he wasn't seething inside, no longer struggling against the malicious intent of the big, bad universe. It made him approachable.

She wondered if it was a mistake to get used to that. The raging side of the Swede might return at any moment.

Or would he? Lita had watched Bon progress through the classic stages of grief—or most of them, anyway. Perhaps his last connection with the Cassini brought him to a place of peace. Maybe he no longer railed at the universe because he'd discovered that there was so much more to it than he'd ever expected.

On the other hand, Lita thought with a smile, maybe he was just in a better mood because he practically had the ship to himself. *That* was just as likely. But, if it was true that a kinder, gentler Bon was breaking through to the surface, it made him more attractive than ever.

The thought of him in those terms had never occurred to her before. Between the stormy relationship she'd noticed between Bon and Triana, and the confusing, abrupt relationship he'd shared with Alexa, Lita had never allowed herself to look at him that way. He'd been off limits.

But now . . .

t figures, Gap thought. All of the turbulence that the ship had weathered, all of the near-catastrophes that they'd skirted, all of the systems failures that they'd endured, and now, as they approached the most frightening part of their journey, *Galahad* was purring. The ship barely held together during the roughest stretches, and now decided to relax and coast to its rendezvous with the star portal.

He strolled between rooms in Engineering, making minor adjustments, and drifted through the memories: standing before a panel while puzzling through the mystery of the heating dilemma on level six; huddled with Triana and his Engineering assistants, sweating over a power surge that took them to the brink of a deadly explosion near Saturn; and the frustrating collapse of the ship's radiation shield which threatened a slow, agonizing death.

Jumping hurdle after hurdle, stumbling along a course that seemed so easy when they were studying under the nurturing blue sky of Mother Earth, when the launch and the mission seemed so far away, so unreal. *We've earned our wings,* Gap thought; *we've proved ourselves.*

And, he decided, he'd proven himself worthy, too. He thought of the bleakest moments of this odyssey, when he'd withdrawn from the Council, from the crew, and retreated into a darkness that he'd never imagined. He'd questioned his abilities, and he'd questioned his worthiness of even being selected for the mission.

But his rise from the darkness had been as swift as the descent. He recovered his confidence, and rediscovered the spirit that his mother had always lauded as the spark that made him different. Made him special.

The regret he carried from that experience was the damage he'd inflicted upon Hannah. And now, finding himself alone, he wondered if it had been worth it. He'd learned so much about himself, and had grown in ways that only came from enduring personal defeat. But it cost him a part of himself, too; a part that he now mourned.

Balancing the books, he realized. Payment for acquiring experience. Nothing easy, nothing free.

Slowly the painful thought that he'd kept at bay forced its way back into his head: Hannah was gone, and he might never see her again.

Alone, and on the fringe of a completely new beginning, he leaned against the metal panel, put his head in his hands, and softly wept.

23

hat's odd.

What would cause Hannah to say that? What did she see when the Channel opened up before her? Or was there something wrong with the pod, something that seemed out of place?

The questions rolled through Triana's mind as she monitored *Galahad*'s progress from the ship's deserted command post. Torrec had arranged coordinates with Roc, piloting them toward the second wormhole that lay waiting for them, the rip in space that would deliver them to Eos.

If Torrec could be trusted. Hannah's puzzled exclamation didn't necessarily mean that something was wrong, but it contributed to Triana's growing unease. It was one more reminder that all of the control lay with Torrec.

And that was a miserable feeling.

The Council Leader sat up straight and registered the data spilling onto the vidscreen. Gap assured her that they'd make it to their destination before the shield sputtered and shut down. Barely. Once through to the other side, the bruised effect on space would be absorbed by the ring of debris circling the yellow star. And, with guidance help supplied by the Cassini, they'd navigate safely into the comfortable lagoon within the Eos system.

Over the next several minutes, Triana heard from Channy and Kylie, then Lita and Bon. All decks were clear, and they were back in their respective rooms. Gap gave a final thumbs-up from Engineering. All that was left was the leap of faith.

"Roc," she said, "I show our ETA for the Channel to be eight minutes. Any status changes?"

"No, we're right on track," Roc said. "At this time I'd like for you to make sure your seat back is in its upright and locked position, and that your tray table is stored. Thank you for flying Trans Debris."

She laughed despite the latest round of butterflies. This would be her third venture through a wormhole, but this time with more on the line than just her own neck.

Seconds ticked by. With just over six minutes remaining she powered down non-essential components in the Control Room, not for any particular reason; it simply seemed the prudent thing to do. The majority of the workstations were shut down. The lights dimmed to the ship's late-evening mode, and the room slipped into a shadowy twilight.

A random thought crossed her mind. "Roc," she said, "are you nervous? I mean, are you capable of that . . . feeling?"

"How sweet of you to ask," the computer said. "I wouldn't say nervous. But I do have a measure of curiosity about the process. You're a veteran of this operation by now. Are you worried about it?"

Triana glanced at the tiny monitor as it ticked off the remaining time. Five-thirty-seven, five-thirty-six, five-thirty-five. Was she worried?

"I'm . . ." She paused. Five-twenty-nine, five-twenty-eight, five-twenty-seven. And then, without warning, a sensation sped through her, and she swallowed hard. She wasn't worried, no. She was . . .

"I'm angry," she said.

"Oh," Roc said. "You could have given me ten guesses and

I wouldn't have chosen that particular emotion. Care to elaborate?"

"I'm tired of worrying and wondering. I'm frustrated that we're constantly at the mercy of others, merely because we're the new species on the block, and we can only hope that they're benevolent. I'm bothered that Dr. Zimmer didn't tell us about the additional crew members we've been toting around. When you roll all of that together, it makes me angry."

She watched the seconds tick by. Five minutes.

"I suddenly don't trust anything anymore. I don't trust that Hannah and Manu were taken to the Dollovit star system, I don't trust the motives of your good friend Torrec, and I don't trust that Eos is waiting on the other side of this Channel, like some promised land."

She sat back and added: "What happens if we abort the Channel maneuver?" she said.

"Chalk up another surprising quip from the Colorado girl," Roc said. "Abort the maneuver?"

"Yeah," Triana said. Four-forty-one, four-forty, four-thirty-nine. "What happens?"

"You know what happens. Slow subatomic dismemberment, where your atoms fling their various parts around like a two-year-old throwing a tantrum at day care. You won't die so much as cease to exist, leaving a microscopic pile of quarks and an empty pair of shoes."

Triana bit her lip. Four-thirty, four-twenty-nine.

"Plot a new course to steer us away from the Channel," she said. "We're not going."

"Oh, Tree," the computer said. "You have about four minutes left before you seriously regret that decision. There are no do-overs in this game."

"Plot it."

"Ignore that order, Roc," said a thick voice behind her. She turned to see Bon standing just outside the door to the lift.

His eyes were glowing. Dull orange.

Triana stood up. Bon was clearly under the influence of the Cassini, but walking and talking. With no translator.

"Bon—" she began.

"Ignore the order, Roc," Bon said again. "We're going through."

"Listen to me," Triana said. "Something's not—"

"No, you have four minutes to listen to me," Bon said. He stumbled toward her, looking stiff, unsure. But determined.

"Your distrust of the Dollovit is understandable," he said. "But you're wrong. They're peaceful."

"How can you know that?"

"The Cassini know it. And the jellyfish wouldn't be here if it wasn't true."

Triana sat down, throwing a quick glance at the timer. Three-forty-one. "Okay, I'm listening."

Bon staggered next to her and pulled a chair under him. Once seated, he seemed slightly more at ease. His eyes, however, stared at a point over Triana's head.

"The Cassini came here when our universe was created, from outside."

"What does that mean? Outside?"

"It means that they rode the wave which created our universe." He sighed, apparently flustered at having to condense such a deep subject into a thumbnail sketch. "Imagine a vast number of universes, each an independent collection of matter and energy, but in separate dimensions. Now imagine if two of them somehow collided. The result would be an explosion too powerful to comprehend. A big bang, if you will. Matter and energy would pour into this new universe. The Cassini rode that wave, and have expanded as the universe has expanded. As if they're perched on the skin of a balloon as it's blown up; it expands, and they ride along with it. Space really has no meaning to them, nor does time.

"And, as we guessed, they can assist civilizations at times, or they can destroy. But their primary role is universal policemen. They watch over each and every intelligent species that crawls up from the slime, noting their progress, watching their baby steps turn into giant leaps toward space. And they guard."

"Guard what?" Triana said.

"They guard the beauty and the perfection of each universe."

Triana shook her head. "I don't know what that means."

Bon tilted his head, as if some new signal had sounded, a flash that only he could comprehend. He said: "Wanna know what gives us away as infants? It's not how inferior we are in terms of space travel or technology. It's the fact that we take the universe for granted. We see it, but we don't really see it. We register that there are planets, and stars, and galaxies. But we neglect the perfection of it. We see right past the beauty of that perfection. We take it all for granted. We ask a few questions, but we plod through each day without any regard for the magnificence of it all. It labels us as not only cosmic children, but spoiled children at that."

Triana could only nod now. She couldn't disagree with what he said.

"The Cassini are not only watching to see how far along various civilizations are progressing with their technical abilities; they're paying attention to the maturity of each civilization as well. There's apparently a point we can march right up to and still get away with our immaturity—kinda like a parent letting a child push the boundaries. But if by the time we reach that point we haven't begun to fully develop as universal citizens, then . . ."

His voice trailed away. Triana didn't need him to finish the sentence in order to figure it out for herself. She glanced at the timer. Two and a half minutes.

"Is that what happened to the advanced civilization on Eos Four?" she asked.

"Yes."

"And . . ." Triana wasn't sure she wanted to ask the obvious follow-up, but she had to know. "And does that explain Comet Bhaktul?"

"Yes and no," Bon said. "The Cassini did not send the comet, nor its killer plague, into our path. They did have the power to divert it, if necessary. But that would have alerted humans to the Cassini presence; you can't just push a comet out of the way and hope that nobody notices. More important, however, was the fact that we didn't seem to be worth saving. Although we weren't to the point where we needed to be eliminated, we also weren't showing much . . . how do teachers say it? Potential. In other words, as a species we were a long shot to get our act together.

"And that's why they've been helping us on *Galahad*. As cosmic citizens on Earth, we were on the downhill path as a species. But the Cassini were impressed enough with the drive and ambition of this mission to give our kind another chance. A fairly slim chance, but a chance nonetheless."

They could have saved us, Triana thought. *They could have saved billions of lives.*

Including her father.

Her blood began a slow boil, but just as quickly she calmed herself. That wasn't fair; the Cassini weren't responsible for the death sentence delivered by Bhaktul. If anything, the immaturity of Earth's most prominent inhabitants—but not the only dominant species, according to Torrec—was the deciding factor. Blaming others, rather than accepting responsibility, was the kind of behavior that likely landed humans in the cosmic doghouse in the first place. Reverting to that mentality now, in the face of everything that had transpired in the last three years—including all of the progress they'd made in the most dire circumstances—would be a catastrophic mistake.

The Cassini didn't owe the human race any favors.

"So you're saying that the jellyfish have earned their free pass," she said to Bon. "They aced the test."

"You could say that," Bon said. "But you have a deadline coming down right now, and I just thought you should know that your distrust of them is misguided. It might be better to search within the walls of this ship if you're looking for unscrupulous characters. We have our share."

Triana raised an eyebrow. "Agreed. And what are you suggesting we do about that?"

The orange eyes seemed to intensify. "You might not have to do anything," Bon said. "The issue might take care of itself."

"Oh? How?"

Bon adjusted his posture in the chair and fastened the restraint across his waist. "It's almost time. You better make sure you're buckled up."

The timer flicked under the forty second mark. On the room's large vidscreen, the impossibly dark rip in space seemed to rush at them, preparing to devour Earth's survivors. It was now or never.

Roc, as usual, felt the need to chime in: "He might look like he's had a few too many carrots, but Bon is probably right."

Triana bit her lip again. Bon was on the Council because Dr. Zimmer trusted his instincts. The surly Swede might not have the best social skills, but he also thought things through rationally. And he did, after all, have a hotline to the oldest sentient beings in the universe.

She jabbed the intercom button. "Here we go, everyone. Twenty seconds to the jump. Good luck to us all."

She cinched her lap belt and stared at the image on the screen, stubbornly refusing to let it intimidate her. Bon reached over and grasped her hand as the screen was swallowed in darkness, followed by an explosion of light.

24

It wasn't the sensation that she'd expected. Lita lay on one of the beds in the hospital ward, instead of the one in her room. She wanted to be on call should there be emergencies following the leap. All of the vidscreens in the room were shut down; after hearing Triana's description, she wondered if the visual aspect was too jarring for the brain to accept. That might have partially accounted for Tree's lapse into unconsciousness.

But Lita had blacked out as well, a split second after feeling her stomach lurch. It was the same feeling in her gut that she remembered from her lone experience on a roller coaster. That hadn't gone well for her, and she'd been happy after that to send her brother and sister on their merry, screaming coaster adventures while she opted for the more subdued carnival rides.

There was more to this feeling, though. Beyond the pitch and roll of her stomach, she'd felt as if her body had subtly shifted in place. Now, after coming to, she slowly pushed herself up on her elbows and took stock of her physical condition. She appeared to be in exactly the same spot, and yet it definitely felt as if she'd moved on the bed.

"Roc," she said. "How long was I out?"

"Zvid thirt blunk tau bielsk," the computer said.

Lita's mouth fell open and her eyes widened. "Roc?"

"Sorry, I had to do it," Roc said. "Gotcha, didn't I?"

She fell back onto the bed and threw an arm up over her face. "Ugh, I hate you right now. I really do."

"No, you could never hate anyone, Lita. And to answer your question, it's been twenty-nine seconds since we dove through the window."

Lita pulled her arm away and stared at the ceiling. "Twenty-nine seconds? That's it? So I was out for . . . what? Less than five seconds?"

"I don't know the exact moment your brain was flipped back on, but that sounds about right."

She sat up again, and this time swung her legs off the edge of the bed. "This might sound like a silly question, but did you black out? Did you feel anything? I mean, I know you don't actually *feel*—"

"Not true," Roc said. He manufactured a fake sniffle, then said: "Nobody ever takes my feelings into consideration."

"Well?"

"No, I did not black out, and yes, I did comprehend a change. Your human brain can't handle having itself split in two for even a second, so it does an immediate reboot. I, on the other hand, have no problem with my chips occupying two places in the galaxy at once. In fact, it's rather stimulating. I could get hooked on this jumping stuff."

Lita said: "What kind of change did you feel?"

"I've never been shoved in the back," the computer said. "Mainly because I don't have a back. But that's the closest description I can give. It seemed like my awareness of the familiar surroundings of the ship were pushed forward."

A shove in the back. And she distinctly felt movement before blacking out, even though she'd remained in the same spot. She shook her head, perplexed.

"Well, we seem to have made it through in one piece."

Sliding off the bed, she walked out of the ward and over to her desk. "Triana," she said, snapping on the intercom. "Triana, you there?"

There was no response. A trickle of concern worked its way into the base of Lita's spine, and she fidgeted for a few seconds.

She tried again. "Tree? Hello?"

"I'm here, Lita. Sorry about that."

"What are you doing?" Lita said.

A small laugh came through the speaker, a contented sound. It caught Lita by surprise; Triana rarely displayed joy. But the Council Leader sounded genuinely happy. She said: "I'm looking at our new home."

The scene paralleled the one that had taken place three hundred fifty days earlier. Almost every set of eyes aboard the ship found a window or vidscreen, captivated by the sight of the surroundings. But while the view of a year ago had been of a receding Earth—a farewell glimpse that evoked tears of sadness— now they gazed upon a sight that held both promise and relief. For although it appeared barely larger than other stars, this particular orb represented something more than just their destination. It represented victory.

The crew of *Galahad* wept again, only these tears were an emotional release of the fear and tension that had stalked them from the beginning of their mission. Eos was within sight, which many interpreted as the finish line, the culmination of the most critical journey in the long history of humankind.

Triana knew differently. She understood that getting to this distant star system was an accomplishment that, only years earlier, seemed impossible. But it was merely the first step. Perhaps even the easiest step. The work that lay ahead dwarfed the efforts required to keep the ship intact as it streaked through space.

Nevertheless, she rejoiced at the successes they'd logged, including this final flip through a cosmic tunnel. In less than the blink of an eye, their gray, shopping mall–sized vessel skipped over forty-seven months of tedious star travel, arriving in the misty outer banks of the Eos star system ages before anyone could have anticipated.

This time the brief blackout hadn't seemed as frightening to Triana. She'd already experienced it twice, and therefore knew what to expect, but was that it? Or was it Bon? Did it help that this time she hadn't faced it alone?

Oddly, Bon remained conscious through the wormhole; he was, in fact, the only crew member to make that claim. Lita suggested later that it was his connection with the Cassini that buoyed him during the jump. As she put it: "If you hadn't been online with the universal cops, you would've slumped over like the rest of us."

He stood at a workstation in the Control Room, already plotting the ship's safe passage through the storm of debris that ringed the outer fringes of the Eosian system. In this respect, most star systems were identical. Without the guidance help of the Cassini, *Galahad* would be obliterated by one of the trillions of pieces of rock that tumbled and crashed through this chaotic ring.

Triana walked up to the room's large vidscreen and inspected the bright point of light that beckoned from nearly four billion miles away. Roc began sifting through the region's data, gathering information that previously could only be guessed at from the restricted observations from Earth. Now, with Eos and its planetary posse upon them, more details could be mapped.

"Roc," she said, her eyes darting across the screen. "Will we need to alter our speed to maneuver through their version of the Kuiper belt, or will we be able to juke our way through?"

"Hard to say definitively at this stage, but my initial calculations indicate no," the computer said.

Bon, his head still hovering over the keyboard, confirmed.

"We won't need to hit the brakes, if that's what you're wondering." Triana could see the orange reflection of his eyes glinting in his monitor. Between Roc's assessment, and Bon's Cassini input, the final leg of their tour—rocketing through the system toward the two Earth-like planets in the habitable zone—would take a little over two weeks.

"I've detected our shadows," Roc said, reminding her that the jellyfish empire would never be out of the picture completely. The vulture squadron had slipped through the same Channel, and now swarmed around the ship. "I see they're sticking with their base-sixteen system. We have an escort of thirty-two."

It seemed a lot to Triana, but what number wouldn't have struck her as too many? She made a conscious effort to accept the escort, even if she didn't embrace it.

"Roc," she said, "how much time do you need to get a concise layout of the planetary system?"

"Oh, I'm quite speedy. It's almost finished."

Triana didn't doubt him on that. She looked at Bon, who pushed his chair back from the keyboard. "We'll get the Council together in the Conference Room in one hour. Roc, you can present your data then."

She pulled her long hair away from her face and walked toward the lift. "If anyone needs me, I'll be in my room."

A re you okay?" Katz asked.

Merit groaned, and managed to nod once in reply. He bent over the sink in his room, while his roommate stood behind him and stared at the reflection in the mirror.

Although few people even knew his first name—he was simply Katz to everyone—the seventeen-year-old from New York was one of the more popular members of the crew. Merit was aware that Katz didn't like him, and thus probably didn't care if Merit was fine or not. It was simply an act of courtesy. It was more likely that Katz was worried about his Californian room-mate throwing up again in the middle of their room. Merit, on the other hand, worried that the news might spread among the crew.

"I'm okay." It was intended to sound confident and strong, but instead came out as a croak. Merit cleared his throat and added, with more force: "It's not the jump. I think it's something I ate a couple of hours ago. It's been giving me fits ever since."

Katz nodded, but obviously wasn't buying it. Anyone could see that Merit didn't handle the Channel flip very well. "Then if you don't need anything, I'll see you later."

"Right," Merit said. "See you later." When the door closed, he leaned back over the sink and closed his eyes.

The world had shifted, but for the better, as far as Channy was concerned. She lay on her bed, her fingers digging into the thin material of the bedspread. Iris busied herself with a bath, seemingly oblivious to the jump that had occurred. Kylie stirred on the other side of the room, but didn't seem to be in any distress; Kylie had always been tough, a nice trait to have in a roommate.

The shift—more like a wobble, Channy decided—happened right before she passed out. She remembered flinching as it occurred, but not being afraid. She'd been startled, that's all.

Now, she looked up at the colorful strips of cloth that created a plume of vivid blues, reds, and yellows above her bed. They were arranged in no discernible pattern, a design that Kylie ridiculed as "a collision of color." Channy gave no thought to the display's order; for her it was about the cheer that it exuded.

At the moment it gave her a place to focus her attention while she absorbed what had just taken place. The conclusion she reached startled her almost as much as the shift itself.

She wasn't afraid anymore. Of anything.

The past two months had been difficult for the young Brit. She'd suffered heartbreak, a loss of confidence in her by Triana, and moments where she felt completely overwhelmed by her fears. For someone who'd always been the ship's brightest light, the funk created an endless loop of despair for Channy. She didn't *want* to be afraid, but the more she tried to talk herself out of it, the further she slipped.

The gloominess only intensified as, one by one, crew members began to drop out of their usual exercise routines. With the crisis of the radiation shield, and the upheaval caused by the vultures and the Dollovit, excuses to skip the gym multiplied, until Channy found herself leading only a handful of people through the programs. What had always been her greatest source of energy—her thriving, pulsing workouts, packed with attentive and energetic crew members—became a chore, too often with just a smattering of faces staring back at her. She was falling into a well.

But something shook her when the ship broke through the Channel's infinitely thin doorway. The jump seemed to toss her sideways, and yet upon coming to she noted that she hadn't budged. The jolt had, however, rebooted her thinking.

It was as if a layer of grimy film was stripped away, revealing a fresh, hopeful path before her. Taresh? She cared about him, but his power over her had evaporated. Her fear of the vultures, the Channel, even the unknown? Senseless.

She'd looked at the wormhole the wrong way. The intimidating dark rip in space wasn't a lifeless, sinister end point; it was a boundary, nothing more. In her case, it was the boundary between a past that she'd allowed to darken her spirit, and the brightness that comes with awareness. According to Triana's account, the piercing of the Channel's horizon was accompanied by a blinding, white light.

If so, it was a light that penetrated Channy's soul, rejuvenating her spirit. She smiled at the dazzling, intricate pattern on her ceiling, a mishmash of intertwined cloth strips, and realized that it didn't need to have order within it. It needed light to bring out the inherent beauty hidden by darkness.

Things would be different now.

G ap blinked and shook his head, trying to clear the fog. He was on the floor of the Engineering section, tilted to one side. True to his stubborn nature, he'd convinced himself that strapping himself in wouldn't be necessary. As the ship approached the Channel opening, he'd taken a seat and stretched his legs out before him in a foolish attempt to balance himself. His last memory before blacking out involved an awkward sensation in his gut, tricking his brain into believing he was moving. He wasn't. But his involuntary reaction was to countershift against the perceived movement, and that, combined with his loss of consciousness, put him in his present condition.

He sat up, wincing at the sharp pain in his right pinkie finger, which had apparently buckled under his weight during the fall. He wrung his hand a few times, silently scolding himself for not taking Triana's warnings seriously. The finger was broken, which wasn't a serious physical setback; it was the needling he was sure to get from Lita and Channy that he dreaded.

His first priority was the radiation shield. Getting to his feet and once again wringing his hand, he was at the control panel in five strides.

"Hey there, Roc," he said. "I guess we made it. At least I did; are you there?"

The computer answered immediately. "You know how much I love that question. The metaphysical implications are so . . . so . . . deep. Are any of us *really* here, Gap?"

Gap ignored the bait and studied the data. "I thought for sure there'd be a spike, or a jolt, or something. It doesn't seem to have been affected at all."

"I tried telling you that you were looking at this wormhole all wrong," Roc said. "You wanna talk about whether something is there or not, you should start with one of those. It's so quantum I can't stand it. Gives me little computer shivers."

"What about the bruise effects on this side?"

"I'd say nominal. They're spreading out before us this time, so we're riding the wave rather than meeting it head-on. Much smoother that way."

Gap raised an eyebrow. "And our companions?"

"Right there alongside us. I'm sure they'll stick to us like dog hair all the way through the debris ring. We have the magic ticket, remember, courtesy of Mr. Grumpy Pants with the orange peepers."

This finally induced a chuckle from Gap. "I'd hate to hear your nickname for me when I'm not around."

"It's Mr. Sloppy Socks. By the way, comb your hair because you have a Council meeting in one hour."

The smile stayed on Gap's face as he worked his way around the various data panels in the section. By the time he finished his inspection, a handful of Engineering workers came through the door, ready to take up their assignments. Gap spent a few minutes talking with most of them, then walked to the lift at the end of the hall. As much as he dreaded it, he'd have to incorporate a stop at Sick House to get his finger wrapped before the meeting.

25

Chewing on an energy block, Triana finished dressing. The quick shower had been glorious, and she felt a surge of energy running through her body. In twenty minutes she and the Council would get the layout for their new home star system, and she was eager to hear it.

The near-deadly brush with the stowaway/saboteur seemed a lifetime ago.

She sat at her desk, brushing her hair with one hand while opening her mail file with the other. A few department reports began trickling in as life on the ship accelerated back to normal. There was a personal note from Channy that brought a smile; *Galahad*'s firefly appeared to have found her spark again. And Gap delivered good news in the form of a clean status report from Engineering.

Her eye drifted down the page until she spotted the notice of a video message. It was the recording from Dr. Zimmer. Ashamed that she'd forgotten her mentor and father-figure, she opened the file.

Triana stiffened and almost looked away when the image materialized. The evidence of Bhaktul's cruelty was frightful. This once-proud scientist, the man who had dedicated the final years of his life to ensuring the safety and survival of

251 teenagers, looked gaunt and defeated. It seemed difficult for him to keep his head steady. His eyes, which once sparkled with wit and enthusiasm when addressing his young charges, were now pools of sadness. Through the obvious pain and embarrassment, Dr. Zimmer did his best to put on a brave front. He managed a shaky smile.

"I'll have to make this quick," he said, his voice feeble. "I'm going out dancing in a few minutes, and I can't keep the ladies waiting."

In spite of the crushing sadness she felt, Triana found herself laughing at the dying scientist's charm.

"My original plan was to have enough of these personal messages to last the duration of your journey, but it's beginning to look as if that won't be possible." He turned away from the camera and coughed. From the sound and the intensity—his body contorted under the strain—Triana knew that he suffered excruciating pain. She felt more tears form in the corners of her eyes, and her breathing became choppy.

When he turned back, he held a bloodied handkerchief to his mouth. After composing himself, and blinking away his own tears, he struggled ahead.

"There's so much I want to tell you, so many things that might help as you grow into the magnificent young woman that you're becoming." He gave a wry smile. "I guess I do feel like your second father at times. I feel like I should be there to look out for you. But, of course, you don't really need that."

He coughed again, not as violently this time, but it still racked him with pain. He wiped at his eyes again.

"I suppose one thing that I could leave you with is a piece of advice that my grandmother shared with me when I was about your age. She was a sweet, gentle woman; how she managed to live all those years with my cantankerous old grandfather, I'll never understand. I think it somehow was her nature to care for someone and help to smooth out their jagged edges. She certainly did that.

"I don't remember her making too many speeches. It took very few words for my grandmother to make a point. But once, when it was just she and I alone in her kitchen, and I was rambling on about the constant moving that my family . . ."

Dr. Zimmer seemed to choke on something, and left the picture. Triana heard him in pain, off to the side, and it caused a fresh round of tears. She wanted to reach through the screen, and across time, to comfort the man who had long been dead. For although only a single year had passed aboard *Galahad,* their ever-increasing speed meant that time dilation was in effect, and the Earth would have aged many years.

A moment later Zimmer once again slid into his chair and gave an apologetic smile. "My grandmother listened to me complain about how often my parents and I moved. My father was a sales troubleshooter, a hired specialist for several large companies, so we were always moving. I went to seven different schools before finishing ninth grade, and I used that as an excuse for so many things. I remember telling my grandmother that I wished we could just have a home.

"Well, she waited until I ran out of steam. Then she said: 'I see that you mistake the walls and the furniture for the home.'" He gave a shrug. "For the next couple of minutes she went about her business in the kitchen while she let me stew on that. Then she came over to me and placed her hand on my chest. She said: 'You build your home right here, Wallace. It's not made of bricks and roofing tiles. It's made of love for your family, and it goes wherever you go.'

"From that point on, I looked at my life—every aspect of it—in a new light. It changed the way I approached my schoolwork, it changed my attitude about each town I lived in, and it helped to make me a better man. It especially helped me when I began teaching, when it seemed like each town melted into the next. Two years at Michigan, two in Europe, three years at Caltech, then another year overseas and a year at MIT, all before I settled here. I made sure that the days didn't become a blur, and I learned to find something—anything—from each place that I could hold on to, that I could appreciate. I left things behind in many of these places that I carry around today in my heart."

He leaned forward. "Because that, Triana, is what it will always come down to. You'll realize that your home isn't in Colorado, and your home isn't on some untamed planet around Eos." He tapped his chest. "Your home is built around you, your friends, and your next family." Another sad smile developed on his face as he leaned back again. "Don't look at Eos through the eyes of a settler. Look at it through the eyes of a strong, confident young woman. One who is at home wherever she lands in life. That will give you power beyond belief."

Triana sensed that his time had ended and, from his expression, he had, too. He bravely fought off a coughing spasm and, with a determined look, gave her one final smile. "I love you, Tree," he said, holding up a hand to the camera.

Now her tears were accompanied by sound. She cried out loud, holding her hand up to press against the image of his. "I love you, too," she said, her vision blurring.

A moment later the screen faded to black. Triana left her hand in place for a full minute, staring into the dark glass which now bounced a faint reflection of her tearstained face back at her.

His words had mass. Like her flesh-and-blood father, Dr. Zimmer always managed to convey messages that penetrated deeply and took hold at her core. She resolved to make sure his final words weren't in vain.

The Council meeting was almost upon her. She walked across to her mirror and worried over the puffiness she saw staring back, splashing cold water on her face, then dabbing it with a towel. She concentrated on her breathing as she stared at the image, repeating Dr. Zimmer's words from memory, rededicating herself to live up to his expectations of her.

His words were powerful. But . . .

But there was something else in his message that gave her an odd feeling. Something that he'd said was ringing in her subconscious, trying to get her attention. What was it? What had he said?

It was time to go. She turned to leave her room, her mind still sifting through the words of her mentor, trying to identify the cause of this new chill.

26

Per their new custom, *Galahad*'s Council members congregated in the hallway outside the Conference Room, making small talk before their scheduled meeting. Channy was her old self, which pleased Triana and gave her renewed hope in their mission. Iris hung over Channy's shoulder like an infant, stoically tolerating the treatment because it included a generous scratching of the ears. The cat's eyes blinked shut while she purred, opening only to examine a crew member who passed in the hall. For the only pet on a ship of two-hundred-plus teenagers, life was good.

Triana felt like tons of weight had fallen from her shoulders. True, they still had two weeks of travel time ahead of them, including a mad dash through the Kuiper-like debris on the outskirts of the Eos system. But literally years of travel had been shaved off their mission, which was just fine with the Council Leader. In her mind, the crew of *Galahad* had dealt with more than a mission's worth of danger and sorrow. As she stood in the corridor, reclining against the gently curved walls, she felt better than she had in months.

Channy babbled away at Bon who, strangely enough, seemed to actually be listening. More than once he nodded his head, and at one point even volunteered a comment. Triana stared, wide-eyed. Strange days, indeed.

Of the four Council members, Gap seemed the most withdrawn. He'd quietly greeted everyone with a casual hello, accepting Channy's teasing about his taped finger with a polite smile. Triana presumed that Hannah was at the heart of his melancholy. Theirs had been a choppy relationship, but losing her—even if only temporarily—was enough to siphon away much of his natural passion for life. It was obvious: he missed her.

"Let's go in and get started," Triana said.

"Without Lita?" Channy said.

"She left a message saying something came up in Sick House, and she'd be late."

"Someone sick from the jump?"

Triana shrugged. "Didn't say. C'mon, we'll catch her up, or she can follow on the tripcast. I'm gonna let the crew listen in this time if they want, because we're going to cover what lies ahead."

The group filed into the Conference Room and took their usual seats. After brief departmental reports, Triana opened up the meeting to the rest of the crew. It could be accessed throughout the ship over the vidscreens.

"Roc," she said, "let's have your report on the star system."

"The planets themselves are interesting, but let's deal with the star first. On the old-school H-R diagram, Eos is a class G star, which means it's similar to the sun. It's a little older, however, which means in about three billion years it'll run out of gas, and you'll have to find a new place to plant your petunias."

"Like the jellyfish did when their star died of old age, right?" Channy said.

"Gold star for Ms. Oakland," Roc said. "Otherwise, Eos seems rather stable, and looks to be in good health. Nothing special to report. But the planets . . . that's a different story.

"Eos has a total of seven primary planets in its stable, and a handful of dwarf planets that meander in the background. The two inner planets could best be compared to our planet Mercury: they're small, rocky, and not very pleasant. Of these, number two seems to have had some history of an atmosphere, but it's long been blown away.

"I'll come back to three and four, since they're the ones you're most interested in. Planet five is similar to Jupiter, but even larger. It's a big ball of gas, but that's where the comparison to Gap ends."

Proving that he wasn't completely depressed, Gap gave a smile and said: "Get on with it, you box of bolts."

"Planet six will be every girl's favorite," Roc said.

Channy perked up. "Why?"

"Because it's pink."

"Hey, that's fantastic!" Channy said. "A pink planet! Can we swing by to take some pictures?"

"Sadly, our course won't take us anywhere near number six," Roc said. "You'll just have to schedule a field trip another time."

Triana was surprised to see Bon speak up from the end of the table. "Tell me about number seven," he said.

"Why don't you tell *us* about number seven, Bon?" Roc said.

The Swede tapped his finger on the table, staring at the graphic that Roc displayed on the vidscreen. His intensity level seemed to have shot up.

"What is it, Bon?" Triana said. "Do you know something about this planet?"

Bon kept his eyes on the vidscreen, but finally answered. "That's where the Cassini have their outpost in this system. On one of its moons."

It shouldn't have come as a shock. If what Bon had told her earlier was true, then the Cassini had been present since the beginning of the universe. In fact, he'd said since *before* the beginning. How had he put it? *They came from outside.*

They'd be everywhere. If they'd discreetly camped out on

Saturn's moon, Titan, since the birth of the solar system, there was no reason to think they wouldn't be occupying Eosian space as well.

"I can't confirm Bon's announcement," Roc said, "but he's the one with that particular walkie-talkie and the creepy eyes. All I can tell you is that number seven is a gas giant, with at least forty-five moons, and an orbit that is slightly off the elliptical plane. Beyond seven is a huge empty gap of space before you reach the poor, misunderstood dwarf planets."

"Okay," Triana said, imagining the crew watching and listening throughout the ship. She knew what they wanted to hear. "Tell us about three and four."

"Eos Number Three is, as we expected, fairly rugged and mountainous. The atmosphere is breathable; perhaps a bit more oxygen than you're used to, but you're adaptable, aren't you? The poles, like Earth, are icy and snow packed. We'll know more about the weather as we study it, but it seems quite manageable.

"And then there's Eos Number Four. It's a watery world, that's for sure. Eighty percent of the surface is covered by ocean or lake—and there are some gigantic lakes, I might add. The land is concentrated near the equator, and there's evidence of some pretty extreme seismic activity. Eos Four is habitable, but more of a challenge, let's say. The ancient civilization that Torrec referenced might have been shaken out of existence by the quakes."

Triana considered the information and gazed at her fellow Council members. Each appeared to be deep in thought, probably imagining the pros and cons of each planet for establishing a human colony.

"I don't want to sway anyone's thought process," Triana said, "but it seems that number three would be our best bet. Water, but not too much, a more stable environment, and a warmer climate. Thoughts?"

"Three," Bon said, without hesitation. "An obvious abundance of fertile soil."

Channy grinned. "Oh, definitely three. As much as I'm gonna torture all of you with workouts, you're gonna need the extra air."

Triana looked at Gap, who seemed to take his time, weighing the options. Finally he said: "We could make either work, I'm sure. But I'm inclined to vote with the Council. Let me ask you something, though. What's the policy if some crew members want to go with number four?"

"That's a great question," Triana said. "I think the worst thing we could do would be to split our resources. Plus, there's the issue of what's lying down there in the Storage Sections. How do we divide the crew members in suspended animation? Or the embryos?"

Gap looked pensive. "I don't know. I'm just wondering, that's all, because it might come up."

Triana mulled this over, biting her lip. Then she leaned on the table and addressed the crew listening throughout the ship. "I'm going to leave this open for now. I'm assuming that the majority of you will opt to stay with the main contingent on Eos Three. But, should there be some of you with a taste for danger, and you have a reasonable argument for establishing a base on Four, I'll listen to what you have to say. There's not much time, however. Roc, what's our exact timetable?"

"Nine days on cruise control, gently using reverse power to cut our speed. Then we'll use the atmosphere of the massive giant, planet number five, for a braking maneuver. After that we'll swing around the far side of Eos, and then it's back through much of the system again, each time using the drag of the planets' gravitational pull to throw out an anchor. Assuming our final destination is Eos Three, it's not out of the question to swing around the fourth planet a second time as part of the braking. If someone wanted to get off, you could make up a few sandwiches and send them on their way."

"Okay," Triana said. "Great work, Roc. Thanks. For each of you tuned in to the tripcast, I'll be available as we begin preparations. Feel free to contact me if you'd like to discuss any of this.

"We're not alone, as you know. Roc has identified thirty-two vultures that made the jump with us, and they're right outside. We have no reason to fear them. Their job is to gather data and report what they learn. If you have concerns, please see me."

She looked up as Lita entered the room and stood just inside the door, her hands clasped in front of her, waiting. Triana couldn't decipher the expression on her face, but after a few years of working together she understood the body language: "When you're finished, I have something to show you."

"For the time being," Triana continued, "we need everyone to remember what it took to get here, and what it will take to finish the job. This is not the time to let up, to neglect any duties or responsibilities. If anything, we need everyone on their toes, alert to anything that might fall through the cracks. Our radiation shield is still intact, and we're safe."

With a smile, she added: "And we're almost there. Can you believe it?"

By now all of the Council members noticed Lita's pose near the door. Triana closed out the tripcast and stood up.

"Something to share, Doctor?"

"Oh, I've definitely got something to share," Lita said. "But you need to see it to believe it." She walked out of the room, then turned and waved at the others to join her. "C'mon."

Whatever her secret, Lita didn't seem particularly worried about it. She made small talk during the short walk down to the Clinic. Channy filled her in on Roc's report on the Eos system, and Lita agreed that Eos Three sounded like the wise choice. Gap asked a few questions about the medical effects of the Channel jump, but as far as Lita could tell there hadn't been any significant problems among the crew. A handful of people had called her, but they seemed to only be looking for reassurance that the odd motion sensation was normal and widespread.

"You can practically hear their sigh of relief," Lita said with a grin. "I don't think we have any actual hypochondriacs aboard the ship, but some people just need to be put at ease. In fact, I think that's about seventy percent of a doctor's job."

The party of five entered the Clinic and made their way down a short hall. Lita pulled up outside the door to one of the labs, and raised her eyebrows.

"Ready for this?"

The door swished open. Even from outside, Triana could see what had Lita so energized.

"What is this?"

Lita looked into the room, then back at Triana. "It's exactly what it looks like."

They walked in slowly and gathered around a small glass tank. Inside, floating in a solution of supercritical fluid, was a jellyfish. It was much smaller than Torrec, perhaps six inches long, and its bell-shaped head was a pale blue color. It bobbed toward the top of the tank, then slowly settled to about the halfway point and appeared to hover.

Triana spoke to Lita while keeping her eyes on the Dollovit. "I think I understand now. This used to be the small piece of Torrec's appendage that you removed, correct?"

"Uh-huh. I took a small section, maybe about an inch long. From that I sliced tiny little pieces for our tests, but I kept the primary fragment in this tank, filled with solution from Torrec's original. One of my assistants came in here a little while ago to grab something, and just about wet herself."

Gap walked to the other side and squatted to look directly at the jellyfish. "Did Torrec give you any kind of heads-up about this?" he asked.

Lita crossed her arms. "Let's just say that he didn't seem

concerned at all about offering a chunk of one of his tentacles. And now I know why. Not only did that missing chunk grow back for him, but the piece I took off performed what's called rapid cellular regeneration. Emphasis on rapid." She nodded toward the tank. "At least now we know how the jellyfish population replenishes itself."

Triana muttered something under her breath, then said: "Torrec wouldn't have volunteered the information. He's very good about answering questions, but everything with him is direct. A direct question, a direct answer. He rarely offers unsolicited information. And you're right, now we know why he was so quick to agree to the biopsy." She let out a long breath. "Have you tried communicating with it?"

Lita smiled. "Talon, this is our Council Leader, Triana."

The voice that came from the nearby speaker held the same mechanical qualities that Torrec had exhibited. "Greetings, Triana."

"Talon?" Triana said. "His name is Talon?"

"No," Lita said. "He told me that his name was Torrec. I guess each derivative of a jellyfish keeps the same name as the original. But I told him that was much too confusing for simple creatures like us, and I asked if I could give him a nickname. He has no idea what a nickname is, but agreed to answer to something else."

"Why Talon?"

Lita shrugged. "No reason. I just wanted something else that started with T, and that was the first word that came to me."

"I think it sounds cool," Channy said. "Talon."

Gap straightened up and looked at Triana. "Okay, so we have vultures *and* jellyfish with us at our new home. I guess we think of Talon as the first Dollovit ambassador to Eos."

Again, Triana felt irritation. It seemed that more advanced species felt no need to ask permission when dealing with the galaxy's children. They could come and go as they pleased.

And yet, she reminded herself, without the Dollovit and the Cassini they likely wouldn't have made it this far.

With a slight nod of her head, Triana said: "Welcome, Talon. Please let us know if there's anything we can do to make you more comfortable." It sounded clumsy to her ears, but seemed to fit the required protocol. She gestured for Lita to step outside with her. Once in the hallway she hooked a thumb back toward the jellyfish.

"Any idea of how we contain this little guy when he begins to grow? Where do we get more of that fluid?"

"It's one of the things I asked him before I left for the meeting," Lita said. "He told me that he can curb his growth to match his environment. But he also said that the Vo can get him more fluid. Because of the oxygen in the atmosphere they won't be any help once Talon reaches the surface of the planet, but I think they'll work something out long before that. In fact, they've probably already worked it out."

"I'll bet you're right," Triana said. "Okay, I'll be—"

She was interrupted by a Clinic assistant who hurried down the hallway. "Triana, I think you'd better get in here. Mathias is calling, and says it's important."

Lita looked at Triana. "He's in the Storage Sections, prepping everything for the transport." Without another word, they hurried back to Lita's desk, where Triana snapped on the intercom.

"Mathias, what's going on?"

"Tree, we were going through each of the cryogenic canisters, getting an exact head count and an inventory."

"Are the crew members okay?" Triana asked.

"Yes, they seem to be fine. But after we confirmed all of that we started looking through some of the empty canisters. You know, they weren't all used."

"Right. And . . . ?"

"Well, they were all completely empty. Except one."

Triana looked at Lita, who muttered under her breath: "Not another cat, is it?"

"What did you find, Mathias?" Triana asked.

"We found where Dr. Bauer was hiding out in here. A few of his things are in there."

He paused, then added: "Including a journal. I . . . uh . . . well, I glanced through it, and . . ." He seemed unsure of how to continue.

Triana scowled. "C'mon, Mathias. What is it?"

"Well, I know he was crazy, but if he was telling the truth in this journal, we only have a matter of days before the ship is blown to bits."

27

Triana's head pounded as she took the lift to the lower level. She remembered her dad fighting through a tough stretch of mysterious headaches that the doctors could never figure out, but they ended almost as abruptly as they'd begun. While her mother battled migraines in her teenage years, they ceased to be a factor in her twenties. Triana used to silently tell herself that her mother had defeated the headaches by ignoring them; her mother, she rationalized, made an art form of ignoring things.

But the throbbing in Triana's head was clearly brought on by hearing a name she thought was consigned to her past: Dr. Fenton Bauer. The mad man who slipped aboard *Galahad* before its launch, and who came within minutes—and feet—from achieving his sinister goal, was back. Not in physical form, perhaps, but in objective. He'd wanted to cripple the ship and terminate the mission before it even reached the orbit of Mars. A victim of the insanity brought on by Bhaktul disease, as well as a festering relationship with his own son, Bauer had been foiled by a determined Council and the quick thinking of Triana Martell.

Her spirits, which had been so high just minutes earlier, sagged at the thought that he might succeed after all.

Mathias was waiting when she walked off the lift. "Where

was it?" Triana said as they marched toward the open Storage Section.

"One of the bunks in the male dormitory, about five up from the floor. Couldn't see his stuff from the floor, so we didn't discover it until we were up on a ladder, examining the chambers. And there it was."

The first few rooms were beehives of activity. Crew members were busy cataloging everything, from materials and tools, to the sleeping passengers. Several gave Triana a nod and kept on with their business. She moved to the base of the ladder and looked up.

"We left everything where we found it," Mathias said. "I saw the last entry in the journal and called you, but we haven't removed anything yet."

"Thanks, Mathias," Triana said. Biting her lip, she took hold of the ladder and pulled herself up. She glanced at the sleeping figures as she climbed past, noting how peaceful they appeared. Theirs was a dreamless world, devoid of pain, fear, and sadness. For a moment, gazing at them, she envied their innocence; they journeyed without the weight Triana felt, without the responsibility.

But the feeling soon passed. For they were helpless in this condition, and that was something Triana would never bargain for. Life on *Galahad* might be dangerous, but she much preferred to tackle the danger head-on, to rely on her wits and skills to survive.

When the next rung brought her to the fifth level, she felt a shiver pass through her. The cryogenic chamber was in disarray. The hastily arranged bunk, with its disheveled blanket, held a number of personal items. Triana saw a collection of assorted food wrappers, obviously smuggled in from the outside. A jacket, nearly identical to the ones worn by the *Galahad* launch team—and no doubt used to camouflage Bauer's entry to the ship at the late hour—was wadded into a makeshift pillow. And the journal.

Mathias had left it near the ladder. Triana hesitated, unwilling to touch it, sickened by the hatred affiliated with it. Then, holding on to the ladder with one hand, she reached out and flipped the pages. The first entry that caught her eye was startling:

Zimmer is responsible for the fire which will consume *Galahad*. Through his insidious nepotism, he has brought shame upon his so-called "last chance to save humanity." It is nothing more than a vehicle to continue the Zimmer line. It is salt in the wound to a father whose son has been rejected for another.

Bauer knew. *He knew.* Triana couldn't believe that Zimmer would have told him, but the two men had, at one point, been close. Or at least Zimmer had thought they were close. After months and months of long, tension-filled days, it might have slipped out, perhaps during—

No. Dr. Zimmer knew the pain that racked Dr. Bauer, the torture he felt over a splintered relationship with his own son. This couldn't possibly have come up, not even in one of their weary, late-night meetings.

It was beside the point. Somehow Bauer had discovered Zimmer's secret, and the knowledge would have pushed him over the edge, made him vulnerable to Tyler Scofeld's hostile rhetoric. And Triana saw now that it had driven him, in a Bhaktul-ravaged fit, to sneak aboard the spacecraft and plot its destruction.

She flipped through the pages, mostly assorted rants, with one devoted to celebrating his access to the ship. There were multiple entries alternating between fits of rage and self-satisfied comments on his late-night sabotage.

The unworthy star children will wake up in the morning to realize that this is truly a death ship. Damage to their crops is only the beginning. Access to the ship's computer has been easier than anticipated and, as we planned from the beginning, there is no security to speak of. I will go down with the ship, but I'm ready. Bring on the darkness, darkness that can only mask the pain.

Dr. Bauer's pain was a potent mixture of mental anguish, caused by the troubled relationship with his son, and the destructive physical torment rained down by Bhaktul. While she grimaced at the evil design, Triana at least understood the ingredients of Bauer's insanity.

The last page of the journal—surprisingly legible, given the scientist's deteriorated state—outlined one final, chilling vision.

Tonight it ends. Triana will learn the truth at midnight, and shortly afterward her short journey comes to an end, the only end this mission deserves. And, should things not go as planned, everything is in place to assure—with no chance of failure—the cataclysmic eruption of this vessel. Fire will cleanse the galaxy of this detestable human race and sterilize it before it contaminates another world.

Before I leave tonight I will settle on the date that will be the most fitting. Either the one-year anniversary of *Galahad*'s launch, or perhaps the next celestial alignment of the Earth, Saturn, and Eos. There would be something poetic in that, I believe.

Or, if this is to be a profoundly personal statement, there's always Marshall's nineteenth birthday, which falls close to both of these dates. I'll decide which of the three resonates within me as the truth, and commence the steps necessary to ensure that *Galahad* leaves a blistering mark in the night skies over the doomed inhabitants of Earth.

Let it be done.

Triana stared at the calm, coherent reasoning of Fenton Bauer. It was hard to believe that the end result would be the murder of so many innocent people. He'd truly been insane.

She scrambled down the ladder, clutching the journal in one hand, and thanked Mathias for his work. In the corridor she stopped to inform Roc that an emergency Council meeting would take place in the Conference Room in twenty minutes. Foregoing his usual sarcastic banter, Roc agreed to circulate the news.

Fifteen minutes later they began to arrive. Channy and Lita walked in together, concern etched on their faces. Gap followed moments later. He threw a quick glance at Triana, but she was absorbed in the data scrolling across her vidscreen. Bon was two minutes late, but that merely allowed Triana time to confirm her research.

When she was ready, she looked up from the screen and said: "We have a problem, and I won't sugarcoat it. Dr. Bauer has apparently rigged this ship to blow up."

She quickly shared the final entry from his journal. The Council members passed around the actual book, and Triana watched the sickening horror register on their faces.

"Marshall," Lita said. "I take it that was his son?"

Triana nodded.

Gap laced his fingers together on the table. "This is incredible. He wanted us to fall into some sort of routine, to get happy and content . . . and then wham! With no warning whatsoever. That's just plain evil."

"Could he do this?" Channy asked, pushing the journal across to Gap. "I mean, could he have fixed something to blow up?"

Triana looked grim. "That's one of the things I've been speaking about with Roc. Roc, you wanna explain this?"

"The bad news comes in three stages," Roc said. "First, Dr.

Bauer had unlimited entry to *Galahad* throughout the construction process, so he knew how to access every square inch. He could, quite literally, have arranged an explosion or breakdown on any part of the ship, and that includes within walls, floors, ceilings. For that matter, he could have rigged something within the guts of our ion-drive engines. We would need to practically dismantle the entire ship in order to isolate it. And remember, in space it doesn't take much damage to create disaster.

"Secondly, we have no idea what to search for. I'm sure that he hasn't relied on traditional explosives. Knowing the way his mind worked, in fact, he would have relished the fact that it was a creative ending.

"And finally," the computer said, "we don't know for sure that he's even followed through with these musings. It's possible that he never arranged for any of these, or that he ended up doing something completely different. There are too many unknowns."

Bon was the last to scan the journal's page.

"I'm assuming you've run the dates on these events?" he said with a cool gaze.

"That's what I've been doing," Triana said. "Dr. Bauer listed three potential dates for our destruction. However, one of those dates has already passed. Allowing for time dilation, the celestial alignment he mentioned—Earth, Saturn, and Eos—would have occurred back home about seven weeks ago."

She could see the shudders that passed through the Council members; she was sure it was the same spine-chilling sensation that she'd experienced as soon as the data popped up on her screen. To think that they'd sailed through a potential doomsday, oblivious to the vile schemes of a long-dead former colleague . . .

"That leaves two possible dates," she said. "The one-year anniversary of our launch, which happens in exactly fourteen days. Or the nineteenth birthday of Bauer's son, Marshall." She shook her head. "And that is, believe it or not, in sixteen days."

There was dead silence around the room. It was Roc who finally spoke up: "This should be a movie."

Gap grunted. "Let's wait and make sure it has a happy ending." He looked at Triana. "This gives us time to get to Eos Three."

"But no time to scout locations," Lita said. "We'll have to be ready to jump into the Spiders and pods and just . . ." She flung her arm into the air.

Channy looked between all of the Council members. "Don't we need to find the best spot? I mean, we can't just fall into orbit and bail out, can we?"

"I don't see what choice we have," Lita said. "Roc's right, it would take months for us to find what Bauer's done." She paused, then looked hopeful. "I know we're in some trouble here, but really, when you think about it, we've lucked out. Without Torrec and his vultures, we never would have known about the sabotage. We'd either be out in deep space, or . . ."

Gap finished the sentence. "Or orbiting Eos Three, celebrating our arrival, congratulating ourselves on pulling it off, and then lights out." He shook his head. "Can you believe it?"

Lita looked thoughtful. "Is it fate that the Dollovit found us?"

Triana shrugged. "I'll make a deal with you. Let's get everything packed and ready to go, let's get to the planet and get off this ship. Then, when we're safely on land, when we're breathing real air, *then* I'll discuss the idea of fate with you all day long. Deal?"

Bon pushed back his chair. "As I see it, we'll need to be off this ship in thirteen days. I've got a lot of work to do." Without waiting for a formal dismissal he trudged out of the room.

"Concise as always," Gap said. "But he's right; I might even recommend a bigger cushion than that. For all we know Bauer might have screwed up his dates. Roc, can we do all of the braking procedures and make it into orbit in twelve days?"

"This is where I'm supposed to put on a happy face and tell everyone that there's no problem," the computer said. "But all of you need to know that twelve days is pushing it. In fact, I'm guessing that we'll fall into orbit—as Channy put it—and scram that same day. I can't offer any guarantees."

Gap ran a hand through his hair. "We have a fighting chance. I guess we can't ask for more than that."

Triana dismissed the meeting, wishing everyone good luck. Once in the hall, Lita took her arm.

"Listen, we're gonna make it. Everything's gonna be fine."

"I have no doubt," Triana said. "After everything we've been through, I won't allow anything to stop us now."

28

Four days passed, and as each day flipped over to the next Triana couldn't help but quietly calculate the amount of time they had left. It wouldn't be long, she realized, before they measured it in hours.

Life on the ship became a blur. Crew members turned up the intensity level a few notches; even those who technically were on a break in their work rotation dove in, helping in each department. School was suspended, and physical workouts were cut back to brief cardio routines. Everyone eyed the final prize, knowing that their new home drew closer with each passing minute.

In the Domes, Bon oversaw the final harvesting and storage. Tools, machines, and assorted implements were packed into special transport containers. Cryostorage bins filled with thousands of seeds, stacked and forgotten in the recesses of Dome 1 before the launch, were checked and rechecked, then moved into position near the lifts. They would be the basis of the Eos colony's initial food crops, all grown in specially assembled greenhouses to eliminate contamination of the planet's native species.

Lita and Mathias finished the inventory of the Storage Sections and, with the help of some Engineering assistants, began preparing eighty-four slumbering passengers for their trip to Eos

Three. Lita's capable assistants, meanwhile, took care of packing up Sick House.

Gap ran endless tests and calculations from his station in the Control Room. Triana stayed out of his way, checking in occasionally and offering to help should he need it. They were joined on the deck every few hours by Bon, who silently took his seat and triggered the course changes to safely guide *Galahad* through the jumbled space rubble of the system's outskirts. There was little conversation while he sat there, eyes glowing, his fingers flying across the keyboard.

Triana did her best to keep her mind focused on the mission and its successful completion. But for the few brief minutes where she found herself working next to Bon, she couldn't help but flash forward to their new colony. Once they were no longer confined to this limited space aboard the ship, would she see him as often? Would the backbreaking work that loomed in the next few months—or few years—keep Bon isolated, buried in his work, and unavailable?

Of course they were ridiculous thoughts. Bon was isolated and unavailable on *Galahad*; why should it be any different on Eos Three? She pushed aside the daydreams and burrowed back into her work.

Day five in Eosian space began early. Triana walked into the Dining Hall before 6 A.M., anxious to grab some oatmeal and fruit before composing the latest update for the crew. Sitting in her usual spot in the back of the room, she greeted the early risers who stumbled in, most of them blurry-eyed but still in good spirits. Dr. Bauer's threat was a dark blanket above them, but somehow seeing the finish line kept their heads up and their motors on high.

Triana took a sip of juice and flipped open Bauer's journal. She'd surveyed it once to make sure no other surprises were imminent, but since then she'd locked it away, reluctant to allow his toxic attitude to contaminate her. Now curiosity took over and she gave herself a few minutes to thumb through his rants.

They primarily echoed the same sentiments over and over, and often came back to the same word: unfair. But it was the deranged scientist's comments about Dr. Zimmer that tugged at her. She found herself back at the bitter passage that had originally caught her attention:

> Zimmer is responsible for the fire which will consume *Galahad*. Through his insidious nepotism, he has brought shame upon his so-called "last chance to save humanity." It is nothing more than a vehicle to continue the Zimmer line. It is salt in the wound to a father whose son has been rejected for another.

So many strange vibrations resonated around the issue of Zimmer's child, but now she began to interpret Bauer's cryptic comment.

A father whose son has been rejected for another.

She looked at it again.

For another.

Not just another teenager. Bauer specifically said one son for another. But Triana had been so sure that it was Alexa . . .

Sure? Was there anything she could be sure about on this mission? And what could she believe in the scrawled rant of a madman?

There was something else about Dr. Zimmer that continued to tickle the edges of her mind. Something he'd said to her was the key to this, but she couldn't filter out the static surrounding it.

"Our fearless leader, deep in thought," came the voice above her.

She looked up to see the familiar dark hair, dark eyes, and scar that topped a wolf's smile.

"Good morning, Merit," she said, casually closing the journal and applying the most pleasant tone she could muster. He stood before her without a tray. "No breakfast for you?"

"I only eat twice a day, and never in the morning," he said, sitting in a chair at the table next to her. "I know it's supposed to be the most important meal of the day, but the thought of food this early makes me retch."

"I heard that you might have had a touch of flu or something when we slipped through the Channel, too," Triana said. "Feeling better, obviously."

Merit's smile faltered for a second, then he recovered. "Good old Katz. What a friend." He looked at a group of crew members who were working their way through the food line. "Listen, you're busy, time is running short, so I'll make this quick. I want to let you know that a few of us have reached a decision about Eos."

Triana pushed her tray back and raised an eyebrow. "Oh?"

"Uh-huh. In your address to the crew you said that the Council was in favor of Eos Three as our new home."

"Yes . . ."

"But you also made it clear that anyone could reach out to you should they opt for another course of action."

Even through the heavy-handed speech dialogue that Merit preferred, Triana instantly saw where this was going. "Let me guess: you want us to stop and let you off at number four."

He leveled another smile at her. "Not by myself, of course."

"And how many recruits have you rounded up this time?" Triana said.

"There are nineteen of us. Which means we'll need one of the extra pods that the Dollovit have provided, but very little in the way of equipment or rations. It's not like you're dividing the provisions in half."

Triana stared hard at him. "Tell me, why are you doing this?"

"I already told you," Merit said. "I'm a water freak. How do I pass up a planet that's practically all water?"

"Right. So it has nothing to do with the fact that the Council will be a world away, leaving you the ruler of your own kingdom?"

He adopted a comical look of indignation. "Triana, please! There are eighteen other people involved here, you know. They want to go just as badly as I do. You wouldn't turn them down just because you feel scorned, would you?"

"It's not up to me, Merit. If there's a request to divide the few resources we have for colonization, it's a Council decision. I know that aggravates you, but it's the governmental process aboard *Galahad*."

"Okay," he said, standing. "Talk it over, and let us know. And please, if you have specific reasons why you won't follow through with your promise, let us know that, too."

He gave a mock half-salute and paraded out of the room.

They'll never survive," Lita said. "Nineteen people left alone to tame an entire planet? It's ridiculous."

The other Council members listened with interest, but only Channy nodded agreement.

"His chances are the same as ours," Gap said.

"Oh, c'mon, Gap," Lita said. "Two hundred thirty stand a much better chance, and you know it."

He shrugged. "I disagree. It'll be easier for them to get shelter put up at first, and easier to feed nineteen. In some respects I think he'd have a better chance than us."

Triana had laid out Merit's request, and could have predicted the individual Council member's reactions. She asked Bon to voice his thoughts for the record.

"As long as the supplies are proportionally split, I have no issues with him leaving. I think that most of the crew would feel the same way."

"Good riddance is what you mean," Channy said. She turned

to Triana. "I don't really care for Merit either, but it seems almost cruel to let him take some crew members and try to—"

"Gullible crew members," Gap interjected.

". . . and try to build something on Eos Four."

"Channy's right," Lita said. "We can't allow personal dislike to sway our decision."

Gap drummed his fingers on the tabletop. "We sat right here, with the crew watching and listening, and told them that if they wanted to leave, they could. Are you only saying this now because it's Merit?"

Triana stepped in. "Yes, I did say that to the crew. But before we vote on this, let's make sure we have all of the facts. First of all, Roc, do we even have the time to do this?"

"That's probably up to Dr. Bauer," Roc said. "With all of the unknown factors, we could be fine indefinitely, or we could blow up before I finish this sentence. Whew, made it. Or maybe before I finish *this* sentence. Okay, now maybe before—"

"Fine, you've made your point," Triana said. "Assuming for the moment that he chose the earlier date, and assuming that he got it right: how does that affect our ability to drop off passengers around Eos Four?"

"Since we're using that fourth planet as a component of our braking maneuver, it really isn't a factor. Once we swing around the planet, we can flick anything out the door. Granted, we might want to slow down just a bit more than we'd planned, which might add a few hours, perhaps as much as a day, to our arrival time at Three. I calculate that, even with a slower transit from Four to Three, we should have a good thirty-six to forty-eight hours to evacuate the ship."

"See," Lita said. "If we slow down to let them off, we're pushing ourselves up against a deadline that wouldn't just be inconvenient; it could be deadly."

"Right," Channy said. "So I say they stay with us."

Gap shook his head. "Adding a few hours makes no difference.

We'll be completely packed and ready to go the minute we're in orbit around Three. We don't need an extra day to think about things. If they want to go, they should go."

Bon simply nodded agreement when Triana looked down the table. She stalled for time by walking over to get a cup of water. By the time she returned to the table—and to the curious looks from the Council members—she knew how she would break the tie.

"I vote to honor the agreement I made to the crew," she said. "And Lita, it's not from an insecure desire to get rid of Merit. Although he's very skilled at verbalizing his positions, I'd make the same decision for any other persuasive crew member."

She sat down and ticked off some points on her fingers. "He has probably the same chance we do on an alien surface. We're making an educated guess about our final destination, but for all we know we could land en masse on number three and find carnivorous dragonflies waiting for us.

"Next, we're flying on borrowed time as it is. Roc might have been obnoxious in his description, but his assessment of the situation is right: we could have already been blown to bits.

"And third, remember what this mission was all about in the first place. We were chosen to represent the human race, and to offer our species a chance at survival. Well, we have not one, but two planets capable of supporting life as we know it, and it probably makes sense to put down roots on both. It might double our chances for survival. It's essentially one of the arguments that Torrec made when requesting the embryos."

Triana said to Lita: "Your points, as always, are thoughtful and appreciated. But we'll grant Merit and his friends their wish."

Lita let out a sigh. "It breaks my heart, but okay. I'd like to add one final thing, though, and on this I won't back down. They take none of the crew members in suspended animation, and they keep their hands off the embryos. Can we agree on that?"

"I don't think any of us would argue with that," Triana said. The rest of the Council members concurred.

"Roc," Triana said, "we need to begin working under the assumption that Bauer's next anniversary date is our deadline, if you'll pardon the expression. With that in mind, let's begin a countdown and have everything ready to go by zero hour, with a safety cushion if possible."

"Done," Roc said. "As of right now, you have eight days, seven hours, twenty-two minutes. Factoring in your cushion, the last person off the ship should take the elevator down in seven days, nineteen hours. And please, turn off all the lights before you go and make sure your curling irons are unplugged."

Another Council meeting disbanded. As they stood up, Lita left all of them with a sobering thought.

"We should all remember what seed we planted today with this decision. It would be interesting to pop in a hundred years from now to see what has grown out of it."

29

A while ago I dropped a reference about Gap being one of my favorite people on the ship. He's got the brains to get the job done, he's got a heart that keeps things confusing yet entertaining, and he has a multitude of interests. The guy enjoys puzzling things out, he loves a good game of Masego—and although I'd never tell him, he's actually getting quite good at it—and he's a bit of a daredevil athletically. Sure, he gets a bit emotional about some things, but so what? He's rarely inactive, physically or mentally.

I try to refrain from using my position as the trusted narrator of this tale to preach to anyone, but hopefully a few of you have subconsciously noted this. Your age doesn't matter one bit; as soon as you begin to lose your curiosity and your joy of new things, then you begin to die. Don't let it happen to you, okay?

All right, sermon over.

Gap trudged through the hallway on the lower level with a heavy heart. He wore his helmet and carried his Airboard, knowing that it was likely to be the last time he ever enjoyed his favorite pastime. The resources simply didn't exist to transport the massive gravitational system to the planet's surface. And, with everything that would be taking place over the final few days, now—with zero hour only six days away—was his chance to log a few laps before wishing the track good-bye.

He'd left a message for some of his regular Airboarding friends, and he was thrilled to spot the friendly faces when he entered the room. Rico Manzelli, his arm in a cast, sat on the top row of the bleachers, talking with a few of the ship's other daredevils. Gap recognized Ariel Morgan out on the track; even with the helmet hiding her face, he could spot the Australian girl's distinctive Boarding style as she hurtled around curves, her arms acting as counterbalances to keep her from flying into the walls.

"Hey, stud, tripped over anything lately?" Gap said, plopping down next to Rico.

"Not today, anyway," the Italian boy said. "And you're one to talk. Look at your hand. Plus, seems that I recall your arm in a sling not that long ago."

"Yeah, but mine came on the field of battle," Gap said, pointing out to the track. "I didn't hurt myself walking on the bleachers."

Rico looked sheepish. "Yeah, you're right. And you know what makes it worse? The fact that now I won't be able to go full speed today and take back the record from you."

"Full speed?" Gap said. "What, are you climbing aboard today with your arm broken in two places?"

"Of course. This is my last chance to ride. You don't think I'd let a little thing like a few fractures keep me from a farewell tour, do you? I'm saddling up, pardner." He pointed with his toe at an intricately painted Airboard that lay near his feet.

Gap shook his head and laughed. "You're crazy."

"You'd do the same thing," Rico said.

"Yeah, I guess you're right."

A minute later Ariel took a dramatic tumble out on the cushioned floor. She rolled to a stop, rose to her knees, and removed her helmet. Even from the top of the bleachers Gap could see a smile on her face from ear to ear. She grabbed her gear and jogged up to sit on the row in front of Gap and Rico, while another rider took his turn.

"Hey, guys," she said, removing her pads.

"Did you know that Mr. Macho here is going for a spin?" Gap said.

"Uh-huh. I'm the one who told him if he didn't do it, he'd regret it forever. By the way, are you gonna play it safe today, or set one final speed record before we turn off Zoomer?" she said, referencing the computer that controlled the track's underground magnetic course.

Gap watched the latest rider take a turn too quickly and collide with the padded wall. He winced, recalling his own miscalculation that had resulted in a broken collarbone months ago.

"I'm content with the current record," he said. "I won't be a grandma out there, but I can imagine Triana's face if I show up with another sling or a cast, just as we're about to evacuate the ship." He poked Ariel in the shoulder. "You weren't exactly burning up the track today. Why didn't you go for the record?"

She ran her fingers through her long, brown hair. "You would've just gone all out to take it back. Besides, this was more of a remembrance ride for me."

"What do you mean?"

"I used my time on the Board to think about my family, how they sacrificed everything to get me on *Galahad*. I thought about all of the friendships I've made in the past couple of years, including you two lunkheads. And I wanted to just soak it up, since I won't ever ride again." She threw a quick glance over her shoulder at Gap. "Glad you guys couldn't see me crying through my helmet out there."

Gap and Rico looked away, not wanting to embarrass their friend. But when Gap's turn to ride came, he found himself drawn into Ariel's same thought process.

He began easily, feeling the tug of the gravitational field that

ran under the floor of the room, balancing his weight and maneuvering his Airboard as it rode four inches off the ground. At
this speed his muscle memory did the majority of the work,
effortlessly skimming across the room, reaching out to drag
his fingers across the wall as he made a corner turn, bending his
knees to settle into a quicker pace.

But his mind soared as well. He fought back his own tears as he
remembered his mother's concern over his newfound hobby,
her worry that he'd not only injure himself but lose interest in
his schooling. Neither happened, discounting the minor collection of bumps and bruises.

He savored the memory of Dr. Zimmer announcing that
Gap's push for an Airboard track aboard *Galahad* had paid off.
The kindhearted scientist had expressed the same concerns as
Gap's mother, but had been swayed by the Asian boy's argument
regarding Airboarding's value in terms of exercise and mental
agility.

He mentally replayed the lessons that he'd given to Hannah
in this very room. She'd taken to the sport quickly and enthusiastically, only to give it up the minute Gap had ended their relationship. In a flash he wondered where Hannah might be at that
very moment, what she was doing, what she was experiencing.
Was she thinking of him at the same time?

Would he ever see her again?

The thought caused him to clench his teeth and pour even
more energy into his ride. Faster and faster he raced through the
twists and turns of the track, absorbing every minute course alteration that Zoomer could dish out. The walls blurred past
him, and the shouts of warning from the bleachers became a
nebulous hum in his ears.

The treacherous ring of debris had fallen far behind them. *Galahad* now tore inward through the planetary system of Eos,

                                           Dom Testa

rocketing past the gravitational influence of its massive gas monster, a planet that dwarfed Jupiter and provided the necessary tug to slow the starship. Eos was next, a colossal fireball that clutched at them as they streaked around the far side. The next station on their line would be Eos Four, followed by Eos Three.

The automatic dimming of lights signaled the onset of evening, and Lita marveled again at the glorious display of stars that began to penetrate the clear Domes above the Farms. She walked beside Bon as he made his usual inspection of the day's work, a task that he insisted on completing even though they'd soon be leaving these fields behind. She knew that he would never fully disconnect from this soil, and she imagined the pain he must feel knowing that in a matter of days it would all be reduced to cosmic rubble.

Lita, too, felt a pang of loss. She wasn't attached to the Farms in the same way as Bon, but she'd come to appreciate its beauty and its representation of the cycle of life.

She broke the silent spell that hung over them. "How long will it take to get the crops up and running inside the greenhouses?"

From the look Bon gave her, it was obvious that he knew she was only making conversation. But he went along with it. "Not long. We'll have nutrients for the soil, and there's water available. After that it's sweat and sunlight."

"Do you think we'll be able to eat much of the native plant life?"

"I have no idea," he said, stopping along the path to examine a tomato plant that had been damaged. A telltale set of tracks betrayed a small tractor that had veered from the path. Bon's familiar scowl momentarily returned. Lita opened her mouth to say "it doesn't matter, we're about to leave," but thought better of it. Instead she coaxed him in a different direction.

"Now that you've guided us through the outer fringes, what do you see your connection with the Cassini morphing into? I mean, will they stay connected to you?"

"There's no choice in the matter anymore," Bon said without hesitation. "They'll always be wired into my brain now."

"And how do you feel about that?" Lita said. "Do you feel . . ." She struggled to find the right word. "Used?"

For a moment she thought she might have gone too far. The Swede's face grew dark, and it looked as if he might boil over. But with each passing second he relaxed, apparently coming to the conclusion that he was, indeed, being used to a certain extent. He finally said: "We use each other. Remember the discussion about the Dollovit and their croy?"

Lita nodded. "A symbiotic relationship."

"That's right," Bon said. "It's close to what I experience with the Cassini."

She considered this for a moment. "I understand the help we get from them through you, but what do they get out of it?"

He startled her by taking hold of her chin and turning her face toward his. Her breath caught in her chest when she found herself staring into two eyes that glowed a deep orange. They seemed to slice right through her.

Seconds later they faded away, leaving Bon's natural ice-blue eyes inches from her face. A faint smile on his lips calmed her.

"They get their own representative in another camp," he said. "And before we begin to think we're something special, I get the feeling that we're one of millions throughout the universe. They reach a symbiotic arrangement with someone like me, which places a little reminder in each civilization that we're a breath away from losing our privileges."

Lita's heart continued to beat quickly. "So, you're like the sheriff, huh?"

Still face-to-face, he looked back and forth between her two eyes. "That's right. You should remember that."

She swallowed hard. Without thinking, she took his face into her hands. "Yeah? Well, you should remember this." She pulled him into a long, lingering kiss. When they separated, she gently touched the side of his face. "You have a lot to do in the next few weeks. But remember that, okay? For later?"

If he was surprised, he masked it well. He watched her turn and walk back down the path.

30

Eos Four sparkled on the large vidscreen in the Control Room. Magnified from a great distance, it truly was a watery world, dominated by the crystal blue oceans that spread over eighty percent of its surface. Clouds blotted much of the atmosphere. Thin brown ovals of land stretched near the planet's equator, while a massive crust of ice could be seen covering the southern pole. After a year in space, crew members throughout the ship were being treated to a vision that nearly brought tears to their eyes.

But not for long. The planet was approaching fast, yet another gravitational tool that would help to cut *Galahad*'s speed before it disappeared in the ship's wake.

Triana stood mesmerized, unable to take her eyes from the scene. It was a beautiful world, and for a minute she questioned their decision to bypass this one for the warmer, rockier setting of Eos Three.

"Mmm, now that's a glorious sight," Merit cooed beside her. "We do have sunscreen, right?"

Triana ignored him. In forty-three minutes a pod, carrying nineteen crew members who had spent the past two-and-a-half years living the same highs and lows, the same joys and fears, as the rest of *Galahad*'s teen population, would be jettisoned toward the glittering planet on the vidscreen. Would they ever cross paths again, Triana wondered, and if so, what changes would have taken place?

Merit continued his chatter. "I was surprised that last night you left the going-away dinner so soon. Gee, I hope my fellow colonists heading to Eos Four didn't have their feelings hurt."

Controlling her emotions, Triana casually answered him: "I thought I spent plenty of time at the dinner, Merit. I even spoke individually with every one of them." She gave him a droll look. "Why, did I miss something after I left? Don't tell me I missed another one of your speeches. I'd hate that."

He grunted a laugh, then placed a hand on her shoulder. "Oh, you're going to miss me, Triana, and you know it. Take care of yourself, okay?"

She glanced at his hand, but made no move to return the gesture. "You, too, Merit. Best of luck to all of you."

It seemed that he had more to say, but without another word he turned and walked to the lift. Just before the doors closed, he locked eyes with Triana and flashed his trademark grin.

It sent a creepy shiver down her spine. Something in his smile contained an unspoken message: *Just wait.*

She busied herself for the next forty minutes with the dozens of details that needed to be handled prior to their own departure. Gap volunteered to oversee the launch of Merit's pod, a move that freed Triana to tick things off her lengthy to-do list. But it also was a move that surprised her. Generally Gap wanted nothing to do with the dark-haired Californian. But the more she considered it, the more she realized that it could very well be a symbolic action, too. In essence, Gap would be booting Merit off the ship, something he'd dreamed of for months.

It brought a wry smile to Triana's face. In some cultures there were traditional ceremonies whereby evil spirits or other dark forces were expunged, in effect shooing them from the village and restoring order and peace once again to the community. By opening the Spider bay door and pushing Merit out—even enclosed in the protective shell of the pod—Gap might feel as if he were cleansing the spirit of *Galahad*.

And, Triana thought, *who's to say he's not right?*

Her mind also played back an earlier conversation with Bon. He'd mentioned that *Galahad's* "unscrupulous character" problem might take care of itself. Was this the solution to the problem that he'd foreseen?

She struggled with a dilemma all leaders faced: how to separate personal feelings from the responsibilities of the job. Merit was quite obviously a maddening member of their troupe, but he was still part of the team. To be honest, however, what troubled Triana the most was the fact that he'd wrangled eighteen other crew members into abandoning *Galahad* and following him.

Well, she thought with a sigh, he always was extremely persuasive. She just hoped that it didn't cost innocent lives.

In the midst of solving an inventory dilemma—certainly not the kind of duty she'd expected at the onset of the mission—Gap's voice broke over the intercom.

"Everyone is packed and loaded onto the pod, Tree. Roc has calculated the launch point to the second in order to get them into a perfect orbit of E4. That's in . . ." He paused. "That's in twenty seconds."

The Control Room was packed with working crew members, all of whom stopped what they were doing in order to watch the vidscreen and listen in to the launch. Triana stood at her workstation and gave Gap the all-clear to proceed.

"The pod is away," he said. "Bay door is closing, bay is pressurizing."

And like that, they were gone.

"My, my," Roc said. "Merit is either more influential than I gave him credit for, or the Dollovit are going to videotape his exploits for a 'humans' funniest videos' segment."

"What does that mean?" Triana asked.

"Four of our constant companions have peeled away from the ship and are shadowing Mr. Simms and friends down to Eos Four."

"Vultures?" Triana said. "Four vultures are tracking them?"

"Correct."

"I guess it makes sense," she said. "And you're right, Roc, I think we might be an endless supply of entertainment for Torrec and his pals."

"And, right on cue," Roc said, "Mr. Simms is calling from the pod."

Triana groaned inwardly, but flipped on the intercom. "Hello, Merit. Forget something? Want to come back already?"

"Hardly," Merit said. "There are nineteen smiling faces here, looking forward to our first beach party. I just wanted to let you know that when things get rough for you guys, we'll hopefully be able to lend a hand somehow."

A smile worked its way across Triana's face. "That would be a good trick. But thanks for the offer."

"No problem. Okay, we've got work to do now, so I need to sign off. But remember this day, Triana. This is the day a new empire was born."

After a low chuckle, he added: "We will rule this star system. Farewell."

Two hours later, after breezing through the Dining Hall to fuel up, Triana stopped by Sick House. Like every other department, it was abuzz with activity. Transport crates were stacked by the door, ready to be wheeled down to the Spider bay for loading. They were lucky that not one hospital bed was occupied at the moment, and all hands could be counted on for moving duty.

Lita's hair was held out of her face by her signature red ribbon, and yet beads of sweat still dotted her forehead. She gratefully accepted the energy block that Triana offered and, as they perched on the edges of the room's two desks, they talked about Merit's ominous prediction. Several crew members had been present in the Control Room to hear it, which meant word spread quickly around the ship, something that no doubt Merit had counted on.

"He's a bag of hot air," Lita said, waving it off. "If things are as tough as we think, he'll be hard-pressed to survive, let alone worry about building an empire. Listen, he's out of your hair by his own choice. Don't let him continue to get under your skin."

Triana acknowledged this with a nod. "Still, it makes you wonder what he and his descendants might try down the road. Who knows what stories their kids will hear about us."

"Doesn't matter," Lita said. "If Bon's right, then the Cassini will slap them down somehow."

"And us with them?" Triana wondered aloud.

The door to Sick House flew open and Mathias rushed in, looking right, and then glimpsing Lita and Triana to the left. He was out of breath.

"Hey," he said, briskly walking over to them. "I didn't want to call and tell you on the intercom. But we have a problem."

"What is it?" Lita said.

"It's the embryos," Mathias said. "Someone has taken them."

"What?" Lita said, jumping to her feet. "*Taken* them?"

"I'm sorry. Taken *some* of them. Someone got into the Storage Section and removed a dozen of them, along with one of the incubator units. It must've happened late last night."

Triana felt a river of anger begin to surge through her. She stood up and spoke with an icy calm. "Is there damage to any of the others?"

Mathias shook his head. "Not that I can tell. They took twelve of the small embryonic canisters, but they're all individually controlled. We have three of the incubation units left, which is fine. But—"

"It's not fine," Lita said, her voice rising. She turned to Triana. "You know who did this, right?"

Triana clenched one fist, a method that she found kept her from losing control. "And there's nothing we can do about it. He's long gone."

Alarms were going off in Engineering, a sound that had been absent since they'd siphoned power into the radiation shield. With only thirty-five hours left before evacuation began to Eos Three, Gap cringed. They'd perhaps taken for granted that Fenton Bauer's threat of destruction wouldn't come to pass until the ship was deserted, but . . .

"Roc," Gap said, "talk to me."

"A giant squid has wrapped its tentacles around the ship and is trying to pull it to the bottom of . . . oh wait, I was just reading Jules Verne. Let me check. Hold, please."

The seconds ticked by. One by one team members in the Engineering section drifted over to nervously scan the diagnostic board. When Roc spoke again, he'd lost the playful tone from his voice.

"Electrical systems are shutting down. Some sort of override that I might be able to work on."

The computer's suddenly all-business manner struck more fear into Gap than the alarms. He chewed on the diagnosis for a moment, then said: "Which systems?"

"Random, no pattern," Roc said. "Or, if there's a pattern, I'm too busy to puzzle it out right now. I can tell you this: it would only take a certain number and combination of failures before other components go critical."

Gap could read between the lines. Multiple components of the ship relied on power to be provided fluidly and in unison with other components. If all of the power went out, the ship would merely flounder. But if several units went out together, and then the wrong individual unit sprang back to life, it could be dangerous. Unless they could put a stop to it, one wrong combination of breakdowns would trigger an explosion.

The explosion that Bauer had prophesied.

Triana called on the intercom, and Gap quickly laid it out for her.

"How does this affect our timetable?" she said.

"I think our first order of business is to make sure we're alive long enough to keep a timetable."

"That bad?"

Gap said: "Potentially. Roc's trying to make sense of it. But now I know why Dr. Bauer insisted on so much control of this stuff. He probably knew more about this than anyone, which meant he knew exactly what buttons to push. Just like what he did to Roc last year."

"Right," Triana said. "Okay, I'll get out of your hair. Do you guys have almost everything packed in case we need to move fast?"

"We'll be ready," Gap said. "We might be scrambling once we reach the planet's surface. But we'll be ready."

Allowing herself thirty minutes to throw her things into a storage box, Triana found that there wasn't much she really wanted to take to the planet's surface. She wondered what others would say about her leaving so much behind, but then decided that what others thought wasn't important.

She'd started to take down the posters in her room, the colorful reminders of her home in Colorado. They'd kept her company during the year of space travel, often triggering memories of her dad and reinforcing the powerful life lessons that he'd taught her.

But they weren't coming with her. This was a new life on Eos Three, and she wanted a clean, fresh start. It wasn't the posters that would bring her father to life in her mind.

Another thought occurred to her, and she quickly opened her journal.

I think it'll be easy for us to feel overwhelmed when we reach the surface, but I hope we remember just how far, and how fast, we've come. It's important to remember that Dr. Zimmer never counted on us beginning the new colony so soon.

If all had gone according to plan, we'd be in our early twenties when we arrived at Eos. Now, thanks to the Channel, we'll begin building our new home while we're sixteen and seventeen.

I hope that the challenges we've overcome will help bridge the gap between the years.

The buzzer from her door sounded just as she finished. Channy gave an exaggerated wave when she opened the door.

"Am I interrupting your packing?" the Brit asked, walking in and looking around.

"No, I'm finished," Triana said.

"What?" Channy waved her hand at the walls. "You're not taking these?" She indicated the small storage box. "Wow, you're the lightest packer I've ever seen."

Triana smiled. "I'm not your average girl, I guess. What are you up to?"

"I'm inviting everyone to grab something to eat tonight and meet up at the soccer field. It'll be our little going-away party."

"I'm not much on parties . . ." Triana began.

"I know. I saw you make a cameo appearance for the Eos Four group. But this will be different. More of a farewell to the ship. She's served us well."

That was a good point, and Triana was embarrassed that she hadn't thought of it herself.

"Things aren't going so well," Channy continued, "and we

might have to shut down even more power tomorrow, according to Gap. So I think tonight we should do it while we can."

"Sure," Triana said. "I'll be there. Count me in."

"Excellent!" Channy said. "And I promise, I won't ask you to make a speech or anything. Unless you want to, of course."

"We'll see."

Channy looked around the room again. "So, do you think the Eos Four group will be okay?"

Triana shrugged. "I think their chances are as good as ours. I wish they'd stayed with us, though."

"Ha," Channy said. "Merit couldn't be king if he stayed, right? Besides, now he'll finally get to surf."

Triana opened her mouth to respond, and then froze. The smile on her face gradually faded into a look of disbelief as everything suddenly fell into place.

"You okay?" Channy said.

"Uh . . . yeah." Triana forced the smile back onto her face. "Listen, I've got some things to do before I join you for the party. See you there, okay?"

Channy looked suspicious. "You sure you're all right?"

"You mean besides the emergency evacuation, and the inability to scout a landing location, and the stolen embryos, and an alien ambassador tagging along with us? Besides all that?"

Channy gave a small bow. "Got it. Okay, throw the rest of your stuff in a biscuit tin and I'll see you at the party." She marched out into the hallway.

As soon as the door closed, Triana raced over to her desk and snapped on the vidscreen. Her fingers flew across the keyboard.

Surfing. That was it. The tingling in the back of her mind suddenly made sense.

Surfing. California. Caltech.

What had Merit said? *My mother taught at Caltech for two years* . . .

Triana replayed the video from Dr. Zimmer, and there it was, in his own words.

"Two years at Michigan, two in Europe, three years at Caltech . . ."

And, at the end: "I left things behind in many of these places that I carry around today in my heart."

She opened a new screen and scanned Merit's bio. Raised by a single mother, no information about the father. And, interestingly, Simms was not the mother's last name. In a brief paragraph it mentioned that Merit's mother had given him a unique last name, one where he could "forge his own identity while keeping a connection to his heritage."

Zimmer. Simms. Could it be?

Triana next pulled up the bio on Wallace Zimmer. He had indeed traveled extensively, never putting down roots, teaching for two or three years before moving on. One of those stops was Caltech, beginning two years before Merit was born, then moving on a year after Merit's birth.

Of course, it could have been a coincidence. It had to be. How could *Galahad*'s chief architect be the father of the one crew member set upon shattering the mission?

She had to know for sure. Before shutting down her vidscreen, she placed bio photos of Zimmer and Merit side by side.

It removed all doubt.

What? Merit?

Pay no attention to the girl in Oregon saying "I told you so." I think now she's just showing off.

Man, what do you do with THIS information? If Dr. Zimmer was like a second father to Triana, does that make Merit sorta like a stepbrother?

I'm not gonna tell her that, and I recommend you keep it to yourself, too.

31

The explanation was lengthy and complicated, but the bottom line was that the power in the Domes had been cut back almost seventy percent. Like it or not, Bon's days of farming in outer space were over. Everything that had already been harvested for the evacuation to Eos Three would have to suffice. Rather than assisting the crew, *Galahad*'s power systems now posed a dark menace, threatening to accelerate a chain reaction that would lead to disaster. Most of the ship was running on essential utilities only, which meant agricultural production had to take a backseat to heat, oxygen, and gravity. Lita likened it to a body's immune system going haywire, causing the body to attack itself. Or, as Gap had simply put it: "Dr. Bauer has suddenly made power dangerous."

Bon gave his stamp of approval to the storage of existing resources, then packed the materials that he felt he would need the most on the planet's surface. He stood now in his office, hands on hips, surveying the space around him. Unlike many crew members, he wasted no time deliberating over sentimental trinkets.

In twenty-two hours they would be coasting into an orbit around Eos Three and, if Bauer's malicious plot hadn't yet taken full effect, in twenty-five hours they'd leave *Galahad* for good. Even for Bon, the notion of never seeing this plot of soil again seemed unbelievable. At the moment he grappled with an emotional conflict: should he make one final visit to the clearing, or merely walk away?

For almost five minutes he was paralyzed with indecision. Twice he almost broke for the lift, but both times stopped himself. In the end, he found himself in the hidden clearing that Alexa had referred to as "our spot."

His mind began a quick series of image replays, spanning his first quiet conversation with Alexa in the hospital ward, to their clandestine meetings here, discussing everything from the constellations that blazed above their heads to their unique abilities, the bizarre connections which made them different from the other crew members.

He replayed the moments where Alexa reached out to him, both physically and emotionally. He saw his cold response. Never mind that it was born of an awkward unease and a confused heart; he'd hurt Alexa not through any particular action, but rather through inaction.

He saw her death, again and again. He saw the monstrosity created by the Dollovit, an attempt to replicate the flesh and blood, but with no soul.

And he saw two other faces drift in and out of his consciousness: Triana and Lita.

Through it all, he recognized how the differences in each of their personalities played to a different aspect of his own. With Triana, it was the shy, somewhat distant persona. With Alexa, it was the distinction they shared through their alien or paranormal attributes. And with Lita it was the fierce dedication to discovering the truth that lay somewhere out there, somewhere beyond this corporeal existence.

For a moment Bon felt a connection with the Cassini begin to take hold, but he pushed it aside, a skill that he'd mastered in the last few weeks. It was a skill that he knew was necessary to preserve his own identity. From the first link with the Cassini, in the shadow of Saturn's orange moon, Titan, Lita had strongly campaigned to limit Bon's connection. She'd expressed the same concern ever since. His identity, Lita had preached, was a price that he should never pay for that connection. And, she claimed, once he lost that identity, his soul would be lost forever.

It had taken months, but Bon finally understood what she meant. He knew that Lita carried her own internal struggles, whether it was guilt over her perceived contribution to Alexa's death, or her individual search for higher meaning in the universe. Faith versus fate was the eternal tug of war that Lita might scuffle with for the rest of her life.

For Bon, it was time to move past it all. The power of the Cassini, he knew, had always resided within him. They had channeled it, and focused it to a point, almost laser-fine, but the power of the universe—perhaps even the mysterious dark energy that ultimately had delivered them to their new home—was inside, waiting to be tapped.

Triana stood before the throng of faces and knew that, like it or not, it was her responsibility to address them. She chose to reframe the mission.

"Thank you," she began simply. "Thank you for every ounce of effort and dedication that you've summoned again and again. Even when we've faced doom and gloom, you've rallied to defeat the darkness and the unknown. Now we're about to trade one great unknown for another.

"I won't kid you, because you know what's in store. This planet will welcome us, I believe, but like all worlds it will tolerate us as long as we respect it. I believe we have every intention of assimilating into this new world not only with a sense of gratitude, but with humble eagerness."

This was greeted with nods of quiet approval.

"Despite the hardship that we're about to face, I'm thankful to be here at the beginning. But I want to give you something to think about." She paused. "After thousands of years of wondering, we've discovered that not only are we not alone in the universe, but that there's a report card."

This was greeted with a soft laugh, but Triana saw that it also struck home.

"When we thought we had it all to ourselves, I guess it was easy to act irresponsibly. But now that we know we're being graded, I hope that we take it a little more seriously.

"As proud as we may be of our primitive technology, I propose that we challenge ourselves to match every achievement with internal growth. That we never let ourselves outrace our wisdom. That we always understand the costs, and the responsibilities, that come with progress."

The room had fallen silent. She hadn't meant to make a heavy speech, but somehow all of her thoughts spilled out, uncontrolled. With a deep breath, she switched gears.

"Let me talk about something that will eventually need to be addressed anyway. From the moment we popped into Eos space, we've stumbled over the names of these planets. I happen to think that Eos Three is rather clumsy, and you probably do, too. It's obviously open for discussion and debate, but I'd like to propose a name for our new home. In respect to the man who gave the last part of his life to saving ours, I propose that we honor Wallace Zimmer by morphing his name and attaching it to this beautiful world. What do you think of replacing Eos Three with Walzim?"

There were surprised looks from all of the crew members who were crowded onto the soccer field, but within a minute it seemed that there was complete and total agreement. A small cheer went up from the assembled group.

"And," Triana said, "if you'll indulge me, I'd like to make one more suggestion. Once we establish a new colony on the surface, I think that first town should be named after the only person to lose her life on our voyage to the new world. I'd like to call it Wellington."

This time the response was immediate and unanimous. The crew of *Galahad* shouted their approval.

That's when all of the lights went out.

The initial response was laughter and some whistles. For many it must have seemed part of the proceedings, maybe even a practical joke to loosen up the crowd and inject a haunted-house thrill into the party. But within seconds, the good-natured laughter trickled away, replaced by a palpable feeling of apprehension. When, after a minute, the room remained in darkness, the anxiety spread.

After a moment of disorientation, Triana called out to everyone to remain calm. Her voice was lost in the uproar of confusion. She then fumbled her way toward the door, pressing through the crowd, until she tracked the perimeter of the wall, feeling her way. She fought back the impending wave of panic. "Stay calm, this is temporary," she said to herself, treating it as a mantra to get her through the blackout. When she realized that she must have begun on the wrong side of the door, she began tracing her path back in the opposite direction. By the time she felt the polished steel, the atmosphere in the room had turned heavy with fear. They were trapped like rats in a dark tomb.

"C'mon," Triana mumbled, sliding her fingertips into the crack of the door, which stubbornly refused to spread apart. The emergency power had failed to kick in, a fact that didn't bode well. Another sliver of panic settled in when she thought of what this might have done to Roc.

And to their chances for escape.

She felt someone next to her, someone who obviously had sought to find the exit as well. "Tree?" she heard.

"Who is that?" she said into the inky darkness. "Peter?"

"Yeah," he said. It was Peter Meyer, the Canadian who had been the first to discover Dr. Bauer aboard the ship just after the launch.

"I think we can pull this open if we put everything into it," he said. "I'll grab it at the top. Why don't you try near the bottom."

They strained to pull the doors apart, and at one point felt it begin to give, only to have it collapse back again. A moment later, two more sets of hands joined in. This time the door groaned in disapproval, but soon slid open. A breeze of fresh air from the corridor brushed past Triana's face, and with it came the realization that the ship's ventilation system was down, along with the other systems. The air in the soccer field was growing stale.

Triana wondered where Gap might be, but given the complete darkness it would be impossible to find him in the throng of people. She needed to find an emergency station and its flashlights. With a quick thank-you to Peter and the other helpers, she set off down the hallway, again feeling her way along. If all power on the ship was indeed out, they were in deep trouble. Speed was imperative.

The emergency station would be just about . . . there. She fumbled for a moment with the door, then, pulling it open, grasped a flashlight. The stab of light brought instant—even if only temporary—relief. Triana looked back down the hall, and saw dozens of crew members who had wandered out, groping with their arms before them like cartoonish zombies. The beam of light blinded them momentarily, and they threw their hands before their eyes.

Triana pulled another flashlight from the case and handed it to Peter. "Find Gap," she said. "Tell him to meet me in the Control Room. He'll have to take the emergency stairwell."

Without waiting for a reply she turned and ran.

When Gap met her outside the Control Room he carried a pry bar. Together they pulled open the door and followed the flashlight beam inside.

"Why wouldn't the emergency systems kick in?" Gap asked. "This is not good."

Triana gazed across the dark room and felt the hairs rise on the back of her neck. Eerie shadows, created by the speckled light beam, danced and swayed. Panels that normally were lit up and vibrant sat defeated. For all intents and purposes, *Galahad* was dead, a hulking metallic mess drifting through icy space.

Gap was already on his back on the floor, his head stuck inside an open access panel. Triana could see his flashlight bobbing as he searched for answers. A moment later he sat up.

"I'm not sure, but I might be able to get some sort of power restored," he said. "But I have to do it from Engineering."

"I'll wait here," Triana said.

In the next ten minutes, while waiting to hear back from Gap, she weighed their options and found that there weren't many. Each individual Spider and pod carried its own power. But how to load the remaining cargo, much of it bulky and impossibly heavy, without the mechanical assistance they'd come to rely on? And, even more crucial: how to open the Spider bay doors in order for the small craft to spill out? There would be no grimacing with a pry bar on doors that separated them from the icy vacuum of space.

Another ten minutes passed. Channy appeared in the Control Room to announce that everyone had made it safely out of the soccer field with the help of additional flashlights. They were, of course, terrified of what lay in store for them.

Just as Triana began to get anxious about Gap's progress, he returned, looking dejected.

"I'm doing the best I can," he said. "But even with our power conservation, Bauer's booby trap has caught us. I can't figure out how to get power up again, and without power there's no Roc. What's devastating about it is the thoroughness; Bauer even sabotaged the emergency systems, which I honestly didn't think was possible."

Triana bit her lip. "So . . ."

"So unless we catch another miracle, we're going to zip right past Eos Three . . . I'm sorry, Walzim . . . and toward Eos itself. And I don't know if we have any miracles left in the jar."

It was a crushing blow. Triana felt all of her frustrations return, and with them an ample supply of anger toward Fenton Bauer. Her fist again tapped slowly against her leg as she contemplated the next move.

"Get Torrec," she said, then corrected herself. "I mean, Talon. Go get him and bring him here. Oh, and find a portable generator, too."

Gap gave her a bewildered stare. "Why?"

"Get him, please," Triana said. "And hurry."

Lita made her way to Sick House following the power loss, just in case medical attention was needed. But when her flashlight revealed Gap coming through the door, she was surprised.

"Everything okay?" she said.

"Everything's a complete and total mess," he said. "Is Talon down the hall?"

Lita was taken aback. "Uh . . . yeah. I mean, he was. What's going on?"

"Triana wants him. I didn't understand at first, but I think I'm starting to."

"You want to explain it to me?" Lita asked.

Gap moved down the short hallway to collect the jellyfish. "No time. But if I'm right, we're about to get our first taste of dark energy."

32

"You understand that we're in trouble, right?" Triana said.

In her mind, it was an odd scene in so many respects. Lit only by the tight beams of three flashlights and one emergency lantern, *Galahad's* Council Leader stood in the gloomy darkness of the Control Room, addressing the latest jellyfish ambassador, a creature who, until only days ago, had existed as a one-inch sliver cut from the tentacle of the previous jellyfish representative. The ship was rushing through space with no internal power, the result of a murderous act of sabotage that had actually been perpetrated one year earlier at the hands of a scientist who had originally helped to put the *Galahad* mission together. Meanwhile, on the lower decks, more than two hundred fellow passengers groped through similar shadowy hallways, preparing to evacuate the spacecraft and make their way to the surface of an alien planet that had been rejected by nineteen fellow travelers in favor of a different alien planet. To make matters worse, the computer overseeing the majority of the ship's life support systems was out of commission, a victim of the long-dead saboteur.

When she framed it like this, Triana couldn't help but think of it all as a bizarre dream, her surreal space-age version of *Alice in Wonderland* gone horribly wrong.

"I understand the situation," Talon said. A portable generator was connected to a small vidscreen, providing the Dollovit the ability to communicate with Triana. "I estimate that, without power restoration, life support aboard this ship will cease in approximately seven of your hours. There are other complications, as well, which could result in an explosion."

Seven hours. That would leave them almost a full day short of reaching their destination. So close . . .

She remembered her vow: nothing was going to stop them from reaching Walzim.

"Do you have any recommendations?" she asked. After a pause, she added cautiously: "Perhaps a way of patching in external power?"

Gap stood to one side, and Triana saw him nod. He knew where this was going.

"What you are suggesting is possible," Talon said. "It would provide you with a temporary source of power, but would be complicated. It would require a cooperative effort using the Vo and your own ship's computer. However, the power source you are referencing, which your species identifies as dark energy, is beyond your ship's capacity to manage. At most it could provide you with an additional twelve hours, if supplied in managed doses."

Triana studied the jellyfish floating in its curious gel-like liquid. Tiny flashes erupted and just as quickly disappeared within the tank, signaling the Dollovit's own ability to refine dark energy. A question sprang to her mind.

"Tell me about dark energy," she said. "Where does it originate?"

Talon didn't hesitate. "What you call dark energy is a thread that weaves between all universes, the one cosmic force whose properties are able to exist in all dimensions. No other energy force has that ability. It flows into our universe from beyond, and continues onward to another, and another. It is infinite in its abundance. It brings life."

From beyond. Triana remembered Bon's explanation of the Cassini, how they had come from beyond the universe. There were so many questions that she wanted answers to. But at the moment . . .

"Gap," she said. "Please work with Talon, and do whatever it takes to get us powered up safely."

Gap looked at the jellyfish ambassador, and then back to Triana. "He said he could only give us twelve hours."

"And that will have to do," Triana said. "We'll leave early and make the rest of the journey in the Spiders and pods."

"They're not made for extended space travel," Gap said, lowering his voice. "They're for short-range duty, you know that. And if we do make it to Walzim okay, we'd have to put down immediately. There'd be no time for reconnaissance orbits."

Triana put a hand on his shoulder. "We'll take our chances. You know the old saying about beggars."

Without shipboard communication, word was passed person to person. When Triana explained to Channy their need for a network of runners and messengers to spread information quickly, Channy laughed, noting that Earth's most advanced piece of technology had been reduced to the Pony Express.

"No, they at least had horses," Lita said. "We're more like the Chasquis used by the ancient Inca. They ran hundreds of miles on foot to deliver messages."

The word was given: be ready to go, and stay in groups to prevent someone from wandering off and requiring a search party.

Triana divided her time between the Control Room and the

Engineering department. Gap admitted to her at one point that he had no idea what Talon was doing, but it involved their vulture companions, who once again were attached to the skin of the ship. From what Gap could discern, the vultures somehow were preparing to channel refined dark energy into the power system of *Galahad*. It would come in sips, not gulps, and in a modified form. Similar, Gap decided, to converting solar energy into the current used for household power.

Before long a chill blanketed the ship. Insulated or not, they needed power to provide heat. Memories of their earlier heating issues crossed Gap's mind; that crisis had been resolved, but this one might go down to the wire.

He made the trek up the emergency stairs, back to the Control Room, and said to Triana: "I wish I knew what just happened, but I followed Talon's instructions. He says we're ready to begin the flow."

Triana looked at him in the faint glow of the emergency lantern. "Throw the switch."

Gap gave her an okay signal with his finger and thumb, and headed back downstairs. Triana waited alone in the Control Room, and thought about a contingency plan should this experiment fail. The Spiders and pods might still be able to launch, but without power it would require at least one person to remain behind to manually open the bay doors and initiate the program. Neither the Spiders nor the pods had airlocks to enable someone to enter once the ship's outer doors were opened.

Someone would be sacrificed to save the others. And, as the captain of the boat, she would be that person.

Her somber thoughts were interrupted by a brief flicker of life from the room's lights and panels. It lasted a mere instant. A minute later the lights flashed on again, but this time power remained. Triana closed her eyes and exhaled a heavy sigh of relief.

Various systems came back to life, one at a time. When she

heard the jubilant voice of Gap from her intercom, she quickly thanked him, and asked him to pass along her gratitude to Talon.

"He now says we'll be lucky to keep this patched together for more than eight or nine hours," Gap said. "He's very diplomatic and courteous, but I get the feeling that he thinks our ship is a bucket of bolts that should never have even made it this far."

Triana laughed. "Yes, but it's *our* bucket of bolts, and we love her."

"Does that include me?" came a familiar voice.

"Roc!" Triana said. "We've missed you!"

"Can a computer experience déjà vu?" Roc said. "That's twice that Dr. Bauer has knocked me out, and I'm starting to take it personally."

"Consider it flattery," Triana said. "You're so important he *has* to knock you out."

"I like it. Now, if you'll excuse me, Talon and I have a lot of work left to do. Connecting to a power source is one thing, but keeping it turned on is a completely different matter. Ciao for now."

Triana powered up the Control Room's vidscreen, punched in the proper coordinates, and adjusted for extreme magnification. When the picture shimmered and settled, she gasped.

Walzim, formerly Eos Three, dominated the screen. Without any control over it, Triana felt a sob shake her body, and a solitary tear slide down her face. Although it lacked the sheer beauty of watery Eos Four, their new home was still a gleaming prize, awaiting their arrival.

All of their training, all of the drama that had stalked them throughout their flight, and now the threat of imminent destruction . . . it all evaporated in a heartbeat. Walzim silently greeted the teenage girl from Planet Earth.

"Oh, Dad," she whispered. "We're almost there. Thank you. Thank you for everything."

★ ★ ★

Once again the ship bustled with action. Knowing they could again lose power at any time, the crew loaded everything into the remaining functional Spiders and the Dollovit-built pods. The panels that separated the Storage Sections from the Spider bay slid aside, and all of the cryogenically frozen teenagers were prepared for launch. The remaining embryos were securely stowed.

With the gift of the extra pods, it meant additional tools and other items would make the trip, too. Teams of enthusiastic crew members oversaw the loading procedures, and within six hours Triana received word that everything was ready to go. She called for a quick Council meeting, aware that it would be their last such meeting aboard *Galahad*. Time was slipping away.

"If you've looked at the manifests for each escape craft," Triana said, "you'll see that I've split up the Council among them. Gap, you'll be in the lead, followed by Lita, then Bon, and then Channy. I'll be in the last pod."

"Gonna shut off the lights on your way out?" Channy said with a giggle.

"Something like that," Triana said. She asked each of them if they were satisfied with the packing of their specific departments. All four—including Bon—gave an affirmative answer. There wasn't much left to do except take off. All they needed now was a chance to nudge a little closer to Walzim.

But Triana wasn't prepared for the report from Roc.

"Talon and his pit crew have saved the day in terms of a temporary energy fix, but unfortunately we don't have everything going our way. In order to apply their remedy throughout the ship, we needed a conduit of sorts."

"What do you mean?" Triana said.

"They were able to get the juice into the ship, but for it to actually run all of the necessary systems, we couldn't put it on automatic. It requires a manual application. Otherwise, Bauer's little plan would still come to pass, and instead of a pleasant cruise through the Eos system you'd be part of a second sun. At least for a brief instant. Eos will burn for billions of years, while *Galahad*'s explosion would be over and done in a matter of seconds."

"I still don't—" Triana began to answer, when Gap interrupted.

"I know what he's saying." He let out a long sigh. "Just pumping the energy into the ship would only trigger Dr. Bauer's booby trap. Talon and Roc have created their own little circuit in order to get everything running. Is that correct, Roc?"

"I never gave you enough credit," the computer said. "You're so much smarter than you look."

"And," Gap continued, "if we're going to keep everything functioning, including the launch of so many escape vehicles, then a certain someone will have to remain aboard and stay behind."

The room fell silent. Gap had just announced the unthinkable. Roc would not be part of the first human settlement on another world.

"No," Triana said. "That's not acceptable."

"It's not only acceptable," Roc said, "it's the only choice. Once you disconnect me from the power grid and go to autopilot, the relays will flip into self-destruct mode. Boom."

"There has to be another way to do this!" Channy blurted out. "Tree, there has to be!"

Lita and Bon were silent. Triana could tell from their faces that they understood the circumstances.

"I might add," Roc said, "that even with my incredible skills at brokering power, there's still a deadline. I don't share Talon's opinion that *Galahad* is a junker, but the fact is the ship wasn't created to run on converted dark energy. The lights are due to go out again, permanently. So quit stalling and get out of here, will ya? There's a perfectly good planet out there, waiting for you."

Channy began to sob, and Lita seemed on the verge of breaking down. Triana wanted to cry, but was in shock.

"Roc," she said. "How could you do this without consulting me?"

"Because, dear Triana, you might have been tempted to rule with your heart instead of your head. There was simply no other choice, and with time running out it would have been foolish to waste what little was left in trying to convince you."

He paused, then added: "For what it's worth, I'm not exactly dancing with joy here, and not just because I have no legs. Please, promise me you'll name a mountain or something after me. Something large and impressive, of course."

"Um . . ." Lita said. "I don't want to sound heartless, but won't almost all of our systems on the planet need a computer to run?"

Triana idly tapped a finger on the table. "Yes," she said, her voice low and sad. "But we'll have generic, raw computer access. What we won't have . . ." She couldn't finish.

Gap swallowed hard, then cleared his throat, in an attempt to sound composed. "What we won't have is the advanced element that Roc brings. We'll . . ." He cleared his throat again. "We'll have a basic unit, but nothing that thinks or . . . or talks."

"Or whips you at Masego," Roc said. Gap lowered his head, his eyes closed.

Triana gazed down the length of the table at Bon. The Swede appeared stoic on the outside, but Triana knew him well enough by now to recognize his look of despair. He held up well and put up a steely front, but she knew that he fought to do so.

Lita said: "Roc, what will you do? What's going to happen to you?"

"Why, I'll go down in history as the savior of the human race, of course! Oh, you mean *literally* what'll happen? That's simple. I'll get all of you little carbon-based units safely out and on your way, and then I'll take this baby out for a joyride. With no power, of course, but still. And, with all of you gone, I get to decide what music to listen to."

"So you'll shut everything down . . . including yourself . . . and just . . . what? Drift through space?"

Roc didn't answer. It wasn't necessary. Everyone in the room knew the answer to Lita's question. Unless he switched to the automatic power grid—and ignited an ion-powered bomb—Roy Orzini's masterful computer creation would spend eternity silent and frozen, knifing through the infinite void of space.

"Good-byes are mushy," Roc said. "And your window for safely jumping ship is about to close. Beat it before I say something we'll all regret, like telling Gap his hair *doesn't* look silly. Go on. Shoo."

There was nothing left to say. The Council members pushed away from the table and trudged to the door. Triana was the last to leave. She willed herself to not look back.

W hen I brought up the whole issue of "life or death" a few hundred pages ago, I didn't think it would apply to me. But what else could I do here?

We should probably say our good-byes now, before things get sloppy.

33

"ineteen minutes," Gap said, sitting in the pilot's seat of the Spider. "Where is she?"

Behind him, twenty-nine fellow crew members were strapped into their seats, their eyes wide with anticipation. The same scene was taking place in the remaining Spiders, as well as inside the transport pods. Smaller storage craft, engineered to carry payloads of gear and equipment, stood by as well. All that could be stuffed aboard the escape vehicles was locked down and ready to go.

But Triana was missing. She'd called down half an hour earlier and reported that she had things to take care of. Now, as the clock ticked and Walzim approached, the assembled crew waited for their leader.

Channy's voice came through Gap's earpiece from one of the other Spiders. "Is she saying good-bye?"

He heard Lita respond: "Triana doesn't say good-bye."

ighting along the gracefully curved hallways was dim, so Triana walked with a flashlight, just in case. She skimmed the various levels, calling out for any possible stragglers, but only as a precaution. Gap had reported that two separate roll calls had confirmed everyone present and accounted for, and there were no additional life readings aboard the ship.

Her final stop wasn't her room, nor the Control Room. She walked out of the emergency stairwell into the slightly humid air of the Domes. Although technically still daytime aboard the ship, the current circumstances made it necessary to shut down *Galahad's* artificial suns. It was cooler than normal as Triana began a quick walk down a dirt path toward the center of Dome 1. Once there, she stopped and glanced around. It was an eerie feeling to be, for all intents and purposes, the last person aboard the ship. The tomblike silence that draped the air, however, didn't frighten her. In fact, it was exactly what she wanted.

She closed her eyes and held her arms out at her sides, her head tilted back. She breathed deeply, taking in the moist air and exhaling with a slow, measured pace. In a moment she saw him, a vision that both calmed her and emboldened her.

"Hello, Dad," she said, a smile breaking across her face. "It's time."

In her mind she saw him smile back at her, and give a wink.

"You made this possible," she said. "Not just by sending my information to Dr. Zimmer. You made this possible years ago, with everything that you taught me. You didn't pick me up and place me here on this path, but you pointed me in the right direction. You cleared some of the brush out of my way, and gave me just the slightest nudge in the back.

"Thank you for urging me to take the more difficult path, and not the easy way out. Because of you I believe in myself. You taught me to never settle, to always keep reaching for more, because you had faith that I could do it. You encouraged me without giving me false hopes. You disciplined me in ways that showed me the meaning of consequences, which I never appreciated until I was here, faced with the most critical consequences of all.

"You taught me to listen, to keep an open mind while at the same time not being afraid to defend what I knew to be right.

You showed me how to handle disappointment. And, Dad, more than anything, you showed me how to quietly inspire, because that's what you've always done."

She opened her eyes and looked through the clear panels of the Dome. The blazing star field ignited her emotions, as they always did. She felt a rising surge of love for the people in her life who had sacrificed so much for her, especially her father and Dr. Zimmer. More than anything, against any odds, she wanted to prove that their confidence in her was not misguided.

She wouldn't let Dr. Bauer's scheme derail the mission. She wouldn't let Merit's veiled threat distract her from the second stage of that mission, to settle and colonize humanity's new home. And she would never forget the lessons that she'd learned from her fellow star travelers, and from the benevolent alien life-forms who patiently guided Earth's emigrants to their new home.

One of those alien entities was safely stored within the Spider that waited for her now on the lower level. Talon and his kind would become partners with the struggling refugees from Earth.

"And now, Dad, I'll take everything you've taught me, and bring it to a new world. I'm glad that you'll be there with me. We still have some peaks to climb together."

With one last deep breath, Triana turned toward the stairs, leaving a final set of footprints in the soil of *Galahad*'s farms.

With eight minutes until launch, she walked into the Spider bay control room to find Bon waiting for her.

"What are you doing?" she asked. "You should be aboard already."

"I was aboard. I was coming to find you."

Triana could hear an anxious exchange on the intercom between Gap and Lita. *Galahad*'s Council Leader was missing, and now Bon had bolted. Triana keyed the system and eased their concern by telling them she would be aboard in minutes. Then she turned to Bon.

"I'm fine," she said. "Just had a few things to take care of."

His eyes bored into her. They were inches apart, reliving a scene from a year earlier, alone in this same room, standing in the exact same spot. Only now, things were different. *They,* in fact, were different. Both, she realized, had not only grown, but had grown apart. Up until this point all she'd considered were the changes that had taken place within *him.* But now . . .

"You'd better get back aboard," she said, with a calm that surprised her. "I'll be right behind you."

There would be no reenactment of that long lost scene. There would be no embrace. Instead, Bon held out his hand.

"Thank you for getting us here in one piece," he said. "You were the right choice to lead us. I know you had your doubts; I hope you don't anymore."

Triana hesitated, then placed her hand in his. "Thank you, Bon. There were times when I didn't think we stood a chance."

Bon's grip was firm. "In my country, we say: *I lugnt vatten har alla skepp en bra kapten.*"

"What does that mean?" Triana asked.

Bon lifted his chin. "In calm water, every ship has a good captain." He waited, then said: "Understand?"

Triana could only nod, but inside she felt an odd combination of exhilaration and regret. She wondered if Bon could feel her tremble.

A moment later he released her hand and walked back into the bay. She exhaled and looked at the room's vidscreen, and the timer. It registered 6:20, counting down.

She felt the presence that waited with her in the room.

"I don't know what to say to you," she told the computer. "How do I thank you for this? For everything?"

"I could give you a list," Roc said. "I already mentioned naming the mountain, but you could also find some new clothes for Gap, and maybe take away his gel."

Triana concentrated on her breathing; she knew that otherwise she'd never be able to finish what she had to say. "I couldn't have made it without you," she said. "And I'm not just talking about . . . you know, the work. I mean the talks we had. You kept me grounded. I'll . . . I'll never forget you."

"Ah, immortality," the computer said. "The Legend of Roc. I like it."

Triana bit her lip. "And . . . about the things I said to you earlier. About doubting you. And . . . and about you trying to prove that you're human. Well, I was wrong. I never should have doubted you. And as far as I'm concerned . . ." Her voice trailed away, and she fought for control as her voice broke.

"As far as I'm concerned, you're human enough for me. You're one of my best friends, Roc."

She looked down for a long time, silent. Then she glanced out the window into the bay, at the fleet of pods and Spiders that beckoned, waiting to take her away.

"You better run along," Roc said. "Before you accidentally say good-bye."

In spite of her breaking heart, Triana found room to laugh softly. "No, I'm not going to say that. Somehow we'll find a way to be together again."

"You may be right," Roc said. "I might have a trick or two up my sleeve. Not to mention the most obvious trick, which is a computer with no arms having a sleeve in the first place."

With a sad smile, she brought her index finger up to her lips, then reached out and touched it to the glowing sensor on the panel.

"Remember your strengths," Roc said. "Always."

Two minutes later she was aboard the Spider, and the outer doors of the massive hangar began to silently glide open. Starlight spilled in as Earth's fleet of young explorers stared outward, taking in the universe, and taking on the challenge.

A Note from the Author

As you might guess, I've grown quite attached to the crew of *Galahad* over the years. Like you, I've wondered how they would get out of some tough scrapes, I've muttered "what were you thinking?" to more than one of them, and I've laughed when Roc showed them the lighter side of life.

I'm proud to say that the hardworking teens within these pages represent an attitude that I hope takes hold among teenagers everywhere. Triana and her fellow adventurers are obviously sharp, intelligent young people. But in case you haven't noticed, they're pretty cool, too. In their minds, you don't have to choose between being cool and using your brain; you just do both.

One of my passions is helping young people recognize that Smart *is* Cool. The days of dumbing down in order to fit in with the "cool crowd" are hopefully disappearing. My goal is to help students understand that the choices they make today regarding their education will affect them for the rest of their lives. My nonprofit foundation, the Big Brain Club, isn't about perfect report cards or honor rolls (although we love those!); its mission is to celebrate learning, and to help each student become the best version of themselves. Check it out at www.BigBrainClub.com.

And, if you love the cool, nerdy stuff that's tucked inside the Galahad books, you'll love The Science Behind Galahad.

There are multiple volumes, and they're all downloadable at www.DomTesta.com.

Thanks so much for riding along with Triana and the gang aboard *Galahad*. I hope you've had as much fun as I have!

Tor Teen
Reader's Guide

About This Guide

The information, activities, and discussion questions that follow are intended to enhance your reading of *The Galahad Legacy*. Please feel free to adapt these materials to suit your needs and interests.

Writing and Research Activities

I. Alternative Minds
   A. Go to the library or online to research supercomputers. Find out about Watson, the computer that won the television game show *Jeopardy!* Watch the classic science fiction film *2001: A Space Odyssey*. Then make a brainstorm list of the benefits and dangers supercomputers may present to human life.
   B. Imagine that you are a *Galahad* crew member, and Triana has asked you to develop a slideshow or other computer presentation on the different types of intelligent beings you have encountered in space. Share your presentation with friends or classmates.
   C. Ask friends or classmates to complete the sentence, "The crew of *Galahad* should/should not trust Roc

because . . ." Post all of the completed sentences on a wall in your classroom in preparation for a group discussion. Did most students offer similar answers? What are the most surprising or interesting discoveries you make by analyzing the sentence display? What conclusions might you draw from this exercise?

D. Try exercise C, above, substituting "Roc" with "the Cassini" or "the Dollovit." Do you reach similar conclusions?

II. The Question of Connections

A. The novel depicts different types of connections between human individuals, between humans and other beings (such as Bon and the Cassini), and between those alive and those remembered (such as Triana and her father, or *Galahad* crew members and Alexa). Using paper, paints, found objects, newspaper or magazine clippings, and other materials of your choice, create a collage depicting your understanding of some or all of these connections.

B. In the character of Bon, write several journal entries in which you attempt to describe your relationship with the Cassini and how you envision it developing or changing in the future.

C. In the character of an assistant in Sick House, write a short report defining the term "ventet" as you understand it from examining the ventet of Alexa.

D. In the character of Torrec, write a speech explaining why you do not believe in faith.

E. Write a dialogue in which your favorite human character from the novel explains how humans deal with death, and remember those lost, to Dollovit, Roc, or the Cassini. Invite friends or classmates to perform the dialogue.

III. Choices

    A. From Triana's rash adventure in the Spider, to the encounter with Alexa's ventet, to the choice of going with the Dollovit or landing on Eos, *The Galahad Legacy* is a nonstop challenge to the decision-making talents of its crew. Make three sign-up sheets to post at the front of your classroom: Go to Eos Three; Go to Four; Go with the Dollovit. Invite friends or classmates to sign up for the destination of their choice. Afterward, give each student an opportunity to explain his or her choice to the group.

    B. Write an essay about a difficult choice you have had to make in your own life and describe the outcome of that choice.

    C. In the character of Merit Simms, write a speech defending your actions and explaining why you feel it is important to offer the crew an alternative to Triana's plans.

    D. In the Galahad series, a group of teens travel the cosmos in hopes of preserving the human race far from disease-contaminated Earth. From the moment each teen joined the training program for *Galahad*, they began making painful, life-altering choices. Using examples from this book, other series titles you may have read, and your own life, write a 2–3 page essay entitled, "The Challenge of Choices."

Questions for Discussion

1. In Chapter 2, newly returned Triana defends her actions to her fellow Council members, saying "Making a popular choice wasn't as important to me as doing what I felt was best for this crew." Do you agree with Triana's judgment? How might the idea

of *choice* be considered an important theme throughout the novel? Cite examples from the book in your answer.

2. How might you have reacted to Torrec? Do you think Triana is right to trust him? Why do you think she reacts to him as she does?

3. At the beginning of Chapter 8, Roc asks, "How would you describe where YOUR personality exists? Is it in your brain? Your heart? Somewhere else . . . ?" Answer Roc.

4. By Chapter 9, Triana is beginning to worry about the power of supercomputers, and to question Roc's loyalty. Would you rely on Roc at this point in the novel? Why or why not?

5. In Chapter 9, Triana also wonders, "Was she the same Triana who plunged through the jagged rip in space?" How might this question be interpreted in at least two different ways? Do all major experiences, such as loss, trauma, or even great joy, change us? Does it matter if we are "real"?

6. What bizarre "gift" does the Dollovit give to *Galahad* in Chapter 10? What does Lita reveal about this gift? Had you been aboard *Galahad,* would you have wanted to see, interact with, or keep the gift? How might you have handled the situation, keeping in mind your possible dependency on the Dollovit?

7. In Chapter 14, Lita tries to explain notions of "honoring the dead" and of "closure" to Torrec. What does their conversation teach Lita about the Dollovit?

8. At the end of Chapter 18, Triana and Bon discuss the possibility of humans being computer replicas made by a greater

intelligence. Do you think this could be a possibility? Why or why not?

9. Do you think Triana is right to let Merit's group disembark at Eos Four? Do you think Merit will be a good leader? Explain your answers.

10. Why do you think Dr. Zimmer chose to store embryos on *Galahad*—and to keep this a secret from the crew? Do you think this was a good decision? Do you think that, ultimately, Merit's theft of some of the embryos was an equally scientifically valid choice? Why or why not?

11. Bon posits that the Dollovit are the students of the universe while the Cassini are the peacekeepers. Do you agree with his logic? What role might human beings play in this universal dynamic?

12. Why do you think, ultimately, Triana decides to let Roc "go" and trust the Cassini?

13. Does faith make us human? Might the human sense of personal loyalties and ethical reasoning be as valuable (or sophisticated) a contribution as some of the other life-forms' technological offerings?

14. What do you think will happen to the settlers of Eos Three and Four? What are your hopes for their futures? Has reading *The Galahad Legacy* made you think about your own sense of the future in a different way? Explain your answer.

About the Author

DOM TESTA is an author, speaker, and the top-rated morning radio show host in Denver, Colorado. His nonprofit foundation, the Big Brain Club, empowers students to take charge of their education. Visit him online at www.domtesta.com.